Also by Simon Hall

THE DEATH PICTURES

'One of the best crime novels I have read.'

'This book was brilliant, I read it in a single afternoon.'

'A gripping and exciting read from the start- the type that
keeps you up until all hours of the night because
you're desperate to find out what happens next!'

'Utterly compelling.'

'A brilliant book which I had real difficulty putting down.'

Evil Valley

Simon Hall

For the women who raised me, for their great love, care and extraordinary reserves of patience; Mum, Nan, Les, Jackie and Maureen D

Acknowledgements

The usual suspects of CID, the media and the medical worlds for all their help, plus my perceptive readers; George Major and Shaun Ebelthite, my excellent website team; Mathew Hooper, Gary Best and Mark Eccles, the Commander of Plymouth Police, Jim Webster, and the unsung heroes of the fine libraries of the South-west, in particular Sue Lancaster, Susannah Everington, Julian Luke and Paul Trainer

Prologue

DEATH WAS STALKING HAVEN Close.

The frosted double-glazing of the front door hardly softened the screaming. It was strangled, penetrating, like a desperate, agonised animal. A woman's voice, hysterical with pain and fear. Again. Lights flickered on in a line along the street, faces pressed to windows, fascinated heads shaking in sadness, but never so appalled as to risk missing the spectacle. Again.

It had become a ritual. Frightening nights, shameful days. A thick layer of the morning's make-up to cover the evening's wounds. Passing eyes avoided in the street. Conversation always shunned. Sunglasses, polo-neck jumpers and jeans to hide the blossoming bruises.

A flashing blue light began to tint the quiet cars and houses and windows of the Close. Tyres slewed, and the gunning engine spluttered and died. Two doors opened and closed fast, two broad silhouettes checked the array of heavy shapes encumbering their bodies. Two long, thin barrels, sleek and menacing. Two shorter, snub-nosed objects. The careful fingers manipulated the cold metal handles, slid in the series of tiny, gleaming cylinders, tested the delicate crescent triggers.

'Good to go?'

'Check.'

The figures nodded to each other, began moving, walking fast, following a straight concrete path bisecting a perfect lawn. A worn and muddy mat bid a welcome to their heavy boots.

Death was edging closer.

More sudden noise inside the house. First, a thud, then a smash, an echoing crash. The screaming rose to a screech. Their heavy knocking forced a pause, a second's hanging silence, then more sounds, vague at first, barely discernible, a soft sobbing, growing louder. Another crash. A fleeting shape in a dark window, moving furtively, like a hunter. Another

1

scream, more hammering on the door, more screaming.

Then it stopped. Just halted. The house froze. No movement, no sound. Nothing.

Seconds slid by in silence.

The figures exchanged glances, whispered together.

'Threat to life?'

'Yep. Clearly.'

'Too dangerous to wait?'

'Yep.'

'We have to go in?'

'Agreed.'

'Baton guns?'

The other figure paused, weighed the bulky weapon hanging at his side. 'Too tight in there. Too constrained. Too risky.'

'Side arms? Pistols?'

'Yep. Have to be.'

Two hands reached for two holsters. One fist hammered again on the glass. The ominous quiet persisted inside.

That was how the operator had described the 999 call. At first, it was a ghost … quiet … the hiss of the phone line … no words … just silence. Now perhaps a hint of shallow breathing … growing … getting louder … a low groan. Then the shock of a sudden scream, a sickening crack, a gurgle … more silence.

The line had gone dead, the number traced, the Armed Response Vehicle scrambled. To find this – an unremarkable address in a modern neighbourhood. A tidy street, an orderly line of cars parked under the amber streetlights, three-bedroom houses, hopscotch grids chalked on the tarmac, safe semi-detached suburbia, all now dancing in the blue shadows of the flashing light from the patrol car.

And death, lingering, always just out of sight, hiding in the half light, but always there, rejoicing in the imminence of his moment.

More whispered urgency. 'You ready then?'

'Yep.'

'You sure this is justified, after … well, you know …'

'The last time?'

'Yeah, the last time. If you … if we … take down another…'

'If we have to, we'll have done our job. That's all. Just like the last time.'

'Yeah …'

A brief silence. A muted thud and the hint of another moan crept from behind the frosted glass door.

'So … we go in? We're absolutely sure it's justified?'

'You heard the 999 call. You heard the noises in the house. It sounds like he's murdering her. We don't have time to mess about.'

'Yeah, yeah, I know. It's just … OK … so … the usual way?'

'Yep.'

One silhouette touched the rim of its cap with a forefinger, breathed out hard. The other rubbed reverentially at a shining, silver crucifix hanging around its neck. They exchanged a fast glance, each nodded. The rituals of luck were complete.

It was time.

'Stand back.'

A heavy black boot thumped into the door. It shuddered, but held. Again, and a complaining creak. Again, and the moan of warping plastic. Harder now and a splitting crash. The door careered open, juddering against a wall.

They edged in, one leading, one covering, both half crouched, pistols poised.

The hallway was narrow, in semi-darkness, pictures hanging at dizzy angles. A sunny Dartmoor landscape. A grey New York skyline. A wood-framed mirror, split with a diagonal crack.

A corner loomed. They slowed, carefully rounded it, step by sideways step. Underfoot a soaking, squelching carpet and a flickering blue luminescence from a smashed fish tank. Fronds of water still trickled, crunching broken glass, tiny golden outlines flipping weak and helpless on the floor.

Another corner. Open space now.

A kitchen, fridge door hanging ajar, a wedge of light

spilling out, more crunching glass on the smooth tiles. Cups and plates cracked and smashed, white shards littering the darkness. A photograph of a young couple, morning suit and a white wedding dress, beaming smiles distorted in the cobweb of shattered glass.

And now movement. A woman, on her knees, a torn blouse hanging from her shaking shoulders, sobbing, begging. A man there too, hiding half in shadow, crouched above her, trembling.

'Armed police, put your hands up!'

His head turned unsteadily, unfocused eyes wild with reflected light, white teeth clenched in a baffled scowl, a heedless welcome to the snub-nosed metal barrel now pointing at his chest.

'Armed police!' Louder now, the barked command booming in the sudden stillness. 'Put your hands where I can see them! Do it now! Do it and you won't be harmed!'

Still no movement. Still he crouched. The fridge juddered into rumbling life. A sobbing moan from the human shape on the floor rose to accompany it. Then a shift, more movement, his arm rising, menacing, gathering momentum …

One shot, a whipping, deafening crack in the cramped, echoing space. Then another.

A confused look spread across his face. No pain, no shock, no time, just pure puzzlement at the end of his life. His light shirt reddening fast from the pumping blood, his eyes wide, his body slowly slumping to the floor as the precious life leaked away. His soundless mouth open, eyes still staring, but sightlessly now.

A serrated, glinting knife clattered onto the tiles, and her sobs rose again to another strangled scream.

It was just as it had been before. The last time, only five months ago. Another traumatised woman, another corpse lying in its own suburban home, created at their hands.

The two marksmen stared, turned, looked at each other.

'We're for it now,' one muttered breathlessly. 'We're bloody for it … you've … we've done it again …'

'We did the right thing,' the other interrupted, then louder, harsher – 'The right thing! Didn't we?'

No reply.

'Well? Well?! Didn't we?!'

Still no reply.

Death nodded and departed Haven Close, his work complete.

She was such a beautiful girl. Her eyelids drooped as she lay back on the pillow, but she was determined to fight the gathering sleep, to hear the end of the poem.

'Don't stop,' she whispered. 'Please don't stop. I want to hear what happens to the poor Yonghy-Bonghy-Bo.'

'All right, but this is the last bit now. Then it's lights off, OK? It's way past your bedtime.'

She shifted her head, that long blonde hair diffusing around her like a golden halo. He had to close his eyes, to stifle the thoughts of what must happen to her. The ordeal he would put her through. But it was necessary. It was too important to reconsider. She was perfect. The plan was laid. He couldn't turn back.

He forced the required jollity into his voice. 'OK then, are you ready?'

She smiled that gappy grin, nodded, reached a hand out from under the duvet to hold his. The guilt formed an instant and dense barrier, made him hesitate, but he took it, swallowed hard, began to read.

'"From the coast of Coromandel,
Did that lady never go;
On that heap of stone she mourns
For the Yonghy-Bonghy-Bo.
On that coast of Coromandel,
In his jug without a handle
Still she weeps, and daily moans;
On that little heap of stones
To her Dorking hens she moans,
For the Yonghy-Bonghy-Bo,
For the Yonghy-Bonghy-Bo."'

The Courtship of the Yonghy-Bonghy-Bo, from Edward

Lear's *Nonsense Rhymes*, her favourite. It was the sole part of their relationship he enjoyed. The simplicity of reading to her. He knew exactly why. It was because he was bringing to a fatherless child that which his own father had never brought to him.

Her gentle grip released. He closed the book, lay it down quietly on her bedside table, turned off the lamp. He turned to the woman standing in the doorway, managed to find a smile.

'She loves you, you know.'

'Yes ...' he wondered what else to say. 'And I ... she ... she's a lovely girl.'

He thanked his perfect planning that the woman was so stupid, didn't notice his reticence. It wasn't luck. He had chosen precisely. She was ideal in her loneliness and dullness and desperation. And her daughter was perfect too, in her beauty and innocence and naivety. When her picture was published, in every paper and magazine, and on every news website, and broadcast on every television station ... when the story of what was happening to her was told – and why – then, at last, everyone would finally understand.

The irritating hours he'd had to spend playing his part would be richly rewarded. The thought was all that had kept him going through the tedium of the slow walks in the countryside, pointing out plants and birds and landmarks. The girl had discovered a delight in nature, and he'd been forced to buy a couple of second-hand books to find the knowledge to entertain her. The skylark had become her favourite bird, hovering in the clear air above Dartmoor, trilling out its song. She always loved to remind him how it sang a different tune, depending on whether it was soaring up into the sky, or down to a hidden nest in the moorgrass.

Even the ubiquitous heather was a joy, her only distress the elusive shortness of its flowering season. Classically, just the month of August, she'd quickly learned, although if the weather was kind, the runs of delicate purple candles could appear in July and survive well into September. She would carefully intertwine the tiny flecks with the vibrant yellow of the gorse, and shout how she wanted him to buy her a new dress of gorse and heather colours. He'd had to steel himself so very hard to avoid enjoying her excitement.

The long days by the beach had grown from building endless sandcastles to paddling in sun-warmed and slippery rock pools, waving the fronds of dark and slimy bladderwrack like swords, and hunting the scuttling Hermit crabs, safely protected within their adopted shells. She'd learnt of the menace of weaver fish, their stinging spines buried in the soft sand, and the extraordinary muscular adhesion of the barnacles and limpets that littered the pitted rocks with their tiny pyramids.

She'd insisted Mum took a photograph of the two of them, trousers rolled up, hunting the shallows for shipwreck treasures deposited by the tide. He'd stared at the picture for long hours that night, fighting so hard not to allow himself to become a part of the scene, only eventually finding the strength to burn it.

At least her love of nature was preferable to the deafening funfairs, all sickeningly swirling lights and grating, joyous screams, the very worst of the damned family horrors he'd had to suffer for the perfection of his beautiful plan. All were ordeals, but all would be worth it. When the time finally came. As it would.

The woman was speaking again, more of her ceaseless chatter. 'She'll be nine soon, you know. I was thinking of getting her that pony for her birthday. The one she's always wanted. You know how excited she gets when we see them on our Dartmoor walks. She'd love it so much. You could join in with … make it a present from both of us … if you liked …'

He got up from the chair, tried not to look at the layers of pictures of ponies, dancing and prancing and galloping across the bedroom walls.

'I'm a bit tight on money at the moment. I'm sorry.'

Her words gushed out to cover the awkwardness. 'No, that's fine. I understand. I really do. I'm always having trouble myself. I mean, it's never easy, is it? Where does it all go, that's what I want to know?'

She reached out a hand to lead him from the bedroom,

looked about to speak again, but he interrupted. 'I should be going. I'd love to stay, really I would, but I've got so much to do …'

She studied him, then nodded. 'I understand. Perhaps another time. I hope …'

'Yes. Perhaps.'

He turned to close the door, couldn't stop himself looking back at the child, knees tucked, wrapped in the enveloping safety of the duvet. She was sleeping with a smile. In that frozen moment, he almost changed his mind. But it was too late for second thoughts. Far too late. He blinked twice, focused his purpose, just as the Sergeant Major had taught him. It was the only way to survive. To complete your mission.

The door clicked softly shut. But the knowledge of what must happen to her still wouldn't leave his mind. He shuddered, but only briefly. Then, he smiled.

Chapter One

HE'D THOUGHT HE WAS being smart, but instead he might just
have put them in danger of getting shot.

Dan Groves, TV Crime Correspondent for the south-west
of England, exchanged glances with Nigel, his long-suffering
cameraman. It wasn't so easy to do when both were hunched
up in balls, trying to make themselves as small as possible
behind the low garden wall. Dan tried giving his friend a
reassuring smile, but the look he got in return said it hadn't
been successful. Nowhere close.

More manic shouting broke the silence. 'Don't come any
nearer! I'll shoot! I swear I'll shoot!'

Dan shifted his weight, tried to ease the pressure on his
aching knees. A police marksman was crouched just behind a
car to their side, the muzzle of his automatic rifle only inches
away from Dan's head. It was glinting under the streetlights,
unwavering in the man's grip.

'Any suggestions?' Dan whispered.

The man's reply was terse. 'Just keep your bloody heads
down. If you don't want to be riddled with shot. Pair of idiots.'

'Well, thanks for those kind and reassuring words,' Dan
muttered to himself.

The Manadon area of Plymouth on a quiet autumn evening,
a pleasant residential estate just a couple of miles from the city
centre. Usually the street would be busy with kids kicking
footballs, the older ones hanging around talking, people
coming and going, perhaps on late shifts from work or
popping to the corner shop for milk, or cigarettes. Standard,
contented suburbia.

Tonight, it was unusually quiet. But then, Dan reflected
uncomfortably, it would be when it was the focus of a major
police operation, had been cordoned off because a man had
barricaded himself into one of the houses and was waving a
shotgun from the window and threatening to shoot anyone
who showed themselves.

And he thought he was being clever. When would he ever learn?

They'd been on a straightforward assignment to film a story about boy racers using one of the nearby roads as a racetrack when they'd been tipped off about the siege by a local gossip. For once, they'd arrived before the police, and Dan and Nigel had walked down the street to see what was going on.

They'd ignored the group of people running away. They'd taken no notice of the venomous yelling from the end of the row of terraces. Even the wise advice from a middle-aged woman, hurrying past with her arm around a crying young boy had been duly ignored.

'Don't you go up there,' she'd panted. 'It's dangerous. He's got a gun and he says he'll use it.'

'Nothing to worry about,' Dan had calmed her. 'It's our job to run towards the sound of gunfire.'

He'd grinned, Nigel had smiled and they'd strolled blithely on. That was until the man's screaming and waving of a very large shotgun had sent them ducking behind the garden wall. There they had stayed. And Dan couldn't help but think their situation had not only turned from bad to worse, but then also deteriorated.

Half a dozen police cars squealed to a halt, their sirens screaming. At both ends of the street the familiar blue-and-white police tape was being hurriedly reeled out, a line of officers guarding it. Local residents were ushered quickly away, crouching to avoid any possible gunfire. And around them had crept a team of police marksmen, some scuttling crablike along the row of cars, dodging from vehicle to vehicle, others snaking up on their bellies. The house had been surrounded, and they were caught between a small arsenal of weapons in what Dan could only think uncomfortably of as no man's land.

'I swear I'll shoot!' came another yell from the house. 'Keep back coppers!'

The policeman's gun barrel tracked back and forth across the house. 'Think I've got him,' the man whispered into his radio. 'In the upstairs window. Shall I take him?'

'Negative,' a voice crackled back. 'He's had a domestic with his wife. She stormed out. It's happened before. He's come out peacefully. Let's see if we can manage the same again.'

'Roger that.'

Dan had covered police sieges before, but always from the reassuring safety of outside the cordon. The cold of the pavement was beginning to seep up his back, making it ache. He shivered, pulled his jacket tighter around his chest. The sky was clear and his breath was fogging the night air.

Dan checked his watch, as unreliable as ever. It said nine, so it was probably more like a quarter past. Wessex Tonight's late bulletin was on air at half past ten. If they were going to get the story on, they'd have to work out a way soon.

'What will the cops do?' Nigel whispered.

'Not a lot. They'll keep him contained and try to talk to him. It sounds like he's on his own in there, so they'll wait. They'll only fire if he starts shooting, or comes out and waves his gun around.'

'So what do we do?'

Dan shifted his weight again. His knees were throbbing hard, they needed to get some pictures and he had no intention of waiting around all night while the police tried to talk the man out. So far, they'd filmed nothing, hadn't had the opportunity. Or the courage, more like. If it came to a choice between winning a TV news award and being peppered with shot, or no award and his precious skin intact, little consideration was required in Dan's mind.

'Well, we'd better try to get some pictures,' he said. 'Lizzie will go mad if we're here and we don't get anything.'

Nigel gave him a look, tapped the camera on his lap. 'By we, I take it you mean me. And I have two young sons. Not to mention a lot of life left to live. In one piece, preferably.'

'Sure. But there must be a way of sticking your head up safely for a few seconds to get some shots.'

'Like what?'

Dan was about to shift his position, see if he could take a

11

quick look at the house when he was interrupted by a voice booming through a loud hailer.

'Mr Anderson … Mr Anderson … this is the police. Please come out so we can talk to you.'

'Never!' came the instant and screeched reply. 'You'll never take me alive, cops!'

The marksman rolled his eyes. Dan too groaned. 'Great. Of all the nutters around, we have to get one who's been watching too many Westerns. Look, we can't just sit here. We've got to do something.'

'Like what?' Nigel asked, annoyingly reasonably.

A couple more marksmen scuttled up the pavement, just across the street. One was wearing a black baseball cap emblazoned with "Police".

Dan stared at them, felt an idea growing. 'Have you got your rain hat?' he asked Nigel.

The cameraman produced a battered old khaki model from his jacket pocket. 'Yep. Why?'

'When I was a kid, I remember reading in a war magazine about an old soldier's trick for when they thought there might be a sniper around. It could just tell us whether it's safe to stick our precious heads above the parapet.'

Dan grabbed a stick from the floor, poked it into Nigel's hat and slowly and gingerly lifted it above the wall.

He flinched, expecting a shot. Nothing. He jiggled the hat up and down, moved it back and forth along the wall, as if its wearer was moving, waited, then did it all again. Still nothing.

'There,' he said, trying to keep his voice calm. 'All safe.'

Nigel narrowed his eyes. 'You sure?'

'Absolutely. That's the situation thoroughly risk-assessed. All boxes of those irritating, endless forms ticked. If only I could operate the camera with the skill you've got, I'd take the pictures myself.'

'Yeah, right.'

Nigel weighed the camera on his knees, shifted it to his shoulder and muttered something under his breath that sounded like a prayer. He popped up, filmed a few seconds of the house, then dropped back down again. Beside them, the marksman watched, his mouth falling slowly open.

Dan tried giving him a winning smile. It wasn't reciprocated. He wondered if he'd just invented a new chapter in the Firearms Tactics manual. Perhaps an appendix entitled, "How To Baffle Your Gunman."

He grabbed Nigel's collar and guided him back along the wall, towards the edge of the cordon and their cars, filming all the way. They could drop the pictures in to the newsroom to make a decent report for the late bulletin, and still have time to get to the pub for a late beer. They deserved it after that.

He had no idea how guns would come to dominate the despair of the next week of his life.

Dan had meant to buy Nigel a drink by way of thanks, but found he didn't have any money, so the cameraman had to get the round. It could have been the definition of the insult being added to the injury.

'You are a disgrace,' Nigel said, walking carefully back from the bar with a couple of pints.

'You may have a point old friend, but it worked, didn't it? We got the shots and the story. And good timing too, the man being talked out just before the bulletin with no one hurt. A rare happy ending all round.'

Dan held up his pint, took a sip of his drink. They were sitting in the Old Bank on Plymouth's Mutley Plain, as the less than creative name suggested it was a converted bank, no atmosphere, but good and cheap beer and ideal to drop into for a quick drink. It was busy, students mostly, attracted by the low prices and curry night, but they managed to find a small table at the back.

'So, how's this new woman of yours then?' Dan asked. 'Going well?'

Nigel screwed up his face. 'She's nice enough, but a bit keen. She wants to get to know James and Andrew better, and I'm not sure I'm ready for that. I think she's got me down as someone she'd be happy to settle with and she's already working at it. She's been divorced for a few years now and I think she's getting lonely and wants to have someone around.

It's been four years since Jayne died, so she reckons it's about time I did the same. It's just … well …'

Dan knew exactly what Nigel was talking about. They'd started working together just a couple of months before his wife Jayne was diagnosed with cancer. The prognosis had quickly grown worse, the word treatment replaced by terminal. The scar of the intensity of the emotion of those last weeks of her life had never left his friend.

'You're still comparing everyone with Jayne?'

Nigel nodded. 'Yep, and I do it with every woman I meet. That's why I haven't managed to make it last with any of them.'

'It'll come. When you're ready. There's no sense trying to rush it.'

Nigel stared into his pint. Dan could hear his thoughts. Four years was hardly rushing it. He knew his friend sometimes felt lonely, and with his sons seven and eight years old he'd love to have a woman around to help him in the difficult years to come. But not just any woman.

'Anyway,' Nigel said, looking up. 'Enough of me. How's life with you? How's it going with Claire?'

'Claire is … fine,' replied Dan slowly. 'Just … fine. When I get to see her, that is. I told you she's been made a full-time Detective Sergeant now?' Nigel nodded, sipping at his beer. 'She was delighted by the promotion, but it's brought loads more work. We try to get together at least one night in the week, and have a day out at the weekend, but with my work demands and hers it isn't always possible.'

'How long have you been seeing her now?'

'A year and a bit.'

Nigel looked thoughtful. 'So it's about the sort of time you should be …'

'Yes,' replied Dan, quickly. 'But we'll tackle that when we have to. Look, shall we talk about something else, other than women? I've never really got the hang of them. Christmas is coming up. In my role as surrogate uncle to the boys, any ideas about what presents I can get them?'

'Sure, yes. Well, I'll probably get …'

Nigel was interrupted by his phone ringing, some grating pop tune, no doubt a gift from his sons. He reached for his belt, but just as he did, Dan's warbled too. They looked at each other. A double call meant trouble, a breaking story and a scramble alert from the newsroom.

'I'll get it,' said Dan. He hoisted the phone up to his ear. 'What? Where? Yep, Nigel's with me. We'll go now.' He cut the call, stood up, Nigel doing the same.

'Let's go. You won't believe this after what we've just filmed, but it's true. The cops have killed a guy. Totally separate incident – in Cornwall, just over the river, Saltash. By my reckoning, that's the second time they've shot someone dead in five months.'

They each had a final gulp of beer, but left the two remaining quarter-full glasses on the table. Now that is the definition of urgent, Dan thought, as they strode out through the pub doors.

Everything was routine that night, as it always was now. He liked routine. Five years of serving his country in some of the world's bloodiest hellholes meant routine was only ever a distant fantasy. Now it was real and he savoured it, delighted in it. Ordered days, everything in its place and at its time, just as he expected it to be. Another day of joyous routine – until the news came on the radio.

The film hadn't been good, but it had passed a couple of hours. Now it was just before midnight, time to wash, clean his teeth and go to bed. It was the perfect time of night to sleep. Quiet in the other flats, quiet in the street outside. He enjoyed that peace, such a contrast to the days of trying to snatch some sleep amidst the shouts and screams and incessant gunfire. The cold too, an enemy almost as dangerous as the unseen rifles and bayonets, hiding in the quiet forest, always ready to pounce and steal away your life.

The toothpaste tube was nearly empty. Sloppy, he chastised himself. He made a mental note to buy some more on his routine Monday morning shop. He didn't need to write it down. The Army experience taught you to remember your tasks. There was more toothpaste in the yellow plastic basket above the toilet, three tubes, all neatly stacked in order of their Best Before dates. But he liked to have plenty of supplies in reserve. It was prudent.

He turned on the radio just as Big Ben's chimes rang out. Perfect. The midnight news. An ordered way to end the day, a round-up of all that he should know. He didn't need to any more, didn't have to be on constant alert to be despatched to some far corner of the former empire, but it was a wise habit to retain.

He washed his face to news of an unexpected rise in interest rates. That was irrelevant, the flat was rented and he had little in the way of savings now, just what he would need for these last days of life. He concentrated on his teeth, brushing gently but firmly, up and down, just as the army dentist had taught them. The money was gone, the preparations made and he had enough to live on until it was time to put the plan into action, however long that took. It was just a question of when. He couldn't predict when it would be, but the time would come and he would be ready.

He rinsed his mouth with the anti-plaque wash to news of a threatened strike in the Health Service. That shouldn't matter to him either, but it might to those he planned to visit. He noticed a slight smile in the mirror at the thought.

He picked up the portable radio and carried it into the kitchen, made his sandwiches to news of another terrorist attack in Israel. Two rounds, wholemeal bread. He'd had cheese and tomato today, so tomorrow's would be tuna and cucumber. An apple and a pear in the lunch box too, along with a bottle of fresh water.

Twenty past midnight, his watch said. Life was exactly on schedule, as ever. He never took the watch off, checked its accuracy each day by the Greenwich time signal, another habit his time in the forces had brought. Another good habit.

Time for bed. Ten minutes laying there, in the dark, then the radio off when the news had finished. Seven hours of sleep, exactly what years of experience and training had taught him his body required.

He lay down, closed his eyes, breathed deeply. Now some breaking news, the presenter intoned. Just a few lines of copy, only thirty seconds of information, but enough to have him sitting upright again, reaching blindly for the light switch.

A man, shot dead in Cornwall by police marksmen. It was believed to be the result of a domestic row. An investigation would be carried out. It was the second such shooting by Greater Wessex police in five months.

His life changed then. It was the long-awaited moment. The beginning of the end. They had done it again. The vicious, murdering, bloodthirsty bastards, killing with their usual easy impunity, never a regard for the effect it had on the lives of those left behind. But, this time, they would be sorry. Now, at last, they would finally be brought to account for what they had done.

He hardly slept that night, the angry memories erupting in his head. The night Sam had saved his life, despite the slashing, puncturing wounds he'd suffered from the merciless knife. His gratitude, the first time he could remember crying since he was a boy, how'd he'd looked after Sam, nursed him through those critical days. How they'd been together until the night Sam had again tried to save him, but this time could not, and had paid with his life.

The dark rage made him brittle as he lay in his bed, unmoving, eyes open, staring at the ceiling but seeing nothing. Even the golden, creeping dawn didn't stir him. The insistent alarm only forced itself into his consciousness after its twelfth set of escalating electronic chimes.

7.25. He reached out, stopped it, but still lay there. It was time. It was sooner than he'd expected, but he was ready.

It was finally time.

Chapter Two

DAN GRABBED THE HANDLE above the door, checked his seatbelt. Nigel had passed his advanced driving course three months ago, and the results could be alarming. The car rocked as they cut straight across a blind bend on the wrong side of the road. Streetlights blurred past. Dan had to resist the temptation to close his eyes.

'We won't produce much of a story if we're dead,' he muttered.

'Perfectly safe,' Nigel barked. 'You should always straighten out bends. I'd have seen headlights if anything was coming.'

He changed down a gear, accelerated to beat a turning traffic light, indicated, pulled off the main road.

Two police cars and a van blocked the entrance to a cul de sac, a double line of flickering blue-and-white tape stretched across the road. A couple of constables patrolled their sentry duty along it. A gaggle of onlookers stared, pointed and gossiped excitedly. A couple were still in dressing gowns despite the chill, a sure sign of the most mawkish, the ones who didn't want to risk missing anything.

Nigel parked the Renault, half up the kerb, by one of the police vans and they clambered out. Dan scanned around, noticed the street was called Haven Close, nudged his friend, pointed to the sign. Irony always made good pictures.

Nigel set up the tripod, slotted the camera on top, Dan helping. Seconds counted. The quicker you got to a scene and started filming the more action you captured.

Even better, night-time shots always looked dramatic. Nigel panned the camera, picking up the images. Wider views of the whole street, the officers on duty, the onlookers, close-ups of the police tape, officers and cars. Good stuff. And they were the first hacks on the scene. Even better.

Just one problem nudged Dan. The house where the shooting happened was hidden around the bend in the road.

They'd have to get pictures of it somehow, but he could think about that later. Some reliable information first. Two police shootings in five months, this was going to be a big story.

He checked his watch. It said just before 11, so probably about ten past. Not for the first time he cursed the back-street Brighton jeweller who'd sold him the cheap Rolex. It hadn't taken long to work out why it was such a bargain, but it looked flash and so couldn't be discarded.

All the Wessex Tonight news bulletins were done for the day, but the 24-hour news channel would want copy filed as soon as he could work out what was going on, the News Online site too. The days of continuous bulletins meant modern deadlines were unrelenting. When Dan had become a TV reporter it was one programme a day, at six o'clock. Now a report could often be demanded as soon as you got to a location. They'd have to work fast.

Start with your best bet, your most indiscreet and trusted source. A senior detective who'd be happy to answer any questions after the time they'd spent together investigating the murder of the notorious businessman Edward Bray, the hunt for the serial rapist stalking Plymouth and their efforts to crack the riddle of the Death Pictures. They'd become good friends, not that anyone else knew that. It wouldn't help either of their careers. Dan fished his mobile out of his pocket.

'Evening, Dan.' Detective Chief Inspector Adam Breen sounded unruffled by the late-night call. 'I was expecting to hear from you. Before you ask, yes I am the duty detective, and yes, I am working on the shooting. But there's not much I can tell you.'

'Hang on,' Dan replied, wedging the mobile under his chin and trying to write some notes with his other hand. He stood back from where a pack of journalists was starting to gather, wanted to keep any juicy details to himself. 'Go ahead.'

'This didn't come from me, of course.'

'Naturally.'

'We got a 999 call here earlier this evening, about nine o'clock. It sounded like a nasty assault, possibly involving a weapon, so we scrambled an armed response vehicle. The

19

marksmen had to kick down the door to get in. Following that a man was shot dead. I can't give you any more details because I'm just here holding the fort. As it's a fatal shooting by the police the Independent Police Complaints Authority are coming in to investigate.'

'Great, that's really helpful Adam, thanks. At least I've got enough to put something sensible in my report.'

'One more thing you should know Dan. The man the IPCA are sending is notorious in police circles. We call him the Smiling Assassin. Be wary.'

He cut the call before Dan could ask anything else. Who the hell was the Smiling Assassin? It sounded like something from a film. And Adam's voice when he said it, those words spat out as if he'd tasted something rank.

He rang the London newsroom and passed on the information. As Dan had suspected, it wasn't enough. Nowhere near. They demanded a report, right now, on the phone. The pressure to be first with any breaking news was intense. They'd use a photo of Dan and a map of where the shooting had happened to cover his words.

'With you in two mins,' came a voice. 'After this package on NHS reform.'

Dan scanned around him, tried to work out something sensible to say. When you didn't have any pictures to show the viewers a TV reporter had to think like his radio colleagues and create the images with words.

'One minute, standby.'

Dan scribbled a couple of notes on his pad. Even with Adam's information, he knew very little. Some padding was called for, and a little drama.

'Breaking news now,' came the presenter's voice down the phone. She sounded animated. Breaking stories were the very soul of the 24-hour news channels.

'A man's been shot dead by the police in Cornwall. Our reporter Dan Groves joins us live from the scene, in the town of Saltash.'

'Cue!' came the director's voice.

'Around me here is a scene of intense police activity,' Dan

began. 'The house where the shooting happened is in a quiet residential neighbourhood of the small Cornish riverside town of Saltash. Tonight, its usual tranquillity has very much been banished. There are scores of police officers here, and the scene has been cordoned off while forensics tests are carried out. Armed police were called here at around nine o'clock this evening after reports of an assault in a house, probably involving a weapon. A senior police source tells me the marksmen were denied entry to the house and had to kick in the door. Following that the man was shot dead, but the circumstances of that shooting are not clear. An independent investigation is already getting underway.'

Dan was thanked and the bulletin was on to the next story, something about a hunt for whales in the Far East. They would have recorded his report as it went out, could replay it for the next few hours. That would keep them off his back for a while. Precious time to get on with the story.

The press pack was gathering, a couple of newspaper reporters, some photographers, a TV crew and a radio reporter, fiddling with her microphone. Dan tugged Nigel away and they walked over to the onlookers to do a couple of vox pop interviews.

They gathered wherever there was trouble. Sightseeing ghouls, human vultures unable to resist the sweet lure of death. Their replies were always the same, 'Oh, it's terrible … shocking … who'd have thought it … in such a lovely quiet area as this too …' But they could never quite disguise their enjoyment. Still, their interviews added useful colour to pad out his report.

'What next then?' asked Nigel. 'I've got as many pictures of the area as you'll need.'

'We wait,' said Dan. 'At some point, someone official will have to come out and give us a statement. When we've got that, we'll have enough to fill a report for tomorrow's breakfast bulletins. Then we can go home and get some rest, though it'll be back here early for more of the same.'

Dan kicked at a stone, thought his way through the story. People and pictures were the golden keys to TV news. Their interviews with the onlookers would do for the human element. Officialdom would comment when it finally deigned so to do, as was its way. They had plenty of shots of police activity, but needed to see the house where the shooting happened. That was the next priority. But how?

A chubby face, wild hair, a looming grin and an enormous telephoto lens suggested there may be an answer. Dirty El, shameless paparazzo, was heading over and he looked pleased with himself.

'Hi Dan! You're late. I was wondering when you'd get here.'

'Ah, El. I should have known you'd be here first. One of your seedy little contacts tip you off, did they?'

El wasn't at all abashed. 'It's a profitable investment, making sure some hard-working officers of the law receive the golden bottles of single malt Christmas gifts they so richly deserve.'

'Get anything good? The police aren't letting us near the house and we need to get some shots of it.'

El's grin widened and he hopped from foot to foot. Dan sensed one of the photographer's dreadful rhymes was about to be born. He wasn't disappointed.

'If poor El can't fly,
But he yearns for the sky,
He must try out a spoof,
To get him up on the roof,
And pep up his cash flow to high!'

Dan sighed. 'Translation?'

'They wouldn't let poor El through the cordon either. But I have the advantage of this beautiful long lens,' he giggled, stroking it lovingly, 'and the old El charm and guile of course.'

'What did you do?' asked Nigel. El's creativity in pursuit of a lucrative picture was legendary.

'See that house over there?' The photographer pointed to a semi-detached, modern building across the road. 'Notice anything useful about it?'

Dan studied the house. It looked absolutely average, except

22

for the roof.

'Have you been up in that skylight?'

'Bingo!' cried El, his grin widening. 'Full house for the man on the TV. Got a lovely shot down the street to the house where the shooting happened. Lots of cops and forensics people outside too. I reckon I'm the only snapper with it. Should be worth a few quid to the papers.'

'How did you get them to let you use the roof?'

'Never underestimate the old El charm.'

'Details?'

'Well, the guy wasn't too keen at first. But then I saw he had a For Sale sign up. The house had been on the market for a few months and there hadn't been much interest, so I said – how about some professionally done photos, perhaps with a nice warm tint from one of my clever filters? I humbly suggested they'd make the place look a whole lot better in a brochure. He nearly bit my arm off.'

'El, you're a filthy genius,' said Dan, with a sly glance at Nigel. The cameraman pursed his lips. He knew exactly what his friend was thinking.

'I don't suppose you could introduce us to the guy, could you?'

'You are being a pain today,' said Nigel, as they thanked their host, and walked back over to the cordon. 'First guns, now heights. And you know I hate them. But you were right, the pictures were good. Right on the limit of what I could get with the zoom, but lots of activity, white-suited forensics people coming and going, and a few cops hanging about too.'

'Good stuff,' mumbled Dan who was chewing a ham sandwich he'd charmed from the man's teenage daughter with the promise of a day's work experience. He'd forgotten he was hungry until they were standing in the attic and he had a moment to think.

One of the policemen on the cordon beckoned to the pack. They moved fast, some jogging over, some striding. Positioning was all in an ad hoc press conference. You needed to be close to the speaker to be sure of getting good shots and sound quality.

'The Independent Police Complaints Authority Commissioner has just arrived,' the officer said. 'He'll make a brief statement for you lot in a few minutes.'

The pack formed a semi-circle in front of the police tape. Nigel and the other cameraman were in the middle with their reporters beside them, holding the fluffy, gun-shaped microphones. Next to them were the radio reporters, two now, and then the photographers and newspaper journalists. There was the usual pushing and shoving as hacks jockeyed for position. It was often called a media scrum, but was sometimes more like a ruck.

'All right, calm down,' called the policeman. 'I'd rather be doing crowds at football matches than trying to keep an eye on you lot.'

Some of the hacks were stamping their feet to keep warm, others rubbing their hands. They sky was still clear and the temperature falling fast. Dan's back was aching from the earlier enforced captivity behind the garden wall. He massaged it with a fist.

A man strode around the corner of the road, smartly suited. He was tall, about six feet, and wiry, but seemed powerful with it. A bald strip ran over his crown, the remaining hair surrounding it cut so short it was almost invisible. His lips were pursed but his face was set in a semi-smile, making him look smug. The Smiling Assassin, it had to be. A cluster of microphones was thrust under his nose and he surveyed the crowd.

'Ladies and gentlemen,' he said, and his voice was high and sibilant, making Dan think of how talking snakes were portrayed in children's books. His teeth were oddly small too, like a child's. 'Thank you for coming here tonight. I'm Marcus Whiting, the Independent Police Complaints Authority Commissioner for the south-west of England. I will be carrying out the investigation into what happened here.'

A newspaper reporter's mobile phone started ringing and Whiting's eyes flicked to him. 'Phones off while I'm speaking,' he hissed. 'That's one of the rules of the game.'

24

The man glared, but fumbled in his jacket and the noise stopped. Whiting watched, then continued.

'You'll want whatever information I can give you, but please remember, it's very early in our investigation so there's a limit to what I can say. Two police officers arrived here at just after nine o'clock this evening following an emergency call. They are members of the Greater Wessex Police Armed Response Team. They forced their way into the property. Exactly what happened then is currently being examined, but I can tell you that one of the officers fired two shots and the male resident of the house was killed. A female was also in the house. She is unharmed, but very distressed.'

He paused deliberately, waited for the hacks to stop scribbling. 'I am in charge here, but will be assisted in my inquiry by a team of detectives which Greater Wessex Police have been asked to provide. It is my duty to establish exactly what happened in the run-up to the shooting and when and why the fatal shots were fired. My report will go to the Crown Prosecution Service for them to consider whether any charges should be brought as a result of what happened here tonight.' His eyes again flicked over the pack. 'I would stress that is standard procedure, and does not it any way imply any wrongdoing by the officers involved. Any reporting which omits to mention that would be highly misleading. I hope you are clear on that point, as it is a very important one.'

There was a mumbling of 'Yes' from the reporters, and the woman to Dan's side started to ask a question, but Whiting cut in.

'I will not be taking any questions tonight and this is all the information I will be releasing for now. There will be an update here tomorrow morning.' His eyes flicked over the journalists again, paused, seemed to consider what he was about to say next.

'There is, however, one more thing to add,' he hissed finally. 'We at the IPCA are committed to going about our investigation as openly as possible. So, I have one further piece of information to impart tonight. And it is another important one.'

Behind him, Dan heard a reporter mutter, 'Spare us the bloody lecture, mate, and get on with it.'

Whiting lowered his voice, making the whole pack lean forward to catch his words.

'You will no doubt be aware another man was shot dead by Greater Wessex Police almost exactly five months ago. Again, I stress this information does not imply any wrongdoing and I must tell you the officer's name will not be released to you.'

He paused again, straightened a cufflink, knew he had the journalists waiting, exactly where he wanted them.

'But I can disclose to you this,' Whiting hissed. 'The marksman who shot dead the man tonight is the same one who fired the fatal shots five months ago.'

It was just after midnight when Dan finally got home. He slid the key into the lock, softly opened the door and just managed to get his hands around Rutherford's snout before the dog could start barking out his welcoming delight. The neighbours wouldn't appreciate that, it was bad enough the antisocial hours he kept himself. He patted and stroked the Alsatian as he whirled mute around him, then pushed him off and watched him scrabble around the corner of the flat and down the concrete steps to the back garden.

He'd left a tape at the studios with the pictures they'd shot in Saltash, along with a voice track and script for the TV breakfast bulletins. Even now, back at home, he still couldn't chase from his head what had happened. A great story was unfolding. Perhaps even a scandal. It'd certainly keep him busy for a few days.

Dan knew he was tired, but didn't feel it. He'd have to be up early tomorrow, to get into the office to look up their coverage of the last shooting before setting off for Saltash and whatever developments the day would bring. He had to get some sleep, but there was little hope with these thoughts buzzing in his mind. They were giving him a false energy. He needed to release them.

Rutherford scrabbled back up the steps. 'Fancy a quick run, dog?' Dan whispered to the Alsatian, grabbing him around the neck. He threw his shirt and suit on the bed in the spare room, donned his trainers, rummaged in the hallway cupboard for Rutherford's lead and they walked over the road to Hartley Park.

He released the dog and watched him sprint off along the line of lime and oak trees, then turn and dash back. Dan started jogging, Rutherford cantering beside him, stopping occasionally to sniff out a scent in the hedgerow. 'Ten laps will do us,' he called to the dog. 'We've got to get some decent sleep tonight.'

By the end of the first circuit, he knew their midnight run was a good idea, could feel the tension leaving him, the thoughts quietening as he went through them.

So ... a police marksman had shot dead two people in five months. It could be a coincidence of course, just a man doing his job. But experience had taught him not to believe in coincidence. The police were certainly suspicious, or why bring in the IPCA so quickly to investigate tonight's shooting?

He'd managed a quick chat with Adam as he drove back to the office. 'I can't say anything, Dan, it's an IPCA investigation. But, if I could ... well, you can see what the talk in the force is, can't you? There's real concern at the highest level. Maybe a rogue officer got through the firearms selection. Maybe he's just a little too keen on that gun he's been given.'

El was relishing the story. Dan had left him fondly imagining 'Police Killer' headlines, with the pictures he'd taken splashed over the front pages.

'Of course, what we really need to find out is the marksman's name,' Dan had said, trying not to make it sound like the suggestion he shouldn't be making. 'That, and get a picture of him. Then we could find out about his past and talk to people who know him, get them to tell us what he's like. It'd be incredibly lucrative ... if someone could get a picture of him.'

The photographer smiled in that sleazy way and stroked the long lens of his camera.

'My thoughts exactly,' he sighed. 'I think El has an

important mission to undertake, one that may require some deep undercover work. It'll be a tough one to crack, but El's got a few ideas.'

By his fifth lap, Dan was feeling relaxed and ready to go home, shower and slump into bed. He knew he wouldn't manage ten circuits; he never quite hit the targets he set himself. But then, why set them otherwise?

It was a beautiful time, of both year and day, the still city on a mellow autumn night. A few clouds drifted overhead, their edges polished silver by a sliver of moon. A patina of stars sparkled around them, the Plough, the only constellation Dan knew, hanging low in the northern sky. There were a couple of planets glittering there too. He remembered from some astronomy lecture at university that you could tell them apart from stars as they had a brighter and steadier light. He wondered which they were.

It was a romantic sight and Dan thought of Claire, what Nigel had said in the pub. Yes, he liked her, very much and she seemed to feel the same about him, as far as he could tell. They hadn't got to the big 'love' word yet, but he'd felt it coming on a couple of occasions, lying in bed together or walking over Dartmoor, his stupid, beloved dog gambolling around them like a pantomime fool.

He'd almost said it, wondered if she'd been feeling the same, but it had never quite happened. And Nigel was right, they were getting to that time in a relationship where it could go on, probably for years, when they'd move in together, maybe even the marriage thing that he'd avoided for so long. That, or the other route, missing the narrow moment and slipping into the slow descent of yet another tearful and tortuous break-up.

Dan knew he didn't want that. But did they spend enough time together to even consider a real, long-term relationship? She was busy with work, ambitious and talented, and his job kept him well occupied too. Could they compromise to make getting together on a more permanent basis worthwhile? The thoughts kept nagging, and he tried to put them aside, doubled his pace for a fast lap of the green.

The park was one of Plymouth's highest points, dominating the surrounding districts of the city. Most of the houses were in darkness, only a little moonlight sliding off the newer slate roofs. Lines of white streetlights marked the main roads, just the odd car rumbling along, relieved to be home. All else was dark, quiet and still. There was a rustling in the hedgerow next to him, a cat probably, maybe a hungry hedgehog or prowling fox. Dan had seen them in the park before, kept the curious Rutherford well away from their steely predators' teeth.

'Come on my classy friend,' he called to the dog, who was cocking his leg against a wall. 'Time we went to bed. Tomorrow's going to be a very busy day.'

Chapter Three

DAN HAD BEEN ON holiday at the time of the last shooting; a week's walking over the Two Moors Way with Rutherford. It was a fond memory, starting in south Dartmoor, finishing on the north Somerset coast in Exmoor. He'd stayed at a variety of old inns and bed and breakfasts, and had deliberately avoided buying a paper or listening to any news. It was a rejuvenating break from the intrusive, everyday world, just him, his beloved dog, pure air and peace.

Dan was polite to people who recognised him, doing his best not to flinch at the dreaded words – "Hey, you're that bloke off the telly," followed by the inevitable jabbing finger and, "What you should be covering is …", or, "What you don't appreciate is …" and he'd managed to evade their attempts to entice him into reporting whatever painfully parochial controversy was enraging the local community. He'd heard about the shooting when he got back, but hadn't looked at in detail, hadn't needed to.

It was just after eight, and he was sitting in the studios' News Library, the tape of the reports from five months ago ready to play. He'd slept surprisingly well last night and promised himself that an evening run with Rutherford would become a feature of those days when he needed to relieve some stress and empty his mind.

It was a healthier option than the usual beer. Claire had had a few words to say about his alcohol intake and Dan had surprised himself by taking notice. It was, he thought, one of the first times he'd realised how much he cared for her.

The first report began with night-time pictures of a street in Bodmin, police tape fluttering, a constable on sentry duty. A man had been shot dead in his own home by a police marksman, the commentary said. The timing was similar to last night, just after nine o'clock. The implication was there had been a violent row between the man and his partner, which had escalated. Details then became sketchy, but a neighbour was quoted as saying the man had a knife and the woman was screaming. There'd been similar instances in the past. He'd seen the police arrive and then break down the door, claiming to have heard two shots.

Dan hit the stop button and sat back. It could have been a replay of last night's shooting. No wonder the police thought it suspicious.

The next report came from the day after. It said the Independent Police Complaints Authority had arrived to carry out an investigation, something that was required by law. A dark-suited IPCA spokesman told the camera it would be thorough, rigorous and impartial. There was another interview with a neighbour who said the couple often had noisy rows, but that the man had been friendly enough when they'd passed in the street.

The most striking sequence was a couple of shots of a woman who the commentary identified as the dead man's sister. She was crying outside the house and managed a few sobbing words to the pack of reporters besieging her. Her brother might have had a temper, she said, but he was a good man who hadn't deserved to be shot.

Dan rewound the tape and looked back on the report. He didn't get the same sense of urgency he'd felt at last night's shooting. Five months ago, the IPCA arrived the day after. It felt like a routine investigation, begun because the law demanded it. The marksman would be exonerated and that would be it, case closed. Last night felt very different.

There were a couple of other brief mentions of the story in the log, the man's funeral being held and an inquest opened and adjourned, to resume after the conclusion of the IPCA investigation. The dead man had been named as Keith Williams, 43 years old, a mechanic in a Bodmin garage. A photograph, passport style, accompanied the funeral report. He had dark hair, a shadow of beard, looked chubby, a slightly crooked nose.

Dan stared into the man's face, wondered what he could have done to make himself the target for a police marksman. Could they have known each other, Keith Williams and the mystery police officer? Could the marksman also have known last night's victim? Was there some link between the three of them? Or was there nothing to connect them at all, just two random strangers who happened to cross the path of a trigger-happy policeman?

He checked himself. What was he talking about? Where was his sacred journalistic neutrality? They didn't even yet know if a crime had been committed. They might find the marksman had done his duty, saved two women from being killed or seriously injured.

Dan couldn't help but suspect not. It just didn't feel right. He knew he was anticipating the story of the rogue police killer. It was a reporter's dream. He ejected the tape, placed it back on the library shelf and headed down to the car park.

Whiting's manner hadn't improved. The night's rest appeared only to have refreshed his talent for being patronising.

'I have a little more to tell you,' he said loftily to the reassembled press pack, standing once again in a semi-circle by the cordon. 'It is part of my duty, after all, to keep the ladies and gentlemen of the media informed.'

As Dan had expected, there were the same faces as the previous night and a few new ones too. Journalists tended to be vain creatures and didn't like to let go of the glory of a big story. No sign of El, though. He must be working on his self-imposed mission, that or celebrating the success of the pictures he'd taken. Dan had flicked through the papers while he was in the office and seen El's snaps in several.

Haven Close was quieter now. The new morning had broken the night-time's lines of cars, many carrying their owners off to the daily ritual of work. It was remarkable how quickly normality returned. The ghouls had devoured their rich fill of the spectacle and were no doubt disgorging the gossip, far and wide.

A weak autumn sun was rising in the sky, doing its best to warm the land. At least it wasn't as cold as last night. Dan had slept in a strange, contorted Z shape to try to ease the ache in his back. It had just about worked, but he was still making a point of standing up straight and not slouching.

'Our investigations are well under way and proceeding smoothly,' Whiting continued, his face set in that strange, smirking half-smile. 'Forensics tests on the house are complete. We believe we have now established exactly where the two police marksmen trod last night. We also know precisely from where the fatal shots were fired. We are not yet in a position to release the dead man's name as not all of his family have been contacted. We have not interviewed the woman who was in the house when the man was shot. She remains very upset, and we will progress that line of inquiry sensitively. We have also not yet interviewed the marksman who fired the fatal shots.' His eyes flicked over the pack. 'That is all I have to tell you for now, although I will hold another briefing here at five o'clock. Do you have any questions?'

'Are you happy having Greater Wessex Police officers working on this inquiry?' asked a young woman. 'Isn't there a conflict of interests there?'

'I have full confidence in everyone on the investigation,' said Whiting smoothly, but Dan thought his voice had risen, grown more sibilant. 'Rest assured, young lady, I will get to the truth of what happened here.'

'Can we have access to outside the house to do some filming?' asked Dan.

'No.'

'Why not?'

'It's an investigation scene. I have to preserve it.'

Dan felt his temper bubble. 'Oh come on,' he said. 'I'm not asking to go into the house. I can understand why that's off limits. But why can't we just stand on the street outside and get some pictures?'

'Because, as I clearly stated, it is an investigation scene.'

'What, the street outside?'

'Yes.'

'Surely not.'

'I assure you it is.'

'But it's not in dispute that the officers drove to the street, parked up, then went to the door, is it? All that's important to

33

your investigation happened inside the house. I can't see any reason why we can't get some pictures of its outside from the street.'

There were a couple of murmurs of support from the other hacks. Whiting hadn't made any allies with the way he was treating them.

'Quite apart from the investigation,' he hissed, 'I also have to consider whether the media coverage might be intrusive and upsetting for the family of the dead man.'

'Which is an entirely different argument from the one you were just using,' snapped Dan. 'Is it your investigation, or the coverage which is keeping us from the house? And if it's the media, isn't it a matter for us to decide what we report? It's nothing to do with you, is it? Not unless we've suddenly become a totalitarian state, which I don't think we have.'

Whiting studied him, his lips parting to reveal those tiny teeth.

'I have made my decision and I am not prepared to discuss it further. Some members of the media have already breached the bounds of good taste by apparently climbing onto a nearby roof to get pictures of the house. I find that distasteful and a sign of all that is wrong with modern so-called "journalism". There will be another briefing at five o'clock.'

He turned and paced his upright stride back towards the house, leaving a host of uncomplimentary muttering in the pack. Hacks began phoning the fresh information into their newsrooms. With a big story like this, the ravenous beast of news demanded continual feeding.

'Pompous arse,' grumbled Pete, the local *Western Daily News* reporter. 'Do you think he was talking about the News? We used that shot El got on the front page this morning.'

'Snap,' Dan replied. 'I thought he was talking about me. We used some high shots too. Ah, let him think what he wants. It's up to us what we use.'

'What's the plan now then?' asked Nigel, taking the camera off its tripod. 'When you gentlemen have finished whingeing.'

'We're here all day,' replied Dan. 'We've got to cut a

report for the lunchtime news, and do a live bit, then the same this evening for Wessex Tonight.'

Dan's mobile rang. Adam, and sounding amused. 'You've met the Assassin then?'

'How do you know that?'

'Because he just came back here to the house fuming about some jumped-up idiot of a TV reporter. I asked what the guy looked like, and the description sounded familiar.'

'He was the one being an idiot, trying to tell us how to do our jobs.'

'Funny, that's exactly what he said about you. That and also that you had no idea about duty. He's got a thing about duty.'

Nigel was nudging hard at his arm, pointing up the street. A blue people-carrier with several people inside had pulled up, another car behind, the door opening, the driver getting out and staring towards them. Dan nodded, held up a finger to indicate he'd only be a minute.

'Adam, got to go in a sec, but tell me something first. You don't seem at all keen to help this guy. What's going on?'

'Oh, I'm helping him,' replied Adam, carefully. 'I'm doing just exactly what he asks. The High Honchos have assigned me to his investigation and I'm doing what he wants. Nothing more, and nothing less.'

'So not exactly busting a gut? Not getting stuck in there, being your usual scrupulous, dynamic self?'

'You might think that.'

'Why?'

'Well two things. One, I've had a look at the circumstances of this shooting, and the previous one. I can't see anything immediately suspicious. So I wonder why we're hounding some guy who's brave enough to carry a gun in the service of his country and use it when it's needed to protect the public. It's not easy for these firearms officers, you know. They're the frontline when there's danger. They never know what they're going to be confronted with and what action they'll have to take. I tried it out when I was in uniform, but it was too much for me and I jacked it in. It's bloody stressful and sometimes just downright frightening.'

Adam paused, and Dan heard footsteps and a rustling on the line. 'Sorry, just needed to get a bit further from the house there,' he said. 'Don't want any stray ears on this. And on the subject of the investigation, you'd be wise to be prepared for some action later. This is strictly not from me, as ever, but perhaps having a camera crew in the Higher Colliford Road area of Plymouth would be wise.'

Dan scribbled a note on his pad, knew better than to ask for more information. Nigel was nudging him insistently, pointing down the road again. A middle-aged woman was in streams of tears, being supported by two men and another woman.

'Adam, I've got to go, but you said there were two reasons for not being keen to help Whiting. What was the other?'

'Murky,' came the reply. 'Very murky. I'll tell you more when we next meet.'

It was still cold to touch, but the hours free from the deep freeze had been enough to thaw it. The skin felt like plastic, giving under his fingers but then slowly reasserting its shape. The bristles were still hard and stiff and scratched against his hand as he ran it over the forehead. The eyes were closed, screwed shut, as though the creature had known its fate and wanted to shut it out, find some escape. The blood of the severed neck was dry, hard, smooth, it flaked a little as he probed it.

He took the small notepad and pen from the table, put them into his pocket. Important those, silence was vital, he couldn't risk a word. Not at this stage. But she would still have to know what it was he wanted. It was almost comical, committing a crime where you had to write down your demands. But they wouldn't be laughing when he'd finished. Quite the reverse. He picked up the stocking too, put in into his other pocket.

He checked the address one last time, but he knew exactly where he was going. He'd carried out the reconnaissance of all his targets thoroughly. That was one of the first things the army drilled into you. Plan well. Be prepared.

Only the letter now remained, lying on the table, neatly

addressed. The white envelope was pristine and he wouldn't fold it. It was too important. It would be delivered as it was now, in immaculate order. He liked the touch of politeness he'd added, too. It showed a certain class, befitting his beautiful plan. Not just "Dan Groves", or "Groves, Wessex Tonight reporter", nothing so crass.

Mr Daniel Groves,
Wessex Tonight,
Crime Correspondent,
And Pig Lover.

He stared at the letter, then turned slowly to the frieze which covered the wall. It was filled with images of Dan, lines of his posed publicity shots from Wessex Tonight, the awkwardness of the forced smile forming its boundaries. Inside was stuffed with a tumble of images, enlarged and photocopied cut-outs of his head, fading articles from newspapers about the cases he'd worked on, a couple accompanied by pictures of Dan kneeling beside Rutherford, the dog's tongue hanging out as he panted at the camera.

The cutting at the frieze's centre was from the *Daily Bulletin*, a full-page splash, detailing how Dan had solved the riddle of the Death Pictures.

'Let's see if you're as good with my little puzzles,' he muttered to the article. 'I hope you are. Because the stakes are going to be so very much higher this time.'

He picked up another photograph from the battered old table, the final touch to the masterpiece of artwork, the pride of his collection. It showed Dan bending down, talking to a party of primary school children, their engrossed faces all rapt in attention. He'd taken the picture himself, when he'd visited the Devon County Show to meet the unknowing star of his planned spectacular doing his reluctant publicity work on the Wessex Tonight stand.

He'd even had a brief chat, nothing more than "Good morning, and keep up the fine work", and shaken hands, struggling to contain his bubbling rapture at the knowledge of what was to come. That had been months ago, and since then he'd wondered so many times if his beautiful plan would ever really come to fruition. But now, at last, it was time.

He paused, then added the photograph to the last corner of the frieze, nodded knowingly and smiled, as if at an old friend.

They both had so much to look forward to in the coming days.

Detective Sergeant Claire Reynolds thought it was the tamest raid she'd ever led. No smashing down of doors with sledgehammers, no sweaty, constricting body armour, no running in and shouting, no desperate struggles with drug-ridden suspects in the semi darkness of paint-peeling kitchens. Just a key in a well-oiled lock and a gentle walk into a pleasantly decorated hallway.

Martin Crouch's home was classic Plymouth suburbia; semi-detached, two bedrooms, probably dating from around 1900. It was well maintained, better than her flat, certainly. The house was a lemon yellow; the guttering a newly painted black to match the front door and wrought-iron gate. The border of roses in the garden was tidily clipped, the lawn even and smooth.

Inside was similarly ordered, a little beige carpeted hallway with a couple of photos of a young woman, a small lounge with a comfortable-looking burgundy three-seater sofa and matching armchair, a standard lamp to the side. Both faced onto a wide screen television with satellite system. A magazine on the square wooden coffee table was open on the week's football fixtures, a couple of games circled in black ink.

In the dining room was a small wooden table with two chairs pushed tidily underneath. A blue glass bowl sat in its middle. In the corner of the room was a computer, its hard drive now removed for further investigations. The kitchen and bathroom were part of an extension and unremarkable. She studied the notes on the front of the fridge. A dentist's appointment, a car service reminder, a postcard from Spain.

'Weather fine, hotel good, beach excellent. Having a great time. Wish you were here, Bill and Carol.'

Nothing of interest. She wondered how long it would be in

this increasingly lazy society before postcards came ready written with such standard greetings, just a quick signature required. That was if email, and text- and photo-messaging didn't render them entirely redundant.

Upstairs, both bedrooms were tidy, the beds neatly made, both with matching duvets and pillowcases. She only knew Crouch slept in the back one from the radio on a bedside table, its glowing red digits measuring the passing time precisely. There were net curtains in both bedroom windows. She ran a finger along one of them. It was surprisingly clean for a man who lived on his own. But, come to that, there wasn't a hint of dust anywhere in the house. Either Crouch had a very efficient cleaner or he was unusually house-proud.

She sat down on the stairs, halfway up, just as she used to as a child at home, closed her eyes, tried to think. There was nothing in this house to indicate even that Martin Crouch was a police marksman, let alone that he might have been rather too interested in guns. And nothing whatsoever to suggest he could have planned to kill someone in the course of his job. They'd been searching the house all morning and found nothing.

She shuffled up against the immaculately painted white banister to let one of the search team pass. Crouch himself was still back at Charles Cross police station. Not under arrest, they had no evidence to justify that. He was there helping voluntarily with inquiries, that was the official line. He'd given them a key to the house, just routine they'd said. But he knew he was under suspicion. Of course he did. They hadn't gone through it with him yet, wanted to get a clear picture of what had happened last night before they put it all to him. That would be for tomorrow.

She looked out of the window above the stairs. It wasn't a bad view from here. You could see Dartmoor off to the north, even as far as North Hessary Tor, the hill with its great transmitter mast. Dan had told her it was put up to bring TV pictures to Plymouth and the surrounding area, despite the arguments that it would mar Dartmoor's natural beauty. For a society so addicted to television, it was an easy debate to win.

They were due to go for a walk on the moor at the weekend, her, Dan and Rutherford. Some decent time together was long overdue. Even now, a year and more on, they hadn't really had enough of a chance to work out whether their relationship had a future. They got on well, had fun, enjoyed each other's company, but ... but what?

The love word hadn't been mentioned, had it? And the relationship had never really been tested, the strength of the bond between them. They'd have to talk about it. She wasn't getting any younger, didn't want to be wasting time in long drawn out dead-end flings any more. She still wasn't sure she wanted to have kids, but if she did she didn't want to be too old to enjoy them growing up.

Would she still be able to manage a day off? Not the way Whiting was going. He was working like he was driven, sending officers out on a series of simultaneous inquiries like a Catherine Wheel shooting off sparks. She deserved some time off, but it was difficult to say no when you were asked to work, not if you wanted your career to stay afloat.

'Claire, you'd better come and see this.' One of the forensics team was looking up at her from the foot of the stairs.

'Found something?' she asked, getting up.

'Two things. One possibly good, one not in the slightest.'

He guided her into the lounge. 'Out there,' he said, pointing through the window.

'Shit!' she hissed. On the pavement outside stood a TV camera, pointing straight at the house, the man next to it focusing his shot. 'Any guesses who he is?'

'One of the boys says he recognises him from another job he was on. Local TV, Wessex Tonight.'

'Shit,' she repeated, sitting down on the armchair. Not just that their search of the marksman's house was going to be on the news, but the inevitable question; how did the media get to hear about it? Only a couple of people in the force knew she was seeing Dan, but if the gossips started, the finger would point straight at her. She hadn't told him, but that wouldn't count for much. She could imagine the High Honchos talking;

"Keep Claire out of anything sensitive, can't trust her to be discreet you know. She's seeing that damned reporter bloke."

She'd have to talk to Dan about it at the weekend. That and the rest of their relationship, whatever that meant.

Not now though, she was working on an important inquiry. 'You said you had two things to tell me about. What was the other?'

'This.' A white-gloved hand held out a small piece of paper. 'It was stuck behind the framer's label on the back of one of the photos in the hallway. It was well hidden. I only found it by accident. I took the picture down, put it by the stairs but it fell over and this slipped out, just a corner but enough to see.'

She looked at the fragment of paper. It was the size of a fingernail, and in black ink was written carefully IWGU/66

'What was the photo?' Claire asked.

'It was a young woman, in her mid 20s. His daughter maybe? Was that important?'

'Maybe.' She made a mental note to check on Crouch's family, twirled the tiny piece of paper in her fingers.

'Any guesses about this?' she asked.

'Looks like a password to me. Probably for a computer. For something very important that needed to be encoded and safely hidden but which he didn't trust himself to remember.'

Dan had no idea who he was about to meet, or what he would be talking about, but it was a familiar feeling. At court cases, road accidents, the scene of a killing, it wasn't uncommon for someone to approach them, choke back the tears and find some moving words for the victim. That, or vitriol for the villain. The TV camera could be both great help and hindrance. If someone was angry and wanted to vent their rage, hit out at an innocent target, they'd usually make for it. But if someone wanted to pour out grief the camera acted as a magnet, and a useful one.

'Hello,' he said, walking slowly up to the group of people and putting on his best warm, but not happy, smile. 'I'm Dan Groves from the local TV News. I'm reporting on …'

41

He struggled for the words, knew what he said might be upsetting, could even lose him something important ' ...what happened here,' he ended lamely.

The men looked at him, stony faces, said nothing. Tears were still flowing down the woman's cheeks and she was whimpering.

'Can I help you in any way?' asked Dan. 'I got the feeling you wanted to talk to me.'

Still none of the group spoke. Then, suddenly, one of the men pulled something from his pocket and slapped it hard against Dan's chest. He flinched back, raised an arm, ready to defend himself, aware that Nigel was by his side, holding up the camera like a shield.

But no attack came. Seconds ticked by with nothing happening. Only the bizarre scene frozen.

'It's OK Nigel,' he said, as calmly as he could, but trying to keep his voice from shaking. 'It's OK.'

The arm hadn't moved, was holding the object against Dan's chest. He looked into the man's eyes, didn't see any wildness, just sorrow. He relaxed a little, looked down. It was a photo, crumpled, but the unmistakeable face of a man.

'It's OK,' Dan repeated. 'I think you've lost someone special, haven't you?' He lifted a hand, laid it on the muscular forearm.

The pressure on his chest eased. 'My brother-in-law,' the man said. 'My brother-in-law and my best friend. And her brother,' he added, putting an arm around the woman. 'We've come to tell you what a great bloke he was. All we've heard so far is that he had to be shot because he was violent and a wife-beater. Well, that's bollocks. Utter shite. We've come to put the record straight.'

Dan sneaked a look over his shoulder. The rest of the press pack hadn't seen what was going on, were too busy gossiping and comparing notes on the story, bitching about Whiting. He could feel an emotional interview coming on, full of tears and anguish. Powerful TV, but even better if it was their exclusive. Nigel had the camera, microphone, tripod with him, they didn't need to go back to their cars.

'Let's go and have a chat,' he said to the man, taking a risk and putting a chummy hand on his shoulder. 'I think we should all go and sit down, have a coffee, and you can tell me what kind of a man he really was. I'd like to hear that. Would you mind giving us a lift?'

They drove a couple of miles to a small country hotel, just outside Saltash. The manager wanted a hundred pounds to borrow the conference room for an hour. Dan could imagine Lizzie's reaction when he tried to claim it back on expenses. She was notoriously tight with company money, still hadn't stopped needling him about the sixty quid he'd paid to two prostitutes, strictly just for an interview, of course.

It was that which got him here in the first place, the reason he was moved to crime reporting from his fondly remembered days as the environment specialist. And that had led him to meet Adam Breen and help the police solve the murder of Edward Bray. Then it was the extraordinary riddle of the Death Pictures, a secret message hidden within 10 paintings by a dying artist attempting to right a long forgotten wrong. And it was during that time he'd started seeing Claire, whatever that might lead to.

The old cliché about it being a life-changing moment was very true. And what a ridiculous one too, paying prostitutes for an interview. How life could turn on a second's whim.

'So then?' The manager's voice brought him back to the hotel reception. 'I think a hundred quid's a fair price for the room. Do we have a deal?'

'I'm sorry, my editor just wouldn't allow that.'

'OK then. Well, if you'll excuse me ...'

'Perhaps I can help in some other way?'

'Like how?'

'Like ... how about us accidentally filming with the hotel's name in the background of the interview? Only about half a million people will see it.'

And here they were, Nigel setting up the camera, him trying to think what to ask a woman who'd just lost her brother to a police marksman's bullets.

43

Richard – or Richie – Hanson was his name. He was 44 years old and a teacher at a local primary school. He'd lived in Cornwall all his life, moving away only for three years to Plymouth for his teacher training. Dan studied the photograph, the one that had been pinned to his chest, while Nigel filmed it.

He was smiling at the camera, holding aloft a pint of beer and a set of darts. The photo was taken in a local pub where he played for the darts team. He was a lean man, ruffled blond hair, a thin face, small round glasses. Dan thought he looked a little like John Lennon, and wondered if he'd chosen the glasses to enhance that.

'The picture was taken last year. The team had won the darts league that day,' explained his sister tearfully. Her name was Jenny Sturrock, and she was holding on tightly to her husband Phil's hand.

Nigel finished filming the photo and clipped a small personal microphone to Jenny's shirt. 'Ready to do the interview when you are,' he said.

'Just … just give me a moment,' she replied, her voice shaking.

'Sure. It's only natural to be nervous,' soothed Dan. 'And I know it's a very distressing time for you. Just take it easy, we've got plenty of time.'

He checked his watch. Almost 11 o'clock it said, so probably ten past. They were on air at 1.30. They had to do the interview, edit a report, work out where to present the outside broadcast and then find something to say in it. Time to get a move on. The interview would have to be short and sharp.

'It's not live, so if we go wrong, we can just do it again,' he said, going through his standard reassuring patter. 'And, as Nigel will tell you, that applies as much to me as it does to you. You should see the number of takes I can get through.' Jenny managed a weak smile. 'Are you ready to give it a go?'

She nodded, and he paused, looked down at his notes; breathing space to frame his questions as sensitively as he could. He had a difficult one to ask too, as his job demanded, but he'd save that for the end. It was good interview tactics. If she took offence and stormed out, at least then he'd still have something he could use. It happened.

'Jenny, I know this is a very difficult time for you,' Dan began, 'so thank you for talking to us. Can I start by asking you about Richie? We know nothing about him. What kind of a man was he?'

She gulped down a couple of breaths, breathed out heavily. 'He … he was a wonderful man. He was kind, gentle and caring. He was the best big brother a woman could have. He looked after me when we were kids …'

Her words trailed off into a gasp at the memory and Dan could feel the tears close now, very close. He didn't say anything, just let the silence run, used it to gently encourage her to keep talking, knew she would fill it. She had her chance to tell the world about her brother.

'I remember one day … one day when I was dumped by my boyfriend. Richie put his arm around me and told me what horrible things men were and that I shouldn't be bothered. He said the guy wasn't anywhere near good enough for me anyway. Then he took me to the pictures to make me feel better. And even after that, he said … he said he'd go and beat the bloke up if I wanted him to.'

Tears began dribbling down her cheeks and she dabbed at them with a sleeve. Dan paused, gave her a few seconds to compose herself.

'I've got a feeling of the kind of man he was now,' he said carefully. 'And if this sounds like a silly question, please remember, very few people watching this will have been through anything like what you have. Can you tell me what it has been like, hearing your brother has been shot dead by the police?'

Dan had expected more tears then, perhaps even for her to break down, but the answer was fast, full of pure feeling. And despite the experience of so many of these interviews, it was one of the most memorable he'd ever heard.

Most people, when asked by journalists about their misfortune or plight, regurgitated the word "devastated". They seemed to think it was expected, had heard it used by others in similar positions so many times. Not Jenny. Her words were original, and all the more powerful for it.

'I felt like I'd been plunged into a sea of icy water,' she said. 'It was such an instant shock. I went cold and shivered and shuddered. And after that, I went numb. It was just like how I imagine it must be drowning in freezing water. I went numb and I couldn't believe what people were telling me. All my family were cuddling me and talking to me, but I was so numb I couldn't feel or hear them. And now I have started to believe it, I've got this burning anger inside me for the person who did it. That's why I wanted to come and speak to you.'

Again, Dan let the silence run, readied himself for the last question. 'Finally, I've got something it's my duty to ask you, and it's a difficult issue.'

Her mouth slipped open, waiting for the punch. He paused once more, heard the whirr of the camera's motor next to his ear as Nigel took his cue and zoomed the shot in for a powerful close-up of her face.

That was one of the great advantages of knowing each other so well. Good television was all about teamwork. The close-up revealed each tremble of an interviewee's lip, or reddening of their eyes, the image every bit as arresting as the words.

'Some people watching this will probably be thinking to themselves that the police don't shoot people for no reason. There are reports that there was a violent confrontation going on between Richie and his wife. What do you say to that?'

Her lips pursed tightly together and she shook her head hard, her eyes full of certainty.

'Never,' she replied, and her voice was emphatic. 'Never in a million years. Never in a million, million years. OK, so he liked the odd drink, but he was a kind and gentle man. He was my brother. I grew up with him. I knew him better than anyone. We were close, so very close. We shared everything. There were no secrets between us. He could never be violent, I promise you that. For him to be shot…'

Again her voice tailed off and Dan thought he'd lose her, that she'd break down, but she found the strength to finish, her eyes wide with anger.

'...for him to be shot – well – something either went terribly wrong, or – or someone had it in for my brother and went out to deliberately get him. And I want to know who ... and I want to know why.'

Chapter Four

THEY GOT BACK TO the cordon at a quarter to twelve and found 'Loud' Jim Stone, the unfailingly grumpy outside-broadcast engineer waiting. His face was set in a way Nigel had once and memorably described as resembling a weatherbeaten sack of rocks. He was wearing a subdued Hawaiian shirt today, rolling sand and palm trees under a cloudless blue sky.

'Coz it's a shooting thing,' Loud explained sullenly, seeing Dan's look. 'Death and all that ... didn't want to wear anything too bright.'

Dan wondered whether he expected thanks for his concept of consideration. Loud's nickname came from his taste in shirts; that and his surliness. In a diatribe in the canteen one day, Dan had originally christened him "Loud and Furrow-Browed," and it had immediately caught on, but was usually shortened for simplicity.

'I was wondering where you two had gone,' he muttered. 'Been off having a nice long breakfast break, no doubt. Not like some of us, working hard, setting up the OB truck so you can broadcast your ugly mug to the poor region.'

Dan took a breath and reminded himself the jollying-along route was usually the best for handling Loud.

'Hi, Jim. Sorry we've taken a while, but we had to do an interview with the family of the man who's been shot. I didn't want to rush it and upset them. I know a sensitive soul like you will understand.'

Loud's bush of a beard twitched suspiciously. 'Suppose that's OK. All right then, what've we got to do?'

'Edit a report and do a live for lunchtime, then again for tonight.' Dan slid into the OB van alongside Loud's bulk, not giving him a chance to protest.

It was an easy edit. The best stories always were. They told themselves.

Dan started the report with the photo of Richie, telling the viewers they could now reveal it was him who was shot dead by the police. After that, it was the part of the interview when Jenny talked about her brother's character. They added a few night-time shots of Richie's house while Dan recapped on how and when the shooting happened. The report ended with the last two parts of Jenny's interview, her talking movingly of how she felt about it and denying that Richie could be violent.

Dan watched her words on the monitors. She seemed very sure her brother couldn't have been a wife-beater. But she would say that, wouldn't she? Of course she'd stick up for him, whatever he was alleged to have done. But then again, she sounded convincingly certain. He found himself starting to believe – perhaps hope would be more honest – that this could really be the story of a rogue police marksman.

He checked his watch. Almost 1.10 it said, so probably nearer 1.20. Time to prepare for the live report. Lizzie had demanded a top and tail; the presenter would read a cue, Dan would come in live with a few words to set the scene, his report would play, then they'd cut back to him for a summing up. He popped the moulded plastic tube that linked him to the studio in Plymouth into his ear and took up a position by the cordon.

'A step to your left please,' said Nigel from behind the camera. 'You've got a lamp post sticking out the top of your head at the mo.'

A voice broke into his ear. 'Hi Dan, this is Emma, directing from the Plymouth gallery. Can you hear me OK?'

He raised a thumb to the camera. Broadcast etiquette dictates minimal use of words, sign language being preferable. It was to avoid any ill-advised asides being picked up by live microphones.

'Good stuff,' she replied. 'We're five minutes to on air. You're top of the bulletin, naturally. The next time we talk to you, it'll be for real.'

Dan realised he had no idea what he was going to say. That interview with Jenny, the row with Whiting, editing the story, wondering if the marksman could be a killer, all the business of the morning had given him little chance to think. He allowed himself a burst of controlled panic and felt the tingling shot of adrenaline clear his mind and focus his thoughts. Stick to the golden rule, he calmed himself. When in doubt, just KISS, the old TV acronym. Keep it short and simple.

'Wessex Tonight can this lunchtime reveal the name of the man shot dead by the police in Cornwall,' read Craig, the presenter. 'He was Richard Hanson, known as Richie, a 44-year-old local schoolteacher. Our crime correspondent Dan Groves is at the scene of the shooting in Saltash. Dan ...'

'Yes, this lunchtime, the Independent Police Complaints Authority are continuing their inquiry into the events that led up to the shooting of Mr Hanson.' Dan gestured behind, to the cordon and the constable on duty. 'But I can tell you his family have condemned the shooting and described Mr Hanson as a kind and gentle man.'

His report rolled, a wonderfully welcome two minutes to think of what to say next.

'That was Mr Hanson's sister Jenny, speaking to me earlier,' he intoned sombrely as the report ended. 'The Police Complaints Authority say they're making good progress with their inquiry. They expect to release more details later this afternoon. We'll bring them to you in this evening's Wessex Tonight.'

They'd had a busy morning and produced some good work, so Dan took Nigel to a nearby pub for a sandwich. Loud declined Dan's half-hearted offer to join them. He never socialised, always preferred the sandwiches Mrs Loud packed for him and a sleep in the back of the OB van.

Lizzie called as they were eating and fizzed about the report. 'Great stuff, the sister's a real tearjerker. I almost blubbed myself. No one else had anything so good. How did you get hold of her?'

Dan debated telling the truth, that it was pure luck, but banking some credit with your boss never hurt.

'Oh, you know, the usual tricks. Working the story. Asking around, talking to people, finding out where she lived, taking it easy with her, giving it the old Groves' charm, talking her into it.' He ignored Nigel's raised eyebrows.

'Right. Good.'

Dan sensed the brief flare of praise was fading, to be replaced instead by one of his editor's favourite spiels. He wasn't disappointed.

'Now, no resting on laurels, do you hear? I want more of the same for tonight. I want another report like lunchtime's. I want another live too. I want those pics of the raid on the marksman's home in tonight's piece. I want the whole caboodle, and I want it good.'

'Of course.'

She sighed with delight. 'Oh what a story! The police shoot a guy dead, then they think it could have been a rogue marksman out to murder – for a second time! It's a news editor's fantasy! I can just see the ratings now.'

Dan picked up his beer to take a swig and clinked it clumsily against the table. He winced at his elementary error.

'What's that?' barked Lizzie. 'You're not in a pub, are you?'

'No … no … never … well, kind of. I've just … err … popped in to pick up a sandwich. It's been a long day already, and we'll need the energy if we're going to get some more good stuff this afternoon. Believe me, I'd rather be out there covering the story. I'm only doing it for the sake of the programme … for you.'

Lizzie laced her pause with suspicion, as only she could. 'OK then, but no drinking,' she snapped. 'This is big news and I want you fresh and all over it.'

'Of course no drinking, never in work time,' Dan soothed, cutting the call, finishing the rest of his pint and nodding at Nigel's offer of another half.

The evening's report was similar to lunchtime's, but ending with an added sequence of pictures of the raid on the marksman's house. It was almost five o'clock. The only concern thought Dan, as he and Nigel waited by the cordon with the other journalists, was if Whiting came out and said

51

something dramatic. That would mean he'd have to re-cut it all, and fast. He didn't like to imagine Loud's reaction.

Dirty El had returned, explaining the national papers were interested in some more pictures. But it was a very different El from the usual model. His normally unruly shock of hair had been cut into a smart and businesslike short back and sides and had gone from dark to blond. He had also bought a pair of small rectangular glasses, which he put on to show Dan.

'There mate, what do you reckon?'

'I reckon El is dead, long live El. You look totally different. If I didn't know it was you, I wouldn't recognise you. You look almost reputable.'

El produced his usual sleazy grin. 'That, my friend, is precisely the idea.'

'What are you up to then? Not changing your image to impress some woman?'

El looked as near to shocked as his mischievous face could manage. 'No! Of course not. Nothing so unproductive. It's all part of that little mission we discussed.'

Dan was about to ask more, but there was a stirring amongst the journalists. Cameras were hoisted onto shoulders and microphones and notepads readied. Whiting was striding towards the cordon. Dan noted the time on Nigel's watch, exactly five o'clock.

'Ladies and gentlemen, this will be a brief update as I have little more to tell you,' he hissed, his eyes flicking over the crowd. They rested on Dan, seemed to narrow.

'Our investigations here at the house are almost complete and I expect the cordon to be removed later this evening. By tomorrow, all parties to the case will have been interviewed. The most important of those are the marksman who fired the fatal shots, the other police marksman he was working with and the woman who was in the house at the time of the shooting. I can reveal no more about those interviews as they're a critical part of my investigation. That's all I have to tell you. Are there any questions?'

'Are you naming the man who died now?' asked Peter.

'No.'

'Despite it being on the TV,' Peter replied sarcastically, with a sideways look at Dan. 'It's scarcely a secret now, is it?'

'I can still not be sure we've traced all of the man's relatives and told them of his death,' Whiting hissed. 'I'm afraid I consider that TV report entirely irresponsible.' He stared straight at Dan. 'It would be a dreadful shock if some of the man's family found out from the television he was dead. Furthermore, I believe the hounding of the relatives of bereaved people by journalists is deplorable.'

'Hang on!' snapped Dan. 'I'm not having that. Mr Hanson's sister approached us and asked to speak because she wanted to pay tribute to him and set the record straight about his character. So don't give me your media harassment rubbish.'

'That may be your version of events, but we've had trouble tracing this woman to speak to, and I'm sure if she ...'

Dan felt a sudden urge to pick Whiting up by the throat. 'Well she managed to find me OK,' he interrupted. 'She just walked up to me and asked if she could talk about her brother. Not my hardest piece of research.'

There were a few laughs from the press pack. Whiting's eyes again flicked over them.

'As I've said ... that ends today's briefing. And I do not propose to hold any more. All further information will come from our press office in Cardiff.'

'I think you've upset him,' chuckled Peter, as Whiting stalked away. 'It looks like he's taking his ball back and doesn't want to play any more.'

Dan tried not to enjoy his moment, knew it was pathetically petty, but failed.

The evening's outside broadcast was another top and tail. The studio introduced Dan, he talked about the investigations at the house being almost finished and his report played. Then he told the viewers the interviews with the marksman and others would be completed by tomorrow, an important stage in the inquiry. He was thanked and the programme moved on to its next report, a crisis in farming caused by a tuberculosis epidemic in cattle.

He got home, took Rutherford for a run, then had some tea, stale toast with baked beans, followed by a yoghurt which was four days past its use-by date. He took the risk to get rid of the taste of the stale bread. He would have to get to the supermarket this weekend, however much he disliked shopping. He could live off takeaways and pub grub quite happily, but more importantly Rutherford was almost out of dog food. The beer cupboard was looking thin too, just a few dusty and long neglected tins of his less favoured ales remaining. Running dry was a frightening prospect.

Dan went to run a bath, but first had to shift a fist-sized spider from its new home by the plughole. He wasn't keen on spiders, but tried never to kill anything. Even a wasp that had landed in his beer last summer had been fished out with a pen and left to dry on the pub table. He'd watched it, expecting it to die of drowning or alcohol poisoning, but it had rallied and then tried to fly off, landing first on his hand and stinging him before managing to make it to the safety of a nearby bush. His hand ached for most of the evening. It was an interesting lesson in life. It doesn't always pay to try to do good.

The spider seemed keen on its new home and impervious to Dan's attempts to help, scuttling back and forth along the length of the bath in an attempt to evade him. It was like a video game. He finally managed to tire and corner it, and with the help of a newspaper ushered it into a jug and popped it outside the front door. 'Bet it comes back tomorrow,' he told Rutherford, who'd been watching the action with what seemed like amusement.

He left the light off in the bathroom, preferred the mellowing half-light from the hallway, and eased into the bath. Rutherford lay down on the floor beside him, and Dan flicked the odd handful of foam at the dog as he told him about the day.

'Great story, mate, but I don't think we've made a friend in that Assassin bloke. I want to know what it was he did that so upset our friend Adam. And I reckon we might get our killer police marksman story you know. The sister of the guy who was shot is sure he didn't deserve it and she was pretty convincing. This one's going to run and run. It'll certainly make our demonic, ratings-hungry, tyrannical News Editor happy.'

Rutherford yawned, but at least had the decency to gently thump his tail on the carpet to feign some interest.

Dan ran some more hot water, and tried not to wonder if his backside was getting bigger. There didn't seem to be as much room in the bath as there used to be. He wasn't exactly over-eating, but he was still probably drinking too much beer.

'Maybe it'll have to be ten laps of the park when we say we're going to do ten in future,' he told the snoring dog. 'We don't want to put Claire off, do we?'

He picked up his mobile from the side of the bath – he always took it with him, knew from painful experience that the moment you least wanted a call was the likeliest it would come – and started tapping out a text message. He hadn't spoken to Claire since the shooting story had broken, had been too busy. He stretched to his side and held the phone over the carpet as he typed. Dropping the last one in the bath had been an expensive mistake.

"Evening m'lady. Sorry no speak awhile, been hectic with the shooting. You still OK for a walk tomorrow or Sun? Lunch on me too. Looking forward to it … x"

Lizzie had said he could probably have Saturday and Sunday off. They'd done well on the shooting story and it didn't look as though there'd be any significant developments over the weekend.

'But keep your mobile on, just in case,' had been her final warning words. 'And I mean wherever, whenever and whatever.'

You were never fully off duty with Lizzie. Dan had a recurring dream, that the day he finally got married, perhaps on some sun-blessed beach in the Caribbean, she'd call, demanding he find a couple of hours to cover a story.

A strange feature of the dream was his bride was always faceless and wearing a black dress. What did that mean? Some relic of Thomasin, the woman he'd loved at university perhaps, and who still haunted him? But he hadn't thought about Thomasin so much this last year. Claire had frightened away her ghost, for most of the time, at least. But not all … he didn't want to think about that. He reached for the hot tap and ran some more water, enjoyed its enveloping flow.

The mobile rang and Dan smiled, reached for it, expecting it to be Claire. It was Adam.

'Hi mate, where are you?'

'I'm at home, in the bath.'

'What?'

'In the bath. If you want details, it's …'

'No thanks,' he cut in. 'Something nasty's happened and we need your help.'

'Go ahead,' Dan replied, wedging the mobile under his chin and hauling himself out of the bath. 'I was going to call you soon anyway. I want to know about what happened between you and Whiting …'

'Never mind that now. We've had an attack on a woman in Plymouth. Well, I say an attack, she wasn't actually harmed, but she is seriously traumatised. It's a bloody weird one.'

'Carry on, I'm just fishing some clothes out.'

Dan started drying himself with the off-white bath sheet, walked into the spare room to check the rack of shirts. Was there a clean one? The end of the week meant they were always scarce.

'A guy pushed his way into her flat after threatening her with a gun. I say a guy, we're assuming it's a man. He wore a stocking over his head. He made her sit on a chair and watch while he used the pistol to smash her TV screen in.'

'Uh huh,' said Dan, putting on a shirt and rummaging through his drawers to find some socks and pants. They were scarce too. 'Nothing much on the box tonight then? It wasn't because I was on, was it?'

There was a brief pause before Adam answered. 'Don't joke. I'm wondering if that might be part of it. Here are the even weirder bits. The guy produced a piece of paper and wrote down what he wanted. He didn't speak, just wrote. He wanted her passport, or driving licence, or birth certificate. She pointed to some drawers and he went through them and took the passport. He didn't go over the house and wreck it like burglars do, looking for anything valuable. He only took the passport and smashed the TV. And here's the really odd bit.'

'Uh huh,' repeated Dan, sitting on his bed and trying to pull on his socks one-handed.

'He had a plastic bag with him,' said Adam. 'And he took a severed pig's head out, and put it in the telly where he'd smashed it.'

Dan stopped fiddling with his socks. 'Blimey, that does sound weird. And no attack on the woman at all?'

'No. She was totally unharmed. Well, physically, anyway.'

'It looks like you've got a nutter on your hands. I take it you want some news coverage to warn people about him? And to put out an appeal for anyone who might have seen anything? The usual stuff.'

'Yeah, we'll certainly do all that, but later. It's not the reason I'm calling you. This bit isn't to go out on the TV.'

Dan was about to grab his coat, but the tone of Adam's voice stopped him.

'No?' he said slowly. 'Why do you want me then?'

'Because the guy left a letter at the scene, on top of the TV in fact. And it's addressed to you.'

Chapter Five

A POLICE CAR PICKED him up, Adam had insisted but wouldn't say why. The flat was just off the city centre at North Hill. Dan hadn't had time to properly dry off, and wriggled in his seat to try to rub some of the clinging moisture from his back. His hair was still damp too, and he dabbed absent-mindedly at it with a grimy handkerchief. His brain was buzzing. Who could possibly want to commit a bizarre crime and leave him a note at the scene? And why was he being escorted there?

There was a pair of police vans and four cars outside the house, uniformed officers jogging up and down the street, a group of neighbours watching. Some looked like students, others older people, a couple of children too. Typical of the area. It used to be popular with families who liked the big town houses, but with the expansion of the university many became flats and bedsits for the students. A sweet smell drifted in the air, the unmistakeable hint of cannabis.

Someone's panicking at this moment, Dan thought, imagining them flushing a stash down a toilet at the sight of all these police officers. He tried to smile, but the expression wouldn't grow. He itched tetchily at his back and attempted to calm a welling concern. Adam had never sent him an escort before.

The car parked and the driver got out and walked with him over to the house, politely insisted on it, despite Dan's protests. Adam was waiting, pacing back and forth along the pavement.

'We can't go in, the scene's been secured and we're checking for evidence.'

And good evening to you, thought Dan, but didn't say so. His friend didn't sound in the mood for humour.

A couple of white-overalled figures were crouching on the path, looking for footprints. Dan knew more would be inside, checking every corner of the flat. The sound of detectives carrying out door-to-door inquiries slipped across from the neighbouring houses, soothing but insistent voices intermingled with alarmed and excited residents.

'I've had a look around and that's all I need for now,' continued Adam. 'The more people who go inside the flat, the more difficult it becomes. We'd have to take a sample of your hair and shoe and finger prints and all that stuff if you go any further. I've got a copy of what was written on the envelope and the letter inside. They're the only bits you need to see.'

Adam put on his teacher's voice, the way he'd come to differentiate between their private and professional discussions. Dan wondered whether he was aware of it.

'Can I emphasise that you're here as a witness?' said the detective. 'None of this is for broadcasting, OK? It could prejudice my inquiry.'

'Sure, but your inquiry? What about the shooting?'

'The High Honchos don't like the look of this one so they've put me on it. I've done about all I needed to on the shooting anyway. Suzanne and Claire have taken over helping Whiting. It's more routine now and doesn't need such a senior officer as me. They can handle it.'

That explains the lack of a reply from Claire, thought Dan. So I probably don't need to worry that she's playing it cool for some fearful reason. But it would be good to hear from her. Dan knew it was just her way not to reply to texts quickly, particularly when she was busy. But it didn't stop it from playing on his mind. He always replied to her as soon as he could.

Dan forced his attention back to the street. 'You don't look entirely distraught at being off the shooting inquiry.'

'Our previous discussions on that matter still stand,' replied Adam coolly. 'Now come and sit in the van and have a look at this letter. That's more important.'

Adam hopped up the van's step, pushed past a uniformed sergeant blowing on a steaming cup of tea and pulled a small table down from the inside wall. He took a piece of paper from the inside pocket of his jacket.

"Mr Daniel Groves,

Wessex Tonight,
Crime Correspondent,
And Pig Lover."

Dan stared at it. The feeling of disquiet was growing. 'Well ...
I've had more pleasant introductions. What ... what do you
make of it?'

'The first thing is – why the hell is this guy leaving a note
for you at all? And then, why address it so formally and
politely, up until that last line? Why not just Dan Groves, or
Dan Groves, TV reporter, or something like that, or just
something more abusive?'

'And pig lover? I like a bit of bacon in a sandwich, but I'm
not noted for being a lover of pigs.'

'That, I think, refers to us, the police. It ties in with the
severed pig's head. Read on to the letter. It's bizarre.'

Adam turned the sheet over.

"Dear Mr Groves,

You'll no doubt be wondering why I'm writing to you.
Well, let me tell you that straight away. It's because I think
you may understand what I'm doing and why.

"Allow me to take a step back before I go on. I've seen you
on the television of course, but what marked you out as
distinctive in my mind was when you solved the riddle of the
Death Pictures. Do you remember all those articles the
newspapers ran on you, and the wonderful pictures of you and
Rutherford? It was then I began to think you might understand
me. Anyone who is a dog lover must be a good person, I
thought.

"But I have to confess I'm disappointed in you. You
haven't just been reporting on crimes, as your job dictates,
have you? You've been solving them – not only the Death
Pictures but also the Edward Bray murder. You seem to have
become very close to the police, very close indeed. And I
don't think that's wise.

"Apologies, I digress. This is what is important. After
today, you and I are both set on the path that I have chosen for

us. The other players we shall require in our drama are merely the supporting cast, although it may not always seem so. There is only one question that remains to be answered, and that is how exactly this will end.

"In fact, that's a little misleading. It implies you have a power over a larger part of the action than is actually the case. Only the very last act in our drama remains unresolved. All else is set. And it is the last act, which will be determined by you, your bravery and intellect. My only regret is that I will not be there to see how it is played out.

"My intentions will become clear over the next few days. Then you will inevitably begin to ask yourself – am I evil? That is a good question, and I think, as so often, the answer depends upon your viewpoint. But whatever, the issue of 'evil' is at the very centre of our dance. I'll leave you to think about that. I'll be in touch again soon.

"Forgive me for not signing this. You will know my name quickly enough, I promise, but not just yet. It would inconvenience my plans."

A silence as both men stared at the paper.

'Whew,' whistled Dan finally, for once not knowing what else to say. He looked over his shoulder, out of the police van, tried to quell the sudden fear that someone was watching him. There was no one there.

'Sounds like … well … a real weirdo,' he said slowly. 'But a weirdo who knows a bit too much about me for my liking.'

Adam studied him. 'Yep,' he replied. 'And he also sounds like a clever and calculating weirdo, who's got some kind of plan. And it looks like you're at the centre of it.'

Dan tried to keep his voice calm, wondered why he felt a sudden urge to look over his shoulder again. 'You're not making me feel any better, mate.'

'Don't think I'm trying to alarm you,' continued Adam, looking him in the eye. 'But I'd like to put a police guard on your flat tonight.'

'What?' Dan leaned back against the wall of the van, suddenly felt shaky. 'What? Really? I mean … he's just a nutter isn't he? Just a harmless nutter who's all talk? Isn't he?'

'Harmless nutters don't tend to have guns and a severed pig's head, and leave detailed and lucid letters in women's flats. You're right, he could be harmless. But then again, he might not be. He might have been watching you and knows where you live. I don't want to take that risk.'

Dan struggled to speak. His back suddenly felt damp again. 'Hell, you … you're serious aren't you?'

Adam didn't need to reply, just held Dan's look.

'OK then,' he said, noticing how thin his voice sounded. 'If you … you really think it's necessary, I'll have a cop on my door. The poor neighbours will think I've become the Prime Minister or something.'

Adam managed a serious smile. 'I think it's the right thing to do. It's only a precaution. Just for a few days, until we catch this guy.'

'A few days? Days?!'

'If that.'

Dan breathed deeply, couldn't ease the twitch that made him want to keep looking over his shoulder.

'OK then … OK. Look, I take it I'm safe here at the moment?' Adam nodded. 'Then take me through the letter and tell me what you make of it. I might at least know something about my stalker.'

Claire checked her reflection in the glass of the door, straightened her jacket and knocked.

'Come in.'

Whiting didn't get up, just motioned her to sit on one of the two plastic chairs. He was scribbling some note with black, spidery writing, his head bowed, the light shining off the smooth strip of pink skin running over his crown.

There was a small pile of coins on the desk too, pennies, five pences, tens and twenties, that peculiarity of his. Every time he sat down he would empty the change from his pocket. She'd heard about it, but this was the first time she'd seen it. She'd heard plenty about Whiting. The station was full of gossip and she didn't believe most of it, but if this was true, what about the rest?

'Sorry to keep you,' he said finally. 'Just something occurred to me that I shouldn't forget.'

'That's fine, sir.'

'Yes,' he hissed. 'It is.'

Claire said nothing, kept her face blank. The gossips were certainly right about what the modern world would call Whiting's interpersonal skills. Humanity might be another way of putting it. DCI Breen wouldn't talk about him and what had happened between them, but other officers did, and the word loathing was everywhere. But that was the past, she reminded herself. He was her boss, for now at least. That meant respect and discipline and no difference in her professional approach or attitude to her work.

'I've called you in, Claire, because I needed to have a word with you in private. I need to know you can be …' he paused, flicked his eyes over her '… relied upon.'

'Sir?'

'As you know, Detective Chief Inspector Breen has been moved to another case, and so you and Sergeant Stewart will be in charge of helping me with the remainder of my inquiries.'

'Yes, sir.'

'How do you feel about that?'

'Fine, sir. We have a job to do. You can rely on me to do it.'

'It's not an easy job though, is it? Investigating your own?'

'No, sir.'

'It can make you unpopular.'

'Yes, sir.'

'And that doesn't bother you?'

'If I'd wanted to be popular, sir, I wouldn't have joined the police.'

He smiled that cold, unfeeling look, those small teeth showing under his thin lips.

'Indeed. So I can rely on you … one hundred per cent?'

'Yes, sir.'

'Thank you, Claire.' He nodded. 'I know this will be a

difficult investigation. I know that some of your fellow officers consider those who volunteer to carry firearms to be very brave. I know some believe we are persecuting them for simply doing their job. I understand that. But I can assure you, as I have them, that we are not. To anyone who questions you, you are simply doing your job too. More, in fact. You are doing your duty. If there is wrongdoing, we will expose it. If not, we will exonerate. It is simply that – a matter of duty.'

'Yes, sir.'

'Thank you, Claire.' He scribbled another spidery note on his paper.

'Is that all, sir?'

'Yes. Thank you, Claire.'

She got up to go, but the feeling lingered that Whiting still hadn't finished. Her hand reached for the door.

'Oh, Claire, one final thing.'

'Yes, sir?' The punch line, she knew it.

'All that we're doing has quite understandably aroused considerable interest in the media.'

She felt herself stiffen, kept her face neutral as it was probed by those flicking eyes. 'Yes, sir.'

'I think it's time we got on with our investigation in peace now, out of the glare of publicity. I know I can rely on you to keep our work confidential, no matter who might ask about it, or what your relationship with them might be.'

Adam loosened the knot on his tie and held up the piece of paper.

'I'm not exactly sure what I do make of it. My hope is it's just a weirdo and we can dismiss it but I just don't think it is. It's too well planned. Too ... I don't know, purposeful, I suppose.'

Dan was feeling shakier, kept wanting to get back to his flat, lock the door, sink some beers, have the faithful and protective Rutherford next to him. He couldn't imagine a policeman standing outside, guarding him. Who could possibly want to harm him? He was a reporter with a small regional TV station, not some big-time celebrity. He couldn't believe it, but Adam's face was anything but joking.

'Let's start with the crime then,' the detective continued. 'Come on, you've got a good mind for stuff like this. We've got a description, but it's basically meaningless. He's about five feet 10, fairly slim and has an athletic build, wore trainers, jeans and a black jumper. That's it. The forensics and fingerprints boys are all over the flat, but so far they've found nothing. It looks like he wore gloves and the stocking will have stopped him shedding any hair. Door to door inquiries have come up with nothing yet either. So let's look at the peculiarities of the crime and try to think through it.'

'Uh huh,' muttered Dan, trying to force himself to concentrate. His back was still damp with a nervous sweat.

'First, he didn't speak. That raises two possibilities. One, that he can't speak, that he has a condition which has harmed his voice. We can check that out with the local doctors and hospitals. Two is that he couldn't risk speaking, because he has a very distinctive voice, perhaps a lisp or something like that, or that he knows the victim and she may recognise it. We can go through that with her when she's up to being interviewed, but it won't be for a few hours. She's in a right state.'

'OK,' replied Dan, who was beginning to feel better at having the distraction of something else to think about. 'That all sounds fair enough. What about the pig's head?'

'It's going to the labs. They can tell me if it was professionally severed by a butcher, how long it's been dead for, if there are any fibres or marks on it, where it might have come from, anything like that.'

'Sure. But given the lack of forensics at the flat, I bet they don't find much. He'd know you'd examine the head. I reckon we'd be better off thinking about its meaning.'

Adam nodded. 'OK. And your guess is?'

'It's a jibe, isn't it? It fits in with the address to me as 'pig lover'. Someone wants to have a go at the police for whatever reason. And I'm a nice high-profile way of doing it. Maybe the guy thinks if he targets me, he's bound to get TV coverage and that's exactly what he wants. A public way of getting at the police. I bet that's why he smashed the TV too, to have a go at me and the police together.'

Adam tapped at his teeth with his pen. 'Good thought. But if we're looking for people with a grudge against the police ...'

'That's just about everyone who's ever been arrested, let alone convicted. And plenty more besides probably. So it doesn't help much. Can we narrow it down a bit? Are there any more potential clues in the letter?'

He scanned the words. 'There, look. He talks about Rutherford. Could it be an animal lover who dislikes the police for some reason? Like ... one of those animal rights protesters who picket research labs. Maybe he thinks the police are protecting the people inside too much?'

'A bit hypothetical isn't it? Besides, we haven't got any animal research labs in Devon and Cornwall. And animal lovers are hardly likely to cut off a pig's head to make a point. We'd better stick to what we know, or can have decent suspicions about for now.'

'OK, fair enough. I was just thinking aloud. So, what about the gun? They're not common in crimes here.'

'Sure. That's worth trying. I can get the team to lean on their informants to see if anyone's bought one in the underworld lately.'

Dan thought for a moment. 'He's obviously got some plan that he thinks he needs a gun for, hasn't he? The letter's full of it. According to him, it's all worked out and proceeding smoothly. The only trouble is, we don't have a clue what it is. Except that it involves me.'

They looked at each other. 'You're right. So we'd better concentrate on what we do know,' said Adam thoughtfully. 'That brings us to the last obvious clue. What he stole. A passport.'

'Something to establish a false identity with?'

'Possible, but unlikely. If so, why not take the driving licence and birth certificate and utility bills too, all that sort of thing? They'd be useful to him and they were all there in the drawers. It was only the passport he wanted.'

'To sell on to criminals to use for a fake passport?'

'Doesn't fit, does it? Yes, maybe if this was an ordinary burglary. But not when you've got a man who leaves a severed pig head and a letter behind. The passport would have to have been taken for some specific reason … something symbolic.'

'Like what?'

Adam shrugged. 'I have no idea.'

'What's her name?'

'Who?'

'The woman who was attacked. Her name? And what's she like?'

'Not for broadcast? I've got to protect her.'

'No, not for broadcast, I promise.'

Adam nodded. 'Her name's Sarah Croft. She's in her mid 50s, small and slight. Divorcee, works in a local chemist.'

'Anything important in that? Is she famous in any way? Could that be what he wanted with her passport?'

'Not that I know of. Totally unremarkable as far as we've managed to find out so far.'

They lapsed into silence, looked at each other. The feeling of wanting to glance over his shoulder started to nag again at Dan.

'I'm still curious what it is you've got against Whiting,' he said, trying to distract his fretful mind.

'Another time,' replied Adam firmly. 'I'm far too busy to think about him at the mo. He's never a priority. Never.'

The way his friend spat out the words made Dan even more curious. But before he could push it Adam interrupted.

'I'd better get back to her flat to see if they've come up with anything. I don't think there's any point you staying. I'll get one of the boys to drive you back home and do the sentry duty.'

Dan suddenly didn't feel like going home at all. He sensed a fear of being alone he hadn't known since childhood.

'OK, thanks, Adam. Will you call me if anything else comes up … please?'

'Of course. But I've got this feeling we'll only have a better idea of what he's up to when he does whatever it is he plans next. And judging by his letter I fear we won't have long to wait.'

Back at home, Dan lay on his sofa, the stereo on, a book open in front of him, but nothing helping to calm the tumble of his thoughts. He felt his heart still racing, his mind running with it. Why me? What have I done? What does he want with me?

He knew the policeman was standing watchfully outside the door, but it didn't stop him turning nervously at every slightest creak in the flat.

Even the pints of Old Venom weren't helping. He'd managed to persuade his police driver to stop at the off-licence on Mutley Plain on the way home. The man seemed to understand easily the concept of needing something to calm the nerves. Normally four bottles of the strong, dark beer would have him dozing nicely, but he didn't feel like sleeping at all. He stroked Rutherford's head and was rewarded with a whine and yawn.

It's ridiculous, he thought. Why should I worry? There's a sturdy policeman on guard outside. Rutherford would kill anyone who tried to get near me. But fear isn't rational. I've never had a stalker before. It's the facelessness that's so scary. It could be anyone, for any reason. And he could be anywhere around me. I wouldn't know, unless he chose to reveal himself. And how would he be likely to do that? Not in any pleasant way.

Something to look forward to, he needed something to distract his spinning mind. There was Sunday and the walk with Claire, but now he wasn't even sure if that was going to be enjoyable. She'd called earlier, just a quick chat, sounded distracted and stressed. She was busy with work too but still wanted to go for the walk, needed to, in fact. There was something they had to talk about, something important. It sounded ominous. He'd begun to convince himself he was about to be dumped.

It hadn't bothered him so much since he'd been seeing Claire, but he could feel the swamp of the depression that had always haunted him lurking on the edge of his consciousness.

It was growing, pulling harder the more the image of the severed pig's head burned in his mind.

Enough. He'd had his fill of the world for the night. He walked out to the kitchen, resisted the temptation to again open the blind and peer out, instead grabbed the whisky bottle from the back of the cupboard, took a blanket from the spare room, lay back on the sofa and pulled it over him.

Dan took one swig, another, then another, felt its liquid fire warm him. He couldn't face going to bed tonight. Sleep felt too vulnerable and lonely and he was frightened of his dreams.

Chapter Six

DETECTIVE SERGEANT CLAIRE REYNOLDS occasionally regretted her choice of career. When the insistent electronic bleeping of the detested alarm penetrated her consciousness at half past six on Saturday morning, she expected that familiar feeling. But it didn't come. There was no rueing another missed chance for a Friday night out, no lamenting the loss of a day's walking on the coast, or DIY, or just reading and relaxing in front of the TV.

Maybe the regret would grow in future years she thought, as she hauled herself out of the warm haven of her bed. At least the central-heating timer in her flat was working now, so it wasn't such a battle to get up. And the new carpets she'd had laid made a difference too, much better than those cold wooden boards, trendy though they might be. She'd take comfort over fashion any day.

Maybe if she'd started to feel that need to have kids, but not fulfilled it, not even met a man capable of doing so, maybe then she'd start to feel some regret. Maybe if she had met that man, did have those kids but never saw them. Maybe if she'd made all those sacrifices, but wasn't a Detective Chief Inspector by then, or a Detective Superintendent.

She flicked on the electric toothbrush and checked the mirror. Hair everywhere, as ever, but that would only take some gel and a few minutes work. No spots, good. Even now, at 30, she was still susceptible to the odd spot and it was embarrassing. The boys in the office teased her about them, but then they teased anybody about anything. It was the CID way.

It'd be so good to see Dan tomorrow. No matter how hard the week, what horrors of death or disaster she'd had to investigate, he could always find a smile somewhere within her. And he had that hidden vulnerability she couldn't help but find attractive. It hadn't taken long to realise she was building a relationship with two people. The public Dan, confident and assured, and the private man, such a contradiction, so oddly full of sadness and uncertainty.

They hadn't spent enough time together lately, even if there was that difficult talk to have. She'd have to be careful how she broached it. But it was necessary if they were to carry on seeing each other and she wanted to. She was sure of that. There were those three words she'd been waiting to say to him, waiting and wanting, but just hadn't had the chance – or maybe not found the courage?

One night, lying in bed together, him snoring gently at her side, Claire thought she'd worked out why. Each major boyfriend in her past – there had only been three, she tended to the longer-term relationships – had said them to her first. She had never been the one to take the biggest emotional risk, expose her heart. But now she had to. She'd whispered the words to Dan as he slept, had to resist a searing temptation to push him awake to hear them.

Claire finished brushing her teeth, reached for the mouthwash. Was he husband and father material? Yes … she hoped. Probably … she thought. Maybe … she feared. They hadn't spent enough time together to be sure yet.

She stepped into the steaming shower, enjoying its pummelling heat. She'd done her training, her two years on the beat – even those were strangely enjoyable, seeing a very different side to life to her public-school upbringing – then straight into CID. 30 years old and a Detective Sergeant now, life was going exactly to plan. No one had seen it and no one would, that little piece of paper containing her vision.

She'd written it just after she joined Greater Wessex Police and it was there, in the drawer, to be retrieved and checked occasionally. DS by 30, tick. Detective Inspector by 34. Detective Chief Inspector by 38. Detective Superintendent by 42/44. They all had a space by their sides, ready for a tick. She still wasn't quite sure why she'd added that leeway to the last rank.

Anyway, even if she didn't make it that far so quickly, she had no regrets. It was an extraordinary life. She'd never believed the old saying about the truth being stranger than fiction until she joined CID. Every day brought a new surprise and she loved it.

And this case had been another weird one. A police marksman under investigation for murder? She turned off the shower and grabbed a pure white bath sheet. She'd have to take her own to Dan's flat sometime, his were so murky and grey and hardly absorbed the water. That was, if she was planning on spending more time there.

She smiled. Enough of that for now. Concentrate on today first, and the big interview with Crouch. They had a good picture of what went on in the house, had interviewed the other marksman and the partner of the dead man, had done all the ballistics and forensics tests. They'd gone through Crouch's background too; a big surprise there, something they had to ask him about and that strange password at his house as well.

Some of it looked suspicious, didn't it? But it could be entirely innocent of course. Well, they'd find out. For all his oddities, his lack of any grace, Whiting wasn't renowned as a man who gave up without finding the answers. And she wouldn't either. Claire was surprised to find herself thinking they might make a strangely effective team.

She chose one of her standard black trouser suits from the wardrobe. A woman could never have too many of those, clothes for all occasions, even CID work. Comfortable, hard-wearing and smart. It would be a fascinating day. Another fascinating day.

Adam pushed open the door of Tom's bedroom, trod softly over the green-and-white Plymouth Argyle carpet and looked down at his sleeping son. His face was soft with a serene dream.

Imagining a win for Argyle today? Or that girl in his class he was working on the geography project with – was it Helen? – the one he'd so shyly spoken about at the only family dinner he'd managed to get to that week. He was nine now, reaching that age when girls stopped being repugnant and took on an unexpected and incomprehensible allure. Adam grinned at the thought of what that would mean in the times to come.

Tom's dark hair was tousled, stuck up and springy over his pillow. He was his father's son, all right. Adam ran a hand through his own hair. It could take ten minutes work in the morning to make it presentable. And when Tom started shaving, he'd no doubt suffer his father's fate as well, the shadow of a beard by midday at the latest.

Adam reached out and gently pushed at Tom's shoulder until the boy's eyes blinked open. He watched the passing seconds in the reflections as his son made sense of the world.

'Good morning, young sleep monster.'

'Hi, Dad. Is it football time?'

'Yes, football in a minute. It'll take us a couple of hours to get to Bristol, so we've got time for some breakfast first.'

Tom struggled upright. 'And a kick-about before we go?'

Adam had been hoping he'd ask. 'I should think so. We've got to practise some of the moves Argyle might try this afternoon, haven't we? It's a big match. A local derby. Your first ... an important moment in a young man's life, eh? Like working on a project with a pretty young lady called Helen?'

Adam ducked the pillow that came flying towards him.

Claire and Detective Sergeant Suzanne Stewart sat next to each other on the plastic chairs, Whiting on the other side of his desk. Claire thought the pile of change was smaller today. Perhaps he'd bought himself a coffee? If so, there was no evidence of it and he hadn't offered to get one for them. The man didn't seem to enjoy any little human comforts. Despite her best efforts not to, in her mind she'd started to characterise him as a machine, an automaton.

Claire caught a hint of Suzanne's perfume, noted her new-looking navy jacket, smiled to herself. This was the woman Dan had described as "your classic dumpy and dowdy plodder of a plod" when telling the story of how he'd first met her and Adam Breen on the Edward Bray murder case. The two of them had never got on, Suzanne believing Dan had no place in a police investigation, Dan saying she was nothing more than an average, unimaginative cop, always playing it safe, filling out the paperwork, following the time-honoured routines and correct procedures in a way he never would.

They'd never even warmed to each other, but one night, after a couple of bottles of wine, Claire had finally got Dan to admit a reluctant respect for Suzanne, and an understanding that police work needed both their approaches. He went for the show business style, the wild leaps of careering imagination, the instinctive insights that explained people's actions. The sacred epiphany moments as he called them, which solved the crime in an instant of vivid realisation. She preferred to build a case slowly and methodically, on the traditional foundations of solid evidence.

Suzanne had changed over the last couple of years. She didn't talk about it, kept her private life very separate, but it didn't take a master detective to sense the influence of a man. Fashionable clothes, a trimmer figure, perfume, a hint of make-up, and, most tellingly of all, the occasional sight of a genuine smile. A new reason to live.

Whiting cleared his throat noisily. 'I wanted to get together so we can have a discussion before we conduct the interview with PC Crouch,' he said, giving them his unfeeling smile and exposing the tiny teeth. 'It is the key moment of the case. Let's take a moment to go through the statements of PC Andy Gardener, the other marksman he was working with on the night, and Ms Chanter, the partner of the dead man.'

Whiting produced a pile of papers from his briefcase and placed them carefully on the desk. They were neatly divided by a red, plastic partition. He pushed a half towards Claire, the other half to Suzanne.

'Let's examine PC Gardener's first,' he said. They began reading.

"PC Crouch knocked on the door. There was no answer", Gardener had said. "We could hear screaming from within, so he knocked again, much harder. There was some light in the house, though at the back, not the front where we were. I believe I saw the shape of a person moving fast, perhaps running past the window in the lounge although I could not tell if it was male or female. I may have seen another person's shape following it, but I cannot be sure as my attention was back on the door. PC Crouch was knocking hard and shouting through the letterbox. He said 'Police! Open up please.' There was still no reply, and I heard more screaming and what I believed to be thudding and banging coming from inside the house.

"PC Crouch and I had a brief conversation. We agreed there was reason to believe a crime was being committed and we feared for the safety of at least one of the people in the house, as there was evidence a weapon may have been involved. We would normally wait and follow the standard procedure of contain and negotiate, but we believed there was an imminent risk to life in the house, and so we had to go in. We briefly discussed our tactics. We agreed we could not use baton guns due to the confined space. The Taser electric stun gun is currently banned from use due to its potential contribution to the death of a woman in the Midlands. Thus we decided pistols would be the most appropriate weapons and we drew them. PC Crouch would move in first. I would follow, covering him. This was our standard way of working. He always liked to go first.

"PC Crouch kicked down the door and we moved slowly into a hallway. It was dark. The only light was coming from the far end of the house, and we continued slowly towards it. The screaming had stopped when we entered the house, but then resumed. It was clear it was coming from the rear, and what looked like the kitchen area. We continued forwards. Ahead, PC Crouch rounded a corner in the hallway and I saw him then raise his gun and shout the standard challenge, 'Armed police, put your hands up! Armed police, put your hands where I can see them!' I remember this warning clearly. Following that, PC Crouch discharged two shots and moved on into the kitchen. The corner in the hallway and its narrowness meant I did not see the actual firing.

"After the shots, I pushed my way forward and saw PC Crouch standing over a man who was lying prone on the floor. He was not moving. A woman was sitting on the floor alongside him crying. She appeared to be injured. A kitchen knife was by the man's body on the floor. I immediately radioed for back-up and an ambulance. We checked the man for signs of life but it was apparent he was dead and attempts at resuscitation would be futile. Other officers arrived at the scene within about eight minutes of my call. Nothing was touched in the kitchen during that time, although the woman was leaned against the sink unit to support her."

Whiting's eyes flicked over them. 'All clear?'

'Yes sir,' they both replied.

'Are there any particular points we need to bring out?'

'The fact that Gardener didn't see the actual shooting,' said Suzanne. 'And particularly why Crouch went first into the house.' She checked the statement again, following the lines with a finger. 'Gardener says he always liked to go first. We'll want to know why that is.'

'Precisely,' hissed the Assassin. 'We must remember we may be investigating not just a possible murder, but also what could turn out to be manslaughter. There may have been no plot to kill, no premeditation. But there may have been recklessness, over-zealous behaviour, or even enjoyment of being in the position of having a gun. Could PC Crouch have been too keen to use it? Wanted to use it?'

Suzanne and Claire both nodded. 'Sir?' asked Claire.

'Yes?'

'I've never been firearms trained. I think I'm clear about how marksmen operate, but given the gravity of this case, can you remind me of the rules they work under? I need to be absolutely clear when we interview Crouch.'

Whiting studied the sheet in front of him before continuing. 'In essence, the rules are these. The first principle is to contain and negotiate. That's why sieges are so common in these cases. Officers would first usually surround a house to make sure the incident could not spread and there was no danger to the public. Then they would attempt to negotiate with the aggressor.'

'But in this case – and the one in Bodmin – it didn't get as far as negotiations?'

'No. If a situation is changing rapidly, or there's an

immediate threat to a member of the public or a police officer, then force can be used immediately.'

'And what are the rules then, sir?'

'The force used must be proportionate, so an officer can shoot if he believes the person he's dealing with is posing a threat to the public or to the officer himself. It's simplest to think of it in terms of the marksman's priorities. His first is to protect the public. His second is to protect himself. His third is to protect the suspect. So, if the marksman has a legitimate and honest belief that members of the public are, or he himself is, in danger, he can fire. The suspect does not need to have a gun, simply some way of being a threat. In relation to this case, a knife is of course sufficient if the suspect is in close proximity to a member of the public or the officers.'

'And the marksman always shoots to kill?' asked Suzanne. 'He doesn't aim for the legs for example, to disable a suspect?'

'It's not called shoot to kill,' said Whiting, 'but that is largely for reasons of public relations. It's officially known as a "shoot to stop" policy. Marksmen are trained and ordered to fire at the body. So even if it's not the intention to kill, that is the likely outcome. The logic is that when a situation has become so grave that a marksman has to fire, he must do so in a way most likely to ensure he removes the threat he faces. That is why he targets the body.'

'And no baton gun in this case?' asked Claire. 'No thoughts about using that to incapacitate rather than kill?'

'You'll see from the statement they did consider using a baton gun but decided not to do so. It's very much bigger and bulkier than a pistol. They believed it could have impeded them in the close confines of the house they were entering. The evidence we have seen so far leads me to conclude – initially of course – that was a fair judgement.'

His eyes flicked over them and Claire and Suzanne both nodded. 'Shall we go on to Ms Chanter's statement? It contains some evidence you may well find distressing.'

'Yes sir,' they both replied and began reading.

*   *   *

Sergeant Dicks had a nagging feeling he recognised the man but wasn't sure from where. Maybe someone he'd met in his days on the beat? Some party? A friend of a friend? Whatever, it didn't matter and he wasn't going to embarrass himself by asking. The guy seemed friendly, knowledgeable and decent. And they didn't get many applicants for the position. Just the one in fact. He was suitable and he'd do. It was only for a few weeks until Mick came back, after all.

'So you're happy with changing the barrels, cleaning the pipes, all that sort of thing?'

'Sure.'

'And you don't mind working with police officers? They can get a bit bawdy sometimes.'

'No problem. I'm sure I've seen far worse in the places I've worked in.'

'Oh, I don't know. You'd be surprised.'

'Well, if there's trouble, I won't have to worry about how long it'll take the police to get here, will I?'

Sergeant Dicks chuckled. This was the man for them, sense of humour a golden indispensable. 'No, don't worry, we look after our little club. You won't have any trouble. OK, if you're happy I'll leave you to it. As I said, I don't know how long we'll need you for, but it's likely to be about a month until the regular barman's leg heals.'

'Sure. That's fine by me.'

'OK then, goodnight and good luck.'

Sergeant Dicks climbed the stairs from the basement, pushed open the fire door, got into his car, the barrier lifted and he drove out of Charles Cross police station. Where did he recognise that chap from? He was sure he'd seen him before somewhere. Well, whatever, he seemed honest enough, a good smart hair cut, even if he hardly looked like a natural blond.

The Sergeant set plenty of store by a good haircut. When he'd joined the force, a short back and sides was obligatory, but now they came in with all manner of odd styles. Anyway, the club bar was covered and that was the main thing, the lads would have somewhere for a cheap drink when they wanted it.

His mind turned to thoughts of the brunch of sausage, bacon, egg, chips and beans awaiting him at home.

It always felt unfair when your birthday fell in midweek, she thought. For an adult, it was just about tolerable. You did your day's work, opened a present or two, and you could look forward to the weekend and the celebratory meal, the drinks out with your friends, perhaps even a little private party. But for an eight, soon to be nine year old, stuck in the disciplined confines of school on your special day, it was near insufferable. So it hadn't taken much pleading before she agreed they could take the bus into Plymouth this fine Saturday morning with the promise of a little advance of birthday money to buy some new jewellery.

The young girl bobbed her head back and forth and counted the passing shops, her pony tail flying. Sitting by her side on the worn seats, Mum calmed her daughter with a kind hand and turned to apologise to the old lady sitting behind them, receiving an understanding smile in return.

'Mum, I think I want some new hair slides.' She waved the plaited golden rope with a hand. 'Some of the other girls say it's out of date like this. They bunch theirs up with slides. I'd like blue … to go with my eyes. Bright blue … and with glitter on too, maybe. Janey's got one of those. It looks lovely. Hers is shaped like a butterfly. I think I know where to get them.'

Mum thought, but didn't say, how she loved the golden pony tail. 'Don't forget you've only got five pounds to spend today.'

She beamed out a grin, exposing the gap between her front teeth. 'I'm rich! Rich, rich, rich!'

Other people on the bus were joining in the smile. Her own face was warming too. It was impossible to resist. Children did that. In even the most sullen of company, their delight in life was infectious.

'And then next week I've got my real birthday to look forward too,' the girl bubbled. 'I'll wear my new hair slide when I open my presents. Can I open them before school? Can I? And can I have my friends round at the weekend, like you said? Can I?'

Mum tugged gently at the flying pony tail to calm her. 'We'll have to see. It depends if you're a good girl or not.'

'And are we there yet? At the shops? Mum, I'm worried they might sell out of hair slides before we get there.'

More smiles from the surrounding passengers.

'We're almost there. And I doubt they'll sell out, don't worry. Look, a hair slide won't cost all of your five pounds. Why don't you work out what else you'd like to buy and let Mum have a bit of peace?'

She nodded hard, the smile fading into a frown of concentration as she began counting off the money on her fingers. 'Hair slide ... necklace ... bracelet ... all matching, of course. Or maybe not ...'

Jo Chanter's statement started with the background to the shooting.

"I was married to Richard, known as Richie Hanson for six years but retained my maiden name. We have lived together for all that time. At the start of our relationship, there was no sign of him being violent. But, about a year ago, he seemed to change and would sometimes hit me. At first, this was largely in the body area. I believe that was so the bruises would not show. He would often hit me on the back with a belt, leaving extensive marks and bruising. About three months ago, his abuse became worse and he would sometimes punch me, not just in the body but in the face too. He would also threaten me with a knife although he never actually attacked me with it.

"On the night of Thursday, 22nd October, I told him I wanted a divorce and we had a row. It escalated and he again hit me, threatened me with a knife and said he was going to kill me. I called 999, but was unable to speak as he attacked me and cut the call. About ten minutes after that, there was a knock on the door. By then, I feared for my life and was screaming. He had cornered me in the kitchen and was still threatening me with a knife. I was lying on the floor to protect myself. He was standing over me, shouting and occasionally kicking me. I was extremely frightened. The next thing I knew, I heard a crash from the front of the house, shouting and then what sounded like two pops. Richard was lying on the floor and there was a police officer, standing over him with a gun, while another officer tried to talk to me to see if I was all right. I was taken away by an ambulance crew and cared for."

For Claire, it always happened when she heard a story of domestic violence. Her mind ranged back to the downstairs neighbour in the flat where she used to live, that night the woman had knocked hesitantly, so softly on her door, as if fearing the reaction, flinched back when Claire had opened it. She had blood trickling through her matted hair, drying on her trembling lips. She'd pleaded for help, her body shaking, endlessly apologising, telling Claire it was all her fault for not getting the tea ready on time.

Of the many corpses she'd seen now, the living dead too; their bodies cut, torn, ripped and battered, hanging on the sheer line between life and death in a hospital bed, that memory was still one of the most vivid and haunting she knew. It was the one that always returned.

Why she wondered? Why so powerful? Because of the words the woman had stumbled out, the desperate pleas, the way she blamed herself for the viciousness unleashed upon her. And because Claire, despite the eternal lesson of not getting involved, had tried to help, had called in a couple of police officers she knew, had rung the crisis lines, the shelters, found the woman a place to stay and hide, a sympathetic detective to investigate. And despite all that, she'd gone back to the flat when he called her and she had refused to press charges.

And that night, more crashes and screams from downstairs. Claire had gone to the estate agents the next day to find a new flat to rent, couldn't bear the images her imagination brought.

'What do we need to follow up there?' asked Whiting, when Claire and Suzanne finished reading.

'It seems consistent with Gardener's statement, sir,' Claire replied, trying to keep her voice neutral. 'I never understand why women don't just get out.'

'That is not the issue we're examining here,' hissed

Whiting. 'Retain your focus, Claire.'

The embarrassment brought a blush to her face and she stared down at her boots to hide it.

'Does the medical evidence tally, sir?' asked Suzanne quickly, to distract Whiting.

'Yes it does, Suzanne. The doctors found old bruises on Ms Chanter's body, consistent with her statement. There were also new injuries on her body and face, which had been inflicted in the last few hours. They were not cuts, but were consistent with her being punched.'

'And what about the ballistics and other evidence, sir?' asked Claire.

'That tallies too. You've seen the computer simulation. The front door is kicked in – we have Crouch's boot prints on it – and the two marksmen move up the hall. We have their prints on the carpet, Crouch taking the lead as the statements say. His footwear is the larger by two sizes. Crouch moves around the corner and then stops, Gardener behind him. Two shots are fired by Crouch, both hitting Mr Hanson in the chest. He dies instantaneously. Ballistics indicate they were fired from exactly the position Crouch says, angling downwards to hit Mr Hanson as he bent over Ms Chanter in the kitchen. He then collapses by her side. Any questions on that?'

They both shook their heads. 'The final evidence we must recap on before we interview PC Crouch is that from the shooting of five months ago,' continued Whiting. 'As you know, the circumstances there were very similar, which is why I was called in to investigate. Again PC Crouch and PC Gardener were on duty together in an armed-response vehicle. They were called to a house in Bodmin at about nine o'clock in the evening, a similar time to the Saltash shooting. Again the call came from the woman who lived there. She said her husband was attacking her with a knife, then the call was cut. Again PC Crouch kicked the door down, again he went into the house first.'

'His statement says he got to the rear of the house, a dining room where he came upon a man threatening a woman with a knife. He shouted a warning but the man ignored it. He feared for the safety of the woman, so again, in that case, he fired twice. The man was hit in the chest, again dying instantaneously. Again PC Gardener did not see the actual shooting as he was behind PC Crouch who was standing in the doorway of the dining room. Again the woman said the man had abused her over a period of years and that they were having a row that night, him threatening her with a knife. Again the medical examinations back that up. Again, PC Gardener's, the woman's and PC Crouch's statements are entirely consistent. Again the forensic and ballistics evidence back them up.'

Whiting paused, stared at both of them. 'So … what do we make of all that?' he asked, his sibilant voice drawing out the start of the sentence.

'It's frighteningly similar, sir,' whispered Claire. 'Just frighteningly.'

'Yes,' hissed Whiting. 'Frighteningly similar. Too similar to be a coincidence, wouldn't you say?'

Claire and Suzanne both nodded. 'Yet how else can we explain it?' Whiting asked. 'Some grand criminal conspiracy between these two women, two police officers with unblemished records and the medical, ballistics and forensics staff whose evidence backs up the accounts of what happened? Because it all tallies, right down to finding each man's fingerprints on each knife he was supposed to be threatening each of the women with. It all adds up perfectly to produce the picture we've been presented with. So a conspiracy does not exactly seem likely, does it?'

'No sir,' they said together.

'So, you see the problem with our interview. That is the point I wanted to draw to your attention. We may have suspicions, but we don't have any evidence for them, apart from not liking the coincidence. In other words – we don't know what we're looking for, do we?'

'No, sir,' replied Suzanne.

'And then we've got those two other factors to inquire about. That strange note we found in PC Crouch's house. It looked like a computer password, didn't it? Greater Wessex

Police's technical division have been all through his computer and have found nothing strange or suspicious whatsoever. No files, emails or web sites that he's visited. But we must still ask him about it. What could it mean? What might it suggest?'

Again the two women nodded. Claire wondered if Suzanne was also starting to feel irritated by Whiting's lecturing manner.

'And then there's the last matter we must investigate,' he said, sweeping the papers from the desk into his briefcase and standing up. 'The fact that personnel and background checks on PC Crouch have revealed nothing unusual or possibly relevant, apart from one thing. Just the one.'

He paused, stared at them before speaking, his eyes narrowing. 'His daughter Marie – his only child – was also a victim of domestic violence … and was killed by her husband in their own home after a row.'

No one spoke, but Claire could see the word in all their thoughts. It was so obvious it could have been painted on the walls of the office. One of the Holy Grails of detective work.

Motive. For murder.

Chapter Seven

PC MARTIN CROUCH HARDLY looked like a killer, but then they seldom did. He was more like an uncle who'd popped in for a cup of tea, Claire mused. There was no hint of tension about him, none of the twitches, fiddling hands or cold sweats the thriller writers would have you believe. If only there were. She'd often thought how much easier it would make the detective's job.

He sat in the interview room, leaned back on the plastic chair, his legs crossed. A cup of coffee stood in front of him and he studied it as he sipped, looking up only when Claire, Suzanne and Whiting walked into the brick-walled, low-ceilinged, whitewashed room.

He appeared younger than his 51 years, no doubt the product of looking after himself well. The firearms officers were regularly tested for fitness, had to be with the amount of gear they carried. He was thin but with a wiry strength, had mousy hair, cut fairly short, grey eyes and a mottled skin, the most noticeable feature his oddly small ears. He was wearing a black polo-neck jumper and jeans. A silver crucifix hung outside the jumper, and his hands occasionally strayed there, stroking a careful finger over it.

He stood up when they walked in, not as tall as she'd expected him to be, about five feet nine or so. He caught her by surprise by reaching out a hand to shake hers, then Suzanne's and lastly Whiting's.

'I don't hold it against you,' he said, and his voice was quiet and calm. 'I knew I'd be placed under investigation after what happened. I know you've got a job to do. All I'd ask is that you appreciate I had a job to do too, and as far as I'm concerned I did it.'

Whiting produced his cold smile. 'Of course. Please sit down PC Crouch and we'll get started.'

'Do call me Martin.'

Suzanne pressed a button on the tape recorder set into the

85

wall and a low metallic buzz filled the room. She identified them all and gave the time, 10.04. Claire pulled her jacket tighter around her chest. It was always cold in the interview rooms, and with the autumn coming on, it smelt damp too. Last year, there had been a move to renovate them, but it had been vetoed by CID. They liked this atmosphere. It encouraged suspects to talk.

Whiting took a couple of pennies, some fives and a ten-pence piece from his pocket and placed them on the table beside him in a pyramid.

'PC Crouch, can I start by asking you to take us through what happened on Thursday night please,' began Whiting, his unblinking eyes fixed on the man. 'We have a copy of the 999 call and the emergency controller's message sending you to Haven Close, so you can start with your arrival at the house. Take your time. It's important you tell us every detail.'

Martin Crouch stroked a finger over his cross, closed his eyes and spoke. His voice was soft and level. He recounted the same story they'd heard a couple of times now, how he and his fellow marksman, PC Andy Gardener, had arrived at Haven Close, agreed there was a threat to life in the house and decided to force their way in.

Whiting listened intently, his fingers on his temples, taking the odd note. Claire recognised the technique. Let the subject talk, relax a little, then interject with a question, then another, increase the pace and pressure of the interview, test his story.

'I stood back and kicked at the door,' Crouch was saying. 'After a couple of blows it gave and we walked into the hallway. Then I ...'

'Your guns were drawn?' Whiting interrupted fast.

'Yes. We didn't know what to expect inside the house so we agreed we should draw them.'

'You went first into the house?'

'Yes.'

'PC Gardener's statement said you always went first when there was a potentially dangerous situation. Why was that?'

Martin Crouch looked down at the floor and stroked his cross again. 'Because I believe I have less to live for.'

'Explain, please?'

'Andy is a family man, with a wife and young son and daughter. I have no one. My wife and I divorced several years ago.'

Whiting sat up straighter, but said nothing, just held Crouch's look. Claire couldn't help but admire his interrogation technique. He'd switched approach, from a staccato burst of short and sharp questions to pressuring Crouch with silence. Clever.

The marksman paused, took a breath and his voice grew quieter. 'And … well … I suppose I have to tell you this?'

More silence from Whiting. Only a look. It was enough.

Crouch breathed out hard again, continued. 'Well … Marie, my only daughter … my only child … she's dead. So if there is something waiting on the other side of a door, or around a corner when we go in, I believe I should find it first.'

Another scribbled note from Whiting. More silence. Then he looked up, pointed at Crouch's cross.

'I see you're a religious man. Is that what makes you feel you should be subjected to danger before PC Gardener?'

Crouch looked surprised. 'I don't see anything religious in it at all. I think it's purely a practical matter. If I should be killed, there's no one who'll suffer apart from me. If you mean – do I think I'll get into heaven by doing so, making some sort of sacrifice, I think you misunderstand faith. You can't bargain with God.'

Claire scratched an ear and looked out of the small, grimy window to hide a smile. One point to Crouch. She knew she shouldn't feel it, that it was unprofessional, but it was nonetheless oddly enjoyable seeing Whiting being lectured. He gave out enough himself.

'Putting aside matters of faith PC Crouch,' hissed Whiting, 'effectively you're saying if anyone was going to be shot, or stabbed, or attacked, it would be better if it was you, as you have no dependents.'

'Yes.'

'Thank you. That was all I wanted to establish. Please continue with your account of the night. We were at your entry into the hallway.'

Crouch nodded. 'We walked slowly up the hall, Andy covering behind me in the standard way. It was dark, but there was a light ahead. The screaming had stopped, but I thought I could still hear a noise. It sounded like whimpering. So I moved slowly forwards. I came to a corner in the wall and moved around it, trying to be as quiet as possible. In front of me was a kitchen area. There was a woman, lying on the floor, her hair straggling over her face. She looked injured. A man was standing over her, holding a knife.'

'Could you see the knife clearly?'

'Yes.'

'What kind was it?'

'It was long-bladed and looked like a chopping knife.'

'How long?'

Crouch held out his hands, stretched them apart. 'About eight inches.'

'And what did you think?'

'I thought he was going to stab her.'

'How could you know that?'

'He was clearly dangerous. His face was angry and covered in sweat and his knuckles were white from gripping the knife. I think his hand was trembling and he had the knife up in a stabbing position. The woman was bleeding and I thought she may already have been stabbed.'

'Did he see you?'

'Yes.'

'What did you do?'

'I challenged him. I can't swear to the exact words, but they were much as we're trained. They were something like "armed police, put down the knife".

'Just the once?'

'Twice. The second time was probably "armed police, put your hands where I can see them".'

'You're sure?'

'Quite sure. It's standard procedure – drilled into us – and I followed it.'

'And then what happened?'

'He didn't drop the knife. He raised it, as if he was going to stab the woman.'

'And then?'

'I fired.'

'Once?'

'Twice.'

'Twice?'

'Yes. It's standard practice to fire twice. In case a shot misses, or the suspect isn't incapacitated.'

'I'm aware of the procedure, PC Crouch,' hissed Whiting. 'I was testing your recollection. And then what happened?'

'The man fell, next to the woman. I moved over to him to check he was no longer a threat. I saw I'd hit him with both shots and so Andy and I tried to administer first aid.'

'With no success?'

'No. I believe he'd been killed almost instantaneously.'

'Been killed? You mean you killed him.'

Crouch twitched at the words. For the first time, Claire thought she heard an edge of irritation in his voice.

'Yes, if you want to put it like that. I killed him. Or rather … I did my job.'

The two men studied each other for a moment, then Whiting asked, 'Where was PC Gardener throughout this?'

'Initially just behind me, in the hallway. After the shots were fired, alongside me in the kitchen.'

'Why was he behind you when you fired?'

'He was covering my back when we went into the house, then he couldn't get past me because the hallway was narrow. He wouldn't try if he saw I had raised my gun as it could affect my aim.'

'I see.'

Whiting sat back on his chair, rummaged in his briefcase, produced a couple of sheets of paper. He slowly looked through them. Crouch watched him carefully. Claire sensed a new angle of attack coming. The papers Whiting was looking at detailed an expenses claim.

The silence ticked on. Crouch said nothing, just rubbed at a knee with his palm. Suzanne shifted on her chair, crossed her legs. Whiting placed the papers carefully back into his case, looked up.

'Are you content with your actions?'

Crouch stared at him, stroked his cross again. Finally he said, 'If you mean am I content I killed a man, then no, of course not. But if you mean – do I think I followed the procedures correctly and fired because it was the last resort left to me and in the protection of the public, then the answer is yes … I am.'

Another silence in the room. Footsteps echoed past in the corridor outside. A cell door clanged.

Whiting nodded slowly. 'Thank you, PC Crouch. That's all I want to ask about this incident, so …'

'It's not all I want to say.'

Whiting's eyes narrowed. 'I beg your pardon?'

'I said, I have something else to say. Something important. Something you need to hear.'

Martin Crouch was sounding increasingly irritated, as if he was being forced to repeatedly explain something patently obvious.

His voice rose, and he nodded to emphasise the words. 'I can see you're sceptical of what we do.'

'I'm not anything …'

Crouch interrupted. 'May I give you an insight into how difficult a job we have?'

'If it's relevant,' Whiting hissed.

'It's entirely relevant. And you should appreciate it. It's very easy sitting in an office passing judgement over a cup of tea and some biscuits. But when a firearms officer is faced with a threatening situation, he has to make a decision within a second or two. He has to accurately assess what is happening, whether there's a danger to the public and himself and how to deal with that. It is by no means simple.'

Crouch paused, but Whiting said nothing.

'He's usually working in a situation which is unfolding and unclear,' the marksman continued. 'He probably won't know exactly who he's facing. Is it a terrorist? A violent criminal? Someone high on drugs? Or someone perhaps who's lost their child in an accident, has got drunk to try to cope and is only making a cry for help? He's got to work that out in an instant. On top of that, most incidents he deals with are in the dark. There's lots of confusion. Probably some shouting and screaming too. And amid all of that, he has to protect the public and has only a couple of seconds to decide how best to do so. Weighing on his mind in those brief seconds is the knowledge that if he does shoot, he'll probably be suspended and put under investigation, something that usually lasts for weeks if not months. And through all that he'll know there's the danger of being charged with manslaughter, and having to face a criminal trial when he was only doing what he thought was his duty.'

Crouch paused again and took a sip of coffee, staring intently at Whiting all the while.

'And that's just one possibility,' he went on. 'Now take it the other way. Suppose he doesn't fire and some innocent member of the public dies. He knows he'll be subject to disciplinary action by his force and no doubt get a flaying in the media too. Why didn't he use the gun he's given to protect the public? That'll be the cry that goes up. Surely it was obvious it was justified to open fire? Can we trust those who are empowered to protect us? It'll be all that sort of thing, all from people who have not the slightest idea of what a marksman has to go through, and all said in the comfort of a safe office with the wonderful benefit of pure hindsight.'

Crouch's face had turned a dull red. 'So yes, I think that is relevant and should be borne in mind by people who have never been in such a situation.'

'Duly noted,' replied Whiting icily. 'Now, as this is my interrogation, we will move on to the first shooting, five months ago.'

He rummaged through his stack of papers, pulled out several which had been stapled together. 'I don't propose to take you back through this case at length PC Crouch. It was investigated at the time and you were exonerated. I have the report of the shooting.'

Crouch nodded. The colour had drained from his face. He

stroked his cross.

'I first want to ask how come you were back on duty so quickly?' said Whiting. 'Is it not the case that most investigations into fatal shootings take several months?'

'Because I was exonerated, as you said. It was a straightforward case and I was found to have done my job, however unpleasant. The police have a policy of trying to investigate such cases much more quickly now. It's becoming widely accepted it's unfair on a marksman to have an inquiry hanging over him for months and even years. That's something I entirely agree with and was grateful for the force's support.'

Whiting scribbled another spidery note on his pad. Claire thought it said, "Was initial investigation sufficiently robust?"

'What concerns me, PC Crouch, is how very similar the two incidents are,' Whiting continued. 'Extraordinarily similar. Particularly that when you fired the fatal shots, PC Gardener was again unable to see exactly what happened. So … in both cases the only witness to your opening fire is a traumatised woman. One who might well be grateful for what you've done and happy to say anything to make sure there are no repercussions for you.'

Crouch leaned forwards on his plastic chair, his face creased in a frown. 'Women often stay with violent partners for years. Life's not all so black and white as you seem to think. So I'm sorry, I don't understand the point you're making.'

'The point I'm making is this,' hissed Whiting, emphasising each word. 'You've told us how important it is for a marksman to make decisions in a second or two. So in this first case, in Bodmin, this is what I'm suggesting. You'd taken up firearms for a simple reason – you wanted to shoot someone. You knew PC Gardener couldn't see what was happening. In front of you was a situation, which wasn't, as you claim, endangering the life of the woman, but just an ordinary row where the man had happened to pick up the knife and – in anger – point it as his wife. You saw the chance to shoot and get away with it. And so you did.'

Crouch was shaking his head in disbelief. 'That is a disgraceful thing to say. That is utterly disgraceful. I want …'

'And then,' Whiting interrupted, speaking fast. 'And then you had another chance in similar circumstances on Thursday, didn't you? So you did it again. You killed another man because you knew you could get away with it. You'd done it before and you'd got a taste for it.'

Crouch's eyes were wide. 'That's an appalling thing to say,' he spat. 'It's disgraceful. It's despicable to suggest something like that. I came here freely to be interviewed, but if you're going to say such things, I am going to call in the Police Federation to come and represent me here, and …'

'Because you've got a motive, haven't you?' cut in Whiting, his voice hard but quiet.

Crouch seemed to recoil. 'What?'

'You've got a motive.'

'What motive? What the hell are you talking about?'

Whiting waited, stared into the marksman's eyes. Claire didn't like the man, but she did admire him. His tactics and timing were precise.

'Your daughter,' he hissed. 'Marie was killed by her violent husband. So when you see a man beating up a woman in their own home, you can't handle it, can you? That's what made you shoot, wasn't it? Maybe once I can believe you needed to shoot a man, PC Crouch … maybe in Bodmin. But not twice. You shot to avenge Marie, didn't you? And because you were sure you could get away with it. You did it in Bodmin, so you decided to have another go in Saltash. That's the truth of this, isn't it, PC Crouch? You didn't open fire out of any duty or necessity. It was simply revenge. And if you're caught, then so what? What does it matter? By your own admission you don't have much to live for.'

Claire studied Crouch. His face was set, a dull red, staring at Whiting. She expected some rage, some outburst of flaring anger, but it didn't come. He closed his eyes and stroked his cross.

'I came here willingly to cooperate,' he said with a strained calm. 'But if that is the kind of suggestion that's going to be put to me, I will no longer do so without the benefit of a Police Federation representative. I am not under arrest so I'm free to go, and I am leaving now.'

He got up, reached for the door, paused. His eyes were set on Whiting, his breathing echoed in the quiet room, fast and shallow.

'It's not me who's a disgrace to the force, Whiting,' Crouch snarled. 'It's bastards like you. Passing judgement in your safe little offices without the guts to do a real job, and get out there and protect the public. You're typical of all that's wrong with policing nowadays.'

'Well?' snapped Whiting, taking the change from his pocket and carefully stacking it into a small pile on his office desk.

Claire looked at him, thought: the Smiling Assassin isn't smiling now. She wondered if he knew his nickname. If so, would he see the irony in him accusing someone else of being an assassin? Someone who she'd say won that bout in the interview room by a fair margin.

'I don't think we've got a thing on him, sir,' said Suzanne, with her usual methodical fairness. 'I agree it was right to put the point about two shootings in such similar circumstances in five months to him, but that's all we've got, isn't it? Coincidence and suspicion. Nothing more.'

Whiting turned to Claire. 'I agree,' she said. 'And the trouble is, all the evidence tallies with his account of what happened. In fact, it goes further. With both cases there's evidence of considerable domestic violence before the actual shootings. So it's entirely possible such an assault was going on when Crouch went into the house and that's what he came up against. Then we're left with the central question; was his opening fire justified? From the evidence, we have no reason to believe it wasn't. I agree his daughter's death looks like a good motive and it's a hell of a coincidence to have two such similar fatal shootings in five months. But we just don't have any evidence to back up our suspicions, do we?'

'But we're still suspicious?' asked Whiting.

'Yes, sir,' they chorused.

'So let's do some more research on him,' hissed Whiting. 'Let's have a look at PC Gardener to see if there's any kind of reason he might enter into a conspiracy with Crouch. And the two women whose husbands were shot too. Let's see if there's any evidence he might have known them or had the chance to conspire with them.'

'And there's that password we found at his house too,' added Claire. 'We didn't get to ask him about that. He, err … decided to leave first.'

'Yes,' said Whiting, ignoring the reminder about how the interview had ended. 'See what you can find out about that Claire. We know it's not his home computer, so perhaps one somewhere else? Were there computers in the houses where the men were shot?'

Suzanne checked a note. 'Yes sir. In both.'

'Then that's a possible lead. Get the technical division to go over them. There might be some connection with Crouch. Claire, please make that a priority. Then we'll get him back in here and talk to him again.'

Whiting's eyes flicked over them. 'There is something very strange about this case, and we will get to the bottom of it,' he hissed. 'It is our duty to do so.'

That Saturday night he dreamt of Sam again and the way he'd died. It was mercifully quick, but so undignified and unwarranted. And he hadn't been there, alongside his friend. He should have been, needed to have been. Soon after, yes, but not at the time, and he would never forgive himself for that. Sam hadn't died with him there and it still hurt. It would never stop hurting. They would pay for that, for Sam's death, all alone, and the eternally haunting memories he had been left with. They would never stop paying.

His raging brain registered a thirst. He got up, walked mechanically to the kitchen, poured himself a glass of chilled water from the plastic jug in the fridge, topped it back up from the tap, returned to the lounge and sat in the armchair for an hour, trying to calm his thoughts. Then he went back to bed, but slept only fitfully.

The living dreams never allowed him to truly rest. The machine-gun fire and mortars blasting around him, more screaming faces begging for the help he couldn't give. He could still smell the mutilated bodies, even in his sleep. He felt the air around him slashed open by the whistling shrapnel, the pops and puffs of the friendly, blossoming explosions, the rank scent of raw death in the freezing air. And the corpses, so many of them, jumbles and tangles of stiffened limbs, testimony to the agonies of their deaths.

It was the young boy, Milan, whose face was always foremost in the panicking crowd, reaching out through the razor wire. Only seven or eight years old, an innocent in this hell, hated for the race he had unknowingly been born into. A target because of nothing he had ever had the chance to do in his brief life. Alone, amid the mass of sobbing, screaming faces, each so desperate to escape the pervading terror. And he, one of the thin line of pathetic soldiers, so close to disobeying the strictest of their orders, not to get involved, as those brown eyes stared at him, the silent mouth trying to find the words to beg for help.

He still wondered whether he would have reached out, if the boy's pleas had lasted a minute or two longer. But the crowd had been silenced by the shock of gunfire. And then, amongst them, the bodies had started to drop, thudding into the frozen mud. And the screaming had begun again, with new fear and desperation. And Milan's chest had exploded, a spray of the hot blood smattering the soldier's face as he bent down to whisper his useless words of comfort.

He'd lunged forwards, tried to breathe life into the dying child, all the while so coldly aware of his futility. He'd only known the boy's name because of the agonised wail of his mother, desperately pushing through the mass to fall across the body of her lost son. She'd screamed out her anguish, cuddling him, holding the fragile, unmoving shape, then looked up and spewed out her fury at the man in the uniform who had been sent here to protect her and her family and the thousands of others in this genocidal slice of Europe.

He'd never understood her words. But he knew precisely

what she was saying.

On the few occasions he found the realisation within himself of the creeping insanity he'd come to welcome, he wondered if that was the moment it had touched him, begun its infectious passage through his brain. The body of the young boy at his feet, the bullets hissing in the air, more lifeless figures falling around him. If he could ever define a moment when the disease struck, began to pervade his life, that would have been it.

It was the point at which the hatred had begun. And it grew so fast, so very quickly. His comrades, his officers, his government, his society. All and everything, except for Sam. The only one he could ever truly rely on. Who he could trust. Would always be there for him. Would never let him down. And then Sam too had been taken by the same faceless forces that had propelled him into this torment. Those who would now pay. Who would never stop paying.

He woke in a panic. It was just after five o'clock. Too early to get up, but he wouldn't go back to sleep. He didn't want to return to the private hell where the dreams always took him. He was afraid.

He sat back in the chair, staring out of the window at the still and silent world. He tried to stay awake but couldn't hold off the creeping, edgy sleep, and the sporadic visions came again, silver lines of vicious razor wire, the dark and evil forest, Sam, lying there, dying, always just out of reach as he tried to help, bring comfort.

He shook himself awake. He felt more tired now than before he'd rested. It was seven o'clock. Time to get up, shower and shave, get ready for work. But first he had to finish the preparations for the next stage of the beautiful plan. The note was written, the pig's heart ready. This part was riskier, but he was confident in his work.

The evening would come around quickly.

Chapter Eight

'I'D RATHER YOU SAID it now and didn't try to soften it. I'd prefer you just got on with it and told me.'

The words tumbled out. He couldn't stop them. He needed to have an answer, however much he feared it. But all he got was bafflement.

'What on earth are you talking about? And what the hell have you got a police guard on the door for?'

Dan pushed the leaping, yelping Rutherford away, out of the hallway and into the lounge and shut the door after him. The dog loved Claire, but this was human time. He hadn't meant to come out with it so soon, but the feeling had been gnawing at him all of Saturday.

He wasn't sleeping, despite another assault on the whisky bottle. The urge to keep looking over his shoulder hadn't faded, and the Swamp was still greedily sucking at his spirit. He couldn't take the fall of going for a walk, starting to enjoy himself, relaxing with her, beginning again to hope for the future, then be told somewhere halfway up a Dartmoor tor their relationship was over.

'You said you had something important you wanted to discuss,' he said, looking into her eyes. She had such beautiful eyes. 'I'd rather hear it now and get it over with.'

She frowned, tilted her head so her dark bobbed hair half fell across her face in that way he found irresistible. He was sure she knew it. 'Well, OK, if you want to, but I don't see why ...'

Rutherford began scrabbling at the lounge door. He hated the thought of missing out on anything, particularly when he sensed a walk.

'Shhh, dog,' Dan said. 'It's because I don't want to go through the "it's not you, it's me, or I'm not ready", or any of that stuff. I've heard it all before, too many times. I'd rather just get it over with.'

She shook her head, ruffling her hair, and looked even

more beautiful. Damn her, he thought. I've been trying to convince myself I don't fancy her, or won't miss her and it hasn't worked at all. Damn, damn, damn.

Claire fixed her hands to her hips. 'I really have no idea what you're talking about. I've just about managed to get a few hours off and I thought we were going for a walk. I've been looking forward to it. That's it.'

She looked genuinely puzzled, but he wasn't going to allow himself hope. It would hurt too much when the brief, kindling flame was ruthlessly extinguished. He might as well say it.

'Dumping me. You said we had something important to talk about. I know exactly what that means. End of relationship. So let's get it over with here, not out on Dartmoor somewhere, so we have to drive back together in a horribly awkward atmosphere, and then do the pathetic "we can still be friends" bit.'

She stared at him, silent. Dan felt himself freeze, ready for the final words, but her face warmed into a smile.

'Oh, you idiot. Is that what you thought?' She wrapped her arms around him in a squeezing hug and he made no move to resist. 'You lovely idiot. It was nothing like that, nothing at all. I've been really looking forward to seeing you.'

'You have?'

'Of course.'

'You sure?'

'Yes!'

'Oh … err … right … then … what did you want to talk about?'

'It's only a work thing. That's all. Just work.'

She leaned back and found his lips, kissed him hard, then stood back and looked at him again.

'You've been worrying about that since we talked?'

'Maybe … a bit … well … just a little … all right, yes.'

'I'm so sorry. It's only a work thing. I really am going to have to find a better way of telling you there's something we need to talk about, aren't I?'

'Yes,' he replied with feeling, wanting to grab her, cuddle into her, hide the prickling in his eyes which told him they were starting to shine.

Dan went to hold her, but a howl echoed through the lounge door, followed by more scrabbling.

'Bloody dog,' he muttered.

'Hadn't you better go and reassure your mad hound that he's not missing out?' Claire asked. 'Come on, let's get going. I need a walk. It's been a hell of a week.' She took his hand, held it tight. 'Where are you taking us?'

Dan realised he hadn't even dared to think about it, but now the rushing, warming relief revived his languid brain.

'Not too far if we haven't got long. Just to the south-west of the moor, about a half-hour drive. I thought I might take us to a place which is famous for its mad dog. Rutherford should fit in nicely.'

They drove north, out of Plymouth and onto Dartmoor. It was a clear but blustery day, high spears of white cloud speeding across the cold blue sky. They crossed Roborough Down, the great granite rock marking the boundary of the old wartime airfield, now home to hundreds of meandering sheep, their white fleeces flecking the yellow gorse and lush green moorgrass. A buzzard watched loftily from the top of a telegraph pole as they passed.

Dan explained about the note addressed to him and Adam's suggestion for the police guard. He tried to make a joke of it, that at least his chaperone didn't have to spoil their romantic moment and follow them onto the moor, but he could see from Claire's look she was concerned. She wanted to talk about it but he changed the subject, didn't want the thought spoiling their time together.

There were none of the usual ponies on Dartmoor, he thought to distract himself, then remembered they'd all have been drifted into farms for the annual sales. It was a story he covered every year when he was the Environment Correspondent, the moor's farmers and landowners coming together for the ritual rounding up of the thousands of semi-feral creatures. The south-west's equivalent of the wild west, he'd called it. It was an amazing spectacle, to see a herd of grey, white, brown and black ponies, their hooves thundering in a gallop as they were corralled by deft riders on horseback and buzzing quad bikes.

Dan expected to feel a sting of nostalgia for his old job, but nothing came. The shadowy realm of crime had sucked him in, the fascination of the lurid underworld that he now dealt in and the detectives who tried to shine the faltering light of justice into it. It was how he'd met Claire too. He stole a glance at her, sitting next to him, gazing out at the view. She was beautiful, there was no other word for it. He still hadn't calmed the welling relief at hearing she didn't plan to dump him, but it was an oddly enjoyable emotion. He wasn't at all sure he'd managed to disguise it.

They turned off the road at Burrator and headed past the great Victorian reservoir. The cheerful blue ice cream van was in its usual place, the road lined with the cars of those who'd come for their weekly escape from the city. The reservoir was low for the time of year, a band of grey shingle fringing the bumpy expanse of wind-battered water.

They crossed the narrow granite bridge and trundled through the hamlet of Sheepstor, following the road as it narrowed, rumbled over a cattle grid and climbed out onto the open moorland. Another slow mile and they reached a small car park by a ford.

'Where are we?' asked Claire, getting out of the car.

'Just east of Burrator Reservoir,' replied Dan, opening the door to allow Rutherford to explode out. The dog ran barking to the ford, then back to the car, then to a hedge, then back to the car, sniffing ecstatically around him wherever he went.

Dan watched, shook his head resignedly, 'Like a canine pinball, that dog.' He pointed south to a hill topped with a ramshackle pyramid of granite rocks. 'That's Gutter Tor. But we're heading east.'

They walked up a well-used, granite-paved track, hedges, occasional wind-beaten trees and rambling dry-stone walls giving way to the open moor. It was a persistent but not aggressive climb. Rutherford spotted a pool just upstream from the ford, sprinted to it and plunged in. He swam across, casting occasional looks back, his mouth open in his smiling face. Claire took Dan's hand and laced it around her waist.

They passed a small dark copse of dense trees, a bright and well-maintained stone cottage nestling into its side. 'That's a scout hut,' Dan explained. 'Lots of groups use it as a base for exploring this part of Dartmoor. I'd like to say I've stayed there, but I'm not great when it comes to camping. I love a good walk, but I also like a hotel at the end of it with a bar, hot bath and soft bed, not a cold tent on some rocky ground.'

Rutherford found a stick and proudly brought it over. It must have been almost four feet long. Claire tried to take it, but the dog locked his jaws and wrestled with her, growling determinedly.

'I will never understand why he brings you a stick, but then doesn't want to let go of it,' she said, releasing her grip. Dan shrugged. He'd long ago given up trying to explain his dog's behaviour. He looked around, saw another stick and picked it up, shouting in delight and holding it proudly, waving it through the ragged wind. Rutherford whirled around, dropped his stick and ran after Dan's. Claire picked up the discarded one and whistled. The dog's look of acute confusion and dilemma made them both burst out laughing.

'So what was this work thing you wanted to talk about?' asked Dan, taking her hand.

'I've been put on the marksman inquiry,' she puffed as they continued climbing. 'You've met Whiting, haven't you?'

'Oh yes. We took an instant dislike to each other. It saved time that way.'

'Yes, I heard you didn't exactly hit it off.'

'How come?'

'You know what cops are like. Word quickly got round about your little showdowns in Saltash. Whiting isn't much liked, you know. Some of the team were delighted you were giving him a hard time.'

'I heard he wasn't popular but no one's told me why. Do you know?'

'Only rumours. Something about an old Detective Inspector whose career he finished with some investigation. I

102

don't know the details. DCI Breen knows much more. The word is that he was this DI's sergeant and learnt the trade from him. They were supposed to be very close.'

Interesting, thought Dan. That would explain Adam's dislike of Whiting. They hadn't been for a beer for a while now, not since Adam had moved back in with his wife Annie and young son Tom. And he'd been seeing Claire too when he had some rare free time.

Adam hadn't said anything about that, and he didn't want to ask what the detective thought. He was protective of his staff and knew too much about Dan's disastrous history of relationships for his liking. Perhaps it was time they had a beer and a chat? After a couple of lubricating pints, Adam might be more inclined to tell him about Whiting. It sounded well worth hearing.

'Anyway, it was Whiting I wanted to have a word about,' continued Claire. 'He had me in his office to talk about the inquiry. It was all routine, but at the end he said something odd. It was about not wanting to see any more coverage in the media, no matter who asked. I can't help but wonder if he knows I'm seeing you and was giving me a warning.'

Dan turned as Rutherford poked another stick into the back of his knees. He pushed the dog away.

'Well … that's going to be tricky, to say the least. It's a big story for us and I'm bound to have to cover more on it. What do you suggest? That we don't talk about it? That'd be a shame. I like hearing what you're up to.'

'And I like telling you. It's an important part of my life, something I want you to share in, not feel excluded from.'

'Sure. So any ideas?'

She stopped, looked around her and hopped elegantly up on a small granite boulder.

'Come here,' she said and he did, standing looking up at her. 'I trust you,' she went on, rubbing the top of his head. 'So I will tell you about the inquiry if you promise not to use it in your reports.'

Months or years ago, that would have been impossible for Dan, to know the fascinating details of a highly newsworthy story but not be able to report them. Now though, he didn't even think about his answer.

'Sure. No problem. Deal.'

'Great. Then that's all sorted then. You can lift me down from my judge's rock now.'

He did, stealing a kiss in the process. 'There is one thing I won't tell you though.'

'Uh huh?' It didn't seem important after that kiss.

'The marksman's name. The High Honchos are paranoid about it getting out and him being hounded when there's absolutely no evidence – yet, anyway – of him doing anything wrong. Is that OK?'

'Sure, but there is one slight problem,' replied Dan, thinking of Dirty El and his mission.

'Which is?'

'A picture of this guy is going to be worth thousands. I know at least one photographer is trying to find out who he is and get a snap. And if it becomes public, Wessex Tonight would have to use it. Probably in one of my reports too.'

Claire tilted her head, the flowing hair falling across her face. 'It hasn't happened yet, has it? Shall we tackle that when we come to it? I've had enough of worrying about work. I need a few hours off.'

They were on higher ground now and the wind gusted around them, flapping noisily at their jackets. Rutherford faced west, instinctively towards the breeze, the invisible power flattening his coat and making it shine in the sunlight.

'Great views from here,' shouted Claire above the wind.

'Yes. You can see the sea at Plymouth,' he said, pointing to the south and the smooth sheet of silver that hugged the jagged coast. 'Over to the west is Bodmin moor. That spire is an aerial, the Caradon Hill transmitter. It brings TV pictures to much of the region and so is blessed with transmitting me most weeknights.'

She chuckled. 'Idiot. I hope it's specially reinforced to cope with your ego. We're pretty high up here, aren't we?'

Dan had been hoping she'd ask. 'Yes, I'd say about …' He paused, picked up a stone, held it at head height, dropped it.

'About 420 metres,' he said finally.

Claire whistled. 'Blimey. That is impressive. How can you tell?'

'I looked it up on the Ordinance Survey map before we came out.'

She ran at him, grabbed him and blew a raspberry in his ear. He caught her and kissed her, and they wrestled together into a hug. Rutherford came running over and leapt up to join them.

What a lovely family picture, Dan thought. Was he happy? He suspected so, but the feeling caught him by surprise. He wasn't used to it and it was more than a little scary. As easily as it was given, so it could be taken away. Those three big words were illuminated in his mind, but he waited and let them fade before they could take hold and escape from his mouth.

'So what does the stone dropping OS map tell us about where we are?' asked Claire.

'Well that,' said Dan, pointing to a series of piles of granite blocks, tumbled together in roughly room-sized rectangles, 'is the remains of the old Eylesbarrow Tin Mine. It was a major tinning centre in Victorian times. The path we walked up is the old mine track.' He took her hand and pulled her over to stand on a small ridge. 'And just down there is one of its old adits, or mine shafts.'

A round black hole, about the circumference of a bus, gaped in the moor. It was like the entrance to the lair of a huge, subterranean beast. A small wire fence complete with danger signs circled it. Dan picked up a stone, threw it in. Several seconds later a hollow rocky clank echoed from the void.

'Most of the old adits are sealed up, but some are still open and you can get into the tin workings,' he said. 'It's not my kind of thing. I'm not keen on confined, dark spaces, but some people explore them. It's a notorious place for illicit sex for youngsters who've got nowhere else to go.'

He gave her a sleazy smile and pinched her bottom. 'Maybe later,' she said. 'Depending on what time we get home and how good you are.'

'Come on then, let's get the walk done so we can get back,' Dan replied with his best winning smile. Claire gave him a look.

They continued up the stony track, growing narrower now and fading into the moorgrass. Dan pointed west. 'Just over there is a place you might have heard of. You know how much of Dartmoor has mystic connections and there are lots of strange place names? There's a famous one down there. That's Evil Coombe – or valley, if you prefer.'

It was small and shallow, like a dry riverbed, pitted with grey granite boulders and yellow gorse. A green tent stood halfway down, ruffling in the buffeting wind. A small stream crossed the valley just below the tent, its flashing, crystal water gushing, swollen by the autumn rains. A couple of crows stared at them from the top of a pyramid-shaped boulder, then hopped effortlessly into the sky, wheeling into flight and mocking them with their cackling calls.

'It's got quite an atmosphere,' said Claire. 'It does feel sinister. I'm almost frightened to ask. How did it get to be called Evil?'

Dan chuckled. 'I'm afraid I'm going to disappoint you there. Your detective's instinct wants to hear some story of murder long ago, or ritual sacrifices by black-robed figures doesn't it? Well, it's nothing like that. The name probably comes from eval, the old tin miners' word for a pick. Lots of Dartmoor names are like that. They sound good, but don't bear closer examination. The Devil's Walk near Princetown is just the same. It was named after a local chap who unfortunately was called Mr Devil.'

They walked up to the top of the ridge and into a renewed battering from the angry wind. There were a few spots of rain too, and the sky was looking leaden and menacing, as if it was glowering at their invasion of the sacred wilderness of the moor.

'Had enough?' asked Dan hopefully, memories of her half-promise still fresh. 'I think we might get soaked if we go on much further.'

'What was this dog thing you were going to show me?'

'Over there,' said Dan, pointing north. 'See that low, boggy area?'

'Yes.'

'That's Fox Tor Mire. It's one of Dartmoor's most treacherous bogs. It's generally reckoned to be where Sherlock Holmes's *Hound of the Baskervilles* is set. I thought it'd be appropriate for Rutherford as a non-fiction hellish hound. But we can do it another day.'

'Fine. I've got to get back to the station this afternoon to do some more work on the marksman case, but your suggestion for spending a little more time together first sounds appealing.' She snuggled into him, whispered in his ear. 'Can we go back to your flat rather than find an adit?'

Dan thought their walk back down the hill was one of the fastest he'd ever managed.

Marcus Whiting sat cross-legged on the bed in his hotel room on Plymouth Hoe, the floor around him covered in sheets of paper. It was a modest hotel, not the standard he was entitled to, but he didn't have extravagant tastes. He worked with public money and it would not be wasted on excess.

On his left were the documents from the first shooting, five months ago. He'd divided them into five piles; witness statements, Crouch's statement, Gardener's statement, the previous IPCA investigation report and background documents on the police officers and the witnesses.

On his right were the papers from the latest shooting, divided into five similar piles. Whiting was staring from one pile to another, eyes flicking from left to right, trying to spin the different details in his mind to see if some settled together. He'd been doing so for four hours now, but still nothing came.

Frustrated, he closed his eyes and laid back on his bed, stretched his aching back. He knew he should go out, find a reasonable restaurant to have an evening meal, but he didn't feel hungry. The investigation did not allow time for luxuries. He would let himself eat when he had answers or ideas. Not before.

He opened his eyes, turned his body, and focused on the red and white hoops of Smeaton's Tower, the old Eddystone Rocks lighthouse, now standing guard over the Hoe. The window rattled as the wind gusted in off the sea. He could hear distant rumbling skateboard wheels on the tarmac and gulls squealing to each other as they soared in the wind, but he scarcely registered them. There was something he was missing, he was sure of it. Something about this case did not add up. Whether it was criminal or not, he would get to the bottom of it.

The suspicion returned. He didn't like it, but knew it could be justified. It had happened before, it could well be happening again. Was his inquiry being obstructed? There was no direct evidence of it, just the suspicion. And if not deliberately obstructed, how about subtly? Was he being shown the whole picture? Were some people protecting others? Were these officers who'd been assigned to help him up to the job? Were they driven enough and sufficiently sure of their purpose to see it through? Would they spot the crucial evidence? Even if they did, would they tell him?

The answer came back the same as always. The only person he could trust was himself. No one wanted him here. It was a familiar feeling. It used to make him lonely, but he was long past that now. He'd forgotten what it was like not to feel lonely. He was used to being alone and couldn't imagine any other way.

He'd learnt that in his childhood; he could trust only himself. So much, so many times they'd moved around. How many was it? He didn't know, just that he'd lost count. It had been explained to him, lovingly and patiently each time, that Dad had an important job to do in a new Embassy and they would have to move. Again.

It was about every year, he thought. A year was just the wrong amount of time for a young boy. Less and he wouldn't have made the friends he loved. Less and he wouldn't have found walks, dens, places to play. Less and he wouldn't have joined clubs and settled at school. Less and he wouldn't have become attached.

If it had been more than a year, the friends and places might have endured. He might have kept in touch, written and phoned, gone back to visit. But it never was. It was always a year in one place, then on to the next, starting all over again. Just the wrong amount of time.

How many times had they moved before he stopped making those friends to whom he would always have to say goodbye in a few months? He didn't know. He suspected it wasn't many. Was it deliberate, or something subconscious, not forming bonds? He didn't know that either, just that it was a thing he didn't do. Yourself, that was all you really had.

There was his duty too, another lesson his father had taught. To be more accurate, initially his father, but then, more importantly, fate. It was duty which meant they had to move again his father had said every year over the dinner table, the young Whiting pulling himself up to his full height to hear the words clearly, looking over the wooden fruit bowl that followed them on each annual move. He must do his duty.

When he was much younger, Marcus Whiting had thought the talk of duty was exciting. It meant his dad was a spy, like those he saw on the television, pitting his life and his wits against enemy agents to save his country. It was only much later he'd found out the truth. He would never forget the deflation and disillusionment.

He knew he had never really understood how someone who worked in the passports and visas section of the embassy could be so driven by duty. But nevertheless, duty was something he had inherited.

Not at first, though. The teenage Whiting had rebelled against it. He smiled faintly at the memory but with indulgence, not warmth. It was the natural thing to do, of course. Boys rebelled against their parents, it had been going on for ever and it always would. He had been a rebel, a frequent visitor to the headmaster's office, caned a couple of times too. He wore the raw weals with pride, delighting in showing the other boys, the nearest he ever got to friends.

Then, there was that clever teacher at his last boarding school, Mr Lewis. He'd spotted the young Whiting's potential he said, and told him not to waste it or he'd regret it. He must work hard and do well at his O levels, particularly the mathematics that he taught.

Mr Lewis had made him a prefect, the old trick of giving the bad boy responsibility. Even then, he'd still been a rebel. Until the night of the accident, that was. Then he'd finally come to understand what his father meant by duty and the importance of it. He had never forgotten.

Another rattling gust of wind drew his mind back to the inquiry. What was he sure of? That he was suspicious, yes, but also that he was making little progress. He gazed around at the ten unsteady piles of documents, the pillars of thousands of pieces of paper.

Was there an answer in them somewhere? He certainly had no evidence, and he still wasn't sure if he was being obstructed. But there could be a way to resolve both those questions. It would be risky, and quite probably dangerous, but it might also be his only chance to find out what really was going on. And he thought he had identified the unwitting person for the role he had in mind, had sensed a similarity of purpose that he could use.

He would go through the papers one more time and decide whether to give it a try, but he knew he already suspected it might be the only way. It had worked before. He sensed he was hungry but he ignored the ache in his stomach. Dinner could wait. Duty was far more important.

It was remarkable how quickly you could get used to something, Dan thought, as he lay outstretched on his great blue sofa that evening, Rutherford on the floor by his side. He'd hardly noticed the policeman at the flat's door when he got home and the thought wasn't taunting his mind any more. He didn't have that urge to keep checking over his shoulder either. Nothing whatsoever had happened to unsettle him over the weekend and he'd begun to convince himself that letter was an idle threat.

The time with Claire had been great too, and for the first time Dan allowed himself to imagine what might happen between them. Could they move in together? Here, in the flat? Why not?

She loved it and she got on well with Rutherford. The place was big enough certainly, larger than most two-bedroom houses. But it was very much his. How would he feel about her stuff appearing, her changing the odd thing around? That would be an invitation for friction. Everything here was perfect as far as he was concerned. Maybe it would be better if they bought somewhere new. That way it would seem more equal, a healthier start to their life together.

He checked himself, blew out a deep lungful of air. What was he thinking about? They hadn't talked about any of this, hadn't even mentioned the love word yet. How could he know she was thinking the same? Don't spoil it by going too fast, he warned himself. Don't push it. Just let it develop naturally.

He did feel so much better than when she'd rung the doorbell this morning. Then he'd been expecting his P45 notice of termination of employment as partner. He was even rehearsing his plan, a day in the pub with the lads, drinking away his sorrow, a roast dinner, anything to fight off the Swamp as best he could. Now he was lying here, feeling relaxed, contented and at peace with the world. There was no sign of the Swamp, fickle foe that it was. Life's clouds had lifted.

He stroked the dog's head with one hand, sipped at a glass of beer with the other. It was remarkable too how little he thought of Thomasin now. She was still there, on the fringes of his mind but without the substance she once had, without the hold and the destructive power. Adam had been right in one of the early pep talks he'd handed out: meet someone else and memories of unfulfilled love fade fast.

Right, time for his last chore of the day, watering the five hapless houseplants which eked out an unfulfilling existence in the flat. He took the green plastic watering can from the top of the fridge and filled it up, added a couple of drops of plant food. He was on the last needy and grateful recipient, the spider plant in the bathroom, when his mobile warbled. He jogged back into lounge, kneed the curious Rutherford gently

111

out of the way. Adam.

'He's done it again.'

'What?' said Dan, thrown by the unorthodox start to the conversation.

'He's done it again. Your stalker. The second attack in his great bloody plan.'

Dan juggled the phone between his shoulder and ear and reached for his notepad and a pen. 'Where? What? When?'

'Plymouth again, in the last couple of hours. It's similar to the other time, but not the same by any means. He's left what looks like a heart this time. I'm assuming it's a pig's.'

'And a letter?'

'Yes, another letter, addressed to you. And another physically unharmed but traumatised woman. He grabbed her in her car this time. But now I think we've got a good lead. I reckon we might be closing in on him. I damn well hope so. I get this feeling he's going to do something far worse unless we get him quickly.'

'What do you want me to do?'

'You'd better get over here.'

'But I've had a few beers. I can't drive.'

'You've got that cop outside haven't you?'

'My personal bodyguard? Yes, he's still there, bored witless I suspect.'

'Entertain him then. Get him to drive you. I'll radio the order through now.'

Chapter Nine

THE YOUNG POLICEMAN, WHOSE name was Tim, emerged from around the side of the flat smelling strongly of cigarette smoke. He jumped into the police car and drove too fast down to the city centre. Other cars blurred as they dodged out of the way. Dan sensed his driver was delighted to be relieved of the tedium of guard duty.

They pulled up at the Central Park Leisure Centre to the usual line of police cars and vans. The building was in semi-darkness, just a couple of lights showing inside its plate-glass front. The car park at the side of the building was cordoned off. It was half past eight on an autumnal Sunday evening and there was still a scattering of cars, perhaps late joggers or dog walkers in the park, that or local residents sneaking a parking space.

At the edge of the car park, a blue Skoda estate was surrounded by white-overalled figures, scrutinising it and crawling over the surrounding area. Three were concentrating on the passenger side door, dusting the paint with brushes and shining flashlights across it. One was on his knees, examining the seat with a torch. An occasional white flare lit the night as a police photographer captured the scene. A couple of uniformed officers were talking to a small knot of people who seemed to want to get back to their cars.

Dan overheard the odd soothing words; 'sure it won't be long, going as quickly as we can, might be an idea to call a taxi if you're going to get cold after that run sir, can't say exactly how long we'll be ...'

He spotted Adam by the car, talking to a group of plain-clothed men and women, most of whom he recognised from the Edward Bray and Death Pictures cases. So, the usual team specialising in hunting killers or other dangerous criminals had been assembled. The High Honchos must be worried. He waved at Adam, who beckoned him across. Dan pointed to the cordon, fluttering in the persistent wind and Adam strode over and walked him under it.

'Very similar to the last one,' he said. 'A woman had been at an aerobics class in the leisure centre. She was on her way home. She'd just got into her car when the passenger door opened and the guy jumped in. He pointed a gun at her and he had a stocking over his head. His description matches the last one, so I'm sure it's the same man. Not to mention what he did next. Let's go and sit in the leisure centre and I'll show you what he wrote.'

They walked past the policewoman guarding the double glass doors and into a café area. Dan could smell chlorine from the swimming pool, something that always reminded him of schooldays and the dreaded weekly swimming lessons. He'd never got the hang of swimming, a pathetic parody of the breaststroke was about all he could manage. The building was quiet and seemed to be deserted. They sat at one of the red, plastic-topped tables, still slightly sticky from the day's spillages of tea and coffee.

'He didn't say anything, just the same as last time,' began Adam, loosening his tie. He looked tired, his face drawn. 'He just pointed the gun at the woman and put his fingers to his lips to tell her to keep quiet. She's not in quite such a bad state as the last one, but she is pretty traumatised.'

'I'm not surprised,' said Dan. 'What else did he do?'

'He produced a note again. But this time it said "Credit card? Bankcard? National Insurance card? Business card?" She was scared stiff, so just fumbled her bag out and gave him her purse. He looked through it, and found her aerobics club card. It was at the front from using it for the class.'

'And he took it?'

'Yeah, he took it, seemed quite happy with it. Even the victim in her state said she was surprised by that. She'd expected him to take her money and bankcards. That ... or worse.'

Dan knew exactly what he meant. A lone woman, a man jumping into her car and holding her at gunpoint, what must have been going through her mind about what would happen? He'd had to interview a rape victim before, heard about the fractured life in shattering detail. He would never forget it.

'And he left another present?' Dan asked.

'Yep, he got it out of a plastic bag again. A pig's heart. He put it on the dashboard. Lovely. And he left a letter too, addressed to you again.' Adam reached inside his jacket pocket. 'The actual letter's with forensics, but this is a copy.'

He unfolded the paper onto the sticky table. On one side it said simply, "Dan".

'Not so formal this time,' mused Dan.

'Indeed.' Adam turned the paper over. 'He goes on to explain why.'

"Hello again Dan,

I hope you don't mind me using your Christian name this time. It's just, I think, because I feel I know you – I've seen you on the television often enough, and have made some study of your career too – and I have now introduced myself in my last letter. So I hope you're comfortable with first name terms."

Dan felt a shudder run across his back. The feeling of wanting to look over his shoulder had returned.

"Have you worked out what this is about yet? Have you managed to add it up? The clues are now all in front of you, if you look hard enough. I don't think it's a riddle quite as clever as that which Joseph McCluskey set you with his Death Pictures, (yes, I did get the idea from him, I happily acknowledge that) and you managed to solve that one, didn't you? – eventually. So you should crack this too, I think. But just to make it more interesting and add a little twist of my own, this time I have introduced a tighter time limit and a far more pressing reason for you to meet your deadline. You will see what that is within the next day or so.

"You'll notice an unusual feature of my crimes is that no one has been injured. I know Mr Breen (yes, I am sure he'll be there with you reading this) will blanch there and say two women have been traumatised. I accept that and would like to apologise to them. All I can say is that I have tried to go about my work in a way which would cause minimum unpleasantness and suffering, and their help was, unfortunately, necessary.

"No one will be harmed in my little game Dan; that is if you beat the deadline I'm going to set you. I'm confident you'll manage it. This is not about attempting to harm. That would make me as bad as those to whom I wish to teach this lesson. This is about justice. As a mere man on the street, I have only very limited ways of achieving that, but I will do the best I can. This – as you will no doubt come to realise – is more or less about making the law be sorry.

"Again I am afraid I cannot sign this, as it would interfere with my plans. But very soon now you will know my name, I promise. Until then."

There was a silence as they both stared at the note. Dan struggled to shift his eyes from it.

'Phew,' he breathed, eventually. 'I mean … well … blimey. I don't know what to say. He's … well, he's getting madder. I take it there's no chance you can still dismiss him as a crank?'

'Not a hope. He's got a plan and he intends to carry it through. We've got to get him first.'

'He says no one will be harmed though. That must be a relief?'

Adam gave him a scornful look. 'I'm not sure I'd believe a word he says, would you?'

No, thought Dan, who knew he was just trying to reassure himself, hoping hard that his stalker meant him no harm.

'So … what do you do?'

'Forensics are going over the car, heart and the letter, though I don't expect we'll get anything. Just like in the flat, I think he's been careful not to leave us any clues. My detectives are working through what might link this woman to the last. It's all the usual things, their friends, hobbies, work, clubs, all that stuff.'

'He knows a lot about me, doesn't he?' said Dan quietly.

'Yes, he does. I'd like that police guard to stay on your flat until we get him.'

Dan tried to hide his relief, but wasn't sure he succeeded. 'So why does he take a sports club card this time?'

Adam shrugged. 'That is baffling. I might have understood a passport, like last time, as possibly being valuable, but not an aerobics club card.'

'It's not the value though, is it? It can't be. If he's leaving parts of a dead pig and talking about some plan, it's got to be a statement, hasn't it? It must be something symbolic.'

'Like what?'

Now it was Dan's turn to shrug. 'Good question. No idea.' He looked hopefully at the canteen bar but it was deserted. Shame, he could do with a strong coffee to give his brain a kick. That, and to keep the creeping fear at bay.

'What do you make of all the talk of deadlines and knowing his name soon?' he asked.

'The next stage of his great plan, I assume. Some grand gesture which will mean his name's plastered all over the media along with whatever perverted message he's trying to get across. But not yet please, you're still here as a witness, not a hack. Any coverage of this now could spawn copycats and muddy the waters. I want this investigation conducted quietly. Hopefully we can get him before he realises we're on to him.'

'Sure. So what's this woman's name and what does she do?'

'She works in the finance department at the dockyard. Her name's Jane. Jane Willen. She's in her mid 30s, married, two kids, lives out at St Budeaux.'

'Nothing remarkable about her?'

'Nothing at all. Another Mrs Average.'

Adam's words had triggered something in Dan's mind. 'Her name's Jane you say?'

'Yep, Jane Willen.'

'And the first woman's name was?'

'Sarah. Sarah Croft.'

He tapped a finger on the table. There was a connection,

117

flitting, teasingly elusive at the edge of his mind, but he couldn't quite catch it. Dan tried a trick he'd learnt from long experience. When you know something's there, don't frighten it off by chasing it through the recesses of your brain, think of something else and it'll come back when it's ready. It was the mental equivalent of playing hard to get. He let his mind wander back to the afternoon, in bed with Claire, that dark bobbed hair falling across her face …

'The Chief Constable,' he said with a start.

'What?' Adam looked baffled.

'The Chief Constable of Greater Wessex Police. Her name. It's Sarah Jane, isn't it? Sarah Jane Hill.'

'Yeah, but so what? Are you saying he attacked these two women because their Christian names make up the Chief Con's?'

'Why not? It fits, doesn't it? He takes apparently unconnected and worthless objects from the women. The only connection is they both have their names on. So he's taking their name, isn't he? That's what he's saying. That's the symbolism. And then there's that bit at the end of the letter about making the law sorry. And there are the pig organs too. He's trying to punish the police for something they did. Or, to be more exact, Greater Wessex Police.'

Adam looked dubious. 'It's worth checking, but it's a bit of a long shot. It could just be pure chance.'

'He doesn't sound like the kind of man who does chance, does he? He sounds like someone who's been planning this for a while. And, if I'm right, it gives you a link between the two women.'

'In which case, he'd have to know them well enough to know their Christian names, wouldn't he?' said Adam thoughtfully. 'Now that is worth checking. You've half convinced me.'

'Well let me try the other half. It could also give you an in to his next attack. I take it the Chief Constable has a middle name?'

'Yes, she does. It's Nicola.'

'There you go then. Nicola's your next victim.'

Adam shook his head. 'Now that is a jump too far. What do you suggest I do? Find all the Nicolas in the area and talk to them? There are thousands. Put out a warning in the media for all women called Nicola to be on their guard as we think they're in danger of being attacked by a madman wielding pig body-parts? Firstly there'd be panic. Secondly I'd look a bloody fool.'

Dan nodded. 'OK, I can see the problem. But it's worth considering isn't it? And if you find the connection between these two women, is there another woman somehow linked to them both called Nicola? If there is, I'd certainly think about putting a guard on her.'

'Yes ... not a bad idea. We'll get onto it. Right, I'd better get back to the inquiry.'

Adam went to stand up, then paused and turned back. 'Just one more thing first. As you're up to your neck in this already, the High Honchos want to know if you'd be interested in helping us out again, like you did on the Bray and McCluskey cases. You can come and join me and shadow the investigation. You can't report anything without my say-so, but the publicity you gave us last time really helped. Do you think you'd be up for that?'

Dan smiled, couldn't help himself. Lizzie had revelled in the reports they'd managed to produce on the two other cases. Exclusive stories, gripping insights into extraordinary crimes, just the sort of thing that saw the ratings soar and her mood with them. And come to that, if he was honest, he'd loved it himself too, hadn't he? And now another bizarre criminal on the loose, and one who seemed to want to use Dan as his messenger.

'I think we'd be delighted, Adam. I'll check with my editor, but you can safely assume she'll bite your arm off.'

'OK then, you can start tomorrow morning. Now I'd better be off ...'

They were interrupted by a man calling excitedly from the doorway. 'Mr Breen! We've got something you should come and look at. It might be our break. The security guard here. He says he thinks he saw a man hanging around and acting suspiciously. He can describe him. And he reckons he saw the car he drove away in too, and he memorised part of the number plate.'

Claire sat in the CID office at Charles Cross police station, looking out on the ruined church below. Many times she'd sat here, at a loss with a case, and stared at the burnt-out stone shell, let her imagination slip back to the Blitz, the sirens and screams, fire and flames rampaging through the city, ravenously swallowing hundreds of years of history in hours. It was a destructive image, but it gave her brain space to absorb and organise the details of a crime. Pounding your head on a computer screen never brought inspiration, but a distraction often did.

Point one: did she even think a crime had been committed? Had Crouch broken the law? She'd been partially convinced by what he'd said, about having to make that split-second decision to shoot, believing someone's life was in danger, doing the duty that society had asked him to perform. But then Whiting's argument was persuasive too, wasn't it? Two cases, so very similar, and a potentially powerful motive festering in Crouch's past.

She wrote "Crime?" on her notebook, and added "possibly" after it, flicked her hair from her eyes. She needed to get it cut, whatever Dan might say about liking it a little longer. Claire added the word "stylist" in the margin.

Point two: did they have any evidence of a crime? There was nothing firm, only suspicions. Crouch went first into the houses. Could he have known a hallway would be so narrow that he could shoot without his partner Gardener seeing it? But then he'd have to be familiar with the house. Which would mean a conspiracy with the woman there. Could they have known each other, the two women and Crouch? Been having affairs perhaps? That was the usual reason for wanting to get another man out of the way. But that would be a hell of a conspiracy, wouldn't it, all three of them bound into it? And Crouch hardly looked the passionate type.

Could he simply have realised the hall was narrow enough

for him to shoot without his partner being able to see it wasn't justified? Would he have gambled on the women not giving evidence against him because they were glad to be rid of the men who'd been beating them? It seemed highly unlikely, far too much of a risk. And anyway, a knife with the man's fingerprints on the handle was found by each body. That would provide a justification to shoot, if, as Crouch said, he thought the women were about to be stabbed. But it was worth checking the backgrounds of the two women, to see if there might be a link with Crouch.

And what about the domestic violence issue? They had good evidence of abuse in the Bodmin case. Neighbours, family and friends all agreed Keith Williams had a temper and could be violent. The evidence was much more mixed in Saltash with Richie Hanson. His wife, Jo, might have said he abused her, but no one else could imagine him raising a fist, let alone to hit her. A kind and decent man, by all accounts.

But Jo had injuries on her body that suggested she was being beaten, some of them going back weeks, according to the doctors. And anyway, who really knew what went on inside a marriage? Plenty of women suffered domestic violence without anyone suspecting it. Hanson's family and friends could easily be wrong about him. Men changed inside marriage. For some, it seemed to transport them to a different world where the normal rules of life didn't apply.

Claire wrote "Evidence?" followed by "thin, if even that".

Point three: did they have any leads? Forensics and ballistics had given them nothing. There were the background checks on the women to do. Was it worth putting a tail, or surveillance on Crouch? On what basis? She couldn't see it being authorised on the case they had at the moment. The only real lead was that string of numbers and letters they'd found at his house. IWGU/66. It looked like a computer password, but there was nothing it might access at his home. But it was the best they had, wasn't it?

She wrote "Leads? One, probably," and flicked at her hair again.

Claire leaned back on her chair and checked her notebook.

An afternoon and evening's work and she'd come to the conclusion they probably had one lead. It was time to go home. She had an idea, but the best way to test it would be at her flat with her traditional Sunday companions, a bottle of wine and some music. That way, if she found nothing it wouldn't be a wasted night.

The bar was quiet tonight, the few people in told him it usually was on a Sunday. Weekdays were busier with more staff around the station, often needing a drink or two in the evening to cope with what they'd been through in the day. Rarely did a police officer's shift pass without abuse or trauma, and more commonly both.

It was a cosy enough little place, if you liked work bars. A couple of soft sofas in the corners, some wooden tables and chairs, groups of friends, colleagues and acquaintances of convenience huddled around them for a drink. The odd pot plant, warm terracotta walls, even some subdued spotlights. At least they'd made an effort. The beer was cheap too and that was the main thing of course, the real attraction, the comforting duvet of alcohol.

He'd learnt a couple of interesting things tonight. There was a speed trap planned for near his home tomorrow. He'd filed that one away, nine points on his licence was quite enough. Any more and he'd be heading for a ban. Drugs raids were also on the cards in Plymouth later in the week, breaking some new supply route from Birmingham apparently. That might be worth a picture. But it was a sideshow. Of what he wanted to hear, there'd been nothing.

He finished pulling the pint of lager the traffic policeman had ordered. His glasses were slipping down his nose again and he lifted them back with his index finger. Never mind, there was plenty of time. Patience was the watchword of the paparazzi. And he didn't get seven quid an hour for most stakeouts he'd had to do either.

'You'd better stay with me for this if you're joining us on the investigation,' said Adam, as a detective brought the security guard over to their table. 'It sounds like it might be our break. If we can get a good description and even a partial number-plate we could lift him tonight. I might even want to get the description out on the TV.'

Adam stood up, shook hands and introduced himself and Dan. The man's grip was thin and feathery and he only made brief eye contact before looking away. His name was Edmund Gibson he said, in a quiet and shaky voice. He seemed to be trembling and had a slight stutter, the words not flowing smoothly.

He was in his late thirties, about five feet ten tall and looked fit. His hair was a dark blond, cut short and neat. He wore blue jeans and a lighter denim shirt, with a grey T-shirt underneath it.

'Ed – can I call you Ed?' began Adam, receiving a nod in return. 'Ed, your information could be very important to us, so I'll make this quick. We will need to talk to you again in more detail, but for now I want to hear what you saw so we can act on it immediately.'

'Yes, OK,' he whispered, his eyes wide.

'You've heard what's happened?'

'Yes. Your … your officers were going around the area asking for anyone who might have seen anything to talk to them,' he said breathlessly. 'They … they told me a woman had been attacked in her car in the car park here. I … I know most of the people here. Is she OK?'

'Yes, she's fine, Ed,' replied Adam encouragingly, looking him in the eye. 'She's upset, but fine. We're looking after her, don't worry. Just tell us what you saw.'

He nodded quickly and took a shaky breath, looked down at his shirt, fiddled nervously with a loose button.

'I told the policeman I saw a man getting into a car and driving off. He looked … he looked like he was in a hurry. He said to come in here and tell you about it straight away.'

His eyes were still wide as he glanced at them, then looked away again. His fingers kept fiddling with the button and one of his legs jigged up and down as he spoke.

'I can't believe … can't believe something like this

123

happens here,' Gibson said breathlessly. 'I'm supposed to make sure the centre's safe.' He looked at them, almost pleadingly. 'I … I won't be in trouble, will I?'

'No, Ed, you won't,' replied Adam resolutely. 'It's not your fault at all. No one will say it is. You can't be everywhere at once. Now, as you were telling us, what did you see?'

The man nodded quickly. 'I was locking … locking up for the night. The last class had finished about 15 minutes ago and I was checking the building over. It's the last … the last thing I do at night.'

He looked up at Adam who nodded, smiled. 'Go on.'

'I was around the side, making sure the gate into the stores compound was locked when I … I saw this man coming across the car park. He wasn't running, but he was moving fast and looked like he was in a hurry. I don't know why, but I … I watched him. There was something about him that didn't seem right, so I … I watched him.'

Adam nodded again. 'Good, Ed, good. And what did he do?'

'He went up to this car and unlocked it. The indicators flashed like … like they do, you know? Then he got in, started the engine and drove … drove off.' Gibson's voice became indignant. 'He drove fast … much too fast for a place where there are children about.'

'Go on,' urged Adam. 'What did he look like?'

'I … I didn't get a good look at him. The car park's not very well lit.'

'Any information you can give us could be vital Ed. What did you see?'

'Well, he was … was fairly tall. I'd say … six feet or so. And he wasn't fat, but he wasn't thin either, if you see what I mean? Sort of … sort of average build.' Adam nodded encouragingly. 'And he had dark hair. I couldn't tell if it was black or brown or what, but it … it wasn't blond. And he wasn't bald either. He had normal hair.'

'Style?'

Gibson rubbed a finger against a front tooth. 'No particular style,' he said finally. 'It was just … just fairly short and

124

ordinary.'

Adam wrote some fast notes. 'And you said you saw his car, Ed? What can you tell us about that?'

'I ... I saw the car better.' His voice sounded more confident. 'I thought there was ... was something odd about the man, so I watched him drive out carefully. I used to be in the ... the army, you see, and they teach you stuff like that. They teach you to ... to notice and remember. It's all ...'

'The car?' prompted Adam quickly.

Gibson looked at him, eyes still wide. 'It was blue. A kind of royal blue. Like your tie.'

'Did you notice the make?'

'I'm not ... not very good with cars. But it had a kind of ... kind of dancing lion on the front.'

'A Peugeot,' said Dan. 'I've got one. It's a Peugeot.'

'And its size?' asked Adam. 'A big car? Small? Estate?'

'Small. Like a ... a mini kind of size.'

Adam looked at Dan. 'Probably a one, two or three series, like mine,' he said.

'And you remember some of the number plate, Edmund?' prompted Adam again.

'I didn't get it all. I'm sorry ... sorry ... I didn't see it all.'

'That's OK, Ed,' Adam coaxed. 'Tell me what you did see.'

'I didn't see it all because I was kind of ... kind of side on to the car. But I got some of the end. It ended with an ... an A. And it had what looked like a C ... a C or an E before that. I didn't ... didn't see the rest. I'm sorry.'

Adam quickly got to his feet. 'That's OK. You did very well, Ed. Very well indeed. You've been immensely helpful. I'm going to take this description and give it to our officers. We'll need to have another chat with you and get an artist to make up a picture of the man you saw, but that can wait until the morning. You can give your address to the detective here.' Adam pointed to the man waiting by the door. 'We'll come round first thing, if that's all right?'

'Yes ... yes.'

Adam strode out to one of the police vans in the car park,

Dan struggling to keep up.

'I want this circulated and cars with these possible endings to their licence plates checked,' he told the sergeant in the van, handing him the description.

Adam turned to Dan, straightened his tie. 'Well, it looks like we might not need your help after all, my friend.' The tiredness seemed to have left his face and he looked full of energy, as if invigorated by the scent he was following.

'That's just the sort of break we needed,' he continued. 'We'll be knocking on some doors tonight when the info comes back from the computer. Give me a call early tomorrow morning to see if you still need to come and join the inquiry, but I reckon we might well have it all wrapped up by tonight.'

In the months to come, looking back on the case and the torment of the next few days, Dan would always remember those words, and how very fateful they were.

Chapter Ten

IT WASN'T OFTEN HE felt good about Monday mornings Dan thought, as they jogged around Hartley Park, but this was an exception. He was joining Adam on another case, and it was fascinating, perhaps the most interesting they'd worked on together. That was saying something too. Despite the police's efforts overnight, they hadn't caught the man, and Adam was desperate to do so today, before he could carry out another attack.

His legs ran without him noticing as he drifted in thoughts about the case. What kind of man left a pig's head with one woman after breaking into her flat, a heart with another after forcing his way into her car, not attacking either, not even speaking to them, and with both stealing some apparently worthless document? And why was he so interested in Dan?

That was the one weight on his buoyant mood, the shadow of fear for a faceless stalker. He could hardly forget it with the ominous sight of the uniformed policeman watching him from the top of the steep grass bank that covered the underground reservoir at the eastern fringe of the park. After last night's letter, Adam had insisted the officer not only watched Dan's flat, but stayed with him too.

He'd told Rutherford they'd do twenty laps – which realistically still meant fifteen – and they'd almost finished, a run of a couple of miles by his calculations. It was a beautiful morning, the air crisp and clear, the grass glistening with crystal dew and the yawning sky a canvas of blue. There was an edge of chill on the breeze and both he and Rutherford left trailing clouds of ballooning breath as they ran.

In a bare chestnut tree, undressed by the shameless autumn, a group of hopping birds squabbled happily. Dan knew he should have been able to name them from his five years covering the environment, but he didn't have a clue. He'd never thought it would happen, had loved the job, but those days had quickly been forgotten, submerged in the exciting new world of crime.

'Just a bit longer, dog,' he called to Rutherford, who was sniffing at the black metal railings guarding the children's play area. 'I've got to be down at Charles Cross by eight thirty to meet Adam. I'm off playing detectives again. I might be late home tonight, darling.' Rutherford's head lifted from the fence and he came sprinting over, dancing his manic jig around Dan, his mouth hanging open in his smiling face.

Dan slowed to a stagger as he lumbered up the slope covering the reservoir, panting heavily but enjoying the challenge. He'd almost reached the top when his foot slipped on the wet grass, his ankle turned and gave and he fell, thudding sideways into the earthy bank, then tumbling down, over and over, gathering leaves and dew as he slid, scrabbled and rolled.

The world stopped spinning and Rutherford was by his side, panting. Dan gave the dog a reassuring pat and spat out some grass. 'It's OK, mate, just a little fall.'

His heart was racing with the shock and he felt winded, but otherwise OK. He pulled himself up and noticed his ankle was aching, a dull throbbing pain. Dan poked and prodded it; tender, but it didn't feel too bad.

'Are you OK, sir?' His policeman bodyguard had come jogging over, his face creased with concern.

'Yes, fine I think. Might just have bruised an ankle, but that's about it. Nothing broken thankfully.'

The officer held out a hand and helped pull him up. Dan could see the relief on his face. It would be embarrassing to have to tell his commanders the idiot he was supposed to be keeping safe had got himself injured.

The ankle was already swelling, but he could walk on it, albeit gingerly. 'No more runs for us for a couple of days I think, dog,' Dan told Rutherford, slipping the lead around the dog's neck. 'Come on, let's get back to the flat. I've got to get showered and dressed.'

The criminal psychologist's report said exactly what Adam had expected, but that didn't make the words any easier. The doctor was known as "Sledgehammer" Stephens, because, unlike most of his kind, he didn't care for subtleties, nuances of interpretation or shades of opinion. He thoroughly enjoyed his job – sometimes worryingly so in Adam's view – and was also in the habit of typing some of his findings in capitals to make the points unmistakeably clear.

"Clear and apparent PERSONALITY DISORDER ... STRONG PSYCHOPATHIC TENDENCIES ... obvious lust for REVENGE under guise of securing justice ... DISTURBINGLY UNBALANCED ... classical loner ... ORGANISED AND CUNNING ... grave dissociation with society ... CONSIDER HIGHLY DANGEROUS!!!."

Adam noted that even capitals hadn't been sufficient for Stephens's conclusion, and that underlining and exclamation marks had been deemed more appropriate.

To decorate his desk further, the night's inquiries had already prompted two complaints and several more were promised, according to a note. Adam glanced quickly at one of the emails.

"It was outrageous, the police waking us up at that time of the night. I nearly had a seizure. We thought something had happened to our son, or there was some kind of crazed terrorist on the loose. It is entirely unacceptable behaviour. All our lives we have been law-abiding citizens who go out of our ways to help the police, but now ..."

He didn't bother checking the name and address. They were always retired lieutenant colonels, or senior civil servants, always keen for you to be aware of that, always paid their taxes for his services and always outraged. One day he'd like to ask them if they thought policing should be a nine to five job.

Adam dropped the pieces of paper back on the desk, resisted the temptation to slide them off into the bin. He looked out of the window to the ruined church at the heart of the awakening city. It was a beautiful morning, but he felt shaky and ragged. Two hours sleep was all he'd managed last night, and that in the spare room on its hard single bed.

Annie had pointedly left a note saying she didn't want to be disturbed. That had kept him awake for another hour, despite his tiredness. He hoped so hard that she wasn't regretting the decision for them to get back together. He'd promised to spend more time with her and Tom and for a while it had worked. But then another big case surfaced and here he was again, in the Major Incident Room, just after dawn, no time for anything except trying to catch their man. But what else could he do?

He would have to try to spend more time with them this week. The memory jabbed; that cold one-bedroom flat where he'd spent six months alone after Annie's patience finally fractured. He remembered it as being like a prison sentence. He couldn't live like that again. If he could manage to find the time to be with them then, to find a reconciliation, he could do it again now. But it was always the way, wasn't it? When you didn't have what you wanted, you worked hard to get it. Once there, you eased up on trying.

It wasn't that he'd eased up though, was it? It was the worry. More than that, it was fear, of what this man would do if he wasn't quickly caught.

The psychologist certainly agreed. Adam scanned the pages, turned to the summary.

Stephens had concluded the man was clever, ruthless and calculating. Probably an obsessive, suffering a persecution complex and advanced paranoia. Most likely had invented for himself a mission, which he would now carry out with messianic zeal. Filled with delusions he was some form of omnipotent Angel of Justice. Had lost touch with society and so was capable of just about anything. In brief, a psychopath, someone living in an alternate reality, unstable and extremely dangerous.

Adam rubbed his aching temples, noticed a familiar figure and its upright walk heading along the pavement into the station, the sun glinting from the bald strip on his head. Whiting was always in early as well. He watched the man step precisely up the concrete steps and slide into the automatic doors.

He turned away, didn't need any more irritations at the start

130

of his day. It didn't help having him around, taking valuable staff for his inquiry, preaching the demands of duty to anyone who questioned him. As if he knew what duty really was.

It was a reminder of Chris too. What would he have been now if he hadn't retired? – been forced to retire to be more accurate. A Chief Constable? He knew Chris would never have been interested in such a rank, would have called it Chief Paper Pusher. But a Detective Chief Superintendent certainly, leading the big investigations, tracking down the villains. He missed Chris. A couple of calls a year was about all they managed now since his move to New Zealand.

Enough of that. Perhaps he'd book a table for a family meal at the weekend, take Tom to the football on Saturday. A walk on Sunday somewhere? Annie loved it when they all went out together as a family. Some flowers to take home tonight would be a good start. He'd get them later and not just from a petrol station either, fresh ones from a florist. Along with a packet of tablets for his pounding head.

Almost a hundred checks they'd managed last night before he called a halt. No success, not even a hint of anything suspicious in anyone they'd talked to. The teams had to have time to rest, would be needed again this morning. Tiredness caused errors, he'd learnt that early. And in this job a small mistake could be fatal. His feeling that their man was planning something much worse than leaving pig organs and silently stealing documents had been forcefully enhanced by the psychologist's report.

The trouble was there were so many cars that fitted that description and number plate in and around Plymouth. They'd got a list of those owned by men in the right sort of age range, but there were hundreds. And what if the car wasn't his? What if it was a partner's, or friend's? Or came from outside of the area? Or what if the description or number plate was wrong? That security guard hadn't been a convincing witness.

Whatever, it was their best lead at the moment and they had to follow it. There was no talk about anyone buying a gun from the area's underworld. Checks with the local doctors hadn't revealed anyone with a speech impediment who might be committing the crimes. He did have the list of their usual suspects, the career criminals who fitted the description, but he couldn't imagine it being one of those. This was no mundane criminal. Dan was right. He wasn't playing his little game to make money. It was something far more sinister.

Dan would be here in a while. Adam had been surprised to realise how pleased he was about that. He had an insight into police work and people too, could often see those shady little connections that explained someone's actions. And if this man had a grudge against him, far better to have him safely inside the investigation.

He wouldn't tell Dan about the psychologist's conclusions. He was jittery enough at the thought of having a stalker. And now it looked as if he might be in real danger. Better for him not to know, at least for now.

Claire was woken early by the seagulls' exuberant cries in the sunshine outside her window. She waited for a moment before opening her eyes. Her head was a little sore and there was the hint of a gentle thumping, but not too bad. It was only after getting through three quarters of the bottle and starting to feel tipsy that she'd checked its alcohol content. Fourteen and a half per cent. Wines were getting stronger, particularly the New World reds she liked. She'd made a mental note to be more wary in future.

Still, it had been a productive evening. She'd worked through a comprehensive list of inquiries on all the internet search engines she could think of using all the possible permutations of words. She'd found thousands of sites devoted to domestic violence, so many it took her by surprise. She'd expected dozens of course, but never this many. It was an unsettling insight into the reality of many women's lives.

Once she'd discounted the pornographic sites set up to titillate – a shocking number of those alone – she'd come down to a few dozen covering Britain. Then it was a question of refining the searches; to Devon and Cornwall, Bodmin, Saltash, Plymouth, Truro, Exeter, Barnstaple, anything that might throw up a dedicated site for victims of domestic violence anywhere in the south-west of England.

Eventually she'd narrowed it down to a couple. You Don't Have To Take It and DiVorce, the D and V highlighted to emphasise Domestic Violence.

Both sounded hopeful. She still didn't quite know what she was doing, but Chief Inspector Breen had told her, told all of them, to always follow a hunch. She'd read through the sites and seen some agonising stories. Perhaps that was why she'd drunk the wine so fast. There was also advice and help on offer, as well as discussion groups. But first you had to register and tell a little of your own story, in confidence of course.

This was the point at which she hesitated. If all this got to trial, what would the defence barrister boom across the courtroom?

"Entrapment, Your Honour ... this alleged officer of the law did not just break the law, she shattered it ..."

What was she thinking about – if it got to trial? She was playing a hunch, nothing more. They were nowhere near an arrest, let alone a charge. If ... if she made any progress, then she would worry about the law. Claire closed her eyes, imagined who she was, what had just been inflicted on her, and began typing.

"I'm so desperate. Please, please help me. He's given me such a hiding tonight. I'm so scared, I'm shaking, I'm bleeding. It was the belt again, he whipped me with the leather belt. THE BELT! My back's covered with scars. I don't know how much more I can take. If it goes on like this, I think he's going to kill me. HELP ME!!"

Claire stopped, a little shocked at herself. She poured another glass of wine, let her hand linger over the keyboard, then submitted the form. She got up, changed the CD, chose a compilation of the Rolling Stones. It was their earlier stuff, around the time of 'Paint It Black'. Dan had introduced them to her collection, played the song to make a joke of telling her about the swamp of the depression that he suffered.

Claire had known how big a confession that was, had believed him when he said no one else knew, apart from Rutherford of course. That was the way with Dan, the serious stuff always had to be dressed up in some fun, as though he needed it to protect himself. It could be endearing, but it could be infuriating too.

She'd thought she understood what he was saying when he'd talked about the Swamp. He was warning her of how he could suffer, saying it was random and arbitrary and not caused by her. He was telling her he wanted the relationship to work, and if he was sometimes down or moody, it wasn't her fault. It was something that had always haunted him, probably always would.

Claire had thought she understood – perhaps hoped might be a better word? But, as ever, he hadn't made it clear, hadn't told her that he wanted her beside him, to help him through, hadn't asked what effect his moods had on her, hadn't said those words she'd been waiting almost a year to hear.

She'd felt sentimental last night and almost called him. Almost, but not quite. She knew the wine was having its magical effect and it was well past midnight. Better to go to bed and get some sleep. She could check to see if she'd registered with the sites in the morning. It was hardly an urgent line of inquiry and she still didn't really know what she was doing.

Claire hauled herself out of bed, switched on the computer. Two emails were waiting, both from the sites saying she'd successfully registered. No time to log in now, she had to get in to work to meet Whiting, something she was oddly looking forward to. He was an abrupt, graceless and often irritating man, but an impressive investigator.

She would go online later. Anyway, she'd need a few hours to perfect her new identity. She could already feel poor Zoë forming in her mind.

It was still dark when he woke from the fitful, shallow sleep. He was breathless at first, blinked hard in the half-light, unsure where he was, remained rigid, still in his bed, tensed, ready to run or fight, ready even to die. It was back with him again, so clear, so vivid he could have been there, back in the forest, scared, so scared, only Sam there to comfort and reassure him.

The rows and balls of razor wire glinted silver against the icy mud. It was cold, so cold. It always felt cold there. That was one of his sharpest memories, the cold. No matter how many layers of clothes, how quickly he trudged, the cold penetrated his body with its bitter insistence. Even the times by the fire, buddies huddled around, they were only brief respites from the clinging cold.

Even when they'd originally been despatched in August, the country's hottest month, even then his first impression had somehow been the cold. It pervaded his memories.

The vicious cold. That, and the dark and silent forest where death so often lingered in the innocent trees.

The forest had become the enemy. The forest and the spirits that flitted within, always unseen, but you knew they were there. Spirits with guns and lovingly honed knives, always watching you, always ready to take you. You could feel their hatred.

Sam could feel it too, he knew. They were so close they understood each other's moods. But here in Bosnia there was only one mood. Survival. See out the day, that was their unspoken mission. Each day alive is another closer to return. See out the day. Survive.

Life had been good before the day the order came. July 23rd 1995. Or had it? He wasn't so sure now. His certainty had diffused. Perhaps it had just been better. Or different.

In his mind, his life was divided into four phases. There was the carefree time he and Sam had together before Bosnia. That felt warm, his favourite memory. It played in his mind with an amber glow.

Then there were the cold, crawling days of duty. Duty and survival. They were tolerable because they had each other, although they always looked blue in his imaginings, perhaps tinted like the light through the forest. The steely colour of the razor wire.

Then there were the days after it happened. They were oddly smudged memories, perhaps because of the shock, or the tears he had to hide. Or the uncertainty of not knowing what would happen, whether the outcome would be life or death.

The times back in Devon were the clearest. They weren't an exciting life, nor a luxurious one, but they were warm and comfortable. They were both safe and alive and they were together. They'd managed what so many others didn't. They had survived. They'd both brought home their wounds, but they'd lived. He wondered how much his surroundings and how he had spent his days mattered at that time. All that was important was being together and being alive, away from the icy forest and the lines of silver razor wire.

And then there were the times of now. The times after the shooting. He hadn't known what to do at first. It was as if two mighty surges of emotion swelled in his brain, broke free, careered together, battered and beat and pounded into each other, becalmed their furies.

One was revenge, a tide of raging heat so powerful it could propel him anywhere. The other was grief, so heavy and dampening it rendered him lifeless. Together they'd left him sitting in his flat and staring out of the window, not thinking, just looking, his mind blank, a void.

How long had that time lasted? He wasn't sure. He could find out if he searched his memory, but there was no need. It didn't matter. It wasn't important now. It had been a time of automation.

He'd carried on with his job. He'd carried on with his life, what was left of it. But it was like living under anaesthetic. There had been no feeling. He'd sleepwalked through the months, not noticing the changing seasons. How had he survived? His experience in Bosnia? His ability to see out each day? Just to survive.

Then had come the resolution. He wasn't sure how it happened, had no idea why, but that wasn't important. Like an angel, it had come. In all its detail and splendour. Revenge had won the battle for his future. He felt alive again, newly awake, energetic with his purpose. He had a reason to live, a belief in existence that had been lacking for so long. And a reason to die.

The angel had brought with her a plan, beautiful in its

inspiration and detail. All that remained was to put it into action. He'd relished doing so. He'd left his job and found another that the mission demanded. He'd made the preparations. He'd made the friends. He'd bought the gun, the dead pig, the hacksaw, the tent, the old car and the quad bike. He was ready. All he needed now was the catalyst.

Last week it had come.

This morning, the mission would enter a crucial stage. Not the endgame he thought, but the end of the middle game. It was the most dangerous time, the most risky, but he was sure it would work. All the preparations were laid.

It was time. Monday morning. All would be complete within a few days. He and Sam would be reunited. He would have his revenge. He tried a smile, but couldn't quite remember how.

Dutifully, he followed the morning's routine; the shave, the wash, the breakfast radio. But still he couldn't shake loose the memory.

The forest had been a silver silhouette that night, the razor wire glowing in the wedge of moon. They'd trudged back and forth as they always did. The cold had made the ground hard, silent under his boots. They were frightened but they scarcely noticed, were so used to it. And they had the reassurance of being together.

He hadn't heard the fast footsteps coming out of the forest until they were upon him. He'd seen the night's new flash of silver as he turned, the gleaming steel, the vicious tapering point raised ready to end his life. He'd known he had no time to react, could see it plunging slowly towards his throat, could feel the imminence of death surrounding him.

But Sam had sensed it. He was leaping, twisting, white teeth bared, jaws reaching, searching for the flesh, taking the full force of the flying knife in his flank, yelping, breathless, crashing back to the hard earth, that new, unnatural limb jutting from his beautiful fur. It was time enough to draw the gun and puncture the black mass of man with three, four, five spurting red holes, until both he and the dog lay gasping on the icy ground.

Chapter Eleven

THE YELLOW LIGHT OF the rising autumn sun had made no inroads on warming the day. The people he passed as he drove wore coats and hats and scarves, and many kept their hands plunged deep into their pockets, or arms hugged around their chests. Dan set the car's heating to maximum on the drive to Charles Cross, but still he felt cold. Winter was edging inevitably closer.

He'd been resisting it for several years now, saw it as an obvious and regrettable mark of growing older, but perhaps it was time to do as his mother had always told him and buy some vests. He wondered what Claire would think. No matter how you tried, it was simply impossible to undress erotically when wearing a vest.

The sharp attention of the cold was a problem he'd always suffered. A doctor once told Dan that he should think himself lucky. Low blood pressure was good for your health. It helped to prevent a range of illnesses the man said, with one of those unconvincing medical smiles. But not an apparent permafrost in your hands and feet in the winter months, Dan had countered.

Adam hadn't helped. He'd climbed into Dan's Peugeot, grimaced, and immediately turned the heating down and opened a window.

'We didn't get anything in the night,' the detective said, pointedly fanning at his face with a hand. 'The teams are back out now checking the rest of the list of possible cars and people for your stalker, but there are hundreds. It'll take a while.'

Dan changed gear, indicated to pull off the main road. 'So where are we going?'

Adam had hardly let him get a word in since he picked the detective up from Charles Cross police station. It was as if he was thinking aloud, the ideas tumbling out of him.

'First, we're off to meet Gibson at his flat in Stoke. I want to see if I can get any more details from him about the car or the man. We've got a police artist coming over later too to make up an impression of the guy.'

Dan found Tamar Road and the small block of two-storey flats where Gibson lived. It looked relatively new, probably built in the seventies. The pain in Dan's ankle stabbed as he got out of the car and he winced. He could feel how much it had swollen through the thick socks and boots he'd put on to protect it.

'You OK?' asked Adam as they walked though a gate and up to the flats. 'It's number four, just along here.'

'Yeah, just about. I twisted my ankle taking Rutherford for a run this morning. It aches a bit but it's not too bad.' Dan gritted his teeth and tried not to limp.

They climbed a flight of echoing, concrete stairs and found a yellow wooden door marked with a number four. The paint was chipped and the corridor smelt of cats. Adam knocked but there was no answer. He knocked again.

'Bloody hell, where is he?' the detective growled. 'I told him it was important we saw him first thing and he said he'd be in. He'd better not have gone off shopping or something ridiculous like that.'

He knocked again, much harder this time and the door creaked and slipped open. Adam pushed and it swung back to reveal an off-white hallway, some strips of paint peeling by the greying ceiling. A strange smell crept over them, like rank rotting meat.

'Hello,' he called, stepping in to the hall. 'Hello! Mr Gibson! It's the police … Chief Inspector Breen … you met me last night. I'm calling as we arranged. Hello!'

They passed an open door to the kitchen, a small two-hob cooker and grill, a large grimy fridge. One of the taps above the sink was dripping, fast and rhythmic. There was a wooden chopping board by the sink, its pitted surface scarred with dark red fingers of stains.

'Hello, Mr Gibson,' called Adam again, his words echoing around the flat. Dan was sure there was no one here. It felt empty. They passed another open door, to a bedroom this time.

The faded floral curtains were thin and half-drawn, a pile of sheets stacked neatly on the bed. A set of dumbbells was propped up in the corner. The room smelt damp.

There was another open door in the hallway. Adam leaned in, Dan following. A bathroom, white toilet, bath and shower, frosted window streaked with dull, green mould.

'Mr Gibson, hello!' shouted Adam, much louder now, making Dan start. 'It's the police. Hello!'

They came to a final door, light blue, closed this time, cracked paint peeling in patches. The rotting smell was stronger now, cloying the fetid air. Adam turned to Dan, swallowed.

'You might not want to come in here,' he whispered.

'What? Why? What do you mean?'

Adam raised his eyebrows. 'What I mean is … he was in a bit of a state last night, wasn't he? He seemed a nervous type. He's ex-army too, and that can mean people have seen sights which make them fragile and … well, prone to doing extreme things. I'm wondering about what we're going to find on the other side of this door and whether you'll want to see it.'

Dan still hadn't got it. 'Like what?'

The detective sighed. 'Well … you're not exactly good with blood and guts, are you?'

'What? What are you talking about?'

Adam held up a finger, ran it across his throat.

'Ah,' said Dan, suddenly feeling queasy. He took a hasty step back, then another and the pain in his ankle throbbed anew. Adam nodded, paused, and pushed the door open.

'Jesus!' the detective gasped. 'Fucking hell!'

Dan turned away, his imagination running with the horrors inside the room. A shotgun lying on the floor under a rigid hand, a body slumped in a chair, flies swarming around, a destroyed head, blood-splattered scarlet, drying across the walls …

A swirling sickness enveloped him. He'd always hated gore.

He looked up at Adam who was shaking his head, still staring into the room, holding tight on the door-frame, his knuckles white. 'Shit,' the detective whispered. 'I don't believe it. Just … shit.'

Adam breathed out heavily, his chest heaving. Dan knew his friend had seen plenty of mutilated corpses before, it went with the job, but this must be particularly horrific. He wasn't going into that room, didn't want his sleep of the next few months destroyed by the sight returning to him.

'You'd better come and have a look at this,' Adam said, turning to him. 'Don't touch anything, just come and look.'

'Are you sure? I don't fancy … I mean, I don't like blood and guts and …'

'It's nothing like that. Not a damned thing like it. Come and have a look.'

Dan hesitated, then hobbled reluctantly over and joined Adam in the doorway, steeled himself for what he was about to witness.

For a moment he was speechless, couldn't believe what he was seeing. 'What? What?! It's … it's … oh, shit!' he stammered eventually, feeling his stomach spin. 'I mean … hell! Shit!'

They both stared in disbelief. On the wall facing them was a large frieze. Exactly in the middle was a huge photograph of Dan's head, about three feet high. It was grainy, looked like it had been photocopied from a newspaper and enlarged. Around it was a series of cuttings, headlines, scribbled notes.

One was a full-page article from the Daily Bulletin about how Dan had solved the riddle of the Death Pictures. Another was a feature in the *Western Daily News*, about the Bray case. His self-consciously smiling face from the Wessex Tonight publicity shot peppered the display and made up its edges. Newspaper photos of Dan and Rutherford were interspersed with other articles, including one about a talk Dan had given to the Women's Institute in the tiny Cornish village of Blisland.

How the hell had his stalker found that? It was taken from a tiny Bodmin freesheet. Only one answer occurred to him, and Dan didn't like it at all. The man must have been scouring all the region's local press for any news of him, no matter how tiny or trivial.

Dan breathed out heavily, tried to resist the familiar temptation to wheel around, check who was behind him. He forced his concentration back on to the frieze. There were a couple of pictures of Adam too, posed and as smart as ever, it looked like they'd also been clipped from a paper. All around the display were pinned cheerful and colourful Wessex Tonight car stickers.

One photograph made Dan shudder. He stared at himself bending down, talking to a party of schoolchildren at May's Devon County Show. There had been no press photographers allowed in the Wessex Tonight tent that day. The only way the snap could have been taken was by the man who created this … he hesitated to let the word form in his brain, but couldn't find a more palatable substitute. This … shrine.

He must have been standing just feet away. Watching him. Studying him. Perhaps even so close as to be touching him. And Dan had been absolutely oblivious, as the man stood there, gazed at him, took his photo and no doubt enjoyed his fantasies about what was to come.

And on the table, rotting meat, the source of the rank, overpowering smell pervading the tiny flat. Pig meat. Four trotters. Some bones, and pink, bloody flesh.

'I just … hell!' Dan managed. 'It's … well, it's him, isn't it? Last night was all a damned act, wasn't it? It's him.'

Adam was still staring at the frieze, didn't reply.

'You know what the bastard did, don't you?' Dan gasped, suddenly winded by the realisation. 'He described me. That description he gave us of the guy who broke into the woman's car. It was me. And the numbers of the registration plate and the car. They're my bloody car. I don't believe it. The bastard. The devious bastard.'

Adam still said nothing, just pointed across the room to a small, battered wooden table by the window. There was a letter on it, propped up against a vase.

Dan screwed up his eyes, forced them to focus. On the front was written, "Dan."

Karen Reece watched her daughter and her friends skip their

way along the road towards school. So happy, so joyful, she rarely stopped thinking what a wonderful time of life it was. Had she been like that once? She supposed she must have been, not that she could remember it now. Those blue-sky days of no troubles or responsibilities. Not like trying to run a house for them both on the government allowances and the income from her part-time job. Talking of which, she'd better stop standing here staring, and get ready.

It shouldn't be too bad in the store today. Mondays tended to be quieter. Most people didn't stock up on their food until towards the weekend. It was enough of a struggle to get through a Monday, without the extra hassle of fighting your way around a supermarket.

She'd got something to look forward to this week too. Andy would be working tomorrow. She wondered if they'd find time for a bit more chat and flirting. It depended on how busy they were, him with the shelves, her with the never-ending stream of miserable-faced customers at the check-out. They usually managed a few smiling exchanges though, didn't they? Had been for a few weeks now and, she had to admit, she was enjoying the attention.

She hadn't encouraged him at first, had wondered if her relationship with Ed would ever grow. It was only fair to give him a chance, he'd been so kind to her and Nicola. But it had never really happened. He seemed happy just to be friends, and that was fine by her. He was a good man for a chat, the odd outing to the seaside or Dartmoor and Nicola loved him. But she had to think of herself. She'd been on her own long enough now, and maybe, she thought, maybe it was time for a man in her life again. And perhaps Andy was the one.

She always made sure she looked her best on Mondays, a good pair of shoes, a little more make-up than normal. Not that it was easy to look good in those uniforms they gave you, but she did what she could. The only question now was – would he ask her out? They'd found out they were both single and there was an obvious attraction. It wasn't easy meeting men when you were bringing up a young daughter on your own. He was a nice guy, a little older than her, but well-spoken, kind

143

and funny. She liked a man who could make her laugh.

If they went out, where would they go? For a meal? A drink? She could offer to cook, but that wasn't quite right for a first date, was it? Somewhere neutral – like a pub – was better. Somewhere with no pressure on either of them, where they could just chat and see how they got on. Would she be able to get a babysitter? One of the neighbours would probably help. They owed her a favour. Well, that could wait. He hadn't even asked her yet. And when he did, she'd have to be careful not to accept too quickly. She didn't want to look desperate.

She checked the clock. Time to get ready. The girls were almost out of sight around the corner, very near the school now.

Nicola was growing up fast, but they did these days, all the other mums agreed. She'd put on a little make-up for that school disco, heavily supervised of course. She'd worn her best clothes and blushed so hard when that boy – was Jack his name? – had come to sit on the wall outside the house, trying his best to pretend he was just having a rest, but couldn't stop glancing over his shoulder.

She was on the cusp between pure childhood and her first tentative steps into the adult world. The contradictions in her were amazing. One minute she wanted to talk about make-up and clothes, the next whether she could have a pony for her birthday.

Well, she had a wonderful surprise coming on Wednesday when she reached the great age of nine. Not a pony all to herself – how would they look after it? – but a share in one, courtesy of a kindly breeder, a friend of a friend. She planned to pick Nicola up from school and drive her to see the sleek, chestnut Dartmoor pony, that diamond splash of milk on his nose, munching happily at the grass in his paddock. The riding gear for her first lesson would be waiting. She could imagine Nicola's face.

How quickly the years had slid past, how very quickly. Nine now, and they'd been alone together for seven. At first she'd thought she would never cope, agonised about how Nicola would grow up with just her to provide for their needs, teach, love and look after. But it had become natural and they'd grown to be friends, comforts to each other.

How she'd cried that last Mother's Day. Nicola had come home from school with a card, not the usual, to a wonderful mum, the best mum in the world, not that. She'd written "to Mum, my best friend." Karen Reece had lain awake that night, listened to her daughter's soft breathing from the room next door, unable to stop the tears welling in her eyes.

It was remarkable how quickly you stopped worrying, she thought, as that bobbing rope of Nicola's blonde hair disappeared around the street corner, her slight, grey-coated figure skipping amongst her friends. It was only a few weeks ago, at the start of term that she'd given in. Yes, OK then, you can walk to school with your friends, but any hint of mischief and I'll be taking you again. The school was only half a mile away, and there was always that lingering fear of strange men, hanging around. But she'd read in a paper it was a wildly exaggerated danger and you had to let go at some time, didn't you? Start to give them some freedom? It was one of the greatest dilemmas of being a parent, when to loosen the reins.

She was nearly nine now, her friends walked, she could walk with them. There were lots of other mums around, and quite a few dads too – these modern times! – and they all knew each other. She'd be quite safe, of course she would. The school was just around the corner, really. But it hadn't calmed the butterflies those first few times her friends came calling. Nicola didn't know it yet, would have been mad with the embarrassment, but Mum had followed, at a discreet distance, unseen, on the other side of the road, for the first week, just to be sure. She was fine. She'd been well taught, to be careful of the road and never, ever to go with a stranger.

Time to get changed then, and work out what to wear today to leave something smart for tomorrow, something Andy hadn't yet seen. Something tight around the top, she thought. A girl had to emphasise her assets. Nicola would be fine.

'The bastard,' Adam growled. 'He really took me in. I can't believe it. He was there, sitting in front of me, cool as you like and I didn't realise. What a devious bastard.'

He pulled open the top button of his shirt, loosened his tie, sat down heavily on the concrete steps outside Gibson's flat, his face taut. 'A right bloody fool he's made of me.'

'Me too,' agreed Dan. 'I should have realised he was describing me and my car. He's made an idiot of me too.'

'Yeah, but you're not the Detective Chief Inspector here, are you? You're not the one who's going to get a rollocking from the High Honchos and who's going to be the laughing stock of the force. I wouldn't be surprised if there's a disciplinary for this.'

There was a silence. Adam tapped a foot on the ground, then shook his head, lifted his hunched shoulders. 'OK, enough of this feeling sorry for ourselves. It's not going to help us get him. I'll take the rap for it later. We've got forensics coming over to do the flat. They can look at the letter first, then we can open it and see what he's got to say for himself this time. I've called the search teams off the hunt for the mystery man and put everyone on alert for Gibson. But where is he, that's the problem? Where's the bastard gone? Is there anything else we can do to find him, do you think? The key question is – what does he plan to do next?'

'Yep,' agreed Dan. 'If he's planning to do anything. Are you sure he won't just take off and hide?'

'I wish I could believe it. But everything he's done so far tells us he's got a plan and he's going to stick to it. I'd like to think we've disturbed him and put him off his track, but that doesn't stand up. He deliberately made sure we talked to him last night with that false info he gave us, so he knew we'd be onto him by this morning. Whatever it is he's planning to do, he's either done it already or he's sure the fact that we know it's him won't stop him. And I just know he's upping the stakes with what he did last night and showing us his flat. He's about to deliver his sick little masterpiece and I don't even want to think about what it'll be.'

Dan was quietened by the force of his friend's anger. Finally, he said, 'Well … like what do you think? What could he be planning?'

'How the bloody hell should I know?' snapped Adam, rubbing a sheen of sweat from his forehead. 'If I did, I could bloody stop him, couldn't I?'

Dan had an urge to snap something back, but pursed his lips. He could feel the pressure on Adam. If something happened now – some attack, perhaps some rape or murder? – the detective would never forgive himself. He had a chance to arrest Gibson and he missed it.

'I'm sorry,' Dan said softly after counting to five in his head. 'It was a stupid question.'

'No. I'm sorry. I shouldn't take my frustrations out on you.'

'OK, forget it. Right … is there any way I can help? Anything we can get out on the TV to warn people to watch out for him?'

Adam looked up. 'Now there's an idea. That could help no end. But you don't usually do any old police appeal, do you?'

'No, there are too many of them and they're not usually interesting enough. But if we have a quick think we should be able to come up with something that Lizzie would go for. All we need to do is dress up a little story so you can get a description of Gibson out.'

Adam nodded. 'You're the expert. That's what you're here for. What do you suggest?'

Dan felt a momentary qualm, as if Lizzie were watching him. He knew what he was doing, and by no means for the first time. It was exactly what she'd warned him against, again and again: getting so involved he was crossing the line between reporting and becoming part of the investigation. She was spot on, as usual, but so what? What was the right thing to do? Behave like the impartial observer a journalist should be, or try to catch a man who might just be about to commit a terrible crime?

'Well, what we – sorry you – put out, will have to be true, but also limited, so as not to cause panic, or hamper the investigation,' Dan said slowly. 'So what about something like … like … you're hunting a man you believe to have assaulted two women in the last few days? You've got a description of him and you fear he could strike again.'

Dan stopped for a quick think. It wasn't striking enough to get on TV, to lure the viewers into taking notice and helping.

'But you'll have to go a bit further than that to get some real interest,' he continued. 'How do you feel about releasing the fact that he's left a couple of notes taunting the police? That'd probably be good enough. It's certainly dramatic. And what about the pig's head and heart stuff? All the media would go for that. It'd make a really good splash.'

'OK,' said Adam. 'It'll bring all the cranks out claiming it was them, but if you say it'll work and get us a load of publicity, let's do it. The more people we've got keeping an eye out for Gibson the better.'

'I'll ask for the outside broadcast truck. Can you do us a live interview?'

'Yep.'

Dan again felt Lizzie watching him, remembered he should think like a hack, occasionally at least. 'And can we have it first, as an …'

'An exclusive?' interrupted Adam, his glowering face almost lifting. 'Yes, I suppose so.'

They'd stopped, put down their satchels and rucksacks and were playing hopscotch around the cracks and joins in the pavement by the post box. Four of them, as usual. Perfect. He knew they'd stop here, had watched them often enough. They always had a quick game of hopscotch before the final couple of minutes walk into school, just as countless thousands of young girls before them had. He calmed himself, started the car, drew up alongside.

'Hello Nicola,' he said cheerfully as he wound down the window.

'Hello Ed,' chirped the blonde girl with the bobbing ponytail.

'Are you winning today?' He tried to keep his voice steady, sound normal, friendly.

'No.'

She shook her head, the plaited rope of hair flipping back

and forth, skipped over to the car, pointed to another girl. 'Vicky is. She always does.'

The others looked over, smiled and waved, went on with their game. Perfect. They were used to him, trusted him, had seen him at the leisure centre enough times on their swimming lessons. He'd even driven them back and forth to school when the usual bus driver was sick or on holiday.

He always made a point of talking to them then, but not too much of course. He didn't want to arouse any suspicions. He'd stopped here to chat to them often enough too, all part of the plan, a friendly adult on his way to work. All those tedious times spent with Karen Reece as she yapped away relentlessly about work, or whatever problem or moan or ailment was bothering her had finally been worthwhile. Even those endless hours of the fixed smiles during the excruciating outings to the beach, or Dartmoor, or the Cornish countryside. All now at last worth it, all part of the slow, careful plan, finally nearing its delicious end.

'It's your birthday in a couple of days, isn't it Nicola?'

She beamed a sparkling smile, that slightly lopsided look of hers, showing the gap in her front teeth. It was cute, but he had to put that feeling aside. He couldn't afford to like her.

'How did you know that, Ed?'

'Mum told me.'

'Yes, and look what I've got already.' She delved in her bag, found a glittering blue hair grip. 'We bought it on Saturday as an early present. I'm going to wear it in drama class this afternoon.'

'That's lovely. You'll look just like a princess.'

He was almost there now, it was going perfectly. Just keep calm, don't look around, betray your nerves, just smile, be natural, ignore the shuddering trembles coming from inside, the urge to grab her and go, just a few seconds more now.

'Well, it's funny you should talk about early presents,' he continued, wondering if he sounded as breathless as he felt. 'Because Mum has asked me to help her. She said I was to come and get you to take you to choose your birthday surprise.'

He'd expected suspicion, hesitation, a need to explain, persuade. But it would have to be quick, he didn't have long. He was ready with the next rehearsed words, ready to convince her …

'Is it the pony?' she gushed first, her face still beaming. 'Am I going to pick a Dartmoor pony? Is it going to be a black and white one?'

'You know I can't tell you that,' he said, managing a smile. 'It'd spoil the surprise. But hop into the car and I'll take you and we'll see.'

She picked up her bag and walked around to the side door. He opened it and she climbed in. He thought his chest would burst with his heart's furious pounding, but he kept his voice calm, as calm as he could. It had worked. Perfectly.

Just as it had with Dan Groves and Adam Breen, the night before. The raging nerves faced down. The script followed flawlessly. Another brilliant performance. A tribute to himself and the righteousness of his beautiful plan.

He allowed himself the luxury of a smile.

'Wave goodbye to your friends now, Nicola,' he said.

Chapter Twelve

THE FORENSICS TEAM RUSHED through their sweep of Gibson's flat. Adam gave them half an hour. He overruled their protests about the time it required to do their work.

'I understand all that science being slow stuff, but he's going to commit his next crime within hours,' the detective told them. 'So you have only got minutes to find something that might give me a clue what it is. I don't need evidence to convict this guy. He wants us to know it's him. I need to know what he's planning. And arguing is wasting your time, so get going now. Now!'

Adam paced up and down outside the flat, fiddling with his tie, while the white-overalled figures flitted around it. They'd examined the letter first, then opened it and brought it over in a sealed plastic bag for Adam to read. Then they'd spread out over the rest of the flat taking scrapings and samples from the floor, checking furniture for powders, fibres, residue, anything that might give a hint about what Gibson planned.

The letter was the longest message so far, neatly written on both sides of an A4 sheet.

"My dear Dan,

It was, may I say, an absolute pleasure and a privilege to meet you and Mr Breen, even though I had to adopt a little character to do so and we couldn't talk about all the things I would have liked. Another time perhaps. Or then again, probably not. I'm afraid I don't think we'll have the chance now. A great pity."

Adam let out a long hiss.

"Did you like my little personality? I'm wondering what you thought of me. The idea of the security guard was to be an old and slightly eccentric soldier who'd been a tad battle scarred, making him a nervous although still dependable person. I did some drama at university and was told I was rather good at it. Did it work for you? The character was how I got the job. The centre managers seemed to like the idea of employing someone who'd been in the forces, and the position was ideal for my purposes. I knew what I needed and could not have hoped for better.

"Is it becoming clearer to you what my plan is? Have you managed to add it up yet? I can't go into too much detail, because there is the slight chance you will read this before I've completed the next stage. But you must have worked out the connection between those first two women, the one in the flat and from last night in the car. I could scarcely have made it plainer, could I, hopping in to join her in the car park?

"Yes, of course, they both used the leisure centre and I knew them fairly well. I had to know them for my plan to work."

Dan nodded, said, 'That's why he never spoke in his attacks. Why he had to write notes telling the women what he wanted. Because otherwise they might recognise his voice.'

"You do see why now, don't you?" the letter continued. "Or do you? Perhaps you'd like a hint? I shouldn't, but I'm afraid I can't resist it. I'm enjoying myself! How's your Shakespeare? I'll make it easy, so let's go for one of his most famous plays, *Romeo and Juliet*. What would affect the sweet smell of a rose?"

'What the bloody hell is that about?' growled Adam, his clenched fist pressed hard against the wall.

'It's a riddle,' Dan replied, trying desperately to remember the quotation. He'd studied Romeo and Juliet for 'O' level literature and scraped a pass, but the words about a rose wouldn't come to mind.

'No shit,' grunted Adam. 'Not another puzzle like that damn McCluskey business. I'm sick of them. Why do you attract mad criminals? What the hell does it mean?'

'It's a quotation, I think. Or part of one. We need a

dictionary of quotations. I'll call the newsroom in a while to arrange the outside broadcast and get one of the researchers to look it up. Let's have a look at the rest of the letter first.'

Adam snorted, but again held up the bag.

"Anyway, I digress. Back to last night's meeting. I did have one momentary concern, when I was describing the villain to you Adam (I scarcely need mention I know you'll be reading this together. I saw how close you were last night. You make a lovely couple), and Dan, you so helpfully chipped in with the make of the car. I did just wonder at that moment whether you'd realised I was describing you. It was a risk, wasn't it? A delicious one though, which I'm afraid I couldn't resist. I had a second's worry there, but, Dan, you played your part beautifully. Thank you."

It was Dan's turn to snarl now.

"So then, onto more practical matters. You'll want to know where we're going next in our dance. If you haven't already, very soon now you will find out what the next stage of my plan entails. You'll immediately realise it will mean I have to leave Plymouth. Did I mention to you I recently purchased a car? It was out of necessity – you'll see why soon enough – but I've quite got into driving. I had a look at the map and wondered where I might go.

"Somewhere I've not been to before I thought, somewhere easily accessible, next to a good road. Maybe around Manchester. Or somewhere near, like Denton or Hyde. They look like interesting places. Anyway, wherever I choose, I shall be leaving Plymouth. But this is not goodbye.

"Again my friends, you will be asking yourselves about my motive. Soon now your computers and detectives will bring you all the background on me that you could wish for. It's all in there, and surprisingly simple perhaps. It'll explain to you my need to make the law be sorry, and why you Dan have become involved in this too. You probably suspect already that you're a messenger and I would agree with that. But you'll also see why I chose you particularly, and why I am disappointed in you. We have a passion in common. Or rather, we had.

"Your attempts to trace me will soon become increasingly urgent, like a man seeking the elusive band of gold. Well, all the information you need to find me is contained within the letters I have sent you Dan, if you know where to look and how to interpret. I have every confidence you will. The question is – how long will it take you? And in this you must apply yourself as hard as you know how, for as you will soon realise, time is not on your side.

"Again you will be discussing whether I am evil, or mad, misguided or whatever label you might find easiest to describe me with. I do not see myself as evil, though no doubt it will become a word commonly used in relation to me. I am merely a man who has suffered a wrong, which I intend to point out and go some way towards putting right. If I am evil, I was made so. It was my destiny, and who of us can avoid that?

"Finally, I say this. Dan, if my plan goes as I expect, we shall meet again but unfortunately not under such circumstances as to make a real conversation possible. This I regret, but it is how it must be. I hope when you come to report on all that has happened, you give me a fair hearing and understand a little of why I have done that which I have.

"I can honestly say it's been a pleasure.

"Edmund."

Adam leaned back against the corridor wall and let out a long breath.

'He's barmy. He's absolutely bloody barmy. What the hell is he up to now? What's he on about, going away somewhere? Why's he telling us where? And what's all that about a band of gold? And seeing you again, but not being able to talk to you? What the hell does it mean? And do you really think he's put the answers to what he's up to in his letters?'

'Oh yes,' replied Dan emphatically. 'I'm sure they're in there. He wants to be caught eventually so his big statement can get all the publicity he obviously craves. But it's got to be done his way. What scares me is what he's up to now. Right at this moment if the letter's to be believed.'

The forensics officers had finished and the search team went in. 'Anything you can find that might give us a clue what he's up to,' Adam shouted. 'Anything at all. There's no need to be gentle. He won't be coming back here. Rip the place apart. And do it fast.'

A dozen men and women from TAG, the Tactical Aid Group, all dressed in black, fanned out across the flat, began opening drawers, checking down the sides of the sofa, looking under carpets and pictures, anywhere that anything could be hidden.

Dan slipped his mobile out of his pocket and called the newsroom. Lizzie's number, the red line. He noticed his ankle was aching harder now, making it difficult to stand. He sat down on the concrete steps, felt their dense coldness start to creep up his back.

'Lizzie, it's Dan. I've got something for you, an urgent one.'

'Oh, so you do still work here then? Good.'

He swallowed his annoyance, explained the story. 'Sold,' she said instantly. 'I'll send Nigel and the OB truck. I want it on the lunchtime news. I want a big report. I want a live interview. I want even more later. I want …'

'OK,' he interrupted, rubbed the phone on his shirt to make it crackle. 'Sorry, you're breaking up. I'll sort it out and call back later.'

Adam was involved in a whispered conference with another plain-clothes man Dan recognised from the McCluskey case. He looked over quizzically and Adam beckoned.

'Forensics didn't find anything that might give us a clue what he's up to. But this,' he said, waving a file, 'is the background stuff on Gibson. It makes interesting reading, to say the least.'

Dan took the sheets of paper, wondered what he was about to see. His hand was shaking.

The sheet first was a brief biography.

Edmund Gibson, born July 4th 1969 in Exeter. Father a Colonel in the Devon and Dorset regiment, mother a nurse. Went to a state school in Exeter, then university in Birmingham, read history. Graduated with a first class honours degree. Sponsored at university by the army, ambition to join the same regiment as his father, now retired. Trained as an officer but failed the selection course as not having necessary leadership skills. Moved instead to become a dog handler in the Devon and Dorsets. Passed dog training with distinction. Posted to Bosnia along with a detachment from the regiment in July 1995.

Dan turned the page. There was a brief summary of the situation in Bosnia at the time. It was a vicious civil war. The capital, Sarajevo was under siege by Serbs. It was supposed to be a safe haven, set up to protect the Muslim community, but it wasn't working. The Devon and Dorsets had been sent as part of the United Nations peacekeeping force to try to relieve the city. Dan remembered it vaguely from news reports of the time, continual shelling and bloodshed. Slaughter might be a better word, according to the report in front of him. It detailed widespread massacres.

Gibson's personal file revealed he had been on guard duty one night when there was an attack on the troops' camp. According to his account, a man had attempted to kill him with a knife. His Alsatian had attacked the man, suffering a serious knife wound in the process. Gibson himself wasn't injured. The dog – called Sam – survived, but was disabled and was to be sent back to England to be re-homed. Gibson was, according to the record, "powerfully attached to the dog who he believed to have saved his life", and left the army to go back to Devon with Sam.

Before he went, military psychologists had examined Gibson, and concluded he was unfit for duty. The trauma of the constant attacks and the horrors he had witnessed had what they described as a "profound and damaging effect". The knife attack had compounded that, the report calling it "the classic straw that breaks the camel's back", not uncommon in cases of a sudden, direct and tangible threat to a subject's life. The doctors recommended a course of counselling, which Gibson apparently ignored.

There was no record of anything happening to him in the time after that, until last year. Gibson was arrested and charged with assaulting a police officer. The case went to court and he was convicted. Because of his history of military service and his unblemished record he was spared prison, instead given a suspended sentence, community service and a fine.

Dan turned to the last page, the details of Gibson's conviction. He read it, then leaned back heavily against the wall, rested his head on his chest and closed his eyes. He breathed deeply and read it again. Now he understood. The reason for Gibson's obsession with him was here.

The police had received information that a man was using his flat to deal in drugs. He was reputed to carry a gun for protection. Dan looked down, out of the window. It was the flat neighbouring and below Gibson's.

The police had carried out a dawn raid, a dozen armed officers surrounding the flat, then moving in. But Sam had been in the garden and when he saw one of the men creeping over the fence ... did he remember Bosnia? Think his master was again under lethal attack? Or was it just a dog's natural instinct at the invasion of his territory? Whatever, he'd attacked the policeman with such force the officer had shot him dead. Gibson had heard the barking and the shot, come running down the stairs and seen his beloved dog lying dead in the garden. He'd instantly charged at the policeman and assaulted him. The report said Gibson's fury was so great it took six officers to restrain him.

Dan slowly shook his head as he sank into his thoughts.

He thinks I let him down. He's seen those pictures of Rutherford and me they used to illustrate the story about how I solved the Death Pictures riddle. He's seen I'm a dog lover – more, an Alsatian lover – and he feels betrayed that I work with the very people who are responsible for killing Sam. He's going to make the police pay for killing him and he's going to teach me a lesson by using me to tell the world.

The twitch of wanting to continually turn and look over his shoulder was back and its pull was powerful. The man's a psychopath. What the hell have I got myself into?

Adam was staring at him. 'You OK, mate?' he asked. 'You've gone pale.'

'Yeah,' said Dan with an effort. 'Yeah, just about. I was wondering what was going on in his mind. It's … it's damned scary. I think we can safely say we're dealing with someone who's alarmingly unbalanced …'

The detective snorted. 'Mad might be a simpler way of putting it.'

'Well, maybe. But mad in a cold and purposeful way and I can't help but think that's … well, bloody terrifying, frankly.'

'Yeah, quite,' agreed Adam. 'Well, the teams have found absolutely nothing here to help us work out what he's going to do next, so we'd better have a look at that letter and see if we can see any clues. Did you check the quotation?'

'No, sorry. With all that's going on, I completely forgot. I'll do it now.'

He was interrupted by the plain-clothes man lumbering up the stairs towards them. 'Mr Breen, Mr Breen …' he panted.

'Yes, John,' said Adam, losing patience waiting for him to get his breath. 'Come on man, what is it?'

'A kid …' he managed, between breaths. 'A little girl … abducted. About an hour ago … in Plymouth … description of the man matches Gibson.'

'Oh fuck,' said Adam Breen quietly.

Chapter Thirteen

IT WAS THE BRIEFEST of calms. Adam clenched his fists, began barking orders.

'John, get the description out to every cop and traffic warden and community support officer and military police and anyone else you can think of. I want everyone looking out for Gibson, the girl and whatever details you've got of the car. Then get onto the High Honchos and ask them for all the extra manpower they can raise. I want the helicopter too. Get the press office to issue an immediate media alert with the descriptions. Emphasise that the first few hours are vital in an abduction. If we don't get her quickly, the chances of finding her alive plummet. I'll work out what details of the crime we release in a while. Dan you're part of that. Get your outside broadcast people ready. I want this on air as soon as you can manage.'

He grabbed his phone. 'I'll have to divert them from coming here. Where shall I tell them to go? Where was she snatched?'

'Widey Park Road in Peverell. We'll set up a mobile incident unit there.'

Dan called Lizzie, explained what had happened. The phone buzzed with a gasp of pleasure. 'Wow! Brilliant! What a story! Little girl abducted! How old was she?'

Dan noted the use of the past tense. He winced, but didn't bother saying anything. It was like trying to stand in the way of an avalanche. 'She is – that's IS – eight. Nine in a couple of days.'

Another rattling sigh. 'Great, real tear jerking age. Even better that it's almost her birthday. Real pathos. Right, I want wall-to-wall coverage. I want a picture of her. I want tearful interviews with her parents. I want a description of the perve. I want the cops. I want it all live. It's about time we had another cracking story. The ratings have been sagging a bit recently. This'll pep them up. I knew it was a good idea of mine to let you go off with the police again.'

'Of yours?'

'Yep.'

Dan didn't argue, didn't have time. 'Can we flash it?'

'What?'

'Do a newsflash. It's quarter past ten. We're not on air until half one. Seconds are vital in trying to save an abducted kid.'

There was a pause on the line. 'Well, I don't know. Morning TV is pretty popular, and there are the advertisers to think of …'

Dan was ready for that, had his counter-argument prepared. An unanswerable one too, if he knew his editor. 'If we flash it we'd guarantee to be the ones to break the news,' he interrupted. 'It'll be quite an exclusive to put in our entry to the Royal Television Society awards this year.'

'Done. We'll do a bit of you on the phone. I'll get a graphic made up with a description of the girl. We'll call you back in a min.'

'Sure. Lizzie, can you just pass me on to one of the researchers a sec, I've got something I need to check.'

When he finished the call he turned to Adam who was talking fast to the other detective, studying a map.

'Don't tell me,' said Dan slowly. 'The little girl's name is Nicola.'

Adam stared at him. 'How the hell did you know that?'

'Remember Gibson's letter and that bit about the rose and Romeo and Juliet? The quotation is all about "what's in a name?"'

'And?'

'There's the other link between your victims. Sarah, Jane, Nicola. Your Chief Constable's name. Sarah-Jane Nicola Hill is her full name, I believe? It's just what I thought at the leisure centre last night. It's another way of having a go at you, isn't it? That's why he took the job as the security guard, so he would meet some women whose names would fit his plan. He could get their addresses from the centre's records too. So I'm assuming this Nicola also went to the leisure centre regularly.'

'She did,' said Adam. 'Swimming lessons.'

'So she would probably have known him and trusted him. And so got into his car …'

'Without any fuss or fight,' completed Adam. 'He groomed her for abduction.'

The three men looked at each other. 'We sussed it too late,' whispered Adam. 'Again. A-bloody-gain.'

'Shit, what a bastard,' added John.

Dan's phone warbled. 'You wanted it out on the media as soon as possible,' he said to Adam. 'This is the newsroom now. We're going to flash it. What do I need to say?'

'The description of Nicola, Gibson and what we've got of the car. That's the important stuff. I want as many people looking out for them as possible. Not Gibson's name yet though. Tell the viewers how important it is we find them soon. Tell them if they see anything to call 999, but don't approach the man. Don't mention that we think he's got a gun, just warn people to call us.'

'OK.' Dan answered the call. 'Quick, Adam, give me the descriptions so we can make up a graphic.'

'Coming to you in a couple of mins Dan,' came Emma, the director's voice, down the line.

He took a series of deep breaths, tried to calm himself. It wasn't the kind of story you wanted to make a mess of. Dan tried not to think that a little girl's life might depend on what he was about to say. He massaged his aching ankle, concentrated on the message he needed to deliver.

Emma's voice again. 'Thirty seconds, Dan, standby.'

He felt Adam's eyes on him, turned away, focused his thoughts. A prickling sweat was spreading up his back and the phone was trembling in his hand.

'We interrupt this programme to bring you some breaking news,' intoned Craig in his sternest voice. 'A young girl has been abducted in Plymouth and the police are asking for urgent public help in finding her. Our crime correspondent Dan Groves is with the police investigation and joins us on the line now. Dan, what more do we know?'

'Craig, the girl's name is Nicola Reece. She was abducted

just before nine o'clock this morning while on her way to school in the Peverell area of Plymouth. She's described as about four and a half feet tall, with blonde hair, which she has in a ponytail. She was wearing her school uniform, a navy blue sweater with white blouse, a matching navy skirt, white knee socks and black shoes. She also had on a grey duffle coat. The man who abducted her is about five feet ten tall, with a lean build, in his late 30s with short, dark blond hair. There's little detail of the car he abducted Nicola in, apart from that it was red and not new. The police are launching a major manhunt and they emphasise it's vital that Nicola is found as soon as possible. They ask all members of the public to be on the lookout for her or the man and to call 999 immediately if they see anything. I repeat, call 999 but do not approach the man.'

Craig thanked him, and re-introduced the original programme. Dan found himself leaning heavily against a cold brick wall, listening to tips on making the most of the space in a small kitchen.

'Dan! Dan!' Adam was shaking him.

'Err, sorry. Just … err … recovering …'

'You did good. Thanks. That should help. Right, come on, let's get going. We've got to get this bastard.'

Adam started jogging down the stairs. Dan followed, couldn't help overhearing the quick call his friend made. It was to Tom's school to check he was safely in lessons. The boy was nine years old, almost exactly the same age as Nicola.

The big white outside-broadcast van with Wessex Tonight emblazoned on its side was manoeuvring to park as they arrived. The street was packed with police cars and vans, officers striding and jogging back and forth. Nigel was trying to guide Loud into a space without denting a new Volvo. Uniformed police with clipboards knocked at doors and stopped passers-by to talk to them. The police helicopter buzzed overhead.

'Good,' said Adam, taking in the scene. 'I asked for the works and the High Honchos have given them to me – for once. I'm going to go sort out the inquiry. I'll do a press

162

conference when the hacks have all gathered. Is there anything else you want for now?'

'We'll need a picture of Nicola,' said Dan.

'It's being done.'

'And a word with her parents? That's the most important thing. If you really want to make an impact and get people to take notice, we need to hear from the parents about their turmoil and anguish'

'There's only a mum. She's distraught at the mo, but we'll ask her later.'

'Can I do a live interview with you for the news at 1.30?'

'Sure. I'll come back here to your OB truck.'

Loud had managed to park halfway up the kerb but Dan didn't think anyone would mind today. He grabbed Nigel and they went filming, leaving Loud to set up the satellite link. 'Do you think I should change the shirt?' he'd asked as they left. 'Given the story, you know?'

Today's outfit boasted a glowing rainbow, with white birds flying above and green towering trees and golden sand below. 'Yes,' said Dan firmly. Loud's beard twitched, but he didn't argue.

They filmed a couple of policemen knocking on doors and talking to the people who answered. Then they followed another couple walking down the street, stopping people and asking for their help. Dan interviewed some of the locals, got the usual stuff about it being shocking, who'd have thought it would happen here, what kind of a world is it we live in? It was useful colour for his report but what they really needed was that picture of Nicola and an interview with her mum. People and pictures, always the key to a TV story.

The pack was gathering fast: newspaper reporters from the *Wessex Standard* and, *Western Daily News*, a couple of freelance news agencies. Universal TV had arrived too, and a gaggle of photographers, Dirty El amongst them. They managed a brief chat.

'Any news?'

'On what?' asked El, his sleazy grin saying he knew full well.

'Your little mission.'

'It's proceeding smoothly. Haven't hit the jackpot yet, but the groundwork is complete and I'm confident of a favourable outcome.'

'Well, let me know, I'd be very interested. Aside from work, we must have another beer sometime, mate.'

'Can't at the mo. This little part-time job I've got is taking up all my evenings.'

'What part-time job? That doesn't sound like you. What's that about?'

El's grin grew wider and he warbled a few tuneless bars of a song. Dan sensed a painful rhyme approaching, and was quickly proved right.

'She'd disapprove would his mother,
Of El undercover,
But a police mark-s-man,
He must snap how he can,
'Coz for a pic all the tabloids will love ya!'

Dan was about to ask another question when he was interrupted by Adam striding towards them. Cameras rose and microphones appeared as the pack arranged themselves in a semi-circle, Nigel in the middle as ever. A couple of flashes flared. Adam handed around a clutch of photocopied sheets. A colour picture of Nicola and a description of her, Gibson and his car. Excellent.

'Ladies and gentlemen,' he said, as polite as ever, even under such pressure. 'This will have to be brief as I've got a lot to do, but I do appreciate your help. It's important to us. I can't emphasise enough, public help is vital here. Can everyone who reads, or sees, or hears this please look out for Nicola, or this man, or the car we believe they were in. Each passing moment is vital in trying to find Nicola alive. Please help by looking out for her. So far we have no leads as to where she might be. I desperately need information that can help us. That's it for now, but I'll update you again this afternoon. Nicola's mum is also preparing a statement for you.'

*   *   *

Claire grabbed her coat and followed Suzanne out of the CID office. Whiting hadn't hesitated when the call came through. 'Go,' he'd hissed. 'A live child takes priority over an investigation into two dead men. We can reconvene when the child has been found. Go.'

She'd just about finished her emails anyway. She hadn't told Whiting what she was doing, just that she was going through some of the interviews and trying to work out if there might be a pattern. He'd accepted it, if with one of those questioning looks of his. It wasn't as though they had much else to work on. Suspicion, that was still just about it. Suspicion and the possibility of a motive, but no evidence, just the persistent question of what that password they'd found in Crouch's house could mean.

There were computers at all the homes. One in Bodmin, one in Saltash and Crouch had one. Could that be the connection? It fitted with the password. But then, what home didn't have a computer nowadays? It wasn't a great lead but it was all they had. It had to be worth investigating.

She wondered if she'd see Dan at the abduction scene. He was bound to be there. A story like that, he'd be sent straight away. It would be the first time they'd met on a job. She still didn't want other police officers to know they were seeing each other, but it was impossible to keep quiet. They went out for a drink, they saw someone she knew, suddenly the word was around the force. Whiting certainly seemed to know, and if he did then everyone did.

Well, whatever, it was up to her what she did with her private life. There was just that question of the effect on her career, how other officers might treat her, whether the High Honchos could worry about trusting her. Suspicion was ingrained in the police. It was their world. She'd just have to face it and, if she were asked, she'd tell them what she and Dan had agreed. They'd discussed it and they'd resolved it, and that was that. If her bosses trusted Dan, of course.

He'd been helpful in her inquiry too, putting her on to Richie Hanson's sister. That was one thing she still couldn't understand. The woman had been adamant her brother was incapable of violence, and despite years of being lied to in interviews Claire had believed her. But how could that evidence fit with the medical reports, about the bruises on Jo Chanter's body and the statements from her and Crouch that Hanson was threatening her with a knife when he was shot? They had Hanson's fingerprints on the knife too. Something was wrong there, she sensed it, but couldn't quite see what. She'd do some more work on it. First, the search for Nicola. That was most important now.

If she saw Dan there, it would have to be polite and professional. He'd understand. They both had jobs to do and couldn't afford to be distracted, not on a case like this. She could text him later to apologise. Claire couldn't show it – knew he didn't like a fuss – but she'd surprised herself with how worried she was about him. What was he getting into, with this madman they were hunting sending him letters? Whatever he might say about doing his job, he wasn't like her and Suzanne and Adam Breen, not paid to take risks and not experienced in it. For all his bravado, she knew how vulnerable he could be.

Claire jumped as she nearly walked into a cleaner crouching beside one of the swing doors, emptying a bin. She mumbled an apology and told herself to get her mind back on the case.

Two hours now Nicola had been missing. Charles Cross was the emptiest she'd ever seen it, none of the usual banter in the corridors, babble from the offices or continual hum of the lift. Everyone was out looking for her. Everyone doing the best they could, but always with that unspoken fear. Who would find the corpse? That was the merciless truth of the statistics. If you don't find the child quickly, you don't find them alive.

What about her case? Was this computer idea really worth following up, or was she chasing a whim? The trouble was, the computer at the house of the first shooting in Bodmin had gone, been given to some charity shop, untraceable, a new one bought. Was that important? It hadn't been checked at the time because back then there were no grounds for suspicion. It was only after the Saltash shooting the High Honchos got worried. The computer there had been checked, but nothing found. And Crouch's own computer was clean too, not a hint of anything amiss. Still, it was a potential lead and they weren't exactly overwhelmed with them. It had to be worth a try.

Just how much did Crouch know about computers, anyway? He must be competent with them to have one. It was something they'd have to put to him in the next interview, whenever that might be. The Police Federation, the officers' union, were weighing in on his side now, so they'd have to take it gently. There had even been talk of victimisation of an officer for simply doing his job, discussion too of some officers refusing to carry guns if the inquiry went on.

It had happened before, in London, over an investigation into two firearms officers. She'd seen the looks she'd got from a couple of colleagues, the way some glanced over when she was in the canteen. Whiting was certainly right about one thing. This inquiry could make you unpopular.

Still, she would do her job. She was pleased with the online personality she'd created, if a little surprised – perhaps even shocked? – at how easily it had come.

"Please help me! Please!" Claire had typed.

"I wasn't sure whether I should give you my name, but I'm so desperate, I just don't care. I'm Zoë, I'm 29, and a teaching assistant. I've been married to Phil for the last five years, and to start with it was all perfect. But now … well, it's hell. I can't think of any other word to describe it.

"I'm sorry if I pour all this out, but no one else knows and it seems to be helping, just getting if off my mind and out in the open.

"It was all so beautiful at the start, just perfect. The wedding was a dream, in a lovely little Cornish church. It was such a happy day, all our family and friends looking on, all a blaze of beaming smiles. We bought a house in Liskeard, not a huge place but plenty enough for us, a friendly modern estate on the edge of the town. It was just … well, idyllic, all that I'd imagined in a marriage. We were happy, so happy. But now…

"It started to go wrong when Phil lost his job. The call-centre in Plymouth closed. The business was being moved to India, the wages are much cheaper there. He looked for other work, but nothing was so well paid, the only possibilities dirty, hard physical labour. He tried it for a while, but couldn't keep up with the stronger men. A couple of glasses of wine in the evening became a bottle, then another, then a few bottles. I guess it was his way of coping. He'd go quiet, become withdrawn, then turn on me. At first it was shouting and screaming, and that was bad enough. But then one night – one terrible night – he slapped me.

"I remember that moment so well. Afterwards, he stood still, staring at his hand as if it was a stranger's, not a part of him. He looked at me, head bowed, sobbing and burst into tears. We hugged and cuddled and made up. But the next night it happened again, and the next, and this time it was a punch."

Claire paused, leaned back from her computer, let out a low whistle. She didn't want to think about where the words were coming from. She got up, made herself a strong coffee, continued typing.

"It's been going on for months now. You know what? I can't say how many exactly. The days just pass in a haze of misery. And it's got worse – if that was possible. He's become cunning. He hits me in the body and legs where the cuts and bruises won't show.

"I've tried everything to get through, talk to him, try to get him to counselling, but nothing's worked. He's become impenetrable. He sits silently, drinks the red wine, then attacks.

"I wasn't going to say this, but I will. I'm losing hope. I haven't told anyone, not family, not friends. You're the first to know. I've … I've thought about suicide – in fact, I've already started collecting packets of tablets from the supermarket. They're hidden away in the cupboard under the kitchen sink, along with the cheap bottle of whisky. Some days it seems the only way out. I open the cupboard door and stare at the pills and the lovely glow of the whisky. Sometimes I imagine what it would be like just to swallow and drift away, never to have to come back to this hell.

"Then I saw a poster on the supermarket notice board. It advertised a support group, but said anyone who couldn't come along could always make contact online, so I looked up Domestic Violence on the net. You know what? Finding out how many other women were also suffering was a shock, but it gave me strength too. For once, I felt I wasn't alone.

"I've got to go now, he'll be home in a minute. So … can anyone help? Please! You might just save my life."

Claire noticed her hands were shaking as she finished typing. She had to go for a long walk over the cliffs around the Hoe to calm herself. But, even then, Zoë was with her still.

This evening she would see whether she'd got any replies. She still wasn't quite sure what she was doing, just that she was following a hunch. For now though, there were far more urgent matters. She climbed into the car, Suzanne started the engine and they drove fast out of Charles Cross, past the ruined church and towards Peverell.

A cold drizzle had begun drifting from the darkening sky. It made Dan's ankle throb with a renewed ache and he trod carefully on the slippery paving slabs. He exchanged glances with Nigel. Neither of them liked working in the rain.

'Have we got enough pictures?'

Nigel nodded. 'Plenty for lunch. I'll do some more if we need them, but it'll just be the same stuff, cops wandering around talking to people.'

'I'll start editing then. You stand by and keep an eye out for any more action.'

He slid into the OB van alongside Loud. The engineer had changed into a plain navy shirt. Dan had to look twice to make sure it was him. 'Just in case the kid turns up dead,' Loud explained. 'How touchingly considerate,' Dan thought, but didn't say.

He began the report with the picture of Nicola, the most important part of the story, talking about her being on the way to school that morning when she was abducted. Then they edited in the shots of policemen knocking on doors, talking to local people, while Dan spoke of all available officers being

169

scrambled to join the hunt, the police helicopter brought in too. They used a couple of bits of interview of people talking about their shock, then finished with the descriptions of Nicola, Gibson and the car. They didn't edit any pictures over that part, the graphics would be dropped in when they sent the story back to the studios.

Adam arrived at 1.20. 'Any news?' Dan asked.

'Not a bloody thing. No sightings at all.'

'Any guesses?'

'None. He could be anywhere. He had an hour's head start on us, at least. That's time enough for him to be 70 miles away if he hit the motorway. It's clear he had some plan, so I'm sure he's not just running. He's up to something, but what it is I don't know.'

'Nicola's probably safe though, isn't she?' said Dan, without much belief. 'He said he didn't want to hurt anyone.'

Adam shook his head. 'I hope you're right, mate, I really do. But remember we're dealing with a madman here. He could do anything.'

Dan eased himself gently down from the van, protecting his ankle. He slipped into his ear the moulded plastic tube that would link him to the studio. Nigel has set up the camera facing the mobile incident vans. The drizzle was still drifting steadily down.

'What do you want to say in the interview?' Dan asked.

'I don't want to go into anything about Gibson. If he sees it, it might panic him. We'll leave that for now. I just want to appeal for public help really, that's the important thing. I've got a favour to ask too, but we can talk about that after the broadcast.'

Something in Adam's voice sounded ominous, but Dan didn't have time to ask.

'Fine. OK, stand by,' he said. 'There'll be a studio link, then I'll pick up and set the scene. Then my report will play. It's a minute and a half and features the picture of Nicola and the descriptions you gave us. Then I'll interview you.'

Adam straightened his tie and checked his reflection in a car window. 'Sure.'

The opening titles of the lunchtime news rumbled in Dan's ear.

'A major police hunt is under way this lunchtime,' said Craig, sounding more animated than his usual relaxed self, 'after an eight-year-old girl was abducted in Plymouth. Hundreds of officers are scouring the city for signs of Nicola Reece, but so far nothing has been found. Our Crime Correspondent Dan Groves can tell us more …'

'Craig, I'm in the Peverell area of the city where the hunt for Nicola is being coordinated,' Dan picked up, gesturing to the police vans behind him. 'And the police are asking for urgent public help in finding her. They say every passing second could be vital.'

His report played. 'With me now is Detective Chief Inspector Adam Breen who's leading the hunt for Nicola,' he said. 'Mr Breen, how can the public help you?'

'We need their eyes,' began Adam, and Dan could tell he'd been rehearsing his sound bites. Short, sharp and memorable, straight from the 'How to be on TV' handbook.

'I've got all the police officers I can searching for Nicola, but they're just a tiny fraction of the number of people out there who can be looking for her too. I would appeal to people – you've seen the picture of Nicola and heard the description of the man and his car. Please, please, look out for them and if you see anything, contact us immediately. This is very much a team effort. We all need to work together to get Nicola home safely.'

They got an all clear from the studio and Dan popped out his earpiece.

'Very good, that worked fine. So … what was it you wanted my help with?'

'Between us,' replied Adam, 'I'm guessing he's gone to ground somewhere with Nicola. It'll be a place he's prepared beforehand, which'll make it very difficult to find. He's probably got food and water there, so he doesn't have to venture out. I'm guessing he might have a TV, but I'm sure he'll have a radio at least. He'll want to be able to check on the media coverage to see his plan is working.'

171

'So? What are you thinking?'

'I think the best hope of finding him might be in those letters he sent you. He says it's all in there in some form of code, so we've got to take that seriously. It seems to fit with the game he's playing. I've got some code-breaking experts from SOCA, the Serious and Organised Crime Agency on their way. They've already had a look at some copies we've sent. They say it's nothing obvious and they could do with some more clues. Bearing in mind what Gibson said about us being up against the clock, I don't think we've got long to find Nicola, so I want to try something straight away. I'd like to release the fact that the letters were addressed to you.'

'That'd mean that all the media would want to talk to me,' said Dan thoughtfully. 'I'd become part of the story.'

'Exactly. And I'd want you to say that you'd tried to crack his codes but couldn't, and could you have another clue? It seems the only way to reach him and perhaps get us a break.'

Smart, thought Dan, very smart. But how will Lizzie feel about it? How can she say no if there's a chance it'll help find Nicola? More to the point with Lizzie, how can she refuse if it makes Wessex Tonight feature in the story? It'll be all over the national papers, great publicity for the programme and bound to lift the ratings.

'I'll have to check with my editor. But I think I can persuade her. She'll see it as a hell of an angle.'

'Good,' said Adam. 'One more thing, though. I've got something else to tell you, so you're clear what you're getting into. I wasn't sure whether to, but I don't want there to be any doubt about this. It's only fair. But strictly not for broadcast, OK?'

'OK,' answered Dan, wondering what he was about to hear. Adam's face was set and his voice sombre.

'Firstly, I've got a psychologist's report on Gibson. I won't go into detail, but basically it says he's … err … very bad news.'

Dan tried to hide a gulp. 'OK. I think I kind of suspected that.'

'Secondly …' Adam paused, seemed to be struggling for

172

the words. 'Well, I think he's even more devious and dangerous than the psychologist reckons. We've managed to get some information from Nicola's mum. She's in a terrible state, but she did tell us she knows Gibson. More than knows, in fact. She thought he fancied her and wanted to have a relationship. They've been out together lots of times, her, him and get this – Nicola too.'

Adam hesitated again, studied his impeccably polished brogues. 'Well … apparently Gibson wanted it that way. He used to tell Nicola's mum that if it was going to work between them he wanted to make sure he could bond with Nicola as well so he could look after them both. The girl loved him and wouldn't have hesitated to get into a car with him. And given his past, the things he's seen in Bosnia and the effect it had on him, the intricacy and detail of his plan, the time he's spent working on it and the fact that he's got a gun and knows how to use it …'

Adam let the words linger. 'Well, I don't think I need to say anything else.'

Dan drew in a breath and scratched his ear. 'Hell,' he said quietly.

'Quite,' Adam replied. 'Now you know exactly what we're dealing with. We've got to get him and fast. There's no telling what he might do. Nicola's mum is going to do a press conference this afternoon. She's still in a dreadful way, but she'll manage to read a statement at the very least.'

Chapter Fourteen

TWO YEARS HE'D BEEN doing the job now and Dan had already faced countless numbers of these ordeals. There was no other word for them. Bereaved parents, partners, sisters or brothers, lamenting their loss, sometimes those desperately searching for the disappeared, hoping in the face of the uncaring odds that they might one day see them again. Occasionally it was even those who'd suffered themselves, victims of attacks or abuse, for some reason he never understood wanting to share their pain with the world through the hungry media. But always it came down to the same basic elements. Tears and trauma.

No matter how many of these stories he'd covered, he'd never grown used to it. Tonight Dan knew he'd get home, cuddle Rutherford, lie on his great blue sofa, drink whisky, stare at the passing sky and try to forget what he'd seen. But he never would. Many stories he covered were mundane, fillers, forgotten as soon as they were aired. These were different, marked by their raw humanity.

He could remember every single one. Arthur Bray had been the first, an old man sobbing for the loss of his son, blasted at close range by a shotgun in a revenge attack. Then there had been Katy Graham, facing the cameras in hunched anguish, desperate for news of the fiancé who had disappeared. To this day, there had been no sign of him, no hint of his fate. Dan wondered what Katy was doing now. Still hoping, her life on hold? Or had she finally moved on?

Then it was Lisa Pinecoffin – he would never forget that name – crying for the elderly mother murdered in a break-in at her cottage, pleading for anyone who could help the police find the killer to come forward. The appeal had worked, a man jailed for life for the murder after information from a criminal friend he'd boasted to. Adam had said at the time there was occasionally honour amongst thieves.

Then … countless others he didn't want to think of.

Sometimes a tearful face and their sobbed words would drift through a dream, passing ghosts he knew would never be exorcised. Such searing emotion did that. It etched an indelible mark.

Dirty El sidled in to the press conference and pushed his way through to the front, next to Dan and Nigel. He was sporting the biggest lens he could fit on the front of the camera and sharing precisely none of Dan's sentiments.

'I want to get right in there on her face. I need to see those beautiful tears dripping in a big, shocking close-up. That's what sells the picture to the papers. Great story eh? It's going to bring me a fair few quid.' He stroked the bloated lens lovingly. 'It broke so fast the national papers couldn't get their own snappers down here in time, so they've all been on to me booking the shots.'

Dan wondered what El would say when he heard Adam's statement about who the letters were addressed to. He could see his own picture in the papers tomorrow too, wasn't looking forward to it. He didn't photograph well. Lizzie had agreed and eagerly, on the proviso he kept a couple of exclusive details back and only aired them when he was live in the studio tonight. He still had to negotiate with Adam exactly what they would be. It was going to be a long day.

'And another thing,' whispered El, looking at his watch. Dan checked his too. It said quarter to four, so it was probably about five to. 'What do you reckon to it being Mum who's done away with the girl after all, and invented this story about an abduction? That's what usually happens. You know the old hacks' saying?'

Dan did, but suspected he was going to hear it again anyway. In fairness, it was often proved absolutely true. 'Look for who's crying the loudest in the press conference,' continued El, 'and there's your killer.'

A door ground open at the side of the room and Dan had to duck the swing of El's lens. Nigel spun his camera too. A policewoman walked slowly out, holding the arm of another woman who was leaning heavily against her. A blaze of photographers' flashes lit the room and she looked up and blinked heavily, seemed to shrink from the blinding flares. The tears were already running down her cheeks. The policewoman guided her to a table at the front. She sat on one side, Adam the other, dark blue boards sporting the Greater Wessex Police badge behind them.

The room was packed with journalists, photographers and camera crews, a line of microphones set up on the table pointing at the woman. She was in her mid-thirties guessed Dan, plump, with shoulder-length dark hair. He couldn't make out much of the detail of her face. The crying had blurred its definition. It was swollen and looked smudged. She was wearing a black jacket and white blouse, obviously her best.

'Ladies and gentlemen, this is Karen Reece, Nicola's mum,' began Adam, surveying the crowd. 'As you'll appreciate, she's very upset and is being extremely brave in managing to talk to you at all. She will read a prepared statement and then leave. There will be no questions. After that, I also have a statement for you, which I'm sure you'll find interesting.' Dan caught his look, suppressed a shiver at the words. His part in the growing drama.

Adam turned to his side and touched the woman's shoulder. She looked down at a piece of paper, took a deep, gulping breath and began falteringly to read. More flashes strobed around the room.

'Nicola … Nicola is my only daughter … my only child. She's a beautiful girl. She's bright and kind and loving … just … everything you could want from a young girl. But she's more than my daughter. Much more … as she's grown older, she's become my friend too … my best friend. It's not always easy, being two women alone trying to get on in the world, but we … we look after each other and when one of us is down, the other one picks her up. Nicola is … she's my world and I love her with all my heart. She's all I've really got in life.'

Karen Reece's voice faded. Adam reached out an arm and wound it around her shoulders. Dan thought he looked angry and guilt-ridden, as though he felt he was responsible for her suffering. Was he thinking of Gibson, sitting in front of him at the Leisure Centre, going through that act, how he could have stopped all this if he'd realised?

She dabbed at her tears with a sleeve, continued. 'Nicola is … she's a … a kind and gentle person. To the man who has her, I say she would never harm anyone. Never. So please … please … don't harm her. Please … see how much I'm suffering and how desperate I am and … please … let her go. Let Nicola go.'

Now, for the first time she lifted her eyes from the piece of paper and looked at the press pack leering down upon her, the cold, unblinking eyes of the cameras, the eager microphones, the scribbling notebooks. Her eyes widened and she choked on a breath.

Adam squeezed tighter and she steadied herself. 'Please … please, please, let her come home safely to me … my little girl … my Nicola.' Her voice faltered, was lost in her helpless sobbing.

The policewoman quickly got up, took Karen's hand and led her back out through the door. Adam watched them go, drumming a finger on the table, his face set. Dan felt a lump in his throat and swallowed hard. He heard a gentle sigh from Nigel too, knew his sons would get a big hug when Dad returned home tonight.

'Right … ladies and gentlemen, I've got a couple more things to update you with,' said Adam, looking around the room. 'Firstly, we still have no reported sightings at all of either Nicola, the man or the car. We desperately need some, so I renew my appeal to the public. If you think you've seen something – whatever it might be – please come forward.'

Adam waited while the journalists noted that down. Dan knew exactly what was coming next and took a couple of deep breaths. He'd never been in a situation remotely like this before.

'Secondly, I have another important piece of information,' said Adam. 'Can I ask Dan Groves from Wessex Tonight to come and join me at the front please?'

Dan did, sat down at the table with Adam. He tried to ignore the buzz of puzzled conversation that rumbled around the room and the flaring of more camera flashes.

'I can now reveal the man who we believe abducted Nicola left a series of messages in the form of letters. They were addressed to Dan. It seems the man saw him on the television and formed some kind of attachment to him. The man claims the letters contain a code giving clues about where Nicola is.'

Dan tried hard to keep a straight face as the journalists, cameramen and photographers stared at him. El was shaking his head hard, but it wasn't stopping him from aiming that long lens right in Dan's face. He felt a prickling sweat spreading from the base of his back.

'It's highly unusual, but because of that, I have had to treat Dan as part of this investigation,' continued Adam. 'The letters have been shown to him. You'll appreciate I can't go into detail as it may hamper the inquiry, but Dan has a statement to make. Again there will be no questions and despite his association with many of you here today, I have asked him not to make any further comment, as this could cause problems for the investigation. I know you will respect that. Finding Nicola has to be our utmost priority.'

For the first time, Dan appreciated how intimidating it was to be the subject of the media's insatiable hunger. He'd been part of the pack enough times, safe in its group strength and anonymity, but never before the lonely prey.

All he could see were expectant faces, lenses, microphones, dancing blurs of light in his eyes from the camera flashes. All the countless times he'd stood talking to a camera didn't help at all. Then it had been dispassionate, reporting on something he had no stake in, just doing his professional duty. Now it was intensely personal. He'd been singled out by Gibson as his messenger, and what he did and said could decide the fate of a young girl.

He swallowed hard, reached into his notebook for the statement he'd agreed with Adam earlier. Carefully worded, to give the hacks something to interest them and, more importantly, Gibson too.

'The man says he's an admirer of my work, and that's why he's written to me,' Dan began, wondering at how shaky his voice sounded. 'Within the letters, he claims there are coded references to where Nicola is being kept. He believes I might be able to solve them and find her. I have tried my hardest, but have been unable to. I am, however, keen to help in any way I can, so I make this appeal. If the man is listening, or sees my words reported in a newspaper, I ask this. Please let Nicola go. She is an innocent young girl who has done nothing wrong. Please let her go. If he can't find it in himself to do that, at least please get in touch again with another clue that might help me work out where she is.'

When the press conference was over, Nigel drove them back to the studios. He'd been full of the questions Dan had promised Adam he wouldn't answer. Nigel understood, but left him at the office with some fatherly words. 'It sounds like you're getting drawn into something pretty murky. Just take care, OK? And don't forget which side of the fence – or story – you're supposed to be on.'

As he climbed the stairs to the editing suites, Dan noticed he was still feeling shaky. He'd forgotten about his ankle in the nervousness of the press conference, but it was aching again. He was tired too. He wanted to get the day over and go home, lock himself away, cuddle his beloved dog and have a whisky. The Swamp was taking advantage of his fragility and starting to suck him in again.

He sat with a picture editor and put tonight's story together, interrupted a couple of times by a fizzing Lizzie.

'I knew I'd be lucky one day,' she gushed. 'A great story like this and we've got a personal involvement. I want you on every night telling us about it. That's every night, you understand? The cops need you on this one, and there's going to be a price.'

A long finger extended and a perfectly manicured nail began wagging right in his face.

'It's a story a night, and an exclusive one at that. It's a fair deal. I want wall-to-wall coverage. I want every hint, nuance and detail. I want it live and I want it poignant. The viewers will love it. I want them to know we're the ones with the inside track on the hunt for Nicola. They'll be switching to us

179

in droves. I want the works! I knew it was a good idea of mine to get you back in with the police ...'

'Your idea?'

'Yes, mine. Oh, I can just see the ratings now ...'

Dan couldn't find the strength for any further argument, promised he'd deliver and eased her out of the edit suite.

He began the report with the picture of Nicola, then cut to her mother's tearful words. It was classical TV, get the most important, most emotional material in first, true to another of the maxims of the medium – start with a bang and make sure the boring, basic data always comes later.

Then it was pictures of the police carrying out door-to-door inquiries in the street and a couple of clips of interview with local people. After that, a few seconds of Adam, asking for public help, followed by a graphic with the descriptions of Nicola, Gibson and the car. They didn't name Gibson. Adam was holding that back for another story when he might have to appeal directly to him. The thought made Dan shudder again. He knew who'd be doing the appealing, if it came to that.

As he watched the report back, his mind wandered in imaginings of what was happening to Nicola. Where was she? In some cold cellar, alone in the dark, tied up and gagged? Bruised and beaten? Or worse, much worse? Why did men usually abduct children? He didn't want to think about that, distracted himself by picking up his phone and sending a text message to Claire. His body and mind felt strangely cold. He needed the reassurance of some warmth in his life.

After the report, it was his interview in the studio, a two-way, as they were known. Dan didn't often feel nervous when broadcasting live, but this time his hands were shaking. His imagination kept flashing up a picture of Nicola, lying in the corner of that cellar, hungry, terrified, too frightened even to cry. What must she be going through? Almost nine years old, her only experiences of the world love and kindness ... until now.

He'd never so much as met her and he kept trying to suppress the thought, but Dan knew he felt responsible for what would become of Nicola. He wondered if this was how

Adam felt about every case. It wasn't an easy weight to carry, to say the least. And as for himself – if he was honest, what was making it worse was that he had always made a point in life of evading true responsibility. Himself and Rutherford, that had been about it. And now, suddenly a young girl to think of too …

'Well Dan's with us,' said Craig, interrupting his thoughts. 'Dan an extraordinary development this afternoon in the case. And it involves you personally?'

'That's right Craig. The man who the police believe abducted Nicola left a series of letters addressed to me. The detectives called me in, to see what I could make of them. We've agreed not to show the letters, as they're being treated as evidence, but I can tell you they say that within them there are coded references to where Nicola is being kept, hence the police's interest. Now, I'm afraid I didn't manage to come up with any ideas about where it could be. But another thing the letters make clear is that there is only a limited amount of time in which to find Nicola safely. So if the man who took her is watching this, and if he does want to communicate directly with me, I'd ask that he gets in touch again and gives me some help.'

'Dan, thank you,' said Craig. 'Will you join us again tomorrow please to update us?'

'Of course,' he said, not mentioning Lizzie had told him it was non-negotiable, tomorrow and every day until Nicola was found, dead or alive.

Dead or alive …

The short drive home that night felt very long. Because those words wouldn't leave him.

Dead or alive … dead or alive … dead or alive …

Echoing around his head, spinning in his thoughts, as though they were taunting him that he was responsible for which it would be.

Dead or alive …

Marcus Whiting sat on his hotel bed, the same ten piles of papers around him again, statements, background checks,

181

forensic and ballistic reports. He'd lost count of the hours he'd spent reading them. He was tired and hungry, but he hadn't yet come to a conclusion and he would before he could allow himself the luxuries of rest or relaxation. It was a question of priority.

He lay back on the bed, closed his eyes, listened to the wind rattling the window. He wondered if there was ever a day in this hotel when the windows didn't rattle. It was time to be honest. He had made no progress. He had his suspicions, but no case. Circumstance and suspicion did not equate to proof. Was there any other way to proceed?

He shut out the world, retreated into his mind. He let the thoughts run, methodically checking every possible option, rejecting each in turn, his fingers moving by his sides as he ticked them off, one by one. Crouch would have to be reinstated, there was no other choice. There was nothing to justify his continued suspension. So, there was only one option remaining. He had to proceed with the action he had suggested to himself as a last resort. It was all he had.

Was it ethical? Fair? The right thing to do? He was in the grey zone, he knew that, carefully balancing his actions between what was clearly warranted and what was debatable, questionable. Could he justify himself in a court? Perhaps yes, but maybe no. He knew he wasn't sure. But he didn't have a choice. If he was to do his duty.

Whiting opened his eyes, stared out at the dark and blustery night, the line of fir trees outside the hotel bowing low, subservient to the wind's relentless power, the red and white hoops of Smeaton's tower resistant, unmoving behind them. He felt himself relax.

The decision was made. However unpleasant, dubious and difficult, he had no choice. It was the only option. It would begin tomorrow.

Dan spent that night in exactly the way he'd expected. He lay on the sofa at home, Rutherford at his feet, sipping whisky and watching the autumn clouds racing across the bay window. He seldom watched television, only the odd film and some football, but his fingers flipped the channels, finding nothing to interest him. He even tried a documentary about killer whales. Nothing distracted him. The image of Nicola, bound and gagged, lying helpless as Gibson stood over her, laughing manically with triumph like a Hollywood villain wouldn't leave his mind.

He had copies of the two letters Gibson had sent, given to him in confidence by Adam in case he could see any clues. They lay on the coffee table by his side, always nagging at the edge of his vision, as if calling to him. He was surprised to find himself frightened to pick them up. But he knew he had no choice.

The first letter was the one which unsettled him most.

"How will all this end?" Gibson had written. "It'll be determined by you, your bravery and intellect."

Dan took a deep gulp of whisky, felt it burn a passage down his throat. It was holding the Swamp back, but only just. He noticed his hands were trembling as he held the letter and the vision of Nicola returned, helpless and terrified, her tear-stained face desperately searching for a saviour. Was that really the role Gibson expected him to play? What if he didn't? Couldn't?

He pulled himself up from the sofa, walked to the spare bedroom at the front of the flat, peered through the curtains. The policeman was there, a different one this time, stamping back and forth to keep himself warm. Otherwise, the road was quiet. He tried to tell himself he was safe – he knew he was safe, a police guard and Rutherford guaranteed that – but he still felt lonely and vulnerable.

Dan walked back into the lounge, gave the curious dog a pat, had another gulp of whisky. It fired him with some welcome defiance. He picked up Gibson's letters. You helped solve the Bray case, and the Death Pictures too. You can do something with this one. He's getting at you in just the way he wants. Don't let him.

He looked through the first letter, but couldn't see anything that could be any kind of hint about where Nicola might be. There were no place names, no numbers for grid references, nothing. But it was the shorter letter, almost an introduction. Perhaps the second note contained the real clues?

There was that mention of Romeo and Juliet, but they knew now what that meant. What else was odd in there? The talk of leaving Plymouth and perhaps going to Manchester, and Denton and Hyde was bizarre. Surely Gibson wouldn't tell them where he planned to go?

Dan found a map of Britain in one of the bookshelves, opened it on Manchester, scanned the area. The city was sprawling, with scores of suburbs. He went through them; Stretford, Failsworth, Eccles, but couldn't see any that helped. The M60 seemed to form a rough natural boundary, more towns and villages outside, and Gibson had written of visiting somewhere "around" Manchester. Dan looked through the places surrounding the city; Stockport, Oldham, Rochdale, but again none offered any obvious hint about where Nicola might be.

He picked out Denton and Hyde, just to the east of Manchester city centre, at the end of a short motorway, the M67. Again Dan could see nothing which might offer a clue.

He tapped his fingers on the map. What else was a common way of hiding a message? Perhaps it was some kind of anagram?

Dan reached for his notepad and a pen and scribbled the words down, then scrambled the letters. In Manchester he found stream, but nothing else to suggest that could help. What about St? As in abbreviation for street, or a place name, like St Helens? He played around with the remaining letters but found nothing. What about Chester man? Could it be that simple? He didn't think so but it was worth remembering, just in case something else came up that might make it plausible.

What of Denton and Hyde? He found Tyne in there, but nothing else to link with it. He tried mixing the letters from Manchester in as well, but there were too many, it was confusing and he came up with nothing. He put the notebook down in frustration, lay back and rolled his head around to release some of the constricting tension in his neck.

Rutherford got up and padded over to the lounge door, sat

looking at the handle. 'A hint mate?' asked Dan, getting up to let the dog out. He cantered round the side of the flat and down the concrete steps to the back garden, the policeman turning to watch him disappear.

'Evening, sir,' the man said. 'All OK in there?'

'Fine thanks. Having a quiet night. All OK with you?'

'I've been on more challenging guard duty, sir,' said the officer heavily.

Dan made a cup of tea to cheer him up. Strong, with three sugars he requested, but Dan was familiar with police tastes by now. He hadn't met a policeman yet who didn't have at least two.

Rutherford scrabbled back up the steps, Dan let him in, said goodnight to the officer and walked back into the lounge. 'One more try, dog,' he sighed, 'then we're going to get some sleep. I'm whacked.'

He picked up the copy of the second letter again. That reference to a band of gold didn't make much sense. What could that be about? A vague memory of some song flitted around the edges of his mind, but he couldn't bring it home. The "some other shape" reference might mean an anagram. He tried spinning the letters around, but couldn't make them into anything that might be a clue.

Dan took another gulp of whisky, drained the glass and resolved to have no more. For tonight, at least. Gibson had said all the information he needed to find Nicola was in the letters, if he knew where to look. Did he believe that, or was he just being played with? He didn't have to answer. He knew he believed it. The man was out to taunt them, everything he'd done so far made that obvious. Giving them clues they couldn't solve would be an irresistible delight. His imagination could hear Gibson laughing.

Dan groaned and put down the letter. Enough, he was getting nowhere and winding himself up. Enough for tonight. He needed to let it go.

His usual stress release of a run wasn't an option. His ankle was throbbing worse than ever, despite the hot, soothing bath he'd tried. Dan propped it up on a cushion but it didn't help.

'Sorry, Rutherford,' he said. 'I think you're going to have to content yourself with running around the garden for a few days.' The dog opened a slow eye, then closed it again. 'You've had enough of the world today too then, eh?'

The Swamp was gathering its strength, he could feel it encroaching further on his consciousness, growing bolder. He searched for some consolation, something to hang on to, to help fend it off. The highlight of the evening had been that brief text from Claire.

"Sorry can't talk, busy with marksman stuff. All OK and some interesting progress. Heard about your appeal in Nicola case. Be careful! I still need you.. x"

A fatherly talking to from Nigel, now this. Two warnings from two of the people closest to me. I'm not the only one who senses danger. He hadn't stopped wondering what he'd got himself into, making that appeal. How would Gibson react? Who could predict the mind of a psychopath? Dan couldn't help but think they'd find out soon enough.

And what was Adam up to? He'd spent half an hour at the Wessex Tonight studios with a couple of his technical people, talking to some of the company's computer experts. He'd seemed animated by whatever it was, but wouldn't say. Dan lay back on the sofa, cursed his aching ankle and resigned himself to having to wait on that too.

'It looks like a waiting game all round, mate,' he told the prone dog. 'And you know how much I hate waiting.'

This time, Rutherford didn't even bother to open an eye.

The building was free until Friday evening, plenty of time. He'd checked on the internet before he put the final stage of the first part of his plan into effect. There was just the chance a group might have booked in at the last minute, but no, all was well. It was his.

The quad bike had been a stroke of genius, he had to hand it to himself. The whole plan was brilliant in fact, but transport was the part that had caused him the most concern. He knew Nicola's friends would manage a reasonable description of the car and he'd probably only have half an hour's head start, so it would have to be abandoned quickly. But that daunting problem. Where to hide it?

It had taken some work. He'd thought about dumping it, in some woods, running it into a valley somewhere, but they sounded too dramatic, too full of risks. It had to be something quiet and simple and in roughly the area he needed. In the end he'd come up with his little masterstroke. Where better to hide a tree than in a forest? It wouldn't be noticed for a day or two at least, more than enough time for his purposes.

Then it was the quad bike, the most vulnerable point of the plan. He'd been nervous again, almost as much as when he took her. If anything was going to go wrong, surely it was the ride on the bike. But people had behaved exactly as they did when he'd carried out the trial runs. They'd looked, then carried on.

Quad bikes were unusual enough to attract a passing notice, but not so rare as to make them memorable. Perfect. And if there was a bundle on the back, along with some straw, what could that be apart from a farmer going about his business? No one would abduct a child on a quad bike, would they?

And this building, just perfect for his needs. Easy to break into, secluded, quiet, hidden away and in just the right place. A little shed to store the bike, out of sight of anyone who might be passing. He couldn't risk it attracting unwelcome attention.

Inside, he'd expected to have to work in the dark, didn't want to risk showing a light, but the building had a windowless storeroom where he could tune in the little portable TV and radio he'd brought. Luck was on his side.

He'd watched Wessex Tonight and Dan's report on the flickering screen, smiled to himself.

'You're not telling your viewers the whole truth, are you my friend?' he asked the television. 'Where's your journalist's integrity now? And I'm disappointed in you. Again. Surely you're not giving up on my little puzzle so soon? Well, if you need another clue, I'll give you one. It's good to keep in touch after all, now we're such fine friends.'

He took out a notebook and pencil and began writing. It would have to be a telephone call, he could hardly use a post

187

box. That would leave a trail. But he'd anticipated he might need to make a call and the pay-as-you-go mobile worked fine up here. He'd checked that in one of his reconnaissance missions. He knew just when to ring and how to make the call anonymous and untraceable. Perfect.

He began writing. "My Dear Dan …'

Should he give them a clue now? Why not, it wasn't a great hint. It would only tell them he was probably in the Wessex Tonight broadcast area. He could have watched the programme on the internet from anywhere, couldn't he? He carried on writing.

"Hello again! I trust I find you well, although rather busy I suspect. And all for me too! I'm flattered, and I thank you. You're helping my little plan to go exactly as I wished.

"I watched you on Wessex Tonight. A very fine report I would say, and a touching appeal. But I'm afraid I can't just let Nicola go, or our dance won't be complete. So you will have to solve the riddle I've set you. Come on now, Dan, I know you can do it if you try. But are you trying hard enough? Should I give you another hint, I ask myself? How can …"

He was interrupted by a stirring from the sleeping bag. 'Hello, my little lovely,' he whispered, stroking the soft, blonde hair as those innocent eyes opened, blinking in the half-light. 'Hello. Did you have a nice sleep?'

She shook her head, her eyes wide, the movement sending tracks of tears sliding down her pale cheeks. One dripped onto the brown polyester of the sleeping bag, then another.

'I had a scary dream,' she whispered breathlessly. 'I dreamt I was in the sea but I couldn't swim. There were monsters pulling me down, lots of monsters. They wouldn't let me go, no matter how much I screamed and kicked. They kept pulling me down. I was frightened. When's Mummy coming? I'm scared.'

He reached out and dabbed her face with his handkerchief. 'Don't cry. Don't be frightened. You trust me, don't you? I'm Mummy's special friend. I've looked after you, haven't I? We've all gone to the seaside together haven't we? I helped you learn to swim, didn't I?'

She nodded, but her eyes were still shining with tears. 'I've told you, it's all part of our game. Don't worry, it's just a big game, like when we played hide and seek in that wood in Cornwall. Do you remember that? And when we all buried ourselves in the sand in Torquay? It was fun, wasn't it?'

She nodded, hard, some of the colour returning to her face. 'Soon, Mummy will be here soon, don't worry. But we've got to finish our adventure first. You enjoyed that ride on the quad bike, didn't you? Wasn't it exciting?'

She nodded. 'Yes. But I won't have to be tied up again, will I?'

'No, of course not. That was just to keep you safe. You have to do that on quad bikes. It's the law. It's just like wearing a seat-belt in the car. You always wear a seat-belt, don't you?'

'Yes. And I always stop and look and listen when I cross the road.'

'You're a good girl. That's why we're having this adventure. Because we love you and want to make you happy. It's all part of your birthday present. What did you do for your birthday last year?'

She tilted her head as she thought. 'I had a big party tea with all my friends. We had lots of blancmange and ice cream and then we played on a bouncy castle. And I showed everyone my new dolls. I've got one that can talk. Her name's Suzy.'

He tried not to imagine it, those happy, innocent faces smiling, laughing, mums and dads looking on proudly, chatting, glasses of wine in hand.

'And it was a good birthday, wasn't it?'

She nodded, that rope of blonde hair swinging like a golden tail. 'Yes. It was the best birthday I've ever had.'

'Well, your mum and I know that. So we've had to work extra hard to make this birthday even better. That's why we're having this adventure. So it's your best birthday ever. Now, are you warm enough?'

'Yes,' she whispered, and he dabbed at her face with his handkerchief again.

'That's better. You look much prettier without those tears. And have you guessed how our adventure is going to end?'

She angled her head again, managed a small, gappy smile. 'Is it a pony?'

He smiled back, couldn't help himself. 'It might be. But you know I can't tell you yet. It's a surprise.'

'Is it a Dartmoor pony?'

'It might be. But I can't tell you any more. I shouldn't have said what I did, but you're naughty, you know how to make me talk. It's a surprise. But if it was a Dartmoor pony, have you thought about names yet?'

'Yes. I like Brandy, but it depends what colour he is.'

'I thought you wanted a black and white one?'

'I think I might like brown now. I've been thinking about it a lot.'

He smiled at her again. 'Well, we'll have to see what's about when we go looking. Are you hungry?'

'No.' She shook her head, the tail of hair bouncing behind her. 'Are we staying here tonight?'

'Yes. Tonight and tomorrow probably. It's all part of our big adventure for your birthday. We'll stay in here for a while, then when it's the right time we'll go out looking for your surprise.'

'And find Mummy?'

'Yes, we'll find her then. Don't worry, everything's going to be all right. Just remember to be quiet and do as I tell you and everything will be all right. We'll find Mummy and we'll get your surprise. It's all a big adventure … the biggest adventure you've ever had.'

Chapter Fifteen

CLAIRE GOT TO CHARLES Cross just after eight o'clock on Tuesday morning. She'd slept well and felt refreshed, decided to make the most of the fine weather and walked in. It was something she should do more often, she thought. A bit of exercise got the blood pumping around your brain. It relaxed you before the onslaught of the day and softened the stresses of work.

Dan had often said she should come for a run with him and Rutherford in the morning, but she'd always preferred the seductive warmth of her bed. Maybe she'd take him up on it, see how it went. That way, at least they'd get the chance to see each other more regularly.

First, there was the marksman investigation to think about. Was there the hope of some progress now? Did she have a new lead? She might have. She wouldn't go further than *might* at the moment, it was a bit far-fetched after all, but it was possible. The response to her emails had been intriguing. It would be interesting to see what Whiting thought.

The automatic door slid open and she walked in to the front office, all hard grey stone and plate glass. It had to be that way for some of the guests the police entertained. When she'd been in uniform she'd once helped restrain a man who'd been smashing at the glass with a baseball bat. It'd taken eight of them to stop him. The baton gun they'd tried had no effect, the rounds just bouncing off his body, his nervous system not even registering them. He'd been addled with drugs, frighteningly wild.

She cheerily said good morning to the desk sergeant, who told her Whiting wanted to see her immediately she arrived. 'Immediately,' he said, 'the very moment you get in, were his words.' She felt the warmth of her mood wane.

Claire took the lift up the stairs and knocked on the door of his office. He looked up and beckoned her in. There was a pile of newspapers on his desk.

'Sit down,' he hissed, pushing the papers across to her, upsetting the small pile of carefully stacked coins. 'Would you care to explain this?'

Puzzled, she sat down and picked up a paper, the *Western Daily News*. On the front was a banner headline, white on black; "Revealed; The Killer Police Marksman". Beneath the headline was a picture of Martin Crouch. The story accompanying it was thin, just a recap on the two shootings, their similarities and the fact that the Independent Police Complaints Authority were investigating.

The editor had added a few lines of opinion to give the splash more spice. "The police wanted to keep the man's name a secret, but we believe in public accountability, particularly in cases as serious as the shooting dead of two men. That's why we publish PC Crouch's picture today. Rest assured, it is not a decision we took lightly."

Claire picked up another paper, the *Daily Globe*. Its headline was "The Killer Cop". There was another small story about the investigation. She was about to go through the other papers when a hiss interrupted her.

'They're all the same. All the same picture.'

Claire looked up at Whiting. He was leaning forward menacingly across the desk, the top of his head shining under the strip light. 'And what do you have to say about that Claire?'

'I don't understand. I don't see what this has to do with me.'

'Tut tut, Claire. Tut tut. Whatever you may have heard about me, whatever some of your colleagues here may say, one thing I am not is naive.'

She felt a swirl in her stomach as realisation spread. 'You're saying you think I had something to do with this?'

'That,' he said, leaning back but his eyes still flicking over her, 'will be a matter for the investigation to decide. All I am saying is you knew his name, you were in a privileged position in this inquiry, and you have the …' he paused, slowed his voice, '… the contacts to make something like this happen.'

Claire was stunned, couldn't find the words. Those narrow

eyes stared at her. A sudden anger burst through the numbness.

'How dare you?' she spat. 'How dare you? I am a loyal and dedicated police officer without a blemish on my record. How dare you accuse me of leaking details of an investigation because of my private life? How dare you!'

She jumped up from her chair, grabbed for the door. 'I intend to report you for what you've said here. I'm going to find the most senior officer I can now, and I shall call in the Police Federation too ...'

'You don't have to report me,' Whiting said smoothly. 'I am suspending you. I will notify the appropriate senior officers in due course. You will be subject to a formal disciplinary investigation. Now you will go home and not return until you are called. You are forbidden from contacting any other police officers, pending the investigation.'

A brief pause, a more sarcastic tone. 'I suggest you keep away from journalists too. You may leave.'

Dan sat in the corner of the newsroom, his shoe and sock on the floor. He'd folded the sock over to hide the inch-wide hole in the toe. It was time he did some clothes shopping.

Ali, one of the office first-aiders was carefully wrapping a bandage around his ankle. It didn't seem to have stopped the throbbing, but it might give some support and prevent it getting any worse. He'd promised her if it didn't feel better in a couple of days he would go to the doctor. Fat chance, Dan thought. He hated doctors and anyway what spare time did he have with Nicola still missing? A bandage would have to do.

It was curiously relaxing, having someone tending to you like this. It reminded him of his early days at school, in the nurse's office with yet another grazed knee. He was always skinning his knees chasing a football around the playground. The stinging antiseptic wipe of the wound, the soothing white cream, the reassuring words. He didn't mind a bit of attention, so long as he wasn't too badly injured. What man did?

His mobile warbled and he answered it, whispering an apology to Ali. Claire.

'Hello, how are you doing?' he asked, a little concerned. She never called him in the daytime. 'Still busy on the case?' He paused. 'You're what? He's done what? The bastard! He can't do that, of course he can't. Don't worry, we'll sort it out. I'll find out who got the picture, but I think I've got a pretty good idea already.'

Dan pulled on his sock and shoe, thanked Ali and hobbled to his desk. Lizzie wasn't about yet, but she'd be here in a few minutes. She wouldn't take kindly to him working on anything other than the Nicola case. That didn't give him much time, but it should be enough.

He took a couple of newspapers out of the rack, scanned through them. There was the marksman's photo, just as Claire had said. The credit by the side of the picture read Ellis Hughes. Exactly as he suspected. He called El's number.

'Hello?' said a sleepy voice.

'Been out celebrating?' asked Dan angrily.

'Oh, hi, Dan. No, mate, not celebrating. I was busy negotiating with all the papers last night. It kept me up late. I got the name and a snap of the marksman you see.'

'Yes, I'd noticed that. It's caused real ructions.'

El yawned loudly. 'Thought it might.'

'How'd you get it?'

'Between us?'

'Of course.'

'I took a part time job in the cops' club at Charles Cross doing bar work. I reckoned he would come in with some police mates at some point. That was why I had me hair cut and coloured, so they wouldn't recognise me. Well, last night he came in with a couple of others for a drink. I knew it was him because I was keeping an ear on all the gossip in the room and his mates were chatting to him about it. They were giving him a pep talk.'

'And you snapped him?'

'Yeah. It wasn't easy though. I had to hide the camera in the storeroom and get the picture through a little crack in the door so they wouldn't notice. They'd have confiscated the camera if they knew. I kept the shot really tight, just his head, so there wouldn't be any background for them to work out where it was taken. Not that it matters now. I've got the snap and quit the job. But I didn't want them coming after me with some trumped-up charge. You know what they're like.'

'And how'd you get his name?'

'That was the dodgy bit. I thought they might suss me then, but I think I got away with it.'

'What did you do?'

'There were only a few people in the club, so I started with some others and just went around saying I'd been told by the club secretary to check membership cards were up to date. Being cops, they could hardly refuse. Crouch got his out without so much as a whisper. So bingo! One snap, one name, and El hits the jackpot.'

The phone buzzed with a few bars of tuneless warble, followed by the inevitable limerick.

'It made quite a splash,
And raked in the cash,
So now El is flush,
He's feeling lush,
And offering you a good beer bash!'

Dan didn't bother trying to interrupt, felt his anger calming. He could hardly blame El for doing his job and his creativity and persistence were impressive. Plus, it was partly Dan's suggestion which had led to the paparazzo going after Crouch. And if his interpretation of El's awful limerick was correct, he was being offered a free night out on the proceeds.

'OK, mate, but just one thing,' he said, more calmly. 'If anyone asks you how you got it, you'd be able to tell them categorically it was nothing to do with me? You don't have to say how you did, just that I had nothing to do with it.'

'Yeah, sure.' El sounded puzzled. 'That's no problem. It's even true. But why?'

'It's just that I'm working with the cops on this Nicola case, and I need them to trust me. So if a detective calls to ask you about it, you can tell him I was nothing to do with it?'

'Sure.'

'OK mate, thanks for that. I'll let you get back to sleep

then.'

'I'd better get up,' said El through another yawn. 'I want to get down to court. There's a bigamy case the tabloids might fancy. Guy married four women apparently, and none of them knew about the others. The redtops love stuff like that. Dunno how he does it. I can't pull one. Maybe he's got my share.'

Dan tried not to smile. He was about to hang up when he saw Lizzie striding through the swing-doors of the newsroom. Her eyes fixed on him and she immediately headed over. Her heels were high today, four inches he reckoned, a sure sign of danger. It wouldn't hurt for her to overhear this.

'Oh El, just one more thing,' he said, over loudly. 'We'll want to use the picture on the programme tonight. How much?'

'Well mate, I was flogging it to the nationals for a couple of grand a time. I can do you a discount as a pal, but a man's got to make a living, and …'

'Right,' Dan interjected. 'Well, I'll ask again, but this time you might bear in mind the help I gave you in finding the mystery woman in the Death Pictures riddle and the wonderful American holiday that paid for. That, and having an in to the police hunt for Nicola, something which might provide you with lucrative tip-offs if – and only if – I'm in the right frame of mind to do so.'

'Point taken mate,' chirped El. 'It's always useful to have a friend in the know. You can have the Crouch snap on me.'

Dan felt the shadow over him. 'Morning boss,' he said, still staring at his computer screen. He typed a couple of words as though sending an email to the newsroom, telling them they could use Crouch's picture for free.

'Morning,' she said suspiciously. 'What are you up to?'

He looked up and tried for a hurt expression but his face just wasn't built for it. 'I've come in to do some early work on the Nicola case.'

Dan pointed to the papers and Crouch's picture. 'I saw this and as I had the contacts, I thought I'd make sure we got the snap. It's ours, and no charge either.'

'Good,' she said, a stiletto grinding into the carpet. 'I'll take a report on it. We'll put another hack on the case. Not you. You,' she added quickly, jabbing a sharpened fingernail at him, 'back on the Nicola story. I want more. I want lots, lots more. I want every detail. I want every nuance. I want every twist and turn. I want wall-to-wall, and day-to-day. OK?'

Dan hid a sigh, picked up his satchel and hobbled towards the doors.

A crowd of thirty detectives and uniformed officers had gathered in the Major Incident Room – or MIR, in police-speak – at Charles Cross for the morning's briefing. Some had come back from leave or given up rest days to join the search for Nicola. There was a great pride in that, thought Adam. The abduction of a child was unique in bringing police, the community, even the media together. He could feel the edge in the atmosphere, didn't like to think what would happen to Gibson if he even hinted at resisting arrest.

Assistant Chief Constable Alan Hawes stood at the back of the room, keeping as low a profile as he could. But everyone knew he was there, had cleared a circle around him. A case like this would always have the High Honchos hovering close behind. They'd had a brief chat earlier.

'Don't want to get in your way old chap,' he'd said, in his ex-army officer way. 'Just carry on as you would normally. You're one of our top detectives and we trust you to do things your way and get a result. I'm only here to help, if you need more resources, that sort of thing. It makes sense if I'm on the ground, to authorise it straight away.'

The man had almost been convincing. But the High Honchos had heard about Gibson's security guard stunt, of course. Were they wondering if he was still up to the job of finding Nicola? Keeping an eye on him? Preparing to replace him if he didn't get a result quickly?

It was another pressure he could do without and he pushed the thought aside. Finding Nicola, he had to concentrate on that and that alone.

A tactical firearms commander was here too, chatting with a couple of the force's top marksmen. They'd been brought in from a course they were leading and might well be needed. They knew Gibson had a gun and could easily use Nicola as a hostage.

His treasured green felt boards had been set out at the front of the room, all five of them. No matter how much of modern policing became reliant on computers, he would always believe that the only way to feel the vital connections in a case was to see them in front of you, the links between the players physically made real.

Some other detectives thought it was a quirk, a weakness even, but he never doubted its importance. It kept the team focused on who they were hunting and why. It was effectively a mission statement, set out in front of them.

In the centre of the boards was a picture of Gibson, just head and shoulders, the one he'd used in his application for the Security Guard job. Adam stared at it, couldn't help but think the man was smirking at him.

Next to Gibson was a photograph of Nicola. Around the two were postcard-sized notes headlining the various avenues of the inquiry. When one became a positive lead it would move and take the far left board for itself, ready for the other strands of that part of the investigation to gather around it. So far, the board was blank. He needed to fill it, and fast.

'OK, folk, settle down please. We've got a lot to get through and time's against us.' What could he tell them? What leads did they have? Not many was the diplomatic answer. Just about none would be more honest.

'Here's how things stand. We haven't found Gibson's car yet. It's a vital element of the inquiry and we need to. That's out priority today. It'll give us the first hint where he's gone. There was no CCTV near where he lifted Nicola, and the A 38 is just a couple of minutes away. That's a motorway standard road. He had a head start on us of about an hour, so he could be up to 70 miles away.'

Adam pointed to a map on the wall. 'That puts him anywhere from halfway into Cornwall, right up to the eastern edge of Devon. He can't be further. The automatic number plate recognition system would have clocked him as soon as the alert went out. So at least we've got a defined area to concentrate on. We're going through the cameras on all the main roads, but so far we don't have an indication of where he might have gone.' He paused, emphasised the words. 'We need to find that car. It'll give us our best clue.'

A young woman detective at the front put up a hand. 'Yes, Gill?' asked Adam.

'Is there no hint at all of where he might have gone, sir?'

'Not a thing. Our background checks didn't throw up any favourite places or family or friends' houses he'd visit. We've checked the places Karen Reece tells us he went on outings with her and Nicola, but found nothing. Gibson didn't seem to have any real friends. The people he knew and his neighbours haven't been able to help us with anything. They said he kept himself to himself and didn't really talk to them. The search of his flat gave us nothing. He doesn't have a mobile that we know of, so we can't trace it. If you're interested, I'll give you my hunch, though.'

A few replies of 'Yes' rose from the room.

'I don't think he's gone far. I say that because of both the statistics and my feeling about the man. Experience shows us most abductors don't take their victims far at all. And he seems to be motivated by attacking Greater Wessex Police. That's you, me, all of us he's having a laugh with. So I reckon he's still in our patch, and perhaps not even that far from Plymouth.'

'What about the references to the places up north in his letter, sir?' she asked.

'A team of detectives has been sent to each and they're working with the local police,' said Adam, pointing to one of the postcard notes. 'But they've found nothing so far. There's nothing to indicate it's anything but a red herring, although we will still check it, of course. But that leads me on to an introduction I've got to make.'

Adam gestured to a man and a woman standing at the side of the room. 'This is Eleanor Yabsley and Michael Hunter. They've come down from the Serious and Organised Crime Agency to help us with the letters Gibson sent. They're code specialists. Gibson says there are clues in his letters about where Nicola is being kept, but so far we haven't managed to find anything. Eleanor and Michael will be working specifically on that today. Give them all the help they need.'

'Any news on last night's media appeal, sir?' asked a uniformed policeman at the front of the room.

'Nothing yet,' said Adam, 'but I do have to check with Crimestoppers and Wessex Tonight as to whether they've heard anything.'

'What about Gibson's background?' asked the man again. 'Is there anything in there?'

'You've all got the summary of his life?' asked Adam. There was a rumble of 'Yes' from around the room. 'You can see his reason for hating the police in there. It appears he went off the rails after his military service in Bosnia, and seemed to focus on his dog as his only friend. And, as you know, we killed the dog.'

There were a couple of murmurs and shaking of heads. 'Whatever you may think of it, that looks like the reason,' continued Adam. 'And let it be a warning to you. He's not exactly in a normal frame of mind. He's unpredictable and I fear he could do anything – to one of us, if we corner him … and to Nicola.'

The MIR quietened again, heads nodding silently. Adam pointed to Gibson's photo, the calm eyes staring out at them.

'Bear in mind that he's ex-army. He knows how to fight. Also, it's not beyond him to be living rough somewhere with Nicola. He indicates in the letters we only have a very limited time to find her. So he wouldn't have to keep her in comfortable conditions if he had some grand gesture in mind to end all this. What will that gesture be? And why so quickly?'

The room stayed quiet as the detectives thought about it. 'So, as you can see,' continued Adam. 'We haven't got much to go on. As ever, it's down to us.' Adam paused, looked round the room, eye contact for every officer.

'Saving Nicola is down to us. So get out there and worry away at whatever leads you're assigned to. Gibson's taking the mickey out of us. He's playing a game. He thinks he's smarter than us and he's taking the mick. We're not going to let him. Good police work will get this guy. One of you needs to spot the tiny little detail that'll lead us to him. And, as we all know, however careful our criminal, there's always one there. He's been giving us the surprises. Let's work up a big one for him when the handcuffs click on his arms. Go find him team. Go find him and save Nicola.'

Adam stood back and watched as the officers clustered quickly around the boards to be given details of their tasks. He could sense the energy and determination. His little speech had done its work.

His mobile rang and he fumbled in his jacket. 'Hi Dan. That's good timing. I was about to call you. Has anything come in overnight from Gibson? What? Whiting's done what?! Hell, I haven't got time for this …'

Adam flung open the door. It crashed against the wall and juddered. He stalked into Whiting's office.

'I take it you'd like a word,' said Whiting calmly, looking up from some papers he was reading. 'Most people knock.'

'Damn right I want a word. You've suspended Claire Reynolds.'

'Yes, I thought I'd be seeing you fairly soon, Chief Inspector. I know she's a favourite of yours.'

'What I think of her is not the point,' growled Adam, slamming the door behind him and striding right up to the desk. 'But since you ask, she's a very talented, dedicated and utterly reliable officer. That's utterly reliable, Whiting.'

'In a way that I'm not?' he replied, still sitting, his voice deceptively soft. 'You mean that I have a habit of victimising good officers? Is that what you mean? Is that what this is really about, Chief Inspector? Is it about the past?'

'No, it's not about the bloody past, but since you've brought it up, I have never and will never forgive you for what you did with Chris. You hounded a bloody good man out of his job. A good man and a damn good detective.'

Whiting slowly stood up to face Adam and leaned forwards

across his desk. Their faces were inches apart.

'What I did, Chief Inspector,' he hissed slowly, 'was to investigate a police officer for perverting the course of justice. I merely did my duty. I was called on to investigate and I did. In the course of the inquiry I discovered evidence of illegality. I then took the appropriate action. If anyone was responsible for his downfall, it was himself. I did not hound him, I simply did my duty. Can you not understand that Chief Inspector, a man in your position?'

Adam's fist slammed into the desk, making the keyboard rattle and upsetting the pile of coins. Whiting didn't flinch, his face set in that strange half smile.

'Don't give me the duty spiel, Whiting. You wouldn't know what it means. Duty is about catching criminals. It's about getting out there, busting a gut and risking your life trying to catch the real nasties. Not sitting in a nice warm office, sipping tea in perfect safety and calmly passing judgement on brave police officers who were simply doing their job.'

Whiting nodded slowly. 'You really need to move on, Chief Inspector. Move on and realise there's more to the world than the narrow tunnel of a police officer's view.'

Adam went to snap a retort, heard footsteps in the corridor outside, controlled himself with an effort.

'That … is the past Whiting. I don't have time to argue with you about it. I'm trying to find a young girl and I don't have time for this. This is about Claire. She is an utterly reliable, dedicated and loyal officer.'

'I have my doubts I'm afraid,' he hissed. 'You've seen this morning's news reports about the inquiry, I take it?' He pushed the papers towards Adam.

'I've heard about them.' Adam, looked down, saw Crouch's face staring at him. 'What makes you think this is in any way down to Claire?'

'I have heard about her …' he waited to find the word, '… unwise associations. They make her the prime suspect. And this is something I cannot allow.'

'She didn't do it.'

'What?'

For the first time that unfeeling smile faltered and the hissing voice became almost normal.

'She didn't do it. She didn't leak his name.'

Whiting recovered fast, asked smoothly, 'How can you be so sure?'

'Because, like any good cop, I have contacts. I know the photographer who took the shot. He's made trouble for us in the past. He got the picture in the time-honoured paparazzi way of staking out the police station. He knew Crouch would have to come here at some point.'

'And you're sure of this, are you?'

'Quite sure.'

Whiting studied him, sat back down. 'My decision stands,' he said calmly. 'I'm afraid until I have hard evidence, Claire Reynolds remains suspended pending investigation.'

The cold smile slipped back onto his face and the hiss returned to his voice. 'As you'll appreciate, Chief Inspector, it would take someone of much higher rank than yourself to force her reinstatement.'

'Yes, Whiting, I thought you'd say that,' said Adam, for once glad the man he knew hadn't changed. 'That's why I had a word with the Assistant Chief Constable before I came here. He agrees with me. As there's no evidence against her whatsoever, Claire is being reinstated. But she will not be coming back to work with you. She's joining me on the Nicola case, where she's needed for real police work. She's an excellent officer and I'll be very glad to have her.'

Adam didn't give Whiting a chance to reply, turned, walked out and slammed the door behind him. Time to get on with the search for Nicola. That was by far more important than sparring with Whiting. He shouldn't have let the man rile him into a row. He took his mobile from his pocket.

'Claire? DCI Breen. I haven't got time for a chat but you're back with us. Not with Whiting you'll be glad to hear. You're joining me on the Nicola case. Get yourself back in now. I need every officer I can get.'

He listened as the voice buzzed at the other end of the

phone.

'Look, I hear you. It's great you've got a lead. But Crouch is not the priority, right? Just get in here. We've got to find Nicola. I'll talk to you about Crouch when we get a chance. We won't bother Whiting with it. If it comes to something, we'll make it a little surprise for him. I'm sure he'll enjoy that.'

Dan kept his head below his computer monitor to avoid the prowling Lizzie and checked the emails in the Wessex Tonight inbox. There were plenty of comments on some of the stories they'd run last night, most of them favourable. There were also quite a few adverts for sex aids and naughty schoolgirls who needed discipline. Fascinating and tempting though they might be, this wasn't the time to read them.

He typed out a quick email to the Information Technology department to mention he thought the spam filter should be improved. He wouldn't normally have bothered, but his throbbing ankle and Claire's call had left him in a toxic mood. It was cathartic, lancing a little of his venom on the faceless technicals behind the computer system. Dan checked the inbox twice, but there was nothing that might have come from Gibson.

He hobbled down to the post room, taking the stairs gently. Old Jack was in there and had finished sorting the mail; he greeted him cheerily with the rasping voice of the professional pipe smoker. Jack had been at Wessex Tonight since the early days of the programme in the 1960s, always in the post room although he'd now diversified into looking after the studios' garden too.

He should have retired years ago but couldn't bear the thought of leaving. He was a bachelor and TV was his life, however remote he was from the real action. Dan collected his letters, made an excuse about having a deadline to beat and left. If Jack got talking about the old times you could rule at least an hour out of your day.

He had an invitation to a Police Authority meeting, which he binned, and a hand-written letter asking him to be the guest speaker at a Women's Institute lunch. He'd agreed to cover for a colleague several years ago at a similar event and now got invitations roughly every month from the various parts of the region. He did a couple a year to keep the women happy and to tick the "community relations" box on his annual appraisal. He usually got an excellent home-made cake as a thank-you gift too.

There was a press release for the launch of a fisheries project, and another to combat alien weeds – both relics from his days in the environment – but that was it. No hint of anything from Gibson. He hobbled back up to the newsroom to find Ali beckoning.

'It's OK,' Dan soothed, thinking he was about to be sent to a doctor. He tried to walk without limping. 'Really, it is. That bandage has made it a whole lot better.'

'No, no, it's not your stupid ankle,' she trilled in her Scottish lilt. 'There's a message for you on the answer machine.'

He quickly limped over. It had never occurred to Dan that in this age of email and mobiles that Gibson could have left a message on the office answer machine. But then, why not? The newsroom wasn't staffed between midnight and four in the morning, so he could dictate a message without having to talk to anyone. And he could withhold the number of the phone he was using.

He pressed play, heard the familiar voice. "My Dear Dan…"

Chapter Sixteen

THE CASSETTE SPINDLES TURNED, pulling Gibson's voice from the thin metallic ribbon and out to the speaker. How did he sound? thought Dan, as he stared at the cassette. Not triumphant, as he'd expected. Not gloating, not even as though he were enjoying himself. Just flat, normal, everyday. His voice was singsong in a way that made it obvious he was reading from a script.

Four of them crowded around the tape machine in the CID office. Adam stood, hands on hips, glaring at it. Eleanor sat, eyes closed as though deep in thought. Michael looked down at his notepad, scribbled the odd sentence, offered an occasional nervous smile around the room. There was silence apart from Gibson's voice, thin and tinny from the telephone line.

"My dear Dan,

"Hello again. I trust I find you well, although rather busy, I suspect. And all for me too! I'm flattered, and I thank you. You're helping my little plan to go exactly as I wished.

"I watched you on Wessex Tonight ..."

'Yes!' interrupted Adam, raising a fist, then hitting the pause button. 'That's his first mistake and our first real clue about where he is. He's in your broadcast area somewhere. He's in Devon or Cornwall. I knew it. I knew he wouldn't have gone far.'

'How can you tell that?' asked Dan. 'Wessex Tonight is broadcast on the internet. You could see it anywhere in the world.'

'That's what I was up to yesterday evening with your technical people. I asked them not to put it on the web until this morning. But Gibson won't have known that. So he's given us a clue and while it's not a big one, it's a start.'

Adam straightened his tie, pressed play again.

"A very fine report I would say, and a touching appeal," continued Gibson's voice. "But I'm afraid I can't just let

Nicola go, or our dance won't be complete. So you will have to solve the riddle I've set you. How can you be so clueless so soon? You've hardly had time to study my letters. And I expect some effort here, Dan. You managed plenty with the Death Pictures riddle, and I expect the same, at the very least. Because this time the prize is much more important, isn't it?"

Dan felt another involuntary shudder run across his shoulders, had that twitching urge to again spin around, to see who was behind him, watching. His imagination flashed up another vivid picture of Nicola, bound and gagged, face stained with tears, cold and terrified, her time running out because he couldn't solve the riddle. She was begging, imploring him to try harder. He blinked hard to shift it from his mind but he knew it was there, just on the periphery, waiting, ready to attack again, any time he felt he was failing her.

"Time is the key here, isn't it?" continued Gibson's disembodied voice. "You only have limited time, so I imagine you want to know as much as possible as quickly as you can. Very well then, as I'm a fair man I'll oblige you with another clue. But before that, there are a couple of other things I'd like to mention.

"Firstly, Nicola is quite safe. She's warm, well fed and comfortable. I wouldn't say she's happy, but she's not panicked and she doesn't seem particularly frightened. I think that's because she knows me so well, and trusts me. I've told her we're playing a game, which is quite true of course, isn't it? She's accepted that and she's calm. And rest assured, if you play your part, she will remain safe and be returned home to her mother. I thought her appeal very moving by the way, and a clever idea. One of yours I take it Adam? But I'm afraid I can't let her go just yet. I have a point to make first."

Adam let out a low growl and glared at the tape machine.

"You'll have all my personal details by now, Dan. If you're the man I think you are, you'll be wondering about the contradictions in me. What can I say? Have your psychologists examined the letters and my background? Have they concluded I'm a sociopath? A psychopath? I wouldn't blame them. It's something I've wondered about myself, although I've never felt the need to visit a doctor to discuss it. I'm comfortable with what I'm doing. Someone needs to stand up for the little man who always gets trampled on, and this seems to me the only way. Anyway, I digress. Let me give you my explanation, for what it's worth.

"I won't try to do the Freud stuff, but I had a happy childhood. No one stepped on my favourite toy train when I was five. I can't point to any eternally echoing moment like that, which made me what I am. I didn't see my father a great deal – he was in the army as you know, and quite senior– but I was an only child and close to my mother. I did well at school. I was content.

"I think the trouble began when I came to consider a career. The problem was I simply didn't know what to do. I wasn't driven or sure of my direction, unlike many of my fellows. Nothing particularly appealed and it worried me. That was when my father began to bring his influence to bear.

"It started off subtly – 'there are fine careers in the forces you know' – that sort of thing. But the problem with being a military man is that subtlety is a concept long beaten out of you. It doesn't exactly equate with barking out orders to shoot to kill, does it? The pressure became more overt, and so when I was working on my A levels and still without a desire for a direction, I agreed to be sponsored at University by the army. It was the easy way out of the arguments.

"I often look back and wonder whether I knew at the time that it was a mistake. I think I must have felt unease, but that was about all. I was reassured that if I didn't want to join up at the end of university, I didn't have to. I could still find that elusive career in my three college years. At the very least, it bought me time. But nothing came and so, in the absence of an alternative, I joined the army.

"I began training to be an officer, but I quickly realised it was an error. Everyone was bigger, tougher, more determined and more driven. And I … well, I just didn't really care. So, unsurprisingly, I failed. I won't bore you with the reaction of my father, but you can imagine it. All I can say is that no matter what you come up with, it can never be as hurtful as the quiet but choking weight of disappointment I felt came to rest upon me. I was his only son, and a failure.

"I resolved not to waste my training completely, so I looked around for other possibilities. I've never been talented at forming relationships with people – I suspect you've guessed that and no doubt your psychologists have something to say on the matter – and I've never had a girlfriend, but I have always loved animals. We had a pet dog when I was young, a border collie. I loved him greatly. Smudge was his name. But he died when I was five and my father didn't want a replacement. Pets were too much trouble, he said. But I missed that dog and the memory of Smudge made me think perhaps I could work with animals. There were vacancies at the time for dog handlers, so that was what I did.

"It was a revelation. For the first time in my life I found something I wanted to do. For the first time, I had a place where I felt comfortable. I felt valued. I belonged. That had never happened to me before. Not only did I want to be a dog handler, I enjoyed it. You'll see from my record how I trained and was paired up with Sam. And you'll see how his love and loyalty saved my life, how we retired together and then how he was taken from me."

Gibson's words trailed off into silence. Dan and Adam exchanged glances. The detective stepped forward to check the tape machine, but its spindles were still turning, a soft hiss of the phone line leaking from the speaker.

"I'm sorry, Dan," came Gibson's voice again. "The memory still hurts. He was my one true friend. It took a few seconds to compose myself again. It's important for all our destinies – yours, mine and Nicola's – that I get this clear and right.

"Anyway, I was explaining myself. You now have the background to what I've done. But again, Dan, knowing you, I imagine you would have guessed much of this anyway. I expect it's a familiar enough story. What's important now is the more recent past.

"My employment as the shell-shocked Security Guard you

met dates back to a couple of weeks after an infamous moment in the recent history of Greater Wessex Police. It is, if you like, the catalyst. It is what set this sequence of events in motion."

Adam reached out and pressed pause on the machine. 'Any guesses before we go on?' he asked. The two code-breakers shook their heads.

'Dan? He's talking to you here. Any idea what he's going to say? The more you can get into his head and guess what he's thinking, the better chance we have of finding him.'

Images of guns were filling Dan's mind. Guns in Bosnia, guns back in Britain, guns wielded by policemen, used to shoot dogs and more recently people. But then he had the advantage. Despite what Adam had told him on the phone, not to listen to the tape back at the office, to wait until they were together, he had. And not just him either, but Lizzie too.

He'd had to tell her, she was his boss and this was an extraordinary story gifted to them. For once she'd been silent as she listened, her eyebrow hitting a sharp peak of delight at the calm insanity they heard. And then her masterstroke, not just listening to the tape, but making a copy which she intended to use in tonight's programme. He'd thought about it and would probably have suggested it, but wanted her to do it, wanted to be detached from that decision which he knew would enrage Adam.

'A Wessex Tonight world exclusive,' she'd imagined the headline aloud, her voice breathless. 'We can bring you the man who abducted Nicola talking about why he did it.'

He still had no idea how he was going to tell Adam. Don't worry, Lizzie had said, a stiletto grating the carpet tiles. Just tell them we're doing it. The police need us. This guy wants to talk to you and that means we can squeeze the cops for stories. You can negotiate exactly what we use, but we're going to use it. It's the exclusive of the year.

She was right, but Adam was going to go mad, and mad at him, not her. But not for now, that. Later.

'I'd guess it's something to do with firearms,' said Dan finally, trying to sound as though he was thinking it through.

'We know he's got a grudge against the police for killing his dog. I'm wondering if the first shooting of that guy in Bodmin was the catalyst for all this.'

'My thoughts exactly,' said Adam, straightening his already impeccable tie. He reached out and hit the play button. 'Let's see.'

"Do you remember Bodmin and the police shooting a man dead there?' continued Gibson's tinny voice. "That was what woke me. Up until then, my thoughts of revenge had been simmering, but they were only thoughts, vague fantasies. Then I saw the poor man's family on television, crying, saying the police didn't need to shoot him. It was that which made me snap. They shot Sam. They shot this man. They had no need to do either. But they did need to be taught a lesson. I'd been mulling over a plan for quite a while, and I was suddenly sure it was time to put it into action.

"I needed a job where I could meet people and get to know them. I needed to have access to their names and addresses. That security guard position couldn't have come at a better time. I got the job and I waited, built up my little plan, piece by piece. I thought I'd have plenty of time, but that wasn't to be the case.

"Your police force, Adam, was almost too keen for me. I thought it would be years before your trigger-happy, unaccountable marksmen despatched another unfortunate to their grave with their usual impunity. But no. It was only a few months. So I had to act. It came sooner than I expected, but I had the necessary information and so my work began.

"Which brings us to where we are today. We're not at the endgame yet, but we're approaching it. We're almost there. And everything is going beautifully. It won't be long now.

"That's almost all I have to say, Dan, and Adam too. I know you'll be listening in and I hope you don't mind if I call you Adam now? It seems we're getting to know each other very well. We will talk again, but I fear it will be briefly and, as I've said, the circumstances won't permit a detailed conversation."

Adam swore under his breath.

"So I'll sign off now. But don't worry, I haven't forgotten that I promised you another clue. What can I say? All you need to find Nicola and myself is in the letters I have already sent. Look again at what I said about where I might visit. You'll have guessed by now that I'm not there, but it could help you nonetheless. I haven't taken a plane either. And remember what I asked you about the rose. That too could be important. Goodnight for now then, Dan and Adam and whoever else is listening in. Until the next time. Goodnight."

Adam stopped the tape. 'A copy's gone to the labs for urgent analysis,' he said. 'Their preliminary thoughts are already here. It was a mobile he used to call. He withheld the number and it's untraceable. There's not much in the background to help us. The main point they make is that it's quiet, very quiet indeed. There's no hint of cars or planes or mobile phones, or even noise from houses.'

'He's out in the countryside somewhere,' said Dan. 'Somewhere remote.'

'Yep. And that's consistent with his military background. He can go out somewhere he won't be noticed and survive for a few days quite easily.'

Dan thought about what he'd heard on the tape. 'But probably not in a tent from the sound of that. I don't know why but it just felt like he was in a house or building of some kind. It had that kind of hollow sound to it.'

'Agreed,' replied Adam. 'And that's what the labs' analysis says too. But where? We've checked all his bank accounts. There's no payment to anything that might help us. No holiday cottage, nothing like that. We've checked on bookings in case he paid cash and there's anything suspicious, but we've come up with nothing. So what does that leave us?'

'The usual places,' said Dan thoughtfully. 'Dartmoor, Exmoor, Bodmin moor. The more secluded parts of the coast. In other words, a very big area. Huge in fact.'

'Yep. I'm getting the helicopter in again to help us. It's got a thermal imaging camera so it can spot people on the ground. The Tactical Aid Search Groups are ready to go. All force leave is cancelled. We've got as many cops as we can raise ready to go looking. There are also volunteers like the Dartmoor Rescue Team offering their services and we're going to use them. They're good. But we desperately need to narrow down the area we're searching. So, Eleanor and Michael, this is where you come in. He's teasing us with his riddle. Taunting us in fact. Any ideas?'

They were an odd pair, thought Dan. She was older, in her mid 50s, wore a navy cardigan and flowing floral skirt. Her hair had turned silver, but her face was still soft and fine, remarkably unwrinkled, with strong cheekbones and lips, and large, brown eyes. She would have been beautiful once he imagined, and not so long ago either. She still had an alluring quality.

He was much younger, probably in his late twenties, wore ripped jeans, trainers and a black T-shirt. A Celtic band of ornate green tattoo peeked out from under his left sleeve. His hair was spiky and black, looked dyed, and he smiled continually and with a hint of nerves.

'I believe he's telling you the truth,' said Eleanor, and her voice was gentle and warm, like a favourite aunt reading a bedtime story. 'He wants to be caught. That's the whole point of this. His being caught is the final act in his drama. But I don't think he's ready for that yet. He'll tell us when he is.' She looked down at the cassette player, thought for a moment. 'You said he was armed?' Adam nodded. 'Then I'd say he was looking for a showdown. He's probably preparing for it now.'

'We've gone through the letters in detail,' added Michael, whose voice was surprisingly deep for his thin frame. 'There's nothing obvious in there. I've got a computer program that looks for acrostics – you know, patterns in the words, or sentences made up from the first or second letters of the words, or things like that – and it came up with nothing. It checks for anagrams too and didn't find anything there either. So it's more subtle than that.'

Adam stared at them. 'What do you think he means when he talks about not taking a plane?'

'He's telling you to check the airports,' said Eleanor. 'You've got two within your range of an hour, haven't you?

Exeter and Plymouth?'

'Yep.'

'I'd look there. I don't think he'd be hiding there as they'd be too busy and noisy, but you might find a clue.'

Adam scribbled a note. 'Any other ideas? He's keen to talk about Manchester isn't he? But he's not there, we know that now. So why's he still talking about it?'

'Beats me,' said Michael with a nervous smile. 'But I'll look at it again. There might be something in the place names up north that could relate to names down here. I'll go over the maps.'

'That band of gold reference in one of the earlier letters was odd,' added Eleanor, rolling up the sleeve of her cardigan as if about to go to work. 'I'd like to look at that some more. It didn't fit into the flow. I've no idea what it means, but it may be something.'

'I've got an idea,' said Dan. 'It's about the rose thing he mentioned, or the names in other words. You know how he's gone for women whose Christian names make up the Chief Constable's? It's been Sarah Jane Nicola. Well, the Chief Con's surname is Hill. So I reckon he's on or beside a hill somewhere. And I'm guessing now, but given his desire for a showdown, I bet it'll be a well-known hill and that's where this will all end.'

'Good thought,' said Adam slowly. 'But how many hills are there in Devon and Cornwall?'

'Hundreds. But at least it's an idea.'

'I agree. I'll get the search teams working on what we've come up with.'

'What's that?' snapped Whiting, as Suzanne placed the letter on his desk. He looked tired, hunched over his work, his eyes ringed a dull red, a sheen of oily sweat shining on the bald strip over his crown.

Suzanne kept her voice neutral. 'I think it's better if you read it, sir. As one of the officers seconded to your investigation I've been asked by the Police Federation to deliver it to you.'

Carefully he opened the stark white envelope and read, then sat back on his chair and read it again.

'It is a vote of no confidence in me,' he hissed, looking up at her. 'And more importantly it is a notice of withdrawal of cooperation with our investigation. The Police Federation say I have no evidence whatsoever to justify the continued suspension of PC Crouch and that he should be immediately reinstated. It adds that I have demonstrated my ineptitude by allowing his name to leak to the press and wrongly accusing a fellow officer of facilitating that. As such, a motion of no confidence has been passed by the officers of Greater Wessex Police in the investigation and my stewardship of it.

'The only way I can force anyone to submit to my inquiries now, it notes, is if I arrest them. It goes on to say the lack of any evidence denies me that option. As far as the Federation are concerned, the inquiry is at an end. I have been given all reasonable cooperation. To continue now, they say, would be tantamount to a witch hunt, carried out only to placate the hysterical baying of the media and the unwarranted suspicions of senior police officers who have never been presented with the acute dilemma of whether to open fire in the course of their duty.'

Suzanne wondered whether to say she thought the language in the letter rather overblown, but that it had some reasonable points to make. She decided against it, stood upright, waiting, hands behind her back, readied herself for the explosion. But it didn't come. Whiting wiped his brow.

'I don't care about this, Suzanne,' he said, and his voice had lost its usual hiss. He sounded vulnerable and disillusioned. Even, remarkably – almost human?

'I don't care about unpopularity,' he went on. 'That is part of the job. You expect it and accept it. But I do care about doing my duty. The naming of Crouch – and the picture that's been published – is unforgivable. However much I am aware it was not me who caused it, nevertheless it is me who is in charge of the investigation and so I bear responsibility. The Police Federation are entirely correct in that, as they are in another matter. There is no evidence whatsoever against PC

Crouch. All we have is suspicion about what may easily turn out to have been coincidence. I cannot justify the continued suspension and intrusive investigation of a police officer on the basis of that alone.'

Whiting adjusted the pile of change on his desk, taking the tower of pennies and two pences down and forming them into a square. 'Where have we left to go in our investigation, Suzanne?'

She thought for a moment. 'Nowhere obvious, sir.'

'Indeed. There is no forensic or ballistics evidence to give us suspicion?'

'No, sir.'

'And the virtual reconstructions give us no grounds for suspicion?'

'No, sir.'

'And the accounts of all the witnesses and the police officers involved tally?'

'Yes, sir.'

'And there's no hint of some grand conspiracy so beloved by the media? No calls between Crouch and Gardener and the two women, no communications to plot and plan the shootings?'

Suzanne shook her head. She almost felt sorry for Whiting. 'No, sir.'

He stared at her. 'Then I'd say this investigation was at an end, wouldn't you?'

'That's a matter for you, sir,' she replied, controlling her voice to hide her surprise.

He sat back in his chair and adjusted a cufflink. 'Yes.' The hiss was back. 'Yes, I'd say we've reached the end. I shall take a couple more days to reflect on all the evidence we have gathered and then I shall submit my initial report. In the meantime, you can inform the Police Federation that their letter and its contents have been noted. No further interviews will be required of anyone and I will give them a decision on the reinstatement of PC Crouch by the end of the week. But we must be fair, as I know PC Crouch has been under considerable pressure, not least from having his picture published. You can tell the Federation that my interim opinion is to recommend no charges be brought, either criminal or disciplinary, and that he be reinstated.'

It was the first time Dan had been driven in a police car on an emergency call and he couldn't help enjoying it. Initially, he'd just been pleased not to have to use his throbbing ankle to drive himself. Now the pain had been largely forgotten in the thrill of the violent cornering and squealing tyres. He hung on to a handle above the door and tried not to smile. It reminded him of fairground rides of younger days.

The wailing siren bullied the traffic aside as they sped along the main road north out of Plymouth, towards Dartmoor. They were heading for the airport. Gibson's car had been found in one of its extensive car parks.

A white van that had been doing far more than forty in the thirty limit suddenly slowed and slewed out of their path. They accelerated around it, the car's tyres screeching in protest. The van driver watched nervously as they passed, then relaxed in relief as they sped on. Another line of traffic darted aside, like young fish desperately avoiding the snapping jaws of a hungry predator. Adam didn't even look up from his notes. 'This could be our break,' he kept muttering to himself.

The lights on the Derriford roundabout turned green, but the line of traffic approaching froze at their wailing assault. The driver shrieked around the corner towards the airport. Dan gripped the door handle tighter and fought back a temptation to wave to the line of gawping motorists.

Just a couple of minutes and they'd be there. He had to ask Adam now. There'd be no time when they got to Gibson's car. He'd go mad, but it had to be now. He felt a shot of adrenaline pulse its shocking way into his system, the thought of Nicola sobbing helplessly, cold, alone, terrified suddenly back in his mind. He blinked it away and cleared his throat.

'Adam, before we get there …'

'Yes, what?' he snapped, not looking up from his notes.

'Can I get a cameraman to come and film the car?'

'No. I won't want Gibson to know we've found it yet.'

Dan had expected that. 'OK. But my editor's on my back and I do need to know what I can run for a story tonight.'

'OK. You want something new so they can have you in the studio again?'

'Yes. Well, sort of …'

Adam's detective's instinct sensed the discomfort. His head span round.

'What do you mean – sort of?'

'I mean … well … we want to run something from the answer machine message he left.'

The detective's eyes narrowed. 'No chance. It's vital evidence. I can't allow that. Anyway it's gone to the labs for more detailed analysis. We've only got transcripts left.'

Dan took a breath. 'Well … that's not quite true.'

'What? What have you done?'

'Lizzie,' said Dan, carefully distancing himself from her, 'decided we should take a copy of the tape.'

Adam stared at him, and Dan braced himself for the attack. 'In fairness,' he added quickly, remembering what he'd prepared to say, 'Gibson did call us and the tape was our property and we did hand it over to you as soon as we knew we had it and we are helping as much as we can and …'

'OK, that's enough,' cut in Adam, a finger jabbing towards Dan's chest. 'Let's get something straight here. This is my inquiry, not yours. Got that? You're here because I need your help, but what I say goes. It's as simple as that. And whatever you might think, it's not a bloody game either. There's a kid's life at stake. It doesn't get any bigger than this. Do you want to kill a young girl because you think getting some tawdry little exclusive is more important than saving her?'

Dan gulped at the attack. The pain in his ankle stabbed at him, and the thought of Nicola was back, vivid before his eyes. He didn't know what to say, so broke Adam's glare to look out at the planes parked in a neat line through the fence by the side of the road. He gripped harder at the handle above the door.

'I haven't got time to rollock you,' Adam continued. 'I've got much more important things to think about. But consider yourself warned. Don't do anything else without my say so. Ever. Got that?'

Dan nodded and Adam turned back to look at the road ahead, a couple of police cars guarding it.

'Anyway, I don't suppose I've got much choice as we need your help,' he went on. 'I'd have been surprised if you hadn't taken a copy of the tape. I'm used to you bloody devious hacks by now. It's worse than working with criminals. We'll sort out what bit you can run later. But there's going to be a price.'

'Sure,' said Dan trying not to let his relief show. The conversation hadn't been anything like as fiery as he'd feared. 'You know I'll do whatever I can to help you find Nicola. What is it?'

'Eleanor and Michael still haven't come up with anything from the clues Gibson gave us. So I want you to appeal for more help on air tonight. And this time we're going to be waiting overnight in your office to see if we can trace the call. With luck, the combination of that and finding his car might just lead us to him.'

They drew up in a corner of the car park, the rows of vehicles like a spectrum of colour, all obediently awaiting the return of their masters. Gibson's car was surrounded by the familiar cordon of police tape, a couple of uniformed officers on sentry duty. One held up the tape and Adam ducked under it, Dan limping behind.

The driver's door was open and a woman in a white overall was leaning inside, examining under the seat. A couple more white-clad figures worked on the other side and one was under the car at the front poking and scraping at the tyres. It was a red Ford Escort, about six years old, a couple of hints of gathering rust around its doors.

'Any leads, Janey?' asked Adam.

The woman didn't turn around from inside the car and her voice was muffled. 'Not that I can see straight away, sir. We're checking for fibres now in case there might be something revealing, and seeing if there's any distinctive mud on the tyres, but at first glance it doesn't look like it. It's definitely the car he used, though. There are traces of fibres on the passenger seat from the grey coat Nicola was wearing. They're very distinctive and match some we took from her bedroom.' She turned round and pointed to a sealed plastic bag on a white sheet laid out beside the car. 'We also found a couple of long blonde hairs. I'm pretty sure they're Nicola's, but that's subject to confirmation by the labs.'

'We can take a shortcut on that, sir,' came a familiar voice behind them.

They both turned around to see Claire walking towards them. She was holding a DVD.

'I've just been checking the airport's CCTV. It shows Gibson and Nicola driving in here, then it picks them up walking hand in hand towards the airport terminal. They don't go in. They walk past and up that road by the side of the airfield.'

Claire gestured to a lane running alongside the airport, giving Dan a hint of a wink as Adam turned and stared. 'The CCTV loses them before you can see what they do,' she added. 'It's only trained on the area around the terminal.'

'Good to have you back with us, Claire,' said Adam, 'and good work too. Where does the road go to?'

'There are a few more houses up there sir, but it's a dead end after that. It goes on for about half a mile or so, then peters out into a little country lane.'

'Where does the lane go?'

'Take your pick, sir. There are several footpaths that run off it. A couple head back towards the city, the others out on to Dartmoor.'

Adam stared at the road. 'We know he planned all this carefully,' he said slowly. 'So he could have left another car up there for his getaway. Or he could have gone out onto the moor somewhere. That would fit with the quiet in the background of the message he left us. What's your guess, Claire?'

'I don't think he'd want to risk walking far with Nicola, sir. He'd have to have some transport waiting. But by the time he's driven here and switched cars, that must take up 15 to 20 minutes. Which would only leave him half an hour or so to run before he knew we'd be onto him.'

'Exactly,' replied Adam thoughtfully. 'Which means our search radius has just halved. I'm sure he's not holed up anywhere around the airport, but get the TAG teams to do a search anyway. And check for tyre tracks too, although that's probably going to be a waste of time given the drizzle. But we're closing in on him, aren't we? We're getting closer. The question is, what exactly is this deadline he's been on about and why? And how much time have we got?'

Dan looked to the north, at the dark and brooding tors of Dartmoor's hills, their rocky outlines softened by the drifting mist. The opaque light had turned the wilderness a uniform sweep of grey. Miles of secluded loneliness, thousands of possible hiding places.

'He's on the moor,' Dan muttered softly. 'And he's waiting for us to come to him.'

Chapter Seventeen

THE NEWSROOM FELT SOULLESS without the scurrying journalists and technical staff, Dan thought, as he sat on the edge of a desk. It was as though it had lost its voice. It was never quiet, always filled with someone shouting a question or command, telephones with their continual electronic trilling, the burble of computers. But tonight the only sound was their breathing. They'd tried to chat a couple of times to pass the hours but the conversation quickly ebbed, as though they feared they might frighten away that which they were hunting.

A tangle of wires led from the answer machine to a laptop computer, by which stood Zac Phillips, renowned as the most talented of Greater Wessex Police's technical crime – or Square Eyes – division. He fidgeted with the laptop's touchpad as his eyes bounced back and forth, from phone to screen. Green waveforms danced on the display. He'd explained what it meant earlier, in more detail than any of them could take in. Adam summed it up simply. It was working and it was waiting.

Eleanor and Michael sat side by side at the desk. She was reading a book. He was staring at Zac and the screen, occasionally smiling shyly at anyone who caught his eye. Adam wanted them there in case there was another cryptic clue. The undefined deadline was gnawing at him. Dan could see it in the way he stalked back and forth across the newsroom, twitching at every slight sound that could have been the phone readying to ring. If there was a clue, he wanted to start work on it now.

The search teams were in bed, resting ready for the morning, but strictly on call, mobiles by their sides. If they got their breakthrough tonight they would go without hesitation. They didn't know how long they had. They couldn't risk wasting any time.

Dan had brought a book too – some detective fiction he thought would be appropriate – but he hadn't managed to read a page. Who needed imagination and fantasy when you had a case like this?

He'd been interested in what he'd learnt about Michael and Eleanor. He was a cruciverbalist – a crossword addict, he'd explained – and a cryptographer – a code-breaker too. He started doing puzzles at his grammar school in Milton Keynes when the class had been taught about the neighbouring Bletchley Park, the old Second World War Enigma code-cracking centre. He had a natural talent and became the youngest ever winner of the *Daily Bulletin*'s annual crossword puzzle competition. Aged just 20, he had beaten thousands of others and completed the championship grid in under seven minutes. His ability had attracted the attention of what he referred to only as the "government", and he'd been working for them ever since.

Eleanor was very different. Before she retired, she'd been a professor at Kent University, specialising in pure mathematics. Kent police were faced with a serial rapist whom they couldn't catch. She'd read a newspaper report about the case and noticed a pattern in the dates and times when he struck. It was something complex that Dan couldn't follow, but to do with prime numbers. Her work had helped catch the man and see him sentenced to life in prison. She'd been added to SOCA's list of experts and was often called on when there was a crime, which could involve an element of pattern or riddle.

The pair had now worked together on several cases, she said. Three in fact, added Michael, pointing out they'd got results in two, a success rate of 66.6 per cent recurring. This case was important because he wanted to get the average up to 75 per cent, not see it fall back to 50. Dan had noticed Adam's irritated shake of the head at their joviality. All he could see in the detective's mind was Nicola and a ticking clock.

The phone rang, startlingly loud in the empty office. As one they all jumped, eyes spun and fixed on the screen that Zac was monitoring, his face lit green by the display.

'We've got a trace,' he whispered. 'It's an Exeter number.'

'That's in the target area,' hissed Adam, leaning over the laptop. 'Just …'

'Doing the grid on the address now … homing in on the location … just need a few more seconds …'

The answer machine kicked in, Craig's resonant voice. 'This is Wessex Tonight. We're sorry but the newsroom is unstaffed at the moment …'

Dan looked questioningly at Adam, pointed to the phone, but the detective shook his head. He wanted to let Gibson talk to the machine. It was a tight call Adam had said, but if he knows we're here, he'll probably hang up straight away. He left a long message last night. Let's hope he leaves a similar one tonight, gives us plenty of time to trace the call.

' …but if you leave your name, number, and a short message, then we'll get back to you,' the machine recited, followed by a long electronic bleep.

'Got it!' whispered Zac as a map flashed up on his screen. 'It's just outside Exeter. It's …' he paused, looked at the expectant faces surrounding him, frowned. 'It's the headquarters of the fire service.'

'Wanted to let you know we were called out to a small fire in the thatch of a cottage at Topsham, just outside Exeter,' came a cheerful voice from the machine's speaker. 'We put it out with minimal damage. Apart from that, it's been a quiet night. All the best to you.'

Adam let out a long hiss. They settled back in their seats. Dan shifted his weight to try to ease his ankle. It was throbbing again. Maybe he would have to go to see the doctor. It didn't seem to be getting any better. He didn't like not being able to take Rutherford for a run. Plus, was it his imagination or could he feel his waistline growing because of the lack of exercise?

He checked his watch. It said almost five to two. He looked at the newsroom clock, radio controlled and always accurate. Quarter past. He went to wind the Rolex but stopped, didn't see the point. It would always run slow no matter what, and he was used to adding on the missing minutes. Damn that jeweller, his own gullibility and desire to be flash. Quarter past two, but he didn't feel too jaded, despite the chaos of the day.

Lizzie had professed herself "pleased" with the story he'd

produced, quite an accolade on her less than fulsome scale. He'd kept the discovery of Gibson's car a secret, but put in a long section of the tape recording of his call. Even if he did say so himself, it had sounded chilling and made for compulsive viewing. Lizzie had sent a pointed email to the secretary of the region's Royal Television Society, making sure that she watched tonight's programme.

After a long debate with Adam they'd agreed he could use the part where Gibson talked about Nicola being safe, thinking she was playing a game, and the section where he talked about whether he was a psychopath. It sounded highly dramatic and it wouldn't compromise the investigation. Dan sat in the studio to do his live update, mentioned the SOCA experts had been called in before finally appealing for Gibson to get in touch again, just as Adam had asked.

So, now the question. Would he? Earlier in the evening, Dan had been confident, even convinced. Gibson hadn't been able to resist it before. But now, sitting in the dark and silent newsroom, starting to feel cold and the first heavy pull of the tentacles of fatigue, he wasn't so sure. Gibson was a clever man. He must surely have guessed they'd be waiting, ready to trace his call?

He thought about Claire, imagined her curled up in bed in her flat, wondered when he'd next have the chance to lie beside her. This weekend, it would have to be. They hadn't had enough time together lately, and he didn't want them to forget the enjoyment of each other's company. That way lay the disintegration of the relationship, if they forgot it was worth trying. He'd take her and Rutherford for a walk and then have some dinner. That was if his ankle was up to it. And if they'd caught Gibson and found Nicola.

Zac was running his index finger lovingly over the laptop's touchpad, Eleanor calmly reading a book, Michael staring at the floor, one knee jigging up and down. Adam gazed at a health and safety poster on the wall, then began stalking repeatedly across the newsroom again. Dan thought he looked like an expectant father.

He checked the clock. It ticked around to half past two.

Dan hadn't realised how loud it was until he heard its relentless motion in the silence of the night.

The phone rang.

'Withheld number this time,' whispered Zac. 'But it's a mobile.'

Adam was by the screen. 'This is it.'

'Do I answer it?' asked Dan.

'Only if he specifically asks you to. If he's going to ramble on, let him. It gives us more time. Come on Zac.'

'It'll take a few mins. It's more complex to trace than the fire station call.'

' ...then we'll get back to you.' ended the voice on the machine.

'Come on,' hissed Adam bending over the computer.

The answer machine beeped and a familiar voice crackled out, but cheerful this time, almost bubbling.

'Hello, everyone, listening in live, no doubt, trying to trace me. I'm not quite ready to see you again, Adam and Dan, so I'll make this brief. That was a nice report tonight, Dan. Here are your penultimate – yes penultimate – clues. What elements make up a band of gold and in what order, and remember the rose! What's in a name? See you very soon now, but don't forget – your time's running out.'

The machine beeped again as the call was cut.

'Well?' spat Adam, leaning over Zac. 'Well? Did you get him?'

Zac tapped away at a couple of keys. 'Well?' urged Adam again. 'Come on!'

A map flickered onto the computer screen. It was the south west peninsula. Colours spun, some of the land shaded red, most of it blue. The image changed, zoomed in to Devon and more colours covered the screen.

'Well?' hissed Adam savagely, his fists in knots.

Zac pressed a final key, leaned back, breathed out heavily. 'No, we didn't get him.'

'Bollocks!' bellowed Adam, standing up and yanking his tie even further down his neck.

Zac looked up at him. 'But we did narrow it down quite a

bit,' he said, pointing at the screen. 'Look here. This is Devon.'

The phone rang again. 'Ignore it,' growled Adam. 'I don't want to hear about any more bloody thatch fires. Zac, show me what you've found.'

'Well, as I was saying, this is Devon. And if I zoom the screen in a bit, you'll see I can narrow the area down to …'

'Hey, whoa, wait, listen!' yelled Dan.

'Hello again my friends,' came a familiar voice from the answer machine.

'Bollocks!' roared Adam. 'It's him again. Quick, get another trace on it. Come on, man, quick!!'

'Hang on,' pleaded Zac. 'It takes a minute to shut down one program and start up another.'

'I forgot to mention something,' continued Gibson's voice. 'It was to give you an idea of your deadline.'

The line went quiet for a moment.

'Come on, come on, come on!' urged Adam.

Zac's fingers were a blur, flying over the keyboard. 'Almost there,' he gasped. 'Just a few more secs.'

Gibson's voice drifted out from the speaker, but indistinct, muffled, distant from the phone. 'Come on now … come on … do your little speech. It's all part of the adventure. Come on.'

There was another brief silence. Then a young girl came on the phone, shy and quiet.

'Hello … hello Mummy's friends.' The voice was faltering but clear. 'Hello. I'm going to get my pony now. I'll see you tomorrow.'

The line went dead. Adam turned to Zac. 'Get it? Did you get it?'

The technician shook his dark, shaggy hair.

'Bollocks!' bellowed Adam again, slamming a clenched fist into a desk.

Claire hadn't been curled up in bed as Dan had imagined. She was sitting upright, intent on the laptop on her desk, trying to get the email right. The last one had flowed easily, as if she were an actor slipping into a familiar part. But then there'd been no pressure. She was just fishing, not expecting, only chancing. Now she felt the tension of an opportunity.

One reply to her emails, from 'You Don't Have To Take it' had been exactly what she'd expected. You don't have to tolerate it, there are support groups, refuges to help you get out, lawyers on standby to advise you. You can contact us for any advice and you're more than welcome to do so. Here are the phone numbers. If you feel the need for anonymity, just send another email. Predictable, and nothing of interest.

The other, from DiVorce, had been far more enticing, or at least she'd thought so at the time. Now, in the middle of the night, staring at the screen, she wasn't so sure. Perhaps she'd just wanted to read a sinister intent into it? She got up from the desk and walked into the kitchen, put the kettle on. She could do with a caffeine kick, but then she'd never get back to sleep later. She switched the kettle off, poured some apple juice from the fridge instead and sat back down.

Claire clicked the touchpad and scrolled down to the DiVorce email.

"We could load you down with lots of useless advice about the law and refuges and counselling, but we expect you've seen and heard it all before. They're just hollow words. We appreciate it's not that simple – if only it were. We pride ourselves on being utterly straight and honest in a way others aren't. If you're really desperate, it often helps to talk.

"Would you like access to our chat room? Other women with similar problems often visit and we find the talking helps. But one word of caution before you decide to join us. As we said, we don't pull our punches and sometimes the discussions can become very graphic and upsetting. Commonly the abuse described is horrendous, even for someone who's experienced it. And the kind of measures fantasised about to deal with the partner can be extremely violent and shocking, however much we feel they may deserve it. Proceed only if you are prepared for this. Some find it a help, a release. Others that it's not for them. We leave the decision to you."

She began typing.

"Thank you so much for your email. It's good to know that I'm not alone in what I'm suffering. He beat me again tonight. My hands are shaking and I can feel the bruises spreading across my ribs. I'm just about holding back the tears but they keep leaking and dripping onto the keyboard. I don't know whether I want to cry, or scream and shout and hit out. I just don't know what I'm going to do.

"He's gone to sleep after another two bottles of red wine and the kicking he's just given me. He sounds really peaceful and content. I can hear the bastard's snoring from here.

"I hate him, I hate him, I hate him, I hate him, I hate him, I hate him, I HATE HIM!!

"For once I'm not thinking about the pills and whisky I've saved up. I don't want to kill myself. I want to kill him. I want to kill the bastard.

"I've got to go to school tomorrow. I know I won't sleep tonight and I don't know how I'll get through the day. I'm sure my friends know what's happening to me. I haven't told anyone, but I think I can feel them talking about me. I'm sure they know.

"What am I going to do? I haven't got anywhere else to go. If I try to escape, he'll kill me. I can't go on like this. I keep having this fantasy that I could sneak into the kitchen, slip a knife from the drawer, creep upstairs and stick it into his throat as he snores in bed like the animal he is. Is that a terrible thing to imagine? I just don't know what I'm going to do.

"I've got to go, I think I can hear him waking. He'll hit me again if he finds me on the computer. Yes please, I'd like to talk to other women suffering this hell. I need to talk to them. I need to talk to someone. Please help me."

Claire sat back, sipped at the juice and scanned through the words. It was a bit rough, but that was how it should be, the thoughts of a desperate woman. Again she was amazed at how easily she'd slipped back into being Zoë. It came out so fast, so naturally.

She hit the send button, shut down the computer. She needed to get some sleep. They had Nicola to find, which meant another hectic day tomorrow. DCI Breen was pushing them like he was possessed.

Because he had a son of similar age, she wondered, and could imagine what it would be like if he were abducted? Or was it personal, because Gibson was mocking them? Or because he could have stopped the man when he did his leisure centre act? That story had gone round the station fast. Whatever the reason, it seemed more than a professional determination was driving Adam Breen.

She calmed herself and tried some deep breathing. She had to sleep. She needed the energy for another late night tomorrow, a chance to venture into the chat room.

To see what she would find there.

Marcus Whiting pulled his coat tighter around his neck and wriggled his toes to see if he could feel them. His feet were freezing, despite the three pairs of socks. He fumbled a handkerchief from his pocket and wiped at the car's windscreen where his breath kept fogging it. His fingers found a forgotten five-pence piece and he placed it carefully alongside the rest of the change on the passenger seat. Seventy-four pence now, in an untidy pentagon of copper and silver.

The lights were on in the downstairs windows of the house, but there was no sign of movement. There hadn't been for more than two hours and it was now well past nine. How long would he give it? Another hour, maybe two? Surely if nothing had happened by eleven, then nothing would. Would he come back another night? He didn't know.

What had brought him here? Nothing concrete, nothing certain, that was for sure. Just a hunch, a hint, a tickling feeling that all was not as it seemed. It was an itch in his mind and he knew whenever that happened he had to find a way to ease it.

Had it been something to do with that TV report? That one where Richie Hanson's sister had cried for the camera, after the promptings of that irritating reporter. He had to admit it was powerful television and if he was honest with himself – as he always was – she was convincing.

She'd certainly made him doubt her brother could be a wife beater. He'd seen misguided relatives before of course, unable to accept the evils of the ones they loved, defending them passionately. Denial was human nature, a reflex reaction. But she'd seemed different. Claire Reynolds had agreed after she too had interviewed the woman.

But there was more to it than just that. No matter how much he failed to find any evidence, he simply didn't believe in such an apparent coincidence as the one he was investigating. One police marksman didn't kill two men in such extraordinarily similar circumstances in the space of five months. That itch in his mind told him something was wrong and he'd learned never to ignore its prompting.

So what did he expect to find here in Saltash, at this house in Haven Close? He didn't know, just that he'd felt a need to drive here, watch and wait. The lights were on downstairs but there was still no sign of movement. It was a cold Tuesday night in autumn, and the woman inside was probably sitting in front of the television, watching a film, or soap opera, sipping at a gin and trying to forget the guns and death of five days ago.

He checked his watch. Half past nine now. Eleven o' clock would be his deadline. If nothing happened by then he'd drive back to his hotel and get some sleep. He still had his report to complete.

His fingers shifted some of the change around, forming the coins into a hexagon. A car grumbled by, indicated, the yellow lights blinking off the facades of the neat rows of houses in the cul de sac. Whiting slunk down in the seat, his eyes just above the dashboard.

The car was parking a little way up from the house and there were plenty of spaces just outside. He felt himself relax. False alarm. But he kept watching, just in case. There was a dark figure inside the car, waiting, fiddling in the footwell, probably getting his late night shopping together, milk and cigarettes, something like that. Nothing suspicious.

Whiting glanced over to the house. A downstairs curtain twitched. He stiffened, sat up a little.

The dark figure climbed quickly and quietly out of the car, didn't slam the door but pushed it gently closed, walked fast down the street. The door of the house slid open and he was inside.

Whiting sat, waiting, his breath shallow. It could be nothing of course, entirely innocent, a concerned friend or relative checking in. There was one way to find out.

He waited, toying with the pile of change, changing it back into a pentagon, then a hexagon, then a heptagon.

Ten minutes later, a dull light appeared behind the curtains of an upstairs bedroom.

Marcus Whiting allowed himself a rare indulgence. He smiled.

Zac pointed at the screen. 'He's in Devon and in the south-west of the county. That's all I can tell you. He didn't give us long enough to narrow it down any further.'

'And from that second call nothing at all?' asked Adam.

'Nothing. I didn't have time to set the trace programme going.'

'He knew, didn't he?' Adam snarled. 'He knew we'd be looking at what we'd just got from his call and wouldn't be able to trace the second one. And he put Nicola on to taunt us. The bastard is way ahead of us and it's about time we caught up. There'll be no sleep for anyone tonight. We don't have the time. From what he got Nicola to say, I reckon tomorrow is our deadline. Tomorrow … her birthday. That's about as low as the bastard could go. I suppose I should have guessed. Her birthday is our deadline to find her safely. What do you lot think?'

There was some nodding, but no one said a word. Dan could see it in their eyes. They were thinking about what might be happening to Nicola.

'Eleanor and Michael, you start working on what he said about the clues, see if you can pick up anything from it,' said Adam. 'Anything at all. What the hell did that thing about the band of gold mean? We're at the stage where I'm willing to try anything. Dan, come and have a look at the map with me.'

There was a large map of the south-west peninsula on the newsroom wall, filled with the red and green veins of roads and grey blemishes of the region's cities, towns and villages. Dan hobbled over. The pain in his ankle had eased with the rest of sitting and waiting for Gibson's call, but now it jarred sharply back into life.

'Last seen here at the airport,' said Adam, pointing to the north of Plymouth. 'And he's got a radius of half an hour or so to move. I reckon that's about 15 to 20 miles at most, given the roads aren't good. And he's in Devon.'

He drew a rough circle around Plymouth with his finger. 'That leaves us with a fair chunk of Dartmoor, going down into the countryside of the South Hams. It's narrowed it down a bit, but not enough. I need more.'

Adam stared at the map, then quickly turned, strode over to Eleanor. He was moving automatically, Dan thought, robotically. 'Any ideas about the clues he gave? I need to narrow the search area further, as much as I can.'

'That band of gold thing I have no idea about,' said Eleanor. 'Except that it's obviously a term for a wedding ring, but I don't see how that helps. And I don't know what he means by the elements within it. Gold obviously, but what else? Does he mean like those rings that have platinum, or white gold in them too? I really don't know. But it's obviously important. Do you have any thoughts Michael?'

He shook his head and she turned to her computer, began typing. 'I'll start looking band of gold up on the internet and see what references there are that might help.'

'What about the name thing he was on about again?' asked Adam.

'I still think he's talking about the Chief Constable's name,' said Dan. 'Which I reckon means he's on a hill somewhere.'

Adam paced back over to the map, ran a hand through his hair. Dan's ankle throbbed angrily as he limped to join him. A weight of tiredness was suddenly pulling at him and he began to imagine the warmth and safe oblivion of his bed.

Adam stabbed at the board with his finger. 'Hills,' he

muttered. 'Hills. Well there aren't any big hills marked in the South Hams. But on Dartmoor …'

'The moor's all hills,' said Dan. 'It's full of them. And it's quiet, just like in the background of both calls. I didn't say at the time because it was just a thought, nothing to back it up, but when we were at the airport I got the feeling he was on Dartmoor. There are plenty of places to hide. It's not too far from the airport. And with his call … Nicola mentioned a pony, and it's tenuous, but that might be a clue. The Dartmoor pony's the symbol of the moor.'

Adam stared at the map. 'Dartmoor it is then,' he said slowly. 'That's our best guess and I'll take it. We don't have anything else. I'll get the helicopter up first thing in the morning. It'll pick up traces of anyone up on the moor and the TAG teams can follow up the sightings. We'll get the armed response units out too. I don't like the thought of what Gibson could do if he's cornered. We'll go through the villages and see if anyone's seen anything suspicious.'

Adam clenched and unclenched his fists again, his face ruddy and strained.

'We'll get this bastard,' he growled. 'We'll get Nicola back to her mum for her birthday.'

She was such a pretty girl he thought, as he watched her get up from the sleeping bag. Her hair reminded him of … who was it now? He followed the memory back through his mind. That was it, Laura, the babysitter who used to come and look after him, when Dad was briefly home from whatever particular posting it was this time, and he and Mum went out for an evening to celebrate.

Laura had that long, golden hair, sometimes tied up in a ponytail, sometimes flowing free. He always used to guess which it would be before she came round. He liked it best when it was free so he could help her to brush it.

'Do I need to take my bag, Ed?' Nicola was holding out her little satchel to him, the pink pony stencilled on the front.

'What did Mum tell you about your satchel?' he asked, his voice kind.

'She said I should always take it with me wherever I went.'

'Then you'd better take it now. We'll be seeing Mum soon. But first we've got to find you a pony.'

Her little face beamed with that gappy smile. 'I knew I was right. I knew that as soon as it was midnight you'd have to tell me, because then it was my birthday. On my birthday Mummy always tells me I was nearly born on a different day. It was half past twelve in the morning I was born.' She nodded hard to emphasise the point, the tail of blonde hair swinging behind her. 'She says I kept her waiting and waiting and waiting, and she even had to miss Eastenders for me, because I just wouldn't pop out! I took hours!'

She paused, looked up at him and asked slowly, 'Is it a Dartmoor pony, Ed?'

'I promised it would be, didn't I? It's your birthday so you can have anything you want today. But have you decided what colour yet? And what you're going to call it?'

Her face creased back into a frown and she held her head on its side. 'I still can't decide, Ed. I think it's the most difficult thing I've ever had to do in my life. But I think I shall know when I see him.'

'I'm sure you will. Now we're almost at the end of our adventure. We're off outside and we'll be walking for a few minutes, so we'd better wrap you up warm.'

She pulled on the grey duffle coat, fumbling at its shiny toggles. The smile was back, the gap between her front teeth seemed to grow wider with each grin. 'I think I probably want a black and white pony, but I'm still not quite sure.'

'Then we'll have a look at a few and see which one you like the most. That's the best thing. Are you ready to go?'

She raised her arms so he could see her coat was fastened. He pointed to her legs and she looked down, pulled a drooping sock up to her knee. 'I'm ready to go, Ed!' she chirped, marching towards him, swinging her satchel. 'I'm so excited. I don't know when I've ever been so excited.'

'Is that because it's your birthday or because of our adventure, or because of the pony?' he asked, taking her hand. It was so tiny and smooth. He tried not to think what he was about to do with her, where she was going.

'Everything!' she squeaked.

In the shed he pulled the rucksack from the back of the quad bike and slung it over his shoulders. Then he fumbled in his jacket and stuck the tiny note carefully to the handlebars.

'What's that for Ed?' she asked.

'That is a letter to our friends, telling them where to find us. And this,' he said, shrugging the rucksack up his back, 'has got a tent in.' He took her hand again. 'A tent and some food. After our adventure, I'm going to do a bit of camping.'

They walked out onto the silent moor and found the stony uphill track. He looked carefully around, saw no one, breathed out a relieved sigh.

It was a clear night, lit bright by the beacon of a perfect half moon. Dots and pinpricks of silver stars littered the inky sky. Only a breath of wind ruffled the moorgrass and yellow-flecked gorse. A stream chuckled by, the rushing water tumbling over the rugged granite. The air was sharp and cold and the ground crunched underfoot as they walked. Back towards the village an owl hooted out its lonely call. Her little feet sped to keep up with his strides.

'I've never been out at night like this, Ed. It's so exciting,' she whispered, holding his hand tight. 'This is the best adventure I've ever been on. Look, look! There's one.'

He looked towards the brow of a hill, to where she was pointing. Silhouetted against the lowly stars was the dark shape of a grazing pony. 'Is it that one?' she whispered. 'Is that my birthday pony?'

He felt his pulse quicken, pulled her gently along. This was another risky part of the plan, but it was unavoidable. Surely no one would see them at this time of night? They only had to walk for fifteen minutes, if that. But there was just the chance, soldiers on exercise, youngsters on a camping trip, even the police being clever enough to solve his clues. But he didn't think so. Later in the day they'd be on his trail, but not just yet. He'd planned it perfectly.

'I don't know if that's the one,' he whispered back, still gently pulling Nicola along by her tiny hand. 'We'll have to see which you like best. There are lots of them around to choose from.'

She skipped back alongside him, staring over at the pony. They neared the brow of the hill and he saw the familiar shapes of the tumbledown piles of granite blocks. 'Come on, little lady,' he whispered. 'It's this way.'

He guided her through the boulders, then stopped and looked around, north, south, east and west. The moor was shaded silver by the luminous moon and there was no one in sight. Perfect.

They picked their way carefully though another stretch of the granite wreckage strewn carelessly over the moorland. Ahead was the peak of the Tor, but just below it a yawning arch of black vacuum cut into the hillside.

'Come on,' he whispered again. 'We're nearly there now.'

Chapter Eighteen

DAN WAS SURE HE would have fallen asleep if it hadn't been for Adam's continual pacing and prompting. His watch said seven o'clock, so it was probably about quarter past. Dawn was colouring the sleeping sky across the city to the east, and the first steady streams of cars were gathering on the roundabout encircling the ruined church.

They were back at the MIR in Charles Cross, still working on Gibson's clues, ready to direct the teams of searchers gathering with the first light. Dan hadn't slept at all and his mind felt slow, anaesthetised, his body numb and leaden, alive only with the sharp, incessant pain in his ankle.

It was funny, but at times like this he missed Rutherford. The dog was fine he knew, fed and exercised by his obliging downstairs neighbour, always happy to cover for emergencies at the minimal cost of a goodwill case of wine a year. But he missed that stupid tongue-out smiling expression as the dog sprinted across Hartley Park in pursuit of a stick, and he missed the cuddle they always had when he walked back into the flat after a day at work.

He realised Adam was staring at him. The detective's eyes were bloodshot, his black hair spraying untidily and his face taut. The shadow of beard he always carried was rough and dark. Dan felt a sting of guilt for succumbing to his selfishness, getting lost in his own thoughts. He forced his mind back to Nicola.

Was she lying on the floor of some barn or shed or cottage, tied up? Sobbing through a gag? Cold and frightened? Was Gibson leering over his prize, wondering how best to use her to taunt them next? He could see similar thoughts in Adam's unblinking eyes, driving him on.

'Got anything yet?' the detective asked again, his voice hoarse with tiredness.

Michael and Eleanor looked up from their computers, shook their heads, as they had the countless times that he'd asked the question.

'I can't see anything in the band of gold thing,' replied Eleanor softly. 'All I get is references to weddings, dress designers, florists, photographers and wedding planners. Oh, and a song by Freda Payne. I can't see anything in there that helps us. As for the elements in it, well, gold is the obvious answer. I can't see what else it could be. But that doesn't help us either. There used to be some gold mines in Cornwall, but they're way down in the west and we know he's not there.'

Michael threw a paper coffee cup into the bin. It was full of them. 'I've been through all the letters and the hints he says he's giving in his phone calls. I can't see anything at all. I'm sorry.'

Adam ran a hand through his hair and fiddled with the knot of his sagging tie. 'I've just been speaking to the police family liaison officer who's with Karen Reece. She hasn't slept a wink since Nicola was taken. She's sitting in her front room, surrounded by pictures of her daughter, picking them up and holding them, crying incessantly and jumping with fear at every ring of the phone. She's talking about committing suicide if Nicola isn't found safely.'

Adam's voice tailed off and he turned to the window, stared out at the ruined church. 'Jesus, I'd do the same if it was Tom.'

No one spoke. The room was quiet, only the dull rumble of the growing morning traffic seeping through the windows.

'Is he conning us?' rasped Adam, turning back to them. 'Is he just taking the piss, giving us false trails to waste our time and put us off his track?'

'I don't think so,' replied Dan. 'I know I'm no expert,' he added, looking at Eleanor and Michael, 'but he's been playing a game from the start, hasn't he? He used the women's names to set out his pattern, so he's obviously got a plan. I don't think he's going to change that now. And he wants to be caught, doesn't he? He says he'll see us again – although he won't be in much of a position to talk he says – so he obviously expects that. He wants to taunt us. He wants to be able to show that he gave us the clues to find him and Nicola,

239

but we weren't smart enough to get them until he showed us how. I'm sure the answer's in there.'

'OK, where then?' snapped Adam. 'Where the hell is it? Come on then, you cracked that stupid Death Pictures riddle. But that was only a bloody game. Now do something worthwhile. Find the bloody answer for us.'

Dan glared at him, felt his voice rising too.

'For Christ's, sake Adam, I am trying,' he shot back, getting to his feet, suffering another stabbing pain from his ankle. 'I'm trying my damned best. I don't have to be here remember? I'm trying to help you out. I could have just sodded off home and got some bloody sleep like I'd love to. As you've pointed out often enough, I'm a bloody journalist, not a cop. I'm trying to help you find her.'

They stared at each other. 'Now then, come on,' said Eleanor soothingly, getting up from her desk to put a hand on each of their shoulders. 'Come on … we're all tired but we're doing our best. If there's anyone who's not pulling their weight, it's me and Michael. We're supposed to be finding the solutions, remember? So let's calm down and have another go. That's all we can do.'

Adam sat down on the edge of a desk. 'That's what you can do. I'm going up to Dartmoor with the search teams. I want to be at the heart of it.' His voice was calmer now. 'Dan, you can help us with that if you're up to it.'

Dan sat back down too, on a desk facing Adam and massaged his aching ankle. He sensed the disguised apology, accepted it. 'Sure, I'm in for the long haul. I'll come up with you. What have you got in mind?'

'You can have another exclusive for your lunchtime news. You can tell the people out there who we're looking for. And you can say we're concentrating the search on Dartmoor after finding some clues. I want as many people looking for Gibson and Nicola as I can get. I think it's time we named him publicly and told people exactly what kind of a man it is we're looking for.'

Zac had been in the middle of a favourite dream and took

240

some rousing.

She was a new age criminal, a techno villain. She was brilliant, defied the finest minds in the country as they tried to track her down. But she was a moral criminal too, a modern Robin Hood. She only stole from the big banks and most dubious companies, those that exploited Third World workers and levelled the rainforests for profit. And she did it all from her laptop. She'd plug in to a system, dart through its firewalls, raid the treasury, and disappear. The single clue she'd leave was an electronic calling card. The Cyber Minx.

The only problem was he couldn't quite decide on her hairstyle. The rest was easy: slender, tall and elegant, dressed in high-heeled black boots, tight black jeans and a black jumper, which hugged the curves of her swelling breasts. Full and alluring lips, green eyes, and a flawless complexion. It was just the hair that was giving him trouble. It would be dark of course, almost black, but what style?

From the earliest days of puberty he'd always liked women with clinical bobbed hair, cut sharp at chin length. But recently he'd started to turn his head to the current fashion, much shorter and spikier cuts. It was a problem, but only a small one, and it wouldn't be unpleasant to resolve over the coming days and nights. He was looking forward to it.

She'd stolen hundreds of thousands of pounds from a big bank where the Prime Minister himself had an account and SOCA had been called in. But again they'd failed to track her down. Zac shifted in his bed as his mind worked its way into his favourite part of the dream. The government had called for the best computer man in the country, and he, Zac, had been suggested. He'd laid his trap, tracked and caught her.

But when they met, when he knocked on the door of that fine Chelsea flat, then came the dilemma. Continue crime fighting and turn her in, or do as she begged and join her in a moral crusade? So long I've been waiting to meet a man like you, she'd said, waiting so long for someone who's my equal. Come away with me …

He shifted again and his mouth relaxed into a contented smile. It was just the question of her hairstyle.

Something was jabbing at his brain and he couldn't understand what. He was about to take the Minx's hand and walk off into the sunset. It was a perfect Hollywood ending. Who was being so inconsiderate as to interrupt?

He opened one eye and glared at the blue pulsing mobile next to the bed. It was that bloody Adam Breen again, it had to be. Not content with keeping him up all night, he no doubt wanted poor sleepy Zac back in the office to work on another of his mad ideas. He checked the bedside clock. 7.28. He'd only had two hours sleep.

He grabbed the phone. 'Hi, it's Zac.'

'Zac, it's Claire, Claire Reynolds.'

He sat up in bed. Detective Sergeant Claire Reynolds. Claire with the gorgeous dark bob and fine figure. Not to mention the sharp brain. Claire who was part of the model for the Minx. Calling him as he lay in bed. Shit! It was almost worth being woken.

He tried not to stammer. 'Hi, Claire, how can I help you?'

'Zac, it is work but it's a bit of a favour too. After that last case we worked on you said I should ring you if I needed any computer work done? I'm sorry to call you so early but I need your help.'

'Sure Claire, no problem.' Why was he shaping his hair into a reasonable style, he wondered? 'What can I do for you?'

'I'm following a bit of a private hunch, so could you keep it to yourself?'

'Sure, Claire, you know you can trust me.' He hoped he didn't sound too eager. 'What is it?'

'I think there may be some kind of crime going on which involves the internet and a chat room. What I need to know Zac, is if I log into a room and start talking to people in there, can you trace them? And particularly, can you trace whoever's set it up and is monitoring what's said in there?'

Zac ruffled his hair again. It always took some work in the morning.

'Sure, Claire, it's not too difficult to do. It's very similar to tracing a phone call. When were you thinking of doing it?'

'Probably tonight, Zac, if you're free.'

Was he free? That was the sort of question he liked to start the day. A perfect no-brainer. But he'd have to find time to get into town and buy himself something new to wear, wouldn't he?

'I don't think I'm doing anything else tonight,' he said happily.

Adam stood on a dry-stone wall at the edge of the car park and looked down on the crowd. A couple of hundred people had gathered. They'd set up base in the campsite at the back of the Spray of Feathers Inn at Princetown, high up on the open moor. There was a ring of uniformed police officers at the front, with some plain-clothes detectives too. About forty soldiers, in their khaki camouflage fatigues, had been called in from survival exercises to help. There were around a hundred others, all ages, wearing colourful waterproofs, blue and green wax jackets, hats and stout boots, all there to help in the hunt for Nicola.

Nine o'clock on a clear October morning. Nicola's birthday. This had to be the day Gibson was talking about. His deadline. They had to save her today.

Adam's tiredness had fled. He didn't know if it was the coffee, the frosty chill of the Dartmoor air, or the energy and anticipation he could feel from the crowd, but his mind felt alert and his body ready.

'Ladies and gentlemen,' he called, and the rumble of conversation died. 'Thanks to everyone who's come here today to search for Nicola. Your help could be vital. In a moment you'll be divided into teams, each led by a police officer. We've got a large amount of ground to cover and only a limited time before it gets dark, so all I want to say is this. Out there somewhere is a young girl who is in grave danger. It is no exaggeration to say your presence here today could help save her life.'

He paused, let the words settle on the crowd. 'So look for anything suspicious; tents, signs of a camp or fire, discarded clothing, particularly a child's, any unusual activity in a house or cottage or barn, anything like that. The smallest of leads could take us to Nicola. Remember that, and let it guide you in your hunt. Now go, and let's bring her home safely.'

He clambered down from the wall and walked towards one of the police incident vans when a familiar face made him stop.

'Hello, Whiting,' said Adam warily. 'What are you doing here?'

The man diplomatically ignored the stupidity of the question. 'You said you wanted everyone who could to come. I suspected your need would mean even I was not excluded.'

Adam looked at him. That cold smile had gone, as had the hissing voice. 'Well, thanks, for taking the time away from your investigation ...'

'There is no investigation,' Whiting cut in. 'I examined all the facts of the case and my preliminary conclusion is that there is nothing criminal about it. I have submitted my initial report and I expect PC Crouch to be reinstated in the next few days. I did my duty there and now I'm doing it here.'

Adam nodded. 'Thank you. I appreciate it.'

Whiting held his look for a moment, then nodded and walked off to join a search party. Thoughtfully, Adam watched him go.

There was something odd in what the man had said. He'd emphasised the words "preliminary" and "initial" in a strangely meaningful way. It wasn't like him to give up – quite the opposite – nor let word get out about the state of his investigation. He was usually highly secretive. But what did he have to gain by admitting he'd failed?

Adam turned back to the police vans. Maybe he was just being overly suspicious. Whatever, it didn't matter. He had more important things to think about. He pulled himself up into a van, bent over a map of south and west Dartmoor spread out across the table. A helicopter buzzed overhead.

'It's a standard search pattern sir,' said a TAG sergeant, dressed in their all black uniform. 'The helicopter's spotting anything that might be suspicious. They've got the thermal imaging camera working to check for anything that looks like an adult and a child. On the ground, I've divided the moor into a grid and given each search team a square. They'll fan out across it, checking the land and any outbuildings. In the villages there are some of the lads doing door-to-door inquiries. If she's here, we'll find her sir.'

If she's here, thought Adam, gazing out of the van's door on to the open moorland where lines of searchers were heading out. If …

Last night Dartmoor had seemed the obvious place. But now, it looked vast. And there were so many buildings here, barns, farmhouses, cottages, so many woods and valleys, places to hide. And they didn't even have any firm evidence Nicola was here. Just his best guess, nothing more scientific. No more than a considered hunch. How would he feel if they found nothing, then, in a fortnight, the body of a little girl was discovered in a field in the South Hams?

A thought of Gibson as the Security Guard goaded him. The bastard had conned them before.

He couldn't think like that. He'd done his job as well as he could, done what he thought was right. They had to narrow down the search area. They couldn't just look everywhere in the hope of finding Nicola. They had to focus on their best guess. This was it. He'd done the right thing.

How long did they have? It had to be today, didn't it? Today or nothing. If she was out on the moor, how long would she survive? It was bitterly cold. He'd noticed the car's thermometer display on the drive up here. Three degrees it said, but that was without the windchill. It was dangerously cold, icy enough to quickly sap a little girl's strength.

A knock at the van's door interrupted his thoughts. 'Hi Adam,' said Dan.

'Come in, hop up inside,' he replied.

'I'll stay here thanks. My ankle's killing me and I'm trying not to stress it. I'd be out on one of the searches otherwise. Nigel's gone to get some pictures, but I couldn't manage it. How are you getting on?'

'The helicopter's up and the search teams are doing their bit. All we can do now is wait.'

'You're going to stay here?'

'Yeah, unless we get a positive lead. I'm going to stay here and coordinate things.'

'The outside broadcast wagon's coming. I'll cut a report and they want a live interview with you for lunch if that's OK?'

'Sure. I need all the help I can get. I can't stop this bloody feeling growing that we're running out of time.'

It was only when she stopped to tie up a shoelace that Claire realised who else was on her search team. There, at the back, as they walked up the winding path to their start position, his eyes flicking over the moorland. Whiting.

Too late now to turn away, he was almost level with her. 'Hello, sir. Good to see you out here searching.' She thought she managed to keep her voice neutral.

'Good morning, Claire,' he replied, no trace of a hiss in his voice. 'And you don't have to call me sir any more. I'm not your superior any longer. Marcus will be fine now.'

She couldn't imagine ever using his Christian name. 'OK … thank you, sir.'

'And I hope we can forget about what's happened in the past,' he added. 'This is far more important, too much so for any personal feelings to intrude.'

She took a breath to calm herself. 'That's fine. I can live with that. Just so long as you are aware I didn't leak Crouch's name.'

'Claire, please, let us focus on …'

'Stick your focus,' she spat, couldn't stop herself. 'I have never in my career had such offensive accusations levelled at me – not even by criminals – and I want you to know that. I might not have liked what we were doing, but I was professional about it and I was giving it my best.'

Whiting looked surprised, raised a hand in a calming gesture. 'Well, it scarcely matters now,' he said, the hiss back in his voice. 'The investigation is at an end and PC Crouch is likely to be exonerated. It would take a better man than me to find evidence of wrongdoing. After today you will probably never see me again.'

She stared at him, wondered whether to say something about the emails, that hint of a lead. But no, why should she? If it came to something, how sweet it would be for him to know it was her who'd discovered it. A better man than him uncovering the truth, perhaps not. But a better woman?

'Fine by me,' Claire replied, as calmly as she could. She thought he was about to say something, but they were interrupted by the sergeant in charge of their team.

'You all know what you're doing?' he called. 'Walk slowly along in a line, about ten metres apart and scan the ground around you. Make sure the person to each side of you can see further than halfway between you. We cannot afford to risk missing anything. If anyone sees or finds anything they think is suspicious, raise both arms and shout 'here' immediately.'

They fanned out, began walking. Claire made sure she was at the opposite end of the line from Whiting. She recognised the area from one of her Dartmoor walks with Dan and Rutherford. They were near the top of Higher Hartor Tor, about twelve hundred feet up, facing to the south, heading down the valley towards the source of the River Plym. Ahead she could see the grey sprawl of Plymouth and the English Channel sparkling beyond. To the east, another line of searchers paced carefully across the expanse of green.

A rugged wind buffeted and flapped at her coat, stinging her face as she looked from side to side, carefully checking the pockets and tufts of granite, gorse and heather. The windchill was relentless. The cold started to sting her throat and creep into her hands and feet, despite her thick gloves and walking boots.

If Nicola was up here, Claire hoped she had warm clothes and shelter.

'So let me get this straight,' said Lizzie, who sounded worryingly content. 'For the lunchtime news, you're going to name the man the police believe abducted Nicola, tell us a little about his history and why he's so dangerous, and reveal the cops now think he's holding her on Dartmoor.'

'Yep.'

'That's three exclusive lines in one story?'

'Yep.'

The phone went quiet. 'News Editor's heaven,' she sighed finally. 'Just divine. The kids got off to school this morning with no hassle, no forgotten lunches or play club money, and now this. It must be my day.'

She was building up into one of her fizzing crescendos, Dan could sense it.

'The ratings will soar. I can just see them now. Everyone will be watching us, everyone. And hang on, when's the deadline for the Royal Television Society awards nominations? It's tomorrow, isn't it? My God, we can get this into our entry! What a day!'

Dan had been holding the phone away from his ear. 'OK, well, I'd better get on with it.'

'Just one thing,' she interrupted, her voice sharpening. 'Why the hell are they giving you all this? It smacks of desperation to me.'

'I think that's exactly what it is. They're absolutely desperate to find Nicola. It's cold up here, so if she is out on the moor she may not survive long. They need as many people as possible looking for her to give them their best chance of finding her alive.'

'So tomorrow we might have a missing kid found dead story as well, as a follow-up?'

He gave the phone a look. 'That, or a missing child found safe and well.'

'I'll take either,' said Lizzie dreamily.

'Well?' Adam asked the sergeant coordinating the search. He knew he was harassing the man and his incessant questions wouldn't get them any further, but he couldn't help it.

'As was ten minutes ago, sir,' replied Sergeant Wilcox patiently. 'The helicopter's found no traces of anything that looks like a man and child. It's picked up about twenty or so tents though, and the search parties have been directed to check them. We've had four cleared of any suspicion so far. The rest are being completed now. The house-to-house inquiries in the villages haven't picked up anything. We're working through the farms and isolated houses and cottages, but so far nothing there either. We are working as fast as we can, sir.'

Adam patted the man on the shoulder. 'I know, Sergeant, I know. I'm sorry.'

'It's all right, sir. We all want to find her.'

Adam stepped down from the van and checked his watch. It was coming up to one o'clock. Four more hours of searching, at most. Four more hours before darkness closed in and they'd have to give up for the night. His teeth bit into an ulcer forming on the lower lip of his mouth and he winced. He hadn't had ulcers for years.

He walked up to the Wessex Tonight outside-broadcast van and banged on the door. Dan opened it. 'Hop in, mate,' he said. 'Any news?'

'If there was I would have said, wouldn't I?'

Dan stared down at his notes to hide his irritation, managed not to say anything. Adam looked shattered, moved like he was sleepwalking. His face was heavily lined and his eyes were narrow and red. The normally impeccable tie was hanging low around his neck.

'I've done the report,' said Dan. 'Have a look. I'll be interviewing you after it's gone out.'

Adam squeezed past Loud's bulk and into the truck. One of the monitors flashed up a black and white clock with a five second countdown and the report began. It started with pictures of the searchers fanning out across Dartmoor, Dan talking about the hunt now concentrating on the moor and all available police looking for Nicola, along with volunteers and the military. There were a couple of clips of interview of some of the people who'd turned out to help, talking about believing they should rally together and do all they could at a time like this.

After that, there was a picture of Nicola, while Dan recapped on how she'd been abducted. Then there was a photo of Gibson. Dan talked about him being the man that detectives now believed had abducted Nicola. He added a couple of lines about Gibson's army background, which meant he could be living rough on the moor. He wrapped up the report by saying Gibson was considered dangerous and shouldn't be approached, but anyone who thought they had seen him should call 999 at once.

Adam nodded his approval. 'Good,' he said. 'That should make people take notice. And you'll be interviewing me after that?'

'Yep,' said Dan, squeezing the plastic tube that would link him with the studio into his ear. 'Are you ready? We're on in about five minutes.'

They got down from the truck and walked over to where Nigel had set up the camera, looking back on the line of police cars and vans. Dan winced from the stabbing pain in his ankle and tried to keep his weight off it. It was getting worse.

'You've done this with me enough times before,' he told Adam. 'And it's exactly the same as usual. The studio will introduce me, I'll do a fifteen-second scene set, the report will play, then I'll interview you. We've got about a minute and a half for the interview, so I'll probably have time for three questions.'

'OK,' said Adam, straightening his tie. Dan noticed he kept fiddling with the change in his pocket, the first time he'd seen his friend appear tense before going on air. He kept pacing back and forth too, looked like he was rehearsing what he was about to say.

'Dramatic developments in the Nicola Reece abduction today,' intoned Craig. 'Police have begun combing an area of Dartmoor where they believe she may be being held. In a highly unusual move, they've also named the man they believe could have taken Nicola. Our Crime Correspondent Dan Groves joins us from Dartmoor ...'

'Yes Craig, I'm at Princetown, where the hunt for Nicola is being coordinated,' said Dan, gesturing to the expanse of moorland behind him. 'At this moment, hundreds of police and volunteers are out on the moor around us, looking for the little girl.'

The report played and Dan called Adam in to the shot.

Nigel shifted them both around so he could get a good background of the police vans, most appropriate for Adam's interview. 'Ten seconds back to you, standby Dan,' he heard in his ear. 'Five seconds … cue!'

'With me now is the man in charge of the operation, Detective Chief Inspector Adam Breen,' Dan told the camera. 'Mr Breen, I have to ask. Such a big operation as this, the police helicopter up, hundreds of volunteers called in too but no sign of Nicola. Are you getting desperate?'

'We're not desperate, we're just committed to finding Nicola and we'll do whatever we need to succeed in that,' Adam replied calmly, but Dan thought he saw a flare of anger in the detective's eyes. 'I have information she may be on Dartmoor, so we will comb the moor until we either find her or we're sure she's not here.'

'But it's a tough job, isn't it? It's a huge area to search?'

'It is a big area, but as you just pointed out I've got plenty of officers and volunteers from the local community, along with the force helicopter. I'm confident I've got the resources I need to find Nicola.'

'Chief Inspector, you mentioned public help there. Is that still important to you?'

'It's vital. I would appeal to everyone watching to please keep a look out for anyone who looks like Edmund Gibson, the man you mentioned in your report, or Nicola herself. If you see anything, call us. And if anyone is free this afternoon and would like to join in the search for Nicola, we'd be very grateful. Your help could make all the difference.'

They were given the all-clear by the director. Nigel began de-rigging the camera.

'That was a bit over the top wasn't it?' protested Adam, turning on Dan. 'That stuff about us being desperate?'

'It's my job to ask tough questions, you know that. And you handled it fine. You got your appeal in. That's what you wanted, isn't it?'

'Yeah, but you're supposed to be on my side, Dan. It's finding Nicola that's important here, not your bloody stories.'

Dan was cold, tired and his ankle was throbbing badly. He

felt a yearning to get in his car, drive straight home and shut all the doors, lock himself in, take the phone off the hook, cuddle Rutherford and sleep. The Swamp was sucking him down and his friend was making it worse.

'If you hadn't noticed, it's my bloody stories that have been helping you try to find her, Adam,' he shot back. 'For Christ's sake, I've done exactly what you asked in those appeals I made to Gibson for more clues. I've bent over backwards to help you and I don't think a question about whether you're getting desperate is a big issue. You're just tetchy because Gibson's been taking the piss out of you and you can't find him.'

Adam squared up and his finger jabbed at Dan. 'It's nothing to do with that. Not a bloody thing and you know it. This is simply about what's best for finding Nicola. And I don't think …'

'Sir! Sir!' A uniformed sergeant calling from one of the police vans interrupted them.

'What?' barked Adam, wheeling around.

'One of the search teams, sir. They've found something. There's been a break in at a building on the edge of the moor. They reckon Gibson was there with Nicola.'

Chapter Nineteen

THE POLICE CARS BOUNCED and roared over the rough ground of the car park by the ford, just below Gutter Tor. Claire was waiting, pacing, and beckoned urgently. Dan realised it was where they'd walked the last time they'd been out on Dartmoor. He'd parked just here, where the police driver was manoeuvring the car. Rutherford had dived straight into the pond by the ford.

Adam jumped out and strode over to Claire. Dan hobbled painfully behind. He seemed to have been forgotten in the excitement.

'You found it, Claire?' asked Adam as they made their way up a stony path in the green felt of the moor.

'Yes, sir. The hut was hidden in the trees from where we were, up on the moor, but a local farmer told me it was here. It was just a hunch. It looked like a good place to hide. The door was open and I had a look round. There are a few blankets left and a couple of mats to sleep on. I haven't touched anything, but I noticed there were long blonde hairs on one of the mats. There are a few bits of rubbish from where they've eaten too.'

'Any clues about where they've gone?'

'No, sir, not that I could see. But I didn't do a thorough search. I called in as soon as I knew he'd been here.'

'Good work, Claire, well done.'

A small, slate-roofed stone cottage was set into a copse of trees to the right of the path. It had a couple of windows on each side and a wooden door. They walked around to the back where there was a large shed and another, smaller door to the cottage. It was ajar.

Adam studied it, asked, 'What is this place?'

'A scout hut sir. Younger hikers can use it as a base for exploring parts of the moor. It's a haven if the weather gets too rough.'

Dan followed them inside, stubbing a toe on a stone, making his ankle fire with pain. He gasped. He'd have to see a doctor soon.

There was a pair of white-overalled forensic officers kneeling on the floor inside the door. 'You've got half an hour,' Adam told them, checking his watch. 'We've only got enough light for another three hours searching. Don't worry about giving the place a detailed going over. I don't have the time. Just see if you can find any indication of where he's gone.'

In the corner of the hall was a sleeping bag and pile of blankets. There were some wrappings from a loaf of bread, tins of beans and sausages and a small camping stove. A forensics officer picked at the blankets with a pair of tweezers. In a windowless cupboard just off the hall was a small, battery powered television.

'That's how he watched Wessex Tonight then,' said Dan. Adam turned, looked, then stood silent, staring into space.

'So how did he get here?' he asked aloud. 'And where's he gone now?'

'I expect he left after he'd called in with that last message, sir,' replied Claire, looking down at the blankets. 'Just in case we had a chance to trace it. He'd know we were getting close.'

'I think you're right Claire. Which means he can't have gone far. He'd have intended to use this place as a temporary base, then move on to wherever he planned next. Probably the place where he wants all this to end. But where? Are there any traces of a car?'

'No sir. But we haven't looked in the outbuilding yet.'

Adam turned quickly and strode outside. 'Open it up,' he barked at a young police officer standing in front of the shed's double doors. 'Now!'

The policeman jumped, turned and pulled hard at the catch. It groaned, but stayed put. He tried again, harder, and this time it gave. Inside it was dark, but there was the unmistakeable outline of a quad bike.

'There,' growled Adam. 'That's how he got up here.' He walked in to the building and looked over the bike. 'He wrapped Nicola up and put her on the back here. He probably stuck a tarpaulin over her, something like that. Anyone who

254

saw him would think it was a farmer. Get forensics in here to see if they can spot anything that might help tell us where he's gone now.'

'Hang on,' said Claire. 'Look.' She pointed to the front of the bike, at the handlebars. Hanging there was a tiny envelope, the sort that contain gift tags for Christmas presents. It was so small they'd almost missed it in the barn's half-light. On the front was written "Adam."

The detective reached down and picked it off, opened it, his fingers fumbling.

"Adam,

"I thought it was time I sent you a note, as you seem to be struggling. And after all, time is the point. It's almost time now. But for what? And where? All I can say is this. It's in the names and the numbers.

"Edmund."

'What the hell does that mean?' Adam barked, a hand running through his hair.

'It's your final clue,' said Dan. 'He knew we'd be on to him now. He wanted it this way. He planned where he'd go and what he'd do. It's the final chance to work out where he is and what he's doing before the showdown. The deadline's approaching and this is our last chance.'

Adam strode back out of the barn and looked around him. 'Call Michael and Eleanor and tell them what we've found. Dictate the words in the note. Tell them to put everything they've got into cracking it. So where is he now? Where? Where is the bastard?'

'I don't reckon he's gone far sir,' said Claire. 'There's no room in that barn to store a car and he wouldn't have risked keeping one out here in the car park for a couple of days. It'd soon be noticed. I think he must be on foot.'

Adam nodded. 'Which brings us back to where we were. Dartmoor. At least we know for certain he's here now. But where? Are there any other houses or farms around where he could he hiding?'

'All checked sir,' said Claire. 'Nothing.'

'Get them checked again. We might have missed something. I can't risk that. And get the helicopter back to do a sweep over the area.'

'Yes sir.'

'And get the dogs to see if they can pick up a scent. I know he's probably long gone, but it's worth a try. Anything is.'

'Yes sir.'

Adam turned to the east. 'Burrator reservoir's over there, isn't it? Not far away either.'

'Yes, sir.'

'And there are lots of trees and woodland there. Plenty of places to hide.'

'Yes, sir.'

'Get a couple of teams going around the reservoir then. It's worth a shot. We're running out of time.'

The yellow sun was already dipping towards the western horizon.

There was no sight, no vision, it was too dark, perfectly black. There was only the incessant sound. Drip, drip, drip …

A gasping, wavering sob rose above the tinny beat, then another. He tried to ignore it.

The crying faded, and a small, faltering voice joined with the drip, drip, drip …

'I'm scared Ed … I'm so frightened … I don't like the dark.'

He tried again to shut it out, tapped the rhythm of the falling water on his knees.

Drip, drip, drip …

'I'm really scared … Ed, please … please …'

Drip, drip, drip …

Breathless now. 'You're not … you're not going to hurt me, are you?'

It was the first time she'd asked it. He flinched, surprised to find the question penetrated his mind.

'No, of course not, my lovely. I would never hurt you. This is … it's …'

He struggled to find some convincing words. 'It's the very last part of our adventure. It's the most important bit … where you prove you're brave enough to … it's like those stories I read you. You remember those?'

Drip, drip, drip …

'You remember them, don't you? When the hero has to go through the final test before he can claim his great prize? Well, that's what you're doing now.'

Drip, drip, drip.

Drip, drip, drip …

Then her voice. Querulous, fearful. 'How long do we have to stay here?'

He checked the luminous dial of his watch. 'Not long now, my love.' He bit back his reluctance, reached out and took Nicola's hand, squeezed it. 'Not long. I'm sorry we have to spend part of your birthday this way, but I'm afraid it can't be helped. There are some people we need to avoid. They're trying to stop us finishing our adventure and we don't want that, do we? It won't be long before we can go out and choose your pony.'

Drip, drip, drip …

'Really, Ed?'

'Really. You've been such a brave girl. We've almost finished our adventure now, and when it's over we can find your pony. Have you decided which one you'd like yet? For being such a wonderfully brave girl, I'll get you whichever one you want.'

Drip, drip, drip …

Then her voice, calmer now. 'I think I'd like a black one, Ed. I think I'm sure about that now. I think he'll be black and I'll call him Beauty. Just like that book you and Mummy read to me. Will Mummy be here to help me choose him?'

He screwed his eyes shut, tried so hard to shut out her words. It was too late for guilt. Another few hours and it would all be over. But she was such a beautiful girl, so innocent, so trusting. Just a few more hours.

The relentless noise seemed to be growing louder, echoing in his head.

Drip, drip, drip …

Why did it have to be this way? Why couldn't it have been some screaming, spoilt brat who he could easily hate? Why did it have to be a beautiful little girl, with loving eyes, golden hair, a cute gap in her teeth and a smooth hand she'd hold out for a reassuring squeeze? Why did he keep seeing her riding that pony, shrieking in delight, the tail of blonde hair flying behind her?

The answer snapped back. Because he'd chosen her. Because she was symbolic. Perfect.

He thought of her mum, sitting at home, surrounded by friends, family, staring at the phone, willing it to ring, but each time it did dreading what she would hear. What would she be thinking about him? She must be despising, loathing, detesting him. Just as he loathed and detested her. Or was almost sure he did …

Did she really once want to have a relationship with him? Could he have finally managed one with her? Maybe, if she hadn't been a vital part of his wonderful plan.

He hung on to the thought. His wonderful plan. That was what this was about. Not something pathetic and weak, transient and meaningless like a relationship. Something that would live on, be forever remembered, not falter and die, unnoticed by the world.

Drip, drip, drip …

Could he have been a father to Nicola? She'd never had one. She'd mentioned that often enough on their outings. It was just her and Mum. It had always been that way.

That wasn't so very different from his own childhood. He didn't have a dad either, just a man who used that name, someone who would make rushed, flying visits, always on his way somewhere else, always with more important things to do, always too busy to stop and play. When he thought of his father he saw a blur, an undefined image of a half-remembered person speeding in and out of his life.

His imagination brought him that picture again. Nicola, astride the sturdy black pony, wearing matching black riding hat and boots, cantering safely around a grassy paddock, her gappy smile beaming her delight. Would her mum be there beside him, smiling too, perhaps reaching out to hold his hand, share the joy?

Drip, drip, drip …

It was growing louder still, boring into his brain. He ground a knuckle into the rocky wall beside him, felt the skin break, the shock of pain helping him force the thought away. It was too late for regrets. There was only one path for him now, and he was almost there. It was nearly time.

He heard the helicopter buzzing overhead, a couple of voices too he thought, but that could have been his imagination. Everything was going precisely according to the plan. They were looking for him, but he'd out-thought them again. They'd never find him here. They should have discovered the quad bike and hut by now, and they'd be gathering close by. But they'd never find him.

Not until he was ready. Not for a few hours yet.

More words in the blackness. 'My mummy's very pretty, isn't she, Ed? Do you think she's pretty?'

'Yes, I think she's very pretty.'

'Was your mum pretty Ed?'

He wanted to walk away, put his hands over his ears, block out the dripping and that innocent little voice. He hadn't harmed her. He hadn't hurt anyone. He prided himself on that. He'd done what he had to do, and no one had been hurt. No one would be.

The two women he'd visited – that was how he liked to think of it – had been upset of course, but they would get over it. Nicola had cried a couple of times. The ride on the back of the quad bike was the worst, but the tears were brief and she'd been fine afterwards. They'd get over it, all three of them. They'd soon forget. It had been necessary. Someone had to make the statement that needed to be made, and it would be him. It was too late for regrets.

'Yes, Nicola, she was very pretty. She was like a princess.'

He regretted the words as soon as he'd spoken them.

'My mummy says I look like a princess with my hair. She says all princesses have long, blonde hair. Did you know that,

Ed?'

'I didn't, but now you mention it you're right. I've never seen a princess who doesn't have lovely long blonde hair, just like yours.'

'I'll look like a real princess sitting on my pony, won't I? Will it be long now before we can go and get him?'

'Not long now, my love. Not long.'

The guilt came thundering back as he thought about what he had to do next. His father was there, scolding him, a finger pointing, his mother shaking her head, her lips pursed. He tried to block it out but it wouldn't leave him, echoed louder and louder through his head.

He could feel the cold gathering around them, pulled a blanket over her little shoulders, tucked it around her. He didn't want to think about what was coming next, but it wouldn't leave him, whichever way he turned his head, however tightly he closed his eyes.

It had to be this way. There was no choice left now. It was too late for regrets.

Drip, drip, drip …

'Not long now, my love,' he whispered again through the perfect darkness. 'Not long.'

The shadows were stretching further over the moorland, dark fingers pulling at the precious daylight and stealing it away. Dan didn't bother checking his watch, he'd been doing so every couple of minutes for the last hour. It was just after half past four. And the icy cold was sharpening with the gathering gloom.

He'd given up on the letters Gibson had sent, the transcripts of the calls and his hastily scribbled note of that last message at the Scout Hut. He was sure the answer was in the letters and he'd stared at them until the words drifted out of focus. Dan had underlined some parts, sketched asterisks and question marks next to others, but still he couldn't see a solution.

He'd tried anagrams of Denton and Hyde. The best he'd come up with were Done Thy End, Don't Heed NY, Dyed

Then No and Not Dyed Hen. None made any sense. And how could it be an anagram anyway, if Michael's computer program couldn't solve it? It must be something else. But what?

Manchester kept teasing his brain and he'd borrowed a road map of Britain from the Spray of Feathers, gazed at it, wondering why Gibson would mention the city. He'd even looked at Denton and Hyde again, but couldn't see any connection to Dartmoor. They were just ordinary towns, part of the suburbs, towards the end of the M67 to the east of Manchester. So why did Gibson write about them? They knew he wasn't there.

Dan had learned never to ignore his instincts, but eventually he'd given up, taken the map back into the pub, resisted the sweet temptation of the beer pumps and a quiet corner next to the woodburner, instead hobbled slowly back outside to rejoin Adam.

Dan leaned back against a police car, rubbed his eyes. His mind felt numb from the lack of sleep and penetrating cold. But still he worked at Gibson's letters, all the time feeling that each second which passed was another less to find Nicola. Why did Gibson have to single him out as the one who would know how to solve the riddle? What did he do to deserve the torment of this pressure?

He stared again at his notepad, the letters and words dancing in his blurred sight, but he saw nothing. It was as if the enveloping cold and the strain had made his brain seize. The pain in his ankle stabbed at him, but he hardly noticed. He wasn't even thinking of his bed and Rutherford any more. His mind felt blank, empty.

What did that note on the quad bike mean, that the answer was in the names and the numbers? There were no numbers in Gibson's letters. He'd checked each, three times, scrutinised every line but couldn't see any hint of figures. Was it some kind of code? He'd tried giving the individual letters a number, one for a, two for b, three for c and seeing if that made any sense with the first or last letters of each lines of the notes, but they meant nothing.

He'd spoken to Michael and Eleanor, but they'd come to the same dead ends and they were the experts. What chance did that give him? So why was he feeling so angry?

He knew the answer. He'd solved the Death Pictures riddle, and this couldn't be any tougher than McCluskey's mystery. But the Death Pictures had taken him months, and here they'd had only days, now down to minutes. He knew he shouldn't think it, that it wasn't fair on himself, but he felt as though he'd failed Nicola. He could solve a riddle where the prize was a painting. But not when a little girl's life was at stake.

Adam stood in the door of the police van, staring out to the west and the dying sun, as if willing it to linger in the sky. An occasional burst of static and tinny conversation from the radio inside the van made his head snap around, look imploringly at Sergeant Wilcox, receive another slow shake of the head. He'd turn back in frustration, continue glaring at the sunset. His tie was low down his neck and his suit jacket open. He didn't have a coat on, must have been frozen but didn't seem to have noticed the cold.

'We're running out of time,' he muttered again. 'Running out of time.'

The sergeant's voice drifted out of the van, gently pleading. 'I'm going to have to call them back in, sir. There's barely enough light left for them to see anything. I've got to make sure they come back safely. They've been out all day and they're exhausted.'

Adam turned, his voice hoarse. 'Just a few minutes more, Sergeant, please. We've got to give it every chance. Just a few more minutes.'

'Sir, with respect, we've given it every chance. They won't find anything in the dark and they're more likely to be a danger to themselves. Sir, please. We can start again in the morning.'

Adam sat down heavily on the van's step, his head bowed. 'It'll be too late in the morning. We'll have lost her by then. I know we will. Her birthday was the deadline. All we'll find in the morning will be a corpse.'

He looked over at Dan. 'We've lost her. Tomorrow you'll

be doing your story on the discovery of Nicola's body, and Gibson will have what he wanted. He's humiliated us. Me in particular. I might as well write out my resignation now.'

Dan stood up and hobbled over to his friend, put a hand on his shoulder. 'Nothing like it, Adam, nothing like it. Don't talk like that. You did as much as you possibly could. More than that in fact. You did everything. It was me who failed. Gibson picked me to solve his riddle and I couldn't do it. I failed, not you. Let the searchers come home for now. We can look again in the morning. There's still hope.'

Adam stared down at the dusty ground. The land was losing its colour as the light faded.

'It'll be too late then. It was today or never. We've lost her. And to think he stood in front of me and did his act and I never saw it. I could have stopped all this if I'd been thinking. It's my fault. A little girl's out there dying and it's my fault. I could have saved her.'

'Come on, come on.' Dan gently shook Adam's shoulder. 'Let them come back in.'

Sergeant Wilcox stepped down from the van, looked at Adam who stared at him, then, finally, gave the slightest of nods.

'Come and sit in the warm of the Spray of Feathers for ten minutes and let me get you a beer,' said Dan. 'You haven't stopped all day and there's absolutely nothing you can do while the searchers come back in. Come and sit down in the warm for a few minutes. It'll do you good.'

Adam got slowly to his feet and walked alongside Dan, each step laboured and heavy with defeat. He could hear the sergeant on the radio in the van, calling the search teams home.

Dan bought them a couple of pints of Prison Ale, Princetown's finest. He carried the drinks over to the black slate table next to the woodburner where Adam had slumped. The detective was staring down at the table, tracing patterns in the stone with his finger.

'We've run out of time,' he mumbled. 'We've lost her.'

Dan passed the pint across. 'Not yet. Not yet. There's still hope. There's always hope.' He wasn't sure how much belief he managed to force into his voice. 'There are plenty of people out there, still keeping an eye open for her. We're not lost yet.'

Adam took a long sip from his beer, then another. 'We'll start searching again tomorrow at first light, but I reckon we've missed Gibson's deadline. And I don't want to think about what that means for Nicola.'

'Have we any leads left?'

'None. The dogs didn't pick up a scent from the scout hut. The helicopter's found nothing. The house-to-house inquiries found nothing. There was nothing around the reservoir. The search teams combed most of the section of moor where Gibson could have been and found nothing. There were a few tents without people in, but none were suspicious. There was no trace of Nicola. I'm starting to wonder if he is still on the moor with her, or if he's escaped somewhere else. Anything could have happened. He could have killed her, dumped her body and made off in a car he'd hidden somewhere. We'd struggle to find a child's body. There are so many places he could have hidden it.'

Dan sipped at his pint and thought. 'No … that doesn't fit. First of all, and I know you won't agree with this, but the guy's not a killer. He said so in one of his letters, that he didn't want anyone harmed. And his actions bear it out. He hasn't actually hurt anyone …'

'Yet,' interrupted Adam bitterly.

'OK, fair enough. But I certainly don't think he's set out to hurt anyone. And for him, all this is about getting at the police isn't it? It all seems to be building up to some climax, some kind of showdown. I can't believe he'd simply run and not have his moment of insane glory. That doesn't fit. I'm sure he's still around here somewhere and we'll soon find out what the end of his great plan is. He wouldn't allow us not to.'

Adam managed a tired and weak smile. 'That's one of the things I like about you, Dan. You always try to think the best of people. Whereas, me, I've been a detective for long enough to usually think the worst.'

'I'm not trying to paint him as some sort of misguided victim hero type. I don't believe in that stuff. I'm just giving you my best guess about what he's thinking and how he'll behave.'

Dan lifted his ankle onto his knee and gave it a quick massage. It was still aching, but not as badly. Another wave of tiredness soaked his body. He imagined Rutherford waiting at home and his cosy flat. When Nicola was finally found, he'd sleep for a whole day, he promised himself. Then he'd take his beloved dog for a good, long walk, ankle permitting.

'I'd better get back outside in a minute,' he told Adam. 'I've got to do a live broadcast tonight to update the viewers about the search for Nicola. I don't know what I'm going to say.'

'You might as well tell it like it is, mate. That there's no progress and we're getting desperate. You were right at lunchtime. I'm sorry if I snapped at you, but it's just the pressure getting to me.'

Adam paused, swirled the last inch of beer around his glass. 'He has got to me you know. Gibson that is. I realised it this afternoon. I've been taking this personally. He's got to me, with his plan and his riddles. And he's winning. He's been ahead of us all along. He's got what he wanted. He's humiliated us.'

'I don't know about that. You're doing all …'

'Oh, bollocks to him anyway,' interrupted Adam, his voice suddenly stronger. 'Sitting here feeling sorry for ourselves isn't going to help. Come on, you're the one who cracked McCluskey's bloody code. Haven't you got any ideas about what Gibson meant with those riddles of his? I'll take any guesses at this stage. Anything.'

Dan shook his head, finished his pint. 'Not a bloody clue. I've been trying to work on it all afternoon, but I haven't come up with a thing. I had this hunch the stuff he said about Manchester was important, but I can't work out why.' Dan got painfully to his feet, his ankle protesting at being forced to take his weight. 'I'm off to the loo, won't be a minute.'

He limped out of the pub and into the toilets. One of the

things he liked about the Spray of Feathers was the pleasant distraction they offered from the mundane chore of relieving yourself. On the wall above the row of urinals was a large ordnance survey map of Dartmoor.

Dan glanced idly over it, picking out Princetown and Dartmoor Prison in the middle, then going south and west to the Scout Hut where Gibson had hidden. He followed the green line of the old track up to the abandoned Eylesbarrow tin mine, where he'd taken Claire and Rutherford for their last walk. Another walk together this weekend would be very welcome. Some quality time was long overdue. It would be just what he needed, normality and affection, somewhere to hide from these six days of insanity.

The tiredness enveloped him again and he yawned, closed his eyes for a few seconds. He'd present tonight's outside broadcast, then get straight home to a bath and bed. Lizzie was bound to want a follow up story tomorrow and if Adam was right, it could be very bad news. He needed to get some sleep.

Dan was about to leave the toilets when he stopped, turned back to the map. Afterwards, he could never explain what made him do it, just that his subconscious mind must have seen something and prompted him to take another look. He stared at it again. What was he looking for? There was something here he'd missed, something important. He knew it. But what?

The tiredness fled, beaten away by the sudden flare of hope. He was on to something, he knew it. But what? What was it? His instincts said there was something on this map that was telling him where Gibson was. It was so simple, but what was it? He knew it was there, but he couldn't quite see it.

Dan forced himself to look again at the route he'd followed just seconds before. Slowly he traced it across the printed paper. Princetown. No, nothing there. The prison, nothing there. The Scout Hut. Gibson had hidden there, they knew that, but so what? Eylesbarrow tin mine. Nothing there. What was it that he'd seen?

He stared at the map, willing it to tell him. A man walked in and settled into the neighbouring urinal, but Dan didn't notice, just stared on. What was it on the map that was telling him where Gibson was?

What had Gibson said in that final note, the one to Adam? That it was in the names and the numbers. The names didn't mean anything, he couldn't see any connection to where Gibson might be. What about the numbers? The only numbers on the map were the heights of various tors, a couple of roads and the grid references.

His eyes wandered over the tors. Higher Hartor Tor, 420 metres above sea level. Crane Hill, 471. King's Tor, 380. Sheeps Tor, 369. Dan stared at them, but couldn't see anything that gave him a clue.

He raised a finger and traced the few roads crossing the moor. The A386 to Tavistock, the B3212, the main east-west road across Dartmoor, the B3357. He tried to jumble the numbers in his mind, to see if they could mean anything. Nothing.

He felt the brief shot of hope start to wane. One last chance.

Dan traced the grid references along the side of the map. Horizontally they began in the 50s, then moved into the 60s. Vertically they ran from the 60s to the 70s.

Something triggered in his brain. What was familiar about those numbers? The man who had been using the urinal walked past him, out of the door, casting a suspicious look back over his shoulder. Dan didn't see it, was oblivious to everything except the map and his resurgent thoughts. He stood back, leaned against the wall. What was important about those numbers?

It was something recent, something he'd only been thinking about in the last few hours.

But what?

Slow seconds ticked by. Nothing came. He screwed up his eyes, stared harder at the map. Dartmoor, the great wilderness, all hills and valleys, streams and forests. What was it?

A sudden realisation. The road map. That was it. The map of Manchester. He strode back into the pub, quickly pushed past a couple of waiting customers and interrupted the barman.

'That map I borrowed earlier. Can I have it back please?'

'Just a moment, sir, I'm dealing with this lady.'

No time to argue. Each second could be precious. Dan ducked down, under the bar, grabbed for the map. The barman reached out an arm, tried to stop him, but Dan slapped it aside. A wine glass hit the stone floor, shattered.

'Here! What the hell do you think you're doing?'

'Saving a little girl's life.'

The man just stared, open-mouthed. Dan walked quickly back into the toilets, his aching ankle forgotten. He fumbled the map open on pages 92 and 93, Greater Manchester. What was he looking at? Looking for?

What had Gibson said in one of his earlier letters? Something about a trip somewhere around Manchester. He stared at the map. Around Manchester ... around Manchester...

Then he saw it. The motorway circling Manchester. The M60. And here, on the map of Dartmoor there were grid references in the 60s.

Dan felt his pulse quicken. His brain was fresh now, active, eager, the draining lethargy gone. What else had Gibson said? There was that stuff about Denton and Hyde. That had seemed odd all along. Why pick out those places? There was nothing special about them.

He ran a finger over the road map, found them. They were on the M67.

He gazed at the map of Dartmoor, traced the grid references with his finger. Square 6067. What was in it? His hand was trembling. It was where he'd walked with Claire and Rutherford. More importantly, it was close to the Scout Hut.

He was onto something, he was sure of it.

Dan swore loudly. He'd sat in his flat, looking for clues in Gibson's letters, stared at these very bloody motorways and not seen it.

He concentrated, picked out the landmarks in the grid square. Higher Hartor Tor, Plym Steps ... what was there that could mean Gibson was there too?

One place stood out. Dan's eyes fixed on it. At the top of

grid square 6067. A little valley called Evil Coombe.

Gibson had used the word evil several times in his letters, hadn't he? He'd made a point of repeating it. Hadn't he said something like "the question of evil is at the very centre of our dance?"

Hell, he'd walked past it with Claire, even pointed it out to her. Evil Coombe. It was on the side of a hill, and the Chief Constable's surname was Hill. That was it. That was where all this would end, where Gibson would make his final grand gesture.

He ran out of the toilets, threw down the map, grabbed Adam and pulled him up.

'Come on, quick, quick, quick,' Dan panted. 'Quick! I think I've found him.'

Chapter Twenty

IT WAS ALMOST DARK when they reached the car park by the Scout Hut. They climbed quickly out of the police cars and vans and formed a semi-circle. Adam gave a fast briefing. His voice was still hoarse with tiredness, but it was urgent too.

'We think he's up there,' he rasped, pointing along the old mine track, 'in a valley by the side of Higher Hartor Tor called – and get this – Evil Coombe.'

There were about 20 officers gathered around Adam, dressed in black and wearing black baseball caps with checked bands and 'Police' inscribed on the front. It was all that could be gathered at instant notice. Adam ignored the sergeant's request to wait for more, said they couldn't afford the time.

Dan noticed most of the officers were armed. One man next to him, tall and silent, was holding an automatic rifle. Another by his side had a baton gun cradled in his arms. Both wore holsters containing pistols. He backed away slightly, making his ankle throb again.

'I don't need to remind you Gibson has a gun and a young girl with him,' continued Adam. 'I can't afford to let this become a hostage situation. We don't know what state she's in. She may be cold and hungry and very frightened and for her sake, I don't want to have to stay out here for the night negotiating. That's why we're going in now. We need a quick resolution. Our actions will be crucial in ensuring her safety. I'll hand you over now to Sergeant Brand for the firearms tactics.'

The little light that was left was fading fast, the jagged moor now just a black silhouette against the blood-red threads in the sky, the dying embers of the fiery autumn sunset. A portly man stepped forward and addressed the group. He too carried a rifle, slung over his back.

Dan suffered a wave of nausea and tried to breathe deeply. The fatigue was enveloping him again, making him feel light-headed. The sight of all these guns wasn't helping. He bent down to massage his ankle. It was aching unbearably and he wondered if he'd be able to follow the search team. Dartmoor's tors and rough terrain were hard enough to handle if you were fit. He didn't like to think about his own physical state. But he couldn't give up now, not when they could be so close.

He had a sudden idea. It felt insane, but tempting, surely worth trying. The briefing would go on for a few more minutes. He didn't stop to think, just limped over to the stream, sat down on a smooth rock, pulled off his walking shoe and sock and plunged his aching ankle into the freezing water.

A shock of delight rushed through his lethargic body, waking him, banishing the pain in an instant. The release brought an urge to laugh, lay back on the rock and let out wracking great guffaws.

Dan controlled himself, allowed a low chuckle to escape from his chest. What the hell was he doing? Amongst a group of armed police, closing in on a psychopath who was holding a young girl hostage, and he was sitting dangling his ankle in an icy Dartmoor stream. It felt good though, so good. It was liberating, a reprieve from the world of darkness where he'd spent the last unending hours.

He looked around, saw Adam standing rigid, gazing at the sergeant, his eyes wide and intent. He reluctantly pulled his foot out of the stream, dried it on his coat and put his sock and shoe back on, then walked over to the group. The ankle was still aching but felt much better than it had.

'The open moorland gives us a tactical problem,' the sergeant was saying. 'I don't want the risk of any officer being caught in a crossfire, so this is what we'll do. We'll surround the valley, but myself, Chief Inspector Breen, and PC Williams will approach from the front. We will be the talking team. We'll use the standard contain and negotiate tactics. Our side will be designated as white, the front.' He gestured at two men. 'Andy and Bill, you take the right, or red side. Helen and Mike, you're on the left, or green side.'

Dan looked over at the two figures Sergeant Brand was

pointing to in surprise. He hadn't realised any of the firearms officers were women.

'And Will and Stephen, you're on the back, or black side,' the sergeant concluded. 'Now, regarding the problem with the open moor. I want the surrounding officers to take cover as best they can, either lying down or behind boulders.' He looked around the group. 'That is for their own protection. You are not to open fire, unless Gibson makes a run for it, comes in your direction, ignores a challenge and is obviously armed and threatening. Is that understood?'

A low but sharp chorus of 'Yes sir,' came back.

'There is one oddity to this operation,' said the sergeant, beckoning Dan forward. He walked to the front, only hobbling a little now, stood beside Adam. 'This man, you may recognise. He's a TV reporter, Dan Groves, but he's here to help us, at Mr Breen's request. So remember, if it does come to opening fire, we have an unfamiliar face amongst us.'

Twenty pairs of eyes were fixed on him, and Dan felt a stab of fear. Why did it suddenly seem like he had a target painted on his chest? He hoped these people would recognise him, were good at their jobs. Particularly in this darkness. And under this pressure.

'Gibson has specifically singled him out to pass messages to, so Dan could be useful if we have to negotiate,' continued Sergeant Brand. 'That's why he's here.' He looked around the group. The faces were all calm, concentrating, focused, no hint of nerves. 'That's all then. Let's go.'

They began walking fast up the mine track towards the silhouetted pyramid of the Tor. Dan struggled to keep up, his ankle beginning to throb again. The stream had provided only a transient relief. The team moved silently in single file, scanning the land from left to right. A half moon had begun to rise, dusting the land with a silver light. Dan noticed his hands were shaking and his heart beating rapidly.

They crossed another trickling stream and the sergeant held up a hand. He whispered to four black figures at the front of the group and they left the track, heading silently out over the moorland in a line. Dan watched them go, the moonlight reflecting from the rifles slung over their backs. Another few hundred yards up the track and four more were sent the same way. They must be circling, surrounding the valley. Dan took advantage of the brief rest to kneel down and massage his aching ankle.

They carried on up the track. Adam was in front, and Dan noticed he was breathing heavily, marching mechanically. The other men seemed calm, strode precisely. Dan's foot caught a stone and he half fell, righted himself, the pain in his ankle biting hard. He swore silently, concentrated on the black outline of Higher Hartor Tor, a dark looming pile of strewn rocks against the moonlit skyline, tried to put the incessant throbbing out of his mind.

At the top of the track the sergeant again held up his hand. He produced a map from a side pocket, checked it. He pointed down a narrow and shallow valley running to the south of the Tor. The moonlight fell into it like a silver river, pitted only with black boulders of stray granite. Halfway down the valley, just a hundred yards away, was a small tent.

The sergeant beckoned to four more men and they divided, two each slipping down the opposite sides of the valley, well back from its lips. Another four were beckoned and began taking up positions around them, behind the granite rocks.

The sergeant stepped over to Adam. 'We're all in position now, sir,' he whispered. 'We're ready to go. How do you want to play this? We could try going in on the tent to surprise him and lift him before he has a chance to harm the girl. Or we could take it more gently and negotiate. The textbook says we surround, contain and talk, but this isn't a textbook situation. There are big risks in both options, sir, if he's got a hostage in there. I don't want to look like I'm passing the buck, but you're the senior officer here. I'm afraid it's going to have to be your call.'

Dan looked at Adam. The detective stood silently, staring down at the tent. Thank God I have a job where if I make a mistake, the only penalty I pay is a going over from Lizzie, he thought. If Adam gets this wrong and Nicola is hurt, or even dies ... he'll resign from the police and that's just the start of it. He'll never let himself forget it, let alone forgive.

What would I do, Dan wondered? How dangerous is Gibson? We know he's armed. Would he just shoot Nicola, then himself? I was sure he didn't want to harm anyone. But am I that sure? Sure enough to risk a young girl's life? Is this his grand final gesture, the deaths of them both? That would be a way of humiliating the police, wouldn't it? To show how they could have stopped him if they'd been smarter. And it would certainly bring him all the publicity he seemed to crave.

Dan looked down at the tent. It was silent, no sign of movement or life. Above them an owl hooted, making him start. All else was still, but he felt breathless. Was Gibson in there? Holding a gun over a bound and gagged Nicola, waiting for them? Or had he got it completely wrong and the man was miles away, laughing at them?

The cold was seeping into his body, but Dan scarcely noticed it. He knew he was afraid, of all these guns surrounding him, of what they would find in the tent and what would happen in the next few minutes.

He looked again at Adam. The detective was breathing heavily, almost panting, still staring at the tent. The sergeant waited for his word. Then he saw Adam flinch, his eyes widen, the sergeant's face, too, flicking down the valley.

Movement. A ruffling of the canvas, the unmistakeable sound of a zip slowly being drawn down. A figure was emerging from the flap of the tent, crouched at first, now standing tall, looking around. It seemed to nod approvingly.

A hand raised and swung sideways, back and forth in an exaggerated motion. It was a wave, Dan thought incredulously. The man was waving.

'Hello!' A familiar voice cut through the still air. 'Hello, my dear Dan, and Adam too. And lots of others no doubt. Welcome to Evil Coombe. You're just a little earlier than I expected, but I should have known better than to underestimate you. Anyway, it's no trouble. We're all ready for you. Hello, and welcome to my lair.'

There was a silence. Adam, Dan, the sergeant stared down in disbelief. Of all the things they might have been expecting, a friendly sounding, waving Gibson wasn't one.

'Talk to him,' whispered the sergeant. 'He wants to talk. Always get them talking if you can. You're covered if he tries anything.'

'Hello,' called Adam uncertainly, then louder. 'Hello … Mr Gibson.'

'Ah, Adam. Please, I think after all we've been through now we should be on first name terms. Please call me Edmund.'

'Hello, Edmund,' called Adam again, and Dan could hear the tension in his voice. Anger, awkwardness, stress, pressure, anxiety, fear, contempt, loathing, they were all in there.

'That's much better,' came the reply. 'Are you all right, Adam? You sound a little uptight. Hello to Dan too, by the way. I'm sure he's with you. You pair are so close it's touching. Hello, Dan!'

Dan glanced at the sergeant. 'Go on,' the man hissed. 'Try to keep him talking. While he's talking, he's no threat.'

'Hello, Edmund,' called Dan, stepping forwards so he was beside Adam. He felt as if he was walking out before a firing squad. 'Hello.'

'Now that's much better. The two stars of the show are on the stage. Well, three with me of course, but I was being modest. Now, may I ask, how did you find me? I tried to give you enough clues to bring you here, but not too soon. Was it the last hint I left on the quad bike that did it? I wasn't quite sure whether I should give you that one.'

'Yes,' called back Dan. 'Well, that combined with the others. I was in the Spray of Feathers and they had a big map of Dartmoor on the wall. I noticed the grid references coincided with the motorway numbers around Manchester. I should have got it sooner really.'

'I did worry you might have,' shouted Gibson. 'It was a very difficult call, how much to feed you. It was the part of my plan I was most worried about. But anyway, it's all worked out nicely hasn't it? And here we are again, having a lovely chat, just like we did back at the leisure centre.'

An insistent, unwelcome memory surfaced in Dan's mind.

What Gibson said about their final conversation. That it would be short. He felt a growing fear churning his stomach. If Gibson decided to shoot they'd make easy targets, standing here, upright in the moonlight.

'Ask him about Nicola,' whispered Adam.

'How's Nicola?' Dan called, trying to hide the fear in his voice.

'She's fine. Quite safe and very well. She's taken all this in her stride. It's been an adventure for her. She's begun to get a bit upset recently, but she's fine, don't worry.'

'I know you don't mean to hurt her, Edmund,' Dan shouted. 'I know you're no killer. I take it you still mean her no harm?'

'No harm at all.'

Dan felt Adam's foot tap his ankle. 'He wants to talk to you, not me. Keep going on about Nicola. Try to get her freed.'

The crushing weight of responsibility was suddenly back, assailing Dan again, a flare of burning anger too. It was an effort not to turn on Adam, grab his jacket, rant into his face – "I'm only a bloody TV reporter, you're the cops, why do I have to do this? What am I even doing here? Why make me the one who'll decide Nicola's fate? How will I feel if something happens to her ..."

He calmed himself. He had to concentrate, couldn't afford to make a mistake. But what to say? Standing here on Dartmoor, in the cold moonlight, in lethal danger, the life of a nine-year-old girl depending on him. Where was the inspiration, the clever words to save Nicola, and himself and Adam?

'Err ... good, Edmund,' was all he could manage. 'Great ... I knew you wouldn't harm her. So ... err ... what've you been up to?'

'Are we passing pleasantries, Dan?' came Gibson's amused reply.

'No ... I was just wondering ... where Nicola is.'

'She's fine, don't worry about that.'

'Good ... so can we ... err ... see her?'

'Don't you trust me?'

'Yes … of course … well …'

Beside him, Dan thought he heard Adam groan.

'Of course you don't trust me!' called Gibson, his voice still bizarrely jolly. 'I'm a madman, aren't I? I'm barmy! Totally bonkers! I abduct little girls because the police shot my dog! What a nutter!'

Another whisper from Adam. 'For Christ's sake don't wind him up. Get him back on to Nicola.'

Dan found he could hardly breathe to shout. 'So … err … can we see her, Edmund? Just so we're sure she's OK?'

'She's OK, Dan. You can see her in a minute, but you'll have to trust me for now. I think you know me well enough for that.'

'I'm not sure I do, Edmund.'

'Oh, come now. You must have realised I only need to make my little point. I don't want anyone to get hurt. You've been through my history. I'm hardly a killer. The failed warrior. The dog lover whose one true friend was taken from him by the police. I'm not alone in losing loved ones to their bloodlust you know.'

Dan waited, didn't know what to say. Behind him, the sergeant urged, 'Just keep him talking.'

Dan's throat felt very dry. He cleared it awkwardly, shouted, 'Those other two shootings, Edmund? Bodmin and Saltash? Are they what triggered this?'

'Spot on, Dan. I knew I could rely on you. That's why I chose you. I'm trusting you to report why all this happened fairly to the world. Someone needs to say something about what the police are like, and I'm glad it's been me. No one forces them to take up arms you know. They're all volunteers. They eagerly step forward and say, "Oh yes please, give me a nice shiny gun to carry, I want to look like a real man." They don't get extra pay for it. They don't get special promotions either. So there can only be one reason why a policeman wants to carry a gun, can't there? They enjoy it and they want to use it. It's as simple as that.'

'But you carried a gun too, didn't you Edmund? Isn't that

the same? You joined the army.'

'Yes, Dan, but I'm not sure I volunteered. I was pushed into it by my father, and as you know I didn't last long. I didn't like what I found and got out. You can't say that about the police. They seem to enjoy their guns all too much.'

'Well, they are constrained by the law, Edmund,' called Dan. 'They can't just go out shooting with impunity.'

A cold and mocking laugh echoed across the moonlit Coombe, a sinister sound in the still moor. It seemed to echo back and forth from the rocks, dying only reluctantly.

'I beg to differ Dan. As you'd no doubt expect, I've done a little research on police shootings. They've killed more than thirty people in the last dozen years or so in England. Some for terrible, obviously capital offences such as being Brazilian and trying to catch a tube train – poor Jean Charles de Menezez – or carrying a table-leg home after having it mended, like Harry Stanley. And guess how many of our admirable, law-upholding police officers have been prosecuted for those innocents' deaths, Dan?'

'I don't know, Edmund.'

'I'll give you a clue, shall I? It's a round number. Very round in fact.'

'None?'

'Well done, Dan! Exactly zero. The law allows them to go about their killing with complete impunity. And that's just for people. When they kill dogs, no one even raises an eyebrow. They have their guns and no one must spoil their fun.'

'And it's nothing to do with wanting to protect the public, Edmund?' called back Dan. 'Nothing to do with a sense of duty? Maybe the lack of prosecutions shows the law is working well. The officers had nothing to be prosecuted for. They did their duty.'

Dan sensed Adam flinch. 'Careful,' came a whisper from his side. 'I told you not to wind him up.'

'Ah, ever the professional, Dan,' shouted Gibson. 'Doing your job in being Devil's Advocate and putting the opposite view to me? But what is your job now? Are you a fully signed up quasi-policeman, or a journalist?'

Dan felt another surge of anger, tried to cap it, reminded himself a little girl's life could depend on what he said. But Gibson sounded just like Lizzie with those snide bloody digs of hers.

Adam's voice broke the silence. 'I'm the police officer here, Edmund, and I'd like to know if Nicola –'

'Shut up, Adam,' came the sharp reply. 'Don't interrupt. Didn't your parents teach you it's rude? I'm talking to Dan.'

Adam muttered something under his breath. 'What?' Dan whispered from the corner of his mouth.

'Just keep the bastard talking. Try to get him back on to Nicola.'

Dan took a long breath, called, 'So … is that why you chose me, Edmund? Because I let you down? Because you saw how much I love Rutherford, but I can still work with the police … the people who killed Sam?'

'Bingo, Dan! That's it, spot on. I admire and respect you, but I don't agree with you. So I thought you might benefit from a lesson, as well as the police. And here we all are, with our cards finally on the table.'

There was another silence. Dan thought he could see dark figures creeping around the sides of the valley near the tent, but it could have been his imagination. Next to him, Adam stood motionless, unspeaking. Dan suddenly felt very lonely, couldn't stop the thoughts cascading through his mind. Keep Gibson talking, but how? Where's Nicola? What the hell do I say? And what's this lesson he's going to teach me?

'Anyway, as I warned you, this conversation would have to be brief and so it must be,' came Gibson's voice again, but different now, not chatty, no longer amused, but harder, more purposeful. Dan saw the figure move, seemed to rummage at its waist. A hand reached out and waved again, but this time there was an object in it, shiny, with a thin barrel. Another shot of fear pulsed through him.

'This is my gun, Dan, in case there was any doubt. A beauty, isn't she? Not as nice as the ones the police get to carry, but she does a decent job. Not as pretty or modern as their MP5s and their pistols, but she'll do for me.'

Dan heard a hiss from behind. The sergeant. 'Shall we take him, sir?'

'Can you stun him?' whispered back Adam, his eyes fixed on Gibson.

'He's too far away. At that range we can't be sure to hit him and take him down with a baton round. It'll have to be a bullet.'

'Look, Dan, my gun,' called Gibson again, waving it towards them. 'And guess what I'm going to do with it?'

'Keep him talking,' urged the sergeant. 'Keep him looking this way.'

'Err … what are you going to do with it, Edmund?' called Dan, trying to keep his voice from shaking. His heart was pounding and he felt as though he could hardly breathe. He could see tiny red dots hovering on Gibson's chest like lethal flies, precursors of imminent death.

'I'm going to shoot someone, Dan. And guess who it's going to be?'

The figure raised the gun, pointed it towards them. Dan tried to make himself dive to the ground, but he was frozen, couldn't move. He was shaking hard, at any second expecting to feel his chest burst, explode as it was punctured by a bullet, the tension inside him instantaneously released, find himself sliding slowly into dark oblivion.

'Sir?' hissed the sergeant to Adam. 'Sir? Shall we take him? Sir!'

Dan was shaking helplessly, couldn't stop himself. He felt tears pricking at the corners of his eyes.

'Who, Edmund?' he managed, his voice thin, breathless. 'Are you going to shoot me?'

No reply. Slow seconds ticked past.

'Are you going to shoot Adam?'

Still no reply.

Dan found himself shouting. 'Who? For God's sake, who?'

'Sir?' hissed the sergeant again, but Adam was silent.

'No!' called Gibson sharply. 'I'm not going to shoot you, Dan. How could I? Nor Adam, however much he might deserve it.'

He turned back towards the tent, pointed the gun down into it. 'I'm going to shoot this little girl in here. Bye bye Nicola.'

Adam jerked into life. 'Take him!'

'Fire!' barked the sergeant into his radio.

A series of cracks echoed around Evil Coombe, bounced off the silent rocks, rumbled back and forth along the valley. The dark silhouette swayed, staggered, then dropped.

Adam was away, sprinting, tripping on some gorse, stumbling, almost tumbling, righting himself, running hard towards the tent. Dan ran after him, ignoring the agonising pain from his ankle. He could hear the blood's relentless pounding in his ears.

They reached the tent. Adam ignored the slumped, still figure, dropped to his knees and thrust his head inside.

There was a sleeping bag, some pots and pans, but otherwise it was empty. No sign of Nicola.

Adam lurched in, threw the sleeping bag aside, knocked the pots over, scrabbled at the ground sheet. There was nothing.

Dan breathed out heavily, wished his heart would stop thumping. He leaned back on his knees, fought a wave of dizziness. Adam was clawing at the ground, hitting out at the pots with a flaying arm, ripping at the sheet, panting heavily in his wild and hopeless search.

There was nothing. No sign of Nicola. Nowhere she could be hidden.

Stuck high up on the tent pole, Dan saw an envelope addressed to him. He pushed Adam's shoulder, got no response, reached out, grabbed the detective's flailing arms, calmed him. He took the envelope, opened it with shaking hands.

Inside were ten fifty-pound notes bundled together and a piece of paper covered with Gibson's writing.

"My Dear Dan,

"I couldn't resist leaving you one more note. It seemed a fitting end to our dance.

"I'm so very sorry I won't be able to say this in person, but I wanted to bid you farewell. It's been a pleasure. I only regret things couldn't haven't have turned out differently. In another life, we might have been friends.

"Have you managed to add it all up yet? It was simply about making the law bee sorry.

"The money is for Nicola to buy a pony. I promised her one and she certainly deserves it. I hope it's some recompense for what I had to put her through. I trust you to pass it on when you find her. You'll know how.

"My fondest regards and memories,

"Edmund."

'Where is she?' cried Adam, his voice breaking with desperation. 'Where's Nicola? Where the fuck is she?!'

He ducked back out of the tent. Armed police officers were cautiously converging on them. 'Has anyone seen the girl?' Adam cried. 'She's not in the tent.'

One of the marksmen knelt down by Gibson's body, checked the neck for a pulse, stood up again.

'He's dead,' the man said.

'Bollocks to him,' barked Adam savagely. 'I couldn't give a shit. Have any of you seen Nicola?'

Shaking heads, murmurs. 'Then where is she? Where the hell is she?' Adam cried, spinning around and staring at the silvery moorland. 'Get the helicopter back up. She must be around here somewhere. He can't have taken her far. Get the dogs in. I want them following any scent they can find. It's freezing. She won't last the night out here. I don't care that it's dark and I don't want to hear a word about fucking overtime. Get everyone you can and get looking for her. Now!'

'Yes, sir.' The sergeant began dictating orders into his radio.

Another of the police officers put on a pair of gloves and checked the gun lying by the side of Gibson's body. 'It's a replica,' he said quietly. 'It's never fired a bullet in its life. This guy used us to commit suicide. Suicide by cop.'

Adam ignored him. 'Dan, come here.'

Dan couldn't prevent his mind from pleading – no more. Please, no more. Make this ordeal end.

The adrenaline was leaking away, leaving him hollow, floating, lost. His ankle stabbed hard and another warm wave of soporific tiredness took him. He could feel his eyelids drooping, longed for the safety and warmth of his bed, the flat's doors and windows all safely locked, the reassurance of Claire holding him, Rutherford lying on the floor beside them. He still hadn't stopped shaking, or lost the churning in his stomach. He was sweating, despite the penetrating chill of the night. It was all he could manage not to be violently sick.

'Look at the note again,' rasped Adam. 'Look at it. I said – fucking look at it!'

The detective's venom forced Dan's eyes on to the paper.

'He talks about passing the money on to Nicola when we find her and we'll know how,' Adam panted. 'What does that mean?'

Dan made his parched mouth find the words. 'I think … it's probably exactly what it says. He's … he's expecting us to find her. By saying we'll know how, I'd guess he means the clues are all there in front of us again. And probably … in this note.'

Adam pointed a trembling finger. 'Then start thinking about it. Right now! No one's going home until we find Nicola. I'll call Eleanor and Michael and tell them what it says. They can start work on it from their end. You keep going over it until you find anything that might help us. I'll take any guesses, anything. Anything at all. Just come up with something. I reckon we've only got hours to save her.'

Adam turned and aimed a kick at Gibson's prone body, then another, and another. A lifeless arm flinched under the wild assault.

'You bastard,' he hissed. 'You evil bastard. Where is she?'

Chapter Twenty-one

THE KEYBOARD HAD BECOME the weapon of a murder fantasy.

"I want to kill him. I want to feel my fingers around his throat and watch him turn a beautiful blue as he gasps for air and the life ebbs out of him. I want to vent all this humiliation and rage in a wonderful murder. I want to sprinkle cyanide in the wine he loves so much and sit back, smiling as he drinks it. Then I'll count down the last seconds and laugh myself stupid as he pitches forwards, retches, clutches his chest and dies in a slow agony."

Claire stopped typing, sat back, hit the send button. The chatroom had become real.

It was decorated in aggressive red paint, but apart from that it was bare. The floor was cold concrete. A hard, white light hung from the red ceiling, no shade to soften its swinging bulb. Their voices echoed from the stone walls. The three of them were each slumped in the corners furthest from the grey, iron door, fearful of what would enter. One was groaning from her wounds, one huddled in a ball, the other shaking, continually eyeing the door, flinching with every sound that might be the precursor to another kicking.

She'd almost forgotten the long, freezing day on Dartmoor, the frustration, anger and despair at the failure to find Nicola. They'd been stood down and sent home, despite their protests. Come back tomorrow when you're fresh and ready to try again, the sergeant had said. We won't find anything tonight. Whiting had resisted the most, she'd noticed. He sounded as though he would have been happy to spend the night scouring the moor.

She'd got to know the two women in the chatroom over the last couple of hours. It was strange how the faceless computer link and shared suffering allowed you to free your demons in a way that would be impossible over a coffee with a close friend. Both the women told depressingly familiar stories, not so different from the one she'd invented.

Lynn's husband was a professional man, although she wouldn't say what he did. His job was high-powered, his pay breathtaking, certainly compared to what Claire earned as a Detective Sergeant. They had a young son who was a delight, a beautiful modern home near Tavistock on the western edge of Dartmoor.

She spent her days looking after the house, doing the shopping, meeting with friends for lunch, a few hours voluntary work at a charity shop. Much of the time he was a good husband, caring, understanding and attentive. But when he'd had a bad day, a row with a colleague or a competitor, when the little boy was safely in bed, that's when it would start.

At first it was a slap, then it grew to a punch, then a kick. Now his favourite was the cane. It was a thin stick, the kind used by gardeners for twining tomato plants. But it cut the air with a wicked, fearful whip. He'd hit her on her back where the thin wood bit into the tender skin, but the weals wouldn't show. She'd thought about leaving him, but what could she do? There was the boy to think of, the beautiful home too and she had no money of her own, no job, no one to help her, nowhere to go. She was trapped.

Jackie sounded younger. She had two children, but wouldn't say where she was from. She worked part-time in a supermarket, wasn't married, but she and her partner had been together since they left school. He'd beaten her from the start, a punch and a kick after a few beers was his favourite. And he liked his beer too, not quite an alcoholic, but four nights a week at the local was his average. She would lay awake and dread his return. But he was a decent man really, she said. She loved him, so she stayed with him. He only did it when he was drunk. He didn't mean it.

A couple of months ago the assaults had grown worse. He'd got in from the pub one night and called her downstairs. She'd been bad that week he'd said, spending too much money on the housekeeping. He'd taken a carving knife from the drawer. She stood still, frozen, terrified. He made her lift up her nightdress and cut her thigh. And that had become his favourite attack, a thin but bloody cut on the tops of her legs. She stayed with him, had nowhere else to go of course, but she loved him. She was sure he was a good man really, that he would change.

Zac whistled under his breath as he watched Claire's typing, exchanging messages with the two women. It was just after nine and they'd been online for almost two hours. He was trying to concentrate on the screen, but he couldn't help casting sly glances around her flat. He'd imagined being here a few times before, but in very different circumstances. Through the door into her bedroom he could see an inviting looking bed. It wasn't helping that some of Claire's small and lacy white knickers were hanging up on a drying rack in the corner of the bathroom.

'Claire,' he whispered as she waited for a message from Lynn to finish. 'What exactly are you hoping to find?'

'I don't know,' she replied, sipping at a glass of white wine. She'd offered Zac some but discovered he didn't drink. 'I'm just following a hunch. About the only possible link I can see between Crouch and the shootings is a computer. They've all got them and Crouch had a password hidden in his house. Apart from that, I don't know. I was wondering whether – maybe – he could get into these chat rooms and find some desperate woman who he could set up a conspiracy with.'

As spoke, she wondered at how thin it sounded. 'Well, something like that.'

Zac paused, then said, 'So you're playing a part that you hope …'

'He might intrude on, like some kind of guardian angel and offer me a way of getting rid of the man. I'm trying to sound as if I'm at the end of my tether and desperate enough to do anything.'

'Isn't that entrapment?'

She'd worry about that later. 'It might be if it works. For now, think of it as … fishing.'

He nodded, checked the array of electronics he'd linked to the side of her computer, watched her type out Zoë's next message.

"I don't know what to do either. But I suppose I'm lucky compared to you two. I don't have kids to worry about. It's a horrible thing to say, but I just dream about him being killed in a car crash, or some accident at work. I fantasise about the phone ringing and this voice saying "Prepare yourself for some bad news", then telling me he's dead. And instead of being shocked, I'm overjoyed. I just want to be free. I was only half joking with that message about wanting to murder him. I haven't told anyone this, but I've started planning how to kill myself. I just can't take much more."

'Whew,' Zac whistled. 'If that doesn't prompt your guardian angel to come calling, nothing will.'

If he's there, thought Claire. A big if. Her theory was feeling hollow.

They sat back to watch the response. Lynn and Jackie were both very kind thought Claire, the sort of women I'd like to meet. Both sent instant messages telling her never to think like that, not to give up, that something would happen to make life better. She wondered what they looked like, what their children were like, if any of their friends knew or suspected what they were going through. Why had life turned out this way for them?

She began typing a reply, thanking them, telling them they were keeping her going, giving her strength. 'If we don't get anything in the next hour or so, Zac, we'll call it a day,' she said. 'It's only a hunch and I've wasted enough of your time.'

He watched her fingers fly over the keyboard. "...you've made me feel so much better, thank you both. It's good to know I'm not alone. Maybe I will have the strength to plunge that knife into him, then stand up in court and tell the jury why I did it. I wonder if they could really convict me after all that I've been through."

'You sure you don't want a glass of wine, Zac?' she asked, leaning back from the laptop. 'It's the least I can offer you for helping me out.'

'No thanks. I gave up drinking at university.'

'Bad hangover?'

'No, I did something very silly.'

Claire turned to him with that lovely smile of hers, all white teeth and unspoken promise, he thought. 'Oh yes? Tell me more?'

She was interrupted by an electronic bleep from Zac's computer. 'What's that?' Claire asked.

'That,' he said, leaning forwards to see the screen, 'is the equivalent of a fish's nibble on your float. Look.'

There was a message, but in different type from the two women, bold, red letters.

"*Hello Zoë. Don't be alarmed, this is one of the site managers. Just a question. How desperate are you?*"

'It's someone who has superuser powers,' said Zac. 'The others can't see that message. It's just to you. Answer it in the same character you've been playing and I'll see if I can trace where it's coming from.'

Zac began fiddling with the keyboard he'd attached to hers via a tangle of wires and a black box. How do I answer, thought Claire? She could feel a surge of excitement. Not too keen, stay in character, don't frighten them off. Zoë would be wary, wouldn't she?

"Who is this?" she typed. "I thought I was talking to Lynn and Jackie. I didn't know anyone else was there."

The reply was swift. "*It's fine, don't worry. I'm someone who's helped other women before.*"

"What do you mean? How? Why? Who are you?"

"*Don't worry about who I am, just that I might be able to help you. Someone very close to me suffered in the way you are, and I want to try to save anyone else from going through the same.*"

Claire felt another shot of excitement. "How? How can you help me?"

"*Don't worry about that for now. First, I need to know how desperate you are. You must answer me honestly or I won't be able to help.*"

What would Zoë do now, she thought? She might pause, mightn't she? Be suspicious but also interested? Wait a minute to think. Claire forced herself not to type a reply, not yet.

'I've got it,' exclaimed Zac, his head bobbing up from

behind the computer. 'I've got the number it's coming from. But it's a mobile. It'll take a while to trace where exactly it is.'

'What?' said Claire.

'It's a mobile. This person's a site superuser. They've used their special privileges to interrupt and talk to you directly. But they're using a mobile phone and a laptop computer to link to the server.'

'Can you find out where it's being done from?'

'Yep, if you keep them talking for a few more minutes.'

Why would someone use a mobile and a laptop, Claire thought? It must only be so they could hide … because what they were planning was illegal? It could only be that, couldn't it? Crouch? Or was her imagination getting the better of her?

Claire turned back to the computer, began typing her next message. Stay in character, she warned herself. Don't get too keen, over-excited. Zoë would be heartened to find a sympathetic stranger, but still wary.

"I'm really desperate," she typed. "I don't know what to do. I'm thinking about ending it all. I never thought life would be this dreadful. I wake up every morning crying and I cry myself to sleep again at night."

Claire waited, tapped away at the table with a finger, staring at the screen. She reached for the wine bottle, but it was empty.

"*I may be able to help you.*"

She stared at the bold, red words. "How?"

"*I can't tell you that yet. We would have to meet.*"

"How do I know you're genuine? You could be anyone."

"*I'm genuine. I've helped women like you before.*"

"How do I know?"

"*You'll have to trust me. And I would have to trust you. We would both have a great deal to lose if we couldn't trust each other.*"

She stared at the screen. Could it be Crouch? It sounded like him. He typed messages in a similar way to how he spoke. Or was it just some pervert with a new way to prey on vulnerable women? She knew she couldn't stop now, had to find out.

"What would we have to do?" Claire typed clumsily.

"*We must meet. Not now, and not at night, but in a few days, in some place safe for us both.*"

Claire was about to reply when her radio crackled with a tinny voice. 'Emergency. All available officers to Dartmoor to join hunt for missing girl. Most urgent.'

They both stared at it, then Zac whispered, 'What do we do?'

'Shit,' Claire hissed. 'We could be on the trail of a double murderer cop …'

'But it could be entirely innocent.'

'Or we might be able to help find Nicola …'

Zac nodded. 'Nice dilemma. Well, I'm glad I do backroom work and it's not the sort of thing I have …'

'Shhh!' Claire interrupted.

She stood up, stared at her reflection in the mirror. Behind her taut face she could see Nicola, crying, her hands reaching out, begging for help, Whiting, his mouth set in that strange, sinister smile, and Crouch, a gun in his hand, calmly aiming it right between her eyes.

What was going on? The search was supposed to have been suspended for the night. She radioed in.

'Male shot dead, girl still missing,' the harassed operator replied.

A man shot dead. Dan?

'Who?' she gasped. 'Was it … a cop?' Claire hesitated. 'Or someone with the cops?'

'No. Suspect shot dead. Girl still missing.'

She couldn't hide the relief, leaned heavily back against the wall. What state would Dan be in if he was part of the shooting? Did he need her there? Or would he put on one of his typical macho shows and pretend he was better off facing the danger alone?

Where was Nicola? Should she go now and help in the search? She'd found the Scout Hut … maybe she could find the girl. But what about Crouch? If it was him online, this could be their only chance to catch him. She'd love to see Whiting's face if she did …

There was another electronic bleep from the black box next to the computer. 'Got him!' whispered Zac. He clicked at his keyboard. 'The superuser … he's close. He's in … hell, he's just up the road. In the middle of a field, according to this map.'

'What? A field?'

'No, it's not a field, sorry. It just came up green on my screen. It's an allotment. In Lipson. Right in the middle of Plymouth. Just five mins up the road.'

Claire closed her eyes, massaged her forehead with her fingertips. Zac took a couple of steps towards her, stopped. 'What do we do?'

She didn't have the luxury of time to think. 'We go hunting. If we don't get him in twenty minutes we go after Nicola.'

'We? We?'

She grabbed her coat and car keys, then remembered the wine. 'You'll have to drive,' she said.

'Me?' said Zac. 'Where are we going? To the allotment? But I'm a boffin. I don't do field work. I wouldn't know how. It might be dangerous. I've never been on a stake-out. I don't like …'

'Then it's time you learned. It'll help you understand CID better. But how am I going to keep him on line so we can get there?'

'How about … telling him you want to hear more, but you've got to pop away for ten minutes to splash some water on your face and take this in,' said Zac breathlessly.

Claire began typing fast.

Dan had lost his sense of time. All he could feel was a vague, blank hopelessness. He stared up at the half moon, serene in the night sky, the silent, silver moorland around him. He looked longingly down to the south, towards Plymouth, the safety of his flat and beloved dog, the home that would mark the end of these six days of madness. The moon's gentle light was making the sea glitter.

The thundering roar of a hovering helicopter forced him

back to the moor, its pure white beam of searchlight sweeping over him. The marksmen had spread out across Evil Coombe and around Higher Hartor Tor, but they'd found no trace of Nicola. Dan could see the swinging flashes of torchlight as more search teams jogged up the mine track, heard the odd crackle of a radio. Adam's scramble call for every available officer to join them had had instant effect.

An ambulance crew arrived to take Gibson's body away and forensics officers were marking the area around the tent, lighting it with staccato flares of camera flashes. The moonlight faded, softened by some trails of wispy cloud that had gathered in the starry sky. It was growing colder still and his ankle was throbbing with new vigour. He couldn't stop fantasising about the safety and warmth of his bed.

Gibson's last note had been dictated to Eleanor and Michael. Dan too had looked through it, time and again, tried to focus his thoughts but seen nothing. His brain felt numb, sluggish, unable to find the strength to concentrate. He kept reliving the moment Gibson had been shot. It was the first time he'd seen someone die, and so close, right in front of him. The thought made him shudder.

Why him? Why pick on him? Why did Gibson have to invite Dan into his deranged world? And why had he left this final riddle, the last chance to save Nicola, laying the pressure of cracking it so heavily on him? He tried to look again, work through the note, stare at it until he came up with a solution, but the cold and fatigue were weighing him down.

Eleanor had broken the part of the code that was no longer any use to them. Band of Gold and its constituent elements, she'd explained quickly, meant the atomic symbols and numbers of the words. Ba was barium, atomic number 56, Nd was neodymium, number 60, gold was atomic number 79. Combine them and you had 605 679, the exact grid reference of Evil Coombe. She'd worked it out as they were closing in on Gibson, just too late.

Adam stalked up and down by the tent, his eyes wide and wild. The tent had been thoroughly searched, but nothing found that might give them a clue where Nicola was. The helicopter's thermal imaging camera had found no trace of anything that might be a young girl. She must be inside somewhere, Adam had said, shielded from the camera. She had to be …

No one dared to mention the other possibility. That she was lying cold and dead on the lonely moor, her body waiting to be discovered in the morning light.

'We're running out of time,' Adam croaked again to the police officers and volunteers circled around him. 'Every second we waste there's less chance we'll find Nicola alive. Remember that. Be relentless in your searching. The helicopter hasn't seen anything obvious, so check in any buildings or trees that might shield her from the camera. The dogs haven't found a scent either. But she can't be far from here. She can't be.' Adam's voice almost cracked. He sounded pleading.

'He didn't have the time to take her far. So we'll use the tent as the centre of our search and work outwards in square kilometres. And we will continue doing that until we find her. And we will find her alive. Understand?'

The search teams headed off in their assigned directions, black shapes slipping quickly across the moor, flashlights flitting between them.

Dan leaned against a granite boulder by the tent and pulled his coat tighter. The cold was penetrating. He'd lost all feeling in his hands and feet, but not his ankle. It was still throbbing angrily. He had an odd memory of how much heat was lost from the head and wished he owned a hat.

The memory of Gibson's death rose again in his mind. The gunshots echoing, the instantaneous transition from life to death, the fresh corpse pitching forwards in the darkness. He stared down at his notebook, the copy of Gibson's last message scrawled in capitals. Dan tried to force his brain to think, to see the answer, but he was so tired, so very tired. He longed just to lie down on the ground and close his eyes, let the comfort of sleep carry him away from this place of death and despair.

'Come on Dan. Come on … come on … you got the last

one.' Adam stumbled alongside him. His voice was so broken now it was difficult to hear. 'Work on that note … work on it. If ever I needed your help it's now.'

Dan looked down at his notebook again, black letters on silver paper in the dappled moonlight. His eyes could hardly focus. 'I'm doing my best Adam, but I can't see anything. I'll keep trying, don't worry.'

'Don't worry? There's a little girl out there, alone in the freezing cold, about to die, and you say don't worry?'

Dan was too tired to bite back. He felt as though the entire world was watching him, expecting him to solve the riddle, relying on him. His eyes stung and he wondered if tears were gathering. 'I'm sorry, that was a stupid thing to say. I'll keep looking at it, I promise you that.'

Adam paused, looked at him. His tone changed, a moment of realisation. 'You think she's dead?'

It was the first time Dan had heard his friend raise the possibility. They'd all been thinking it, the fear lurked everywhere here, but no one had mentioned it. No one could. They had to hope.

'No, I don't,' he replied as forcefully as he could. 'I don't think Gibson's a killer. I think he wanted to end his own life and decided to do it in a way that would make some sort of statement. But I don't think he's a killer. I think she's alive somewhere.'

'But if we don't find her soon …'

Adam's words tailed off. He looked up at the sky. 'Is there a clue in that last letter?' he rasped.

'I'm sure there is. It's all part of his game. It's not just to taunt you. I know it sounds bizarre with him being dead, but I think it's partly to cover him. It's so he could say that if you don't find Nicola it's because you weren't clever enough to do it, not that he didn't give you every chance.'

'He's been ahead of us so far,' said Adam quietly. 'All the bloody way. He's led us a merry dance. He's taken the piss out of me, that's for certain. He planned the whole thing, right up to his death at the hands of our marksmen. He knew we couldn't risk using a baton gun at that range. He knew we'd have to shoot him if we thought there was a threat to Nicola. Now he's got what he wants and he's out of it, leaving us with the torment of trying to find her. Game, set and bloody match to him.'

'Then let's try and win the final battle and the war,' said Dan, pulling himself up from his rock and trying to dig out an enthusiasm he didn't know how to feel. 'Let's find Nicola. I'll look at the last note again and keep going until I come up with something.'

He was almost real now. She thought if she could just stretch out far enough into the darkness, she could stroke his sleek coat. But the ropes held her ankles tight, wouldn't allow her the freedom to go to him.

She didn't know why she had to do it, just that she did. She kept thinking of the pony. Jet-black he was, tall and strong to carry her around like a princess. A Black Beauty, just like the book Mummy had read to her in bed, back in the summer when the sunlight slipping into her bedroom had made it difficult to sleep. She'd brush him every day and enter him in shows. He'd always win. All the other girls would be jealous of her and Beauty. She couldn't wait to see their faces. And Mum would be so proud.

She'd stopped crying. There was no one to hear, no one to help. She understood that now. It was dark and cold and she shivered in her duffle coat. She had been frightened of the dark, but now she was almost used to it. Back at home she'd been scared of the monsters that lived under her bed. She knew that if she put a foot onto the floor they'd grab for her ankle, pull her down into their world. The thought would keep her awake until Mummy came to scare them away by cuddling her and stroking her hair.

At home the darkness was never complete, not even in the cold winter time. There was always a light under the door, or from the street outside. Here there was no light, and for the first few hours she'd been so scared of the monsters it hid. She'd heard them, the creaks and groans they made and she'd panted in fear, her eyes wide, scanning the blackness for the attack. She sobbed and squirmed and cried out until she understood there were no monsters here. There was nothing apart from her. The darkness was her only companion.

Where had Ed gone? Why had he tied her ankles? He'd said it was to keep her safe, stop her wandering and getting lost. Some of his friends would be back very soon to get her and they had to know exactly where she was. This was the last part of their adventure. When Ed's friends came, he said, they would bring her birthday pony. Mummy would come too and cuddle her for being so brave and clever in her adventure.

Thoughts she hardly dared to face kept coming to her. Did she still trust Ed? The adventure had been strange, and not always fun. But if she didn't trust him, what would happen to her now?

Somehow, she knew she couldn't think it. She focused on the pony, cantering around a beautiful green paddock.

She was thirsty, so thirsty. And she was hungry too. She'd finished the water and bread Ed had left. She thought she'd heard voices and a noise, like a helicopter thundering above, but it had gone away. She'd shouted and cried but no one had come. She'd picked and pulled at the ropes, but they hadn't moved and she'd sat back in the blackness and waited. There was nothing else to do.

There were no monsters, no Ed, no Mummy, no friends, no pony, no one. It was just her.

Another loud creak split the darkness. Before, she'd thought it was one of Ed's friends coming to get her and she sat up, waiting eagerly. But now she'd lost that hope. There were always creaks here, but never a smiling face afterwards to pick her up, wipe the dirt from her cheeks and take her to the pony.

When she got back to school she would beat Vicky at hopscotch. She'd ask Mummy if they could have a grid on the patio in the back garden so she could practice. Mum wouldn't mind. She'd probably want to play too. She liked joining in her games. She loved her mum. She missed her, missed her so much. When she saw Mummy, she could have her hair brushed. It felt tangled. Mum never liked her hair to be tangled. A girl's got to make the best of herself, she always said, got to look good for the world.

She started crying again at the thought, couldn't help it. She wanted Mummy here now, to make the darkness and the cold and the hunger and thirst go away. Tears trickled down her cheeks. It was so dark here. So dark and quiet and scary. Her ankles hurt where they were tied together and her fingers too from picking at the plastic ropes.

She leant over to try again, pulling at the tight knots, trying to find a free end. She thought the ropes were a little looser now, wriggled her feet, found a new inch of freedom. She pulled at the knot, pushed her ankles against the constricting pressure. They were sore where the plastic had rubbed at her skin, but the rope was looser now. A little more and she could free her feet, run to Mummy and her pony. Her ankles wriggled again.

There was another groaning creak in the darkness, and she sat still, listening, waiting, hoping. The long seconds passed, but no one came. No one. It was just her. Alone. In the darkness.

She shivered in the cold and rubbed her head against her shoulder to dry the tickling tear. But another followed it, then another, far too many to dry.

Chapter Twenty-two

ZAC PULLED THE CAR up on the road by the black metal railings. He chose a long space, was too nervous to try to park. Claire was out before he'd even stopped moving, on tiptoe, peering over the fence. He locked the car and jogged over to join her.

The allotment must have been half a mile long, an oasis of tiny plots of farmland in the concrete city. There were rows of beans and cabbages and carrots, all neat and lovingly tended, shaded silver in the moonlight. And there were wooden sheds too, lots of them, at least seven or eight with dull lights glowing. Zac could hardly believe it. Did so many people really come here at night? Why? To escape their miserable homes? They couldn't do much gardening in the dark, surely.

'We haven't got long,' whispered Claire. 'He might get suspicious and give up in a few minutes. Besides, I want to know what's happening on Dartmoor. We'll have to split up to check the sheds.' She pointed to the right-hand side of the allotment. 'You do the four down there. You know what he looks like, don't you?'

'Vaguely,' answered Zac, wondering what he'd got himself into. He'd never been on an operation before and this was a police marksman they were hunting. What if he had a gun? He thought of Claire's flat, those little white lacy knickers hanging up invitingly. He couldn't let her down now.

'Well hopefully he'll still be on a computer,' she said. 'That'll give him away. Keep looking over at me occasionally and I'll do the same for you. If you see him, turn your mobile phone's light on and wave it.'

Zac was going to protest but she was up on the fence, over it, away, striding alongside a line of runner beans, down towards the first shed. He didn't have time to admire her athleticism. He took a deep breath and hoisted himself up on the fence, making sure he didn't catch the new designer jeans he'd bought that afternoon. Zac dropped heavily onto the soft earth and walked fast towards the first shed.

He could hear a radio coming from inside, sneaked slowly up, bent double, alongside a bramble bush. There was a rhythmic wooden thudding in the shed, then a mumbled oath. He slipped up to the grimy, square window, raised his head, peeked carefully in.

A middle-aged man was standing over a replica of what looked like HMS Victory, trying to force a mast into the hull. Zac stared in amazement, then ducked back down and started off towards the next shed.

Claire stumbled over some long dead roots protruding from a compost heap, righted herself. Her first shed was just ahead. She checked the ground, slid towards the thin window. There were old and faded blue curtains drawn, but just a chink of light at the bottom. She lifted her head, looked in.

An old man was leaning hungrily over a workbench, his toothless mouth open, a pornographic magazine spread out before him. She blinked hard, ducked back down, moved quickly towards the next hut.

'Where is she?' moaned Adam, pacing back and forth in a gap between two granite boulders, rubbing his hand through his hair. 'Where the hell is she?'

They'd been searching for two hours and found no trace of Nicola. Adam hadn't stopped moving, his eyes wild, manic, always pacing, continually barking into the radio, demanding reports, updates, any hint of progress.

The moor's ominous quiet had returned, the helicopter completing its thunderous sweeps. The search teams were moving out, further away. Every extra step from here took more time and lessened the chance of finding Nicola alive. But they had to keep trying. Dan checked his watch. It said midnight. His brain registered that meant it was later, but he couldn't focus on the simple sum to work out what the time was.

He leaned against his rock, shivering hard in the vicious cold. A slight wind had slipped in off the sea, waving the moorgrass and gorse and penetrating his coat. His ankle throbbed worse than ever. In his frozen hand he held his notebook, kept staring at it, willing the words to make sense, to tell him where Nicola was, but nothing came. The cold and his tiredness had built a layer of muffling thickness around his mind.

He closed his eyes, then opened them again, knew he couldn't afford the risk of even fantasising about sleep.

'Have you come up with anything yet?' barked Adam.

'No,' Dan managed. He didn't have the strength to say anything else.

'Breen to base,' said Adam into his radio. 'Any news on the efforts to crack the code?'

There was a pause, then the speaker crackled into life. 'Nothing yet, sir. They're still working on it.'

Adam breathed out hard, swore. 'She's dying out there Dan. Dying.'

He didn't know what to say, just stared back down at his notebook and Gibson's final clue. He tried to stop his mind longing for his bed and a cuddle from his dog. He shifted his weight and found his feet unsteady, uncertain how to hold him.

Dan wondered where Claire was. Would she come round to the flat when this was over, hold him, comfort him? He ached for that. He longed for someone to cuddle and warm him, chase away the memory of Gibson's death and the thought of a little girl, frightened and all alone, dying on the freezing moor. He lusted for sleep, but feared the dreams it would bring.

Adam staggered over, put a hand on his shoulder.

'Come on, Dan,' he croaked, his eyes angry red and bloodshot. 'Come on. All those other things we've done together have been games. Just bloody games. Catching a gang of murderers was just a game compared to this. It didn't save anyone, did it? It was only about justice, and that's just a game. Cracking McCluskey's riddle was just a game. A big bloody game. But this isn't. It's about saving a little girl. Come on, mate. Give it one last try. Find her for me.'

Dan nodded, aching with tiredness. He looked back down at his notebook, trembling in his hands. He screwed up his eyes, forced the words into focus. What was here that could tell them where Nicola was? He knew there was a clue, was sure of it.

Something stirred his reluctant brain, something deep in his subconscious, frozen by the relentless cold and numbing fatigue. What was it? A memory of doing cryptic crosswords on trains, long journeys, bored with his book, time to kill. He still did them occasionally when he had the time, mainly on holidays, basking in the glorious sun, dangling his bare feet into a cool, welcoming pool.

He longed for the warmth of that sun now, a relaxing lounger and a pint of cold lager. Sun and warmth, as far from this place of darkness and despair as ever he could be. He gritted his teeth, forced the vision away. He had to concentrate. Adam's imploring eyes were set on him. What was it in Gibson's last note that was teasing him?

He dragged his eyes across the words. "Have you managed to add it all up yet? It was simply about making the law bee sorry."

He nudged Adam. 'There, look. There's something there.'

Adam squinted down at the notepad. 'What do you mean?'

'There's something odd. Look at the spelling. He's written "bee" rather than be.'

'So what? So bloody what?' the detective spat. 'So he's an ignorant bastard and can't spell, so bloody what? We're talking about finding a dying girl here and you're worrying about his spelling ...'

Dan felt a fire of anger burst through him, clearing his brain with its burning energy.

'For fuck's sake Adam, I'm trying to help! He's not bloody ignorant is he? That's the last thing he is. He's planned all this and led us a merry dance. So he's hardly fucking ignorant, is he?'

Adam stared at him, quietened by the outburst. 'OK then ... what are you saying?'

'I'm saying he deliberately spelt "bee" wrongly.'

'Which means what?'

Dan forced his leaden brain to keep thinking, push away

the desire to lie down and stop trying, abandon himself to the temptation of surrender.

'It means,' he said heavily, 'that he had to fit an extra letter into that line. The "e" on the end of be.' He stopped to think again, stared at the notebook. 'It means he's telling us the answer is in there. He wants Nicola to be found, so he's given us a bloody great hint how. Which means it's either an acrostic, or an anagram. It must be. Radio to Eleanor back at base.'

Adam did, told her what Dan was thinking. 'They were working along the same lines,' he said. 'Michael's run the note through his computer programs but he hasn't come up with anything.'

Dan leaned back against his boulder, tried not to let the feeling of defeat take him. But it was close now and strong, growing irresistible. How much longer could he go on, fighting this cold, stupefying fatigue and hopelessness? If a computer couldn't crack it, with its power and vocabulary of hundreds of thousands of words, what chance did he have?

Another thought surfaced, a new hope, bringing unexpected strength. Dan didn't know where it had come from, but he hung on to it. It was a chance, a possibility where before there was none. What if the word they were looking for wouldn't be in a computer's memory?

He forced himself to follow the idea. What could that mean? Only a bizarre place name, surely? The type that Dartmoor specialised in.

He felt a rush of adrenaline, took out a pen. 'It's an anagram,' he whispered. 'It has to be. And you know what? I hate anagrams.'

Dan calmed himself, focused his strength. An anagram … so, what letters was he looking for? What in the note could indicate where the anagram lay?

"Bee" had to be part of it, otherwise why would it be misspelt? He let his eyes run over that line. "Making the law bee sorry." And making could mean "law bee sorry" would form the answer, couldn't it? Spin the letters of "law bee sorry" and you had it.

302

He felt another surge of hope, invigorating his mind with its extraordinary power. It was here, he was sure of it. Dan did as he had so many times when faced by anagrams in crosswords. He took all the letters he thought could be involved and wrote them at random, stared at them.

WORLYEBSERA

Nothing came to him, so he wrote them again in a different order.

BSAWOLEEYRR

Still nothing. Then again, a new order.

ORBEWARSELY

Still nothing. The precious hope was starting to die.
Once more. He had to keep trying.

ELSYBAEWRRO

Dan's eyes locked on the paper, fluttering slightly in the breeze. Now there was a hint of something, he was sure of it. There was a nuance of sense. He could see a pattern. It was here.

Again Dan wrote the letters down in a circle, and this he time saw it.

'Aaagghh!' he moaned, slumping back on his rock. 'Shit! The bastard! It was right in front of me.'

'What?' urged Adam, staring at the notebook, then back at Dan. 'What? Have you got something? What? What is it?'

'It's been staring us in the bloody face. Look.'

He wrote it down for Adam to see. Together they gaped at the word.

EYLESBARROW

'Call the search teams back,' panted Dan, suddenly breathless. 'She's in the old tin mine.'

Zac crept up on the next hut. Music was leaking from inside, but this time it was loud, a thumping bass beat. The shed seemed to be creaking in time with it. He stood up slowly and peered in at the window, then looked away immediately, stepped back and snagged his jeans on a pile of wood.

He swore under his breath. A semi-naked young couple were grappling in a passionate clinch on the shed's patchy carpet, all writhing arms and legs. There was only one thing worse than not getting any sex, and that was having to watch other people enjoying it.

He checked his jeans. No rip thankfully, just a loose thread. They'd cost almost a hundred pounds. Bought to impress Claire, and she hadn't even noticed. He swore again and picked his way carefully towards the next hut.

The shed Claire was sneaking up on was silent. There was a faint light in the little square window, but thick curtains were drawn fast across it. She heard a muffled movement inside and shrunk back, crouched by a line of carrots, tiny explosions of spraying leaves in the dark soil. She waited, but no one emerged. Edged closer. Was it her imagination, or could she hear the tapping of a keyboard?

Claire stood up slowly at the window, tried to look in, but the curtains were tightly drawn. She inched around the side, treading softly in the earth, saw a slit of light escaping from a gap in the wooden slats. She craned her head around and put her eye to it, squinted in, had to raise a hand to her mouth to stop herself gasping.

There, inside the shed, packing up a keyboard was Crouch. He sipped quickly from a flask and buttoned up his anorak. He kept glancing over his shoulder. She got the feeling he was in a hurry. She stepped back from the shed and manoeuvred herself behind a compost heap, knelt down, tried to control her fast, shallow breathing. She watched as he stepped down from the shed, switched off the light, fumbled with a padlock, clicked it into place, then strode off fast towards the line of streetlights on the main road.

She looked around. She couldn't see Zac but she thought he was in the opposite corner of the allotment, safely out of the way.

Crouch got to the fence and hurried out through a gate. He was moving fast. Did he know they were on to him? She hadn't planned it this way, but she couldn't take the risk of him escaping. And she wanted to get to Dartmoor, to Dan and the hunt for Nicola.

Claire picked her mobile out of her pocket and made the call. She'd kept the number in its memory so one day she could tell the man what she thought of him. But this was more important than revenge. Or was it revenge of a sort? No, she knew exactly what it was, but she grimaced at the thought and almost laughed. Almost.

It was her duty.

Chapter Twenty-three

THE BLACK MOUTH OF the long abandoned Eylesbarrow Tin Mine gaped at them, the silver moonlight swallowed by its hungry depths.

'Adit,' said Dan softly. 'The old word for the shaft. And there was Gibson asking if I'd managed to add it all up yet. I was stupid. I should have got it sooner.'

The adit had been partly blocked up with skeletons of rotting timber and great granite boulders, glued together with earth and soil. When they'd first got here Dan had thought he'd been wrong, that the entrance was impassable. He and Adam had exchanged glances and he'd felt the freezing cold and tiredness assail him again, the despair lurking close, a last hope brutally extinguished.

It was only when they walked into the mouth of the tunnel that they saw it. There was a thin gap at the side of the barrier, a little wider than a person and about four feet high. It was why none of the search teams had thought about venturing into the old mine. The entrance was hidden until you were upon it.

Dan peered in but could make out nothing. It was the purest blackness he'd ever seen and it unnerved him. He called out, shouted hello and his words rolled around the shaft, slowly died away.

The search teams gathered at the entrance. 'I'm under orders to wait for a caving expert,' Adam said quietly. 'The High Honchos tell me it's too dangerous to go in alone. Our precious Health and Safety regulations must be obeyed. The tunnels are a hundred years old. They could collapse at any time.'

A man at the back spoke up. 'How long before the expert gets here, sir?'

'I was hoping you'd ask that. A few hours, maybe more.'

A brief silence, some groans and then angry swearing.

'Quite,' agreed Adam with a forced calm. 'So I'm going in. No one else has to, I want to make that plain. But …'

The man at the back interrupted. 'We're coming. We're all coming.'

Adam looked over the group, nodded. 'Thank you. That's what I thought you'd say. Right, we've managed a brief call to one of the Dartmoor Rescue Team who knows this place. I'm told there'll be branches forking off at regular intervals. Gibson can't have taken her far inside. We'll go in teams of two. I'll lead the way and take the first fork, the rest of you continue doing the same until we've covered all the forks we have people for. Just pray we find her before then. Let's go.'

Adam ducked down and clambered into the adit, his flashlight firing blazes of reflections from its damp, granite walls. Dan paused, then followed, his feet sliding on the slippery earth, his ankle stabbing a painful rebuke. He couldn't help but keep glancing at the roof, checking its stability. He could hear the rest of the search team climbing through the wedge of a gap behind him, the odd muttered oath echoing around the tunnel.

As soon as they were all inside the calling began. Loud voices, reverberating in the darkness. Reassuring. Comforting. Hoping.

'Nicola … Nicola … Nicola …'

Dan had expected to have to crouch, but the shaft was tall enough to stand upright. The floor was gravelly, riddled with puddles and pools of still water, the walls jagged where the wound of the shaft had been bored into the body of the moor. It sloped slowly downwards, wide enough for a small hand cart.

Dan imagined the Victorian miners bringing their hard-won tin back to the surface, the rumble of their chatter and the creaking of the cart echoing from the rock. He remembered from his days covering the environment that the hardy Dartmoor ponies were ideal for the task of hauling the precious tin from the mine to the smelting works.

The air was still and silent, tinted with a faint hint of mustiness and damp. The cold enveloped him. Dan hobbled along behind Adam, following his dancing flashlight, glad of the torches of the men behind helping to illuminate his path.

His ankle was hurting hard, an insistent, jarring pain and he kept looking down as he walked, fearful of aggravating it with a slip or glancing blow on the jutting rock. He wondered how long he'd be able to walk. The pain seemed to be stretching further up his leg and was growing ever more difficult to bear. Each step made him wince.

And all around him the voices – 'Nicola … Nicola … Nicola …'

The tunnel turned to the left and narrowed, grew steeper in its descent. Adam stopped, shouted, 'Hello! Nicola!' into the blackness. He waited until the echoes had faded, tilted his head to one side, listened intently. They all did. There was nothing apart from the shallow breathing of some of the search team, the fog of their breath drifting slowly across the beams of the flashlights.

Adam walked on, but quickly came to a fork. To the left the tunnel was narrower. To the right it looked like the main route down into the heart of the mine. Adam stopped again, stared for a moment, then turned.

'Dan and I will go left,' he croaked. 'The rest of you follow the main shaft. Split up and cover any other forks as we agreed.'

Dan felt a knot of fear twist his stomach. He didn't like confined spaces, but hadn't mentioned that to Adam. He hadn't had the chance. No one had asked him if he was OK about venturing into the old mine.

He swallowed hard and limped after the detective, looking back over his shoulder to watch the file of men and their floating flashlights fade into the blackness, their cries following.

'Nicola … Nicola … Nicola …'

The tunnel turned left again and narrowed further. It was just wide enough for a couple of people to walk side by side. Dan felt his fear rise, struggled to control its squeezing grip. He tried to distract himself, imagining the coming weekend, walking Rutherford, cuddling Claire, a few beers. He deserved them. He needed them.

He followed Adam's silhouette down the track, his feet

crunching on the tiny gravel of the pieces of loose rock littering the shaft floor. He studied where he was walking carefully, then lifted the leg of his jeans and stared down at his ankle. Was it his imagination, or did it look swollen under the sock? Adam stopped suddenly and Dan nearly walked into the back of him.

'What?' he whispered.

'Listen.'

The two men stood in silence, listening hard. Adam took a deep breath, yelled, 'Nicola ... Nicola!'

They waited. There was a sound, faintly perceptible, but it was there. They kept waiting, kept listening. It was difficult to make out, but seemed to have a higher pitch, almost melodic. Adam walked quickly on, thirty yards or so, around another corner in the shaft. Dan hurried to keep up despite the pain in his leg. He didn't want to be left alone in this place.

'Nicola ... Nicola ...'

Again Adam stopped. Now they could definitely hear something. It sounded like a child's voice, high and persistent, continually calling. He walked on, faster this time, Dan struggling behind.

The shaft suddenly opened out into a much larger expanse of blackness, like a small cave. The noise was closer now, but it was familiar, too familiar. Dan spun his flashlight up onto the wall and picked out a tiny stream trickling down the shining rock. It was dripping from a crag and carving a shallow bowl into the granite below, the pathetic endeavour of scores of years.

Adam closed his eyes and let out a long groan. 'I thought it sounded like a kid crying. I thought we'd found her.'

'I did too,' replied Dan. 'Wishful thinking, I suppose. We made the noise what we wanted it to be.' He placed the flashlight on the floor, bent down to massage his aching ankle.

'Come on,' growled Adam. 'We haven't got time to stop.'

He set off again and now the tunnel closed in on them, this time sloping upwards for a few yards, then turning back down. It was narrowing too, now only wide enough for one person at a time. Dan felt himself starting to shake, but he wasn't sure whether it was fear of the black, constricting passage or his aching tiredness. His mind taunted him with a memory of a long forgotten story he'd read at school, about a man who went looking for his missing sweetheart in a labyrinth and was never seen again.

He kept his eyes on Adam's figure, watched the flashlight beam slide off the damp tunnel walls. His mind started to drift. Should he have got Gibson's clues sooner? They seemed very simple now he knew the answers. How would he feel if Nicola was hurt when they found her? What if she was dead? Was he even sure she was down here at all?

She must be, he thought. She must be. The clues all made sense, didn't they? But still the doubt nagged at him, wouldn't let go. Could this be Gibson's final triumph, to send them down here on a hopeless quest?

'Nicola … Nicola … Nicola …'

Adam slowed, pressed himself against the wall of the tunnel and slid carefully around a rusting pile of jagged metal. Dan did the same, glancing at it as he passed. There were sharp angles of intersecting, reddened girders and what looked like it had once been a many-spoked wheel, propped up against the shaft wall. Some flaking bolts formed a small pile under its broken circumference.

Adam disappeared into the darkness and Dan moved faster, chasing the floating light, eager to catch up. He was sure the tunnel was narrowing again, stretched out a hand to touch its craggy edge as though wanting to hold it back. He glanced again at the roof, couldn't stop wondering just how stable it was.

How much longer would they keep walking? How much longer could he go on? He was moving robotically, each step of his leaden legs a victory of willpower. The tiredness was washing over him, an insatiable, sapping tide.

How far were they underground? How would they know if another of the search teams had found Nicola? When would Adam decide they'd gone far enough, that she couldn't possibly be here? He knew the answer. The detective would stop only when the passage they were following ended. When

310

he was sure. When he would believe he'd done all he could.

The shaft turned to the right and Adam halted abruptly. Dan followed his darting flashlight and saw that a fork lay ahead. He felt another shot of fear. In the silence he could hear his heart thumping in his chest.

It was what he'd been dreading. A choice to make. Surely Adam wouldn't expect them to split up? How would he find his way back? What if his flashlight gave out in the unrelenting darkness? And if they stayed together, what would they do if there were more forks? How would they know which ones they'd followed? They could be lost down here for days, longer even than that. How would they survive? Dan breathed deeply, tried to calm himself.

Adam hesitated, shouted, then again. 'Nicola! Nicola!'

No response. No sound. Nothing.

The detective stared at the fork, then half turned. 'We'll keep going left,' he croaked. 'If we do that with every fork we hit, we won't go wrong coming back. If we don't find her down here we can check the other passages on the way back.'

I hope you're right, thought Dan, following on. I so hope you're right ... He had no idea of any sense of direction down here, knew how easy it would be for them to get hopelessly lost. The fork to the right was roughly the same size as the tunnel they were following. How could Adam have any feeling this was the best way to go? Luck, they were hoping to pure luck they'd get it right. But the fickle goddess of luck had hardly been with them so far.

Adam stumbled over something and swore. Dan played his flashlight down on the rocky floor. He knelt, and gasped at the scream of pain from his ankle, but ignored it, fumbled for the object. It was a metal water canister, the type the military use. Adam peered at it in the torchlight.

'It's new,' he said and his voice lifted in hope. 'Not rusted. It must be Gibson's surely?' He didn't wait for a reply, set off again down the twisting tunnel.

'Nicola ... Nicola ... Nicola ...'

Dan followed silently, resisting another assault of the tiredness that seemed to permeate every part of his body. He

311

breathed in hard and bit at his jutting lip to try to keep himself going. The ceiling of the tunnel suddenly dropped and they had to duck to pass. Then, just as quickly, it rose again. The downward slope lessened, faded away and they were walking on a level surface. The tunnel began to open out, stretching into another cave.

Adam stopped, played the flashlight over the glistening walls. It was a bigger chamber than the last, about fifty feet or so across and the roof was high. Was this where the tin was collected, hundreds of years ago, wondered Dan? Water dripped rhythmically down one rugged wall, echoing through the chamber, leaving a thin trail of dark stain in its wake.

Around the cave's edges were more piles of ruddy, rusting metal, tangled shapes of black, red and brown, a couple of rotting props of wood. It smelt of decay. Adam ran the flashlight over the litter of debris, scanned the ground for any signs that someone could have been here. Dan followed with his torch beam. There was nothing.

They were about to move on when Adam stopped again, focused his torch on a shadowy recess by the side of a pyramid of rotting timber. Dan's eyes moved hypnotically with the light. There was fallen rubble, but colour as well, the first they'd seen in the monochrome mine. It was something pink, fleshy.

Adam saw it too, strode over, Dan just behind, his throbbing leg forgotten. Something was huddled in the corner, something wrapped up in folds of material. Beside it was a couple of plastic water bottles, some food wrappings.

Adam was on his knees beside the pile, rummaging into it. A small shoulder bag slipped to the rocky floor. A pink pony danced on its front.

'Shit!' he hissed. 'It's Nicola. It's her. We've found her.'

He bent over, pushed the damp blankets away, exposed a pale face with a curl of golden hair lying across it. There was a cake of black, dried blood like a large inkblot on her forehead.

'Shit,' Adam cried, his voice trembling, bending over her. 'She's hurt. Shit!'

He gently shook her shoulders but the little girl was limp in his arms, her eyes still shut. Adam tapped her face lightly, then harder, then harder again, almost a slap. There was no response.

He lifted two fingers to her neck, felt for the artery.

'Fuck,' he moaned. 'No pulse. No pulse.'

He rolled the pliant body onto its back, bent over and began pounding at her heart, blowing air into her mouth, trying desperately to restore her life. Dan watched, paralysed, helpless, lost, not knowing what to do, could only hold the flashlight over them, keep hoping, keep hoping.

Another lock of fine blonde hair slipped across a pale cheek as Adam thumped at the little girl's chest, blew another deep lungful of air into her mouth, felt once more at the artery, moaned again, kept pounding at her chest.

Dan watched, knowing now the true meaning of helplessness. He felt the irresistible tiredness upon him, sucking him down, the deep cold of the hours on the savage moor immersing him again, felt he was watching a dream, that any moment the insistent wet nose of his beloved dog would save him from this black underworld of silent death and perfect despair.

Adam thumped again at the unmoving chest, blew another lungful of air into the mouth of the still child, then stopped suddenly. He hung his head over the lifeless body, as if begging it for forgiveness, turned slowly and looked back at Dan.

His eyes were wide and shining, blood-red in the hard white beam of the flashlight. His knees gave and he slumped down to the cold rock next to the body of nine-year-old Nicola Reece.

'She's dead,' he whispered.

Chapter Twenty-four

THERE WAS A LIGHT in the downstairs window and he could see the shadow of a shape moving quickly back and forth. The rest of the houses in the street were in darkness, the road itself lit only by a line of orange streetlights. They drove on, couldn't risk alerting him by lingering. They didn't have time to wait. They had to go in.

One armed-response vehicle, two firearms officers, that's all he'd been able to assemble in the time. The desk sergeant hadn't exactly put himself out to be helpful – nearly all the available officers were on the moor he said – but Marcus Whiting was used to being obstructed. Unpopularity went with the job. Two armed officers and himself. It was scarcely ideal, but it would have to do.

He'd used the couple of minutes in the car to compose his strategy. It wasn't perfect either, was full of danger in fact and mostly to himself, but it would suffice. There was no alternative. Danger went with the job too, though never before on this scale. But that didn't matter. It was irrelevant. It was his only chance to bring this case to an appropriate conclusion, and it was his duty.

'Park just up the street from his house,' hissed Whiting to the driver. 'We'll go back on foot.'

'Yes, sir,' said the man, but the tone of the words made it sound like abuse. He hoped he could trust these men. He could see they weren't keen to be working with him, could even be friends of Martin Crouch. He had to have them on side, couldn't risk them not doing their jobs.

He laid a hand on each of their shoulders, stopped them getting out of the car. 'I don't care what you've heard about me, and I'm well aware of what you call me. The Smiling Assassin, isn't it?'

That made them pause, glance round at him, just as he knew it would.

'I know you think I persecute innocent officers and I know

this man is one of your own. But let me tell you this before we confront him. I respect what you do. I think you're brave and honourable officers to carry firearms in the service of the public. But there is strong evidence that the man in there has betrayed you all and abused his position to kill. That is what we are dealing with here. We are investigating murder. It is not persecution, it is about the law and justice, those things which you seek to uphold every day. What you are doing here is no different to what you would be doing if you had no idea who this man was. You are doing your jobs ... your duty. Do you understand?'

They both muttered 'Yes, sir.' He kept his hands on their shoulders for a few seconds, then released them. Whiting wasn't sure the little speech had worked, but he'd done his best. It was all he could do. They quietly got out of the car.

'There are two entrances to the house,' he hissed as the officers checked their guns. 'Back and front doors. You,' he said, pointing to one with a moustache, 'take the back. You are authorised to fire if you believe Crouch is armed, attempts to flee and puts up resistance. You,' he said to the smaller man with the dark spiky hair, 'cover me from the front. I am going to ring the bell and attempt to talk to him.'

They walked up the road to the house, waited while the marksman with the moustache slipped around the side to the back garden. A wooden gate creaked and they paused, wondering if the man in the house had heard, but no one emerged. The shadow inside kept moving. The other marksman knelt by the edge of the gatepost, hidden in the hedge, trained his gun on the front door. They were ready.

The silhouette was still moving within the house.

'Your orders are similar, but with one very important difference,' Whiting hissed to the kneeling man. 'This is contrary to your training, but it is my order to you nonetheless and you will obey it. I expect to find Crouch armed. I will try to stand slightly to the left hand side when I talk to him. If he appears a threat to me in any way, you do not fire.' He stared into the man's eyes, emphasised those words. 'I repeat, you do not fire. Only when I lift my hand to scratch my right hip does that mean you should shoot. That is of the utmost importance. Is that understood?'

'Yes sir,' the man whispered.

He hoped the officer had taken it in, but there was still that lingering doubt. His fingers twitched by his hip as he walked carefully up the path. An urge was growing already to scratch it. Whiting flinched as a cat scuttled through the hedge. He stared at the door for a moment, then reached out and rapped hard with the brass lion's head knocker.

A sudden stillness seemed to seize the house. Whiting could sense it. Through the opaque, lead-edged glass he could see the outline of a flight of stairs and some jackets on a rack, the hint of a couple of pictures on the wall. One had concealed that password. He wondered if now he would find out what it meant.

The slow seconds slipped by. He knocked again, waited. This time a dark figure carefully approached the door. He felt himself tense as the latch clicked and the door swung open.

'Whiting,' said Crouch without surprise, staring at him. He was wearing jeans and a light blue denim shirt, a brown leather jacket too, looked ready to leave. A zipped-up black sports holdall stood by the foot of the stairs.

But it was the pistol, pointing straight at his chest, which held Marcus Whiting's attention.

'I should have known,' he continued. 'You don't give up, do you?'

'I nearly did with you, PC Crouch. You were clever … very clever. You covered the tracks of your corruption well.'

'It wasn't corruption Whiting. It was justice.'

'It was corruption. You abused your privileged position. For whatever motive, it doesn't matter. It was corruption … murderous corruption.'

Crouch glared at him, a vein pulsing dangerously in his neck. 'It was justice,' he said quietly, with a false calm. 'In a world that can't seem to manage to find its own true justice. And I'd advise you not to goad me. You're not in your safe little interview room now. You've ventured into the man's world of real policing. Facing a weapon and wondering how to deal with it. Knowing any mistake could be fatal. I never thought I'd see the day, and I almost wonder how it feels.'

Whiting thought it wiser not to go into that. He had a plan, however uncertain, and he needed to stick with it. He had to keep Crouch talking.

'It's certainly ... an experience. But I did expect you to be armed.'

The moment he'd said the words he knew it was a mistake. Crouch took one quick look over his shoulder, the gun never wavering from Whiting's chest.

'In which case ... you'd have brought armed back-up.'

Whiting tried to sound calm. 'Of course.'

'But the news says there's a big armed search going on up on Dartmoor ...'

The IPCA Commissioner said nothing, didn't trust his voice to hold.

'... and it's the middle of the night and I'm threatening you, but no one's taken a shot yet ... and there's no sound from the back garden. So I don't think there are more than one, maybe two marksmen out there, are there?'

Crouch took another look over his shoulder.

'You're surrounded, and ...' Whiting began, but too late. Crouch had turned, began running towards the back of the house.

Marcus Whiting allowed himself one brief second of thought and decision. If Crouch made it outside, he'd be shot dead. And his investigation would die with the man. If he chased Crouch, he put himself in even more danger. But it was the only way to find out what he needed to know.

He felt his legs start running, past a neat rack of coats, a line of family photos. A young woman featured in each, first in a school uniform, then wearing a ripped T-shirt and holding an electric guitar, a robed student proudly bearing a degree, a bride, all smiles, with her groom, and in the same white dress, standing outside a church, alongside a younger, but beaming Martin Crouch. Whiting briefly registered how pretty she was.

Ahead, Crouch kicked open a door, making it judder on its hinges, lunged into a kitchen, knocked a glass from a table. It shattered on the tiled floor, sending splinters of glass skidding across the black and white mosaic. Whiting was through the door too, just a couple of yards behind.

Crouch took a fast glance over his shoulder, didn't break stride. He was heading for the end of the kitchen and another door. The key was in the lock.

Whiting's shoes slipped on the shards of glass. He grabbed at a worktop to right himself. Crouch's hand was on the door handle, jiggling at the key. Outside, all was blackness, but hidden in the camouflage of the night was a police marksman, carbine trained on the house. If Crouch made it outside, he would die.

The key was turning in the door, Crouch pushing at the handle. Whiting didn't have time to think, just threw himself forwards. But the door was opening and Crouch was halfway through, stepping out into the still night.

Whiting could sense the rifle coming to bear on the man's chest, an unseen finger cool on the trigger.

'Armed police! Stop or I shoot!' came the barked challenge from the dark garden.

Crouch hesitated, blinked hard, his head sweeping back and forth across the night. He took another pace forward.

The shout came again. 'Armed police! Drop your weapon!'

Crouch took one more step, his feet crunching on some gravel, the gun still poised in his hand. Whiting knew he had only seconds.

'Armed police! This is your final warning! Drop your weapon! Do it now!'

Lights were flicking on in the house next door, throwing shadows across the garden. There was a small and tidy hedge, a pond, some stone ornaments, a wooden gate. Half-hidden beside it, given away only by the new light glinting from the barrel of his rifle, was the squat form of the police marksman.

Crouch began to raise his gun. Whiting saw the red dot of the laser sight settle on his chest, directly over the man's heart. It wavered, then steadied. The marksman was about to take his shot.

No time to think. Only to act.

Whiting threw himself forwards, careered into Crouch, knocked him off balance. Together they fell onto the damp grass. Whiting felt a stone object thud into his ribs, gasped, winded, but Crouch was already struggling up. That lethal red dot was hovering again, searching for his chest.

Whiting forced himself to his feet, between the marksman and Martin Crouch. From the hedge, he thought he heard the hidden policeman swear. The two men faced each other, both panting heavily.

Crouch raised his gun again, pointed it directly at Whiting's chest. With his other hand, he beckoned, and began backing away, step by careful step.

'Don't move! Stay where I can see you!' came the shout from the hedge. But Whiting ignored it, followed, back into the kitchen, making sure he kept his body between Crouch and the marksman.

Glass crunched underfoot, but Crouch kept backing off, until they were again in the hallway.

Ahead, was the front door, still open, the place Marcus Whiting desperately needed to reach. He managed to prevent himself staring at it, couldn't risk giving himself away. Crouch stopped, halfway up the hall, leaned back against the wall, the pistol never wavering.

The two men stared at each other.

'Can I ...' Whiting began, but his voice failed. He gestured to the flight of stairs. 'Can I sit down?'

Crouch backed away slightly, nodded his head. Whiting stepped carefully across to the stairs, sat heavily, tried to catch his breath. He realised his finger was bleeding and gingerly wiped away some of the blood, held his other hand over the wound.

'I wouldn't worry too much about that,' said Crouch in a sinister voice, the gun still pointing directly at Marcus Whiting's chest.

Whiting was surprised he wasn't frightened. Perhaps he hadn't had the time. He tried to concentrate. He knew what he had to say and do and that he had only this one chance to get it right. Maybe that was keeping the fear at bay. Somehow he had to get Crouch talking, get him over to that open door.

'If that's the case ...' Again, Whiting's voice faltered. 'If things aren't looking too good for me ... can I ask you a couple of questions. Before ...'

Crouch snorted his contempt. 'I think I'll ask the questions. What was it that put you on to me?'

'The computers. In the two houses where you ...' Whiting searched for the words, didn't want to antagonise Crouch. Not just yet. 'Where it all happened. That, and the discovery of the password here.'

Crouch nodded. 'Sloppy. I should have hidden that better. I've always had a problem remembering passwords and PIN numbers.'

Whiting saw the opportunity. Keep him talking. 'What did it stand for? I've never understood that.'

'No, you wouldn't. That was why I chose it. It stood for "I Will Get You", combined with 66, the only year England have won the World Cup. Football's about all that's meant anything to me since ...'

His words tailed off. Whiting interrupted quickly, didn't want Crouch dwelling on wounded memories that could make him even more dangerous. Just keep him talking ...

'In fairness, I should tell you it wasn't me who saw it. It was one of the officers seconded to help my investigation.'

'Well done them. I'm sure they'll go far.'

'I believe you're right.'

There was a pause as they stared at each other. Outside, a car rushed by, white headlights sweeping through the darkness. Whiting wondered how to move the conversation on again. And how long did he have to do it?

'I saw the photos. I take it this is all about Marie, your daughter?'

The pistol rose instantly, moving from his chest to point right between his eyes.

'Don't ... talk ... about ... her ...' spat Crouch, his eyes shining with malice. 'Don't defile her name. Don't ever mention her. Ever. You're not fit to even think about her.'

The gun was pointing straight into his brain. Crouch's

finger was steady on the trigger. Now Whiting felt himself begin to tremble. He imagined what the bullet would do. At that range it would rip through him, right into the centre of his mind, punch a small and neat hole in his brow, rip a far bigger wound from the back of his head as it burst free into the air.

'I'm sorry,' he whispered, raising both palms in a gesture of surrender.

The muzzle of the gun dipped slightly. Whiting tried to make himself breathe slowly, get the man talking again.

'I'd ...' His voice faltered. 'I'd just like to know. I'm guessing you set up that domestic violence web site?'

A pause, then, 'Correct.'

'With its chat room?'

'Correct.'

'So you could see how desperate some of the women had become?'

'Correct.'

'And you monitored their chat?'

'Yes.'

'And contacted them from there. With an offer of help?'

'Yes.'

'And you went round to their houses to see where it could be done? And you found a place where the shooting could be carried out without PC Gardener seeing? So you arranged a time when you knew you would be on shift and so called to the house as the nearest armed-response officers?'

'Correct.'

'And you wiped their computers to leave no trace of the domestic violence site, or the chat you'd had with the women? There'd be no evidence left at all.'

'Correct.'

'And you told the woman exactly how to behave. How to engineer a row?'

'Yes.'

'How to make the 999 call so when you were dispatched to the house, you were told there was a risk to life? So it sounded like the man was armed? So you would be sent straight to them as a priority?'

'Correct.'

'You told them where to collapse, or curl up in a ball and refuse to move? Exactly where you needed them to be so you could shoot the man without PC Gardener seeing it? And that you would be there within ten minutes of their call?'

'Yes.'

'And finally her having a knife there, somewhere on the side, something she'd saved with his fingerprints on? She'd have that somewhere close by where she'd collapsed so you could just nudge it into place on the floor and make it look like he was about to stab her before he was shot? So even if it was still moving, it would look to PC Gardener simply as though the man had dropped it when you shot him? And the knife would have the dead man's fingerprints on, but not yours, because you nudged it onto the floor with your gun, or your arm?'

'Correct. I used my elbow, in fact, but very good Whiting. Very good.'

'And then the stories, yours and the woman's, tie up? And all the ballistics and forensics evidence tally too, along with the man's fingerprints on the knife. And PC Gardener's account as well, even though he's entirely innocent. So all we've got is suspicion about the similarities, but no evidence at all. So we have no choice but to let you go back to your duties?'

'Correct. Well done. You got it all Whiting. Clever you.'

'How many more did you intend to kill?'

'As many as I could, until ...'

'Until?' prompted Whiting, unable to stop himself. 'Until what?'

The gun was still pointing straight between his eyes. Whiting kept his hands raised, sat motionless.

'Until ...' said Crouch slowly. 'Until I started to feel Marie had been avenged.'

Whiting remembered not to use her name. He didn't like the blank look that had slipped into Crouch's eyes. 'And then?'

'Who knows? I did some research on countries with no

extradition treaties with Britain. There are plenty. Or perhaps I wouldn't have fancied that. Maybe I'd just have died trying to get some justice for Marie and women like her. Or maybe now, I'll shoot you – in the name of all the brave police officers you've hounded – then drop the gun, let them arrest me and go to trial. So I can make a real statement about what happens to women who suffer with violent ... bastard ... men.'

Crouch's finger had begun to tremble on the trigger. Whiting kept his hands up, didn't say anything, but wondered how long he'd got before Crouch tired of talking. He knew almost all he needed now. Almost.

He risked a glance along the hallway. How to get to that doorway?

'Anyway, while we're talking, there is one thing I'd like you to know,' said Crouch, his voice changing again, sounding almost friendly. Whiting wondered if that was even more frightening.

'I don't know why I'm telling you this, but it's important to me. No one else knows about what I've achieved, of course, so you might as well.'

'Go on,' said Whiting, curious despite the danger.

'When I set up that web site, I had no intention of doing what I did. I genuinely meant to offer the women a place for support and advice. It was a way of making Marie's death less meaningless. It was only when I started to hear the terrible stories of abuse and suffering that I began to make my plans.'

Crouch's face tightened and the gun wavered slightly. The barrel looked so big, so deadly.

'I never heard it from Marie, you see,' he continued. 'She always hid it. The first time I knew what she'd been through was in court, when it all came out at his trial. Imagine that. The jury, the barristers, solicitors, judge, public, journalists, all getting to hear about what my little girl had suffered. And I knew nothing about it. Me, her father and a police officer.'

He flinched, a tic twitching at his cheek. Whiting could see he was back there in the courtroom. With his free hand Crouch reached up and stroked the silver cross around his neck. But the gun didn't move, was still pointing straight between Whiting's eyes.

'So when I started to hear it from these other women too, I decided to do something about it.' Crouch's voice grew sharper. 'I'd lost Marie. The trial was a joke. He was let off with a suspended ... sentence.' He spat the words out. 'His barrister argued he was a loving husband who'd been provoked, that he was wracked with remorse and the judge swallowed it. He got a suspended sentence. You call that justice?'

The gun barrel was wavering hard now, swaying back and forth. Whiting went to wipe the sweat from his forehead then stopped himself, intensely aware of how his movement could be misinterpreted. He kept his hands raised.

'Anyway, that's enough talking,' said Crouch with sudden decision in his voice. 'It's time to say goodbye.'

The finger was steady on the trigger. Whiting felt a shuddering shock of fear. One more thing needed to be said, just the one. It was dangerous, so dangerous, and if he got it wrong ...

He could feel that bullet bursting through his mind, taking his life in a millisecond of its deadly, obliterating passage.

'Just before you do that, I've got something important to tell you,' hissed Whiting. 'As we're talking about justice.'

'Oh yes?' Crouch said warily. 'Really? Or are you playing for time by any chance?'

Whiting took a shallow breath, all that he could manage. He was shaking and his throat felt painfully dry. He could almost feel that bullet exploding through his brain.

'No. It's important. For me to tell you, if I'm about to ...' He let the words fade. 'And even more important for you to know.'

'What?'

Keep him talking ...

'Look ... do you mind if I get a breath of air? Just, as it might be ... well, you know. My last, and all that.'

Crouch said nothing. 'Just in the doorway there,' Whiting continued, trying to keep his voice calm. 'I'll just stand there while I tell you. You can shoot me any time. I can hardly get away. But I'd like to just breathe some air and see the stars. Before …'

Crouch chuckled, a low, mocking sound. 'How touching. I'd never have thought if of you. Go on then, since you ask so nicely.'

Whiting felt his legs shaking. He swallowed hard, got to his feet, stepped over to the doorway, his eyes set on Crouch the whole time. He had to make the man follow him. And there was only one way.

'You've …' His voice faltered. 'You've been conned.'

Crouch stared at him. 'What?'

'You've been conned. That second woman – Chanter – wasn't being abused at all. She was having an affair. She'd met a man she wanted to be with, but she didn't want to lose the house to her husband. His crying family, the ones that appeared on the TV, they were right. He was no wife-beater. His only crime was spending much of his time drunk, to cope with his disintegrating relationship. I've followed her and got enough evidence to have her calls tapped. She's even admitted it. She was visiting those domestic violence sites to get information to pretend she was a victim. That way she could file for divorce, blame him and get most of the house and money.'

The throbbing pulse was back in Crouch's neck, his voice brittle. 'What? You're lying.'

'I'm afraid not. She was trying to find out what women suffer so she could invent a cover for herself. That's why she was pretending to be so desperate, so other women would tell her their stories. Those injuries we found on her, the ones that looked like they were from beatings – she inflicted them herself. Over several months too, to make them look nice and convincing. A history of abuse. She knew we'd have to examine her and she made sure the evidence was all consistent. Hanson was lying in a drunken stupor half the time, so he didn't notice her wounds, or those screaming fits she put on to make the neighbours think he was beating her'

Still Crouch stood in the hallway, that gun steady. Whiting

325

had to get him to move. And there was just the one way. Dangerous, so very risky. But no choice.

He changed the tone of his voice, made it goading, sneering. 'When you came along and made your kind offer to kill her husband, how could she refuse? You killed an innocent man, Crouch, to help a cheating, scheming woman, not a helpless and desperate victim. Now … how does that fit with your great vision of justice?'

Crouch's face had turned red. He took a step forwards. Whiting inched to his left in the doorway, kept his hands up, very steady, knew he only had seconds left. The gun was still fixed between his eyes and that finger was tight on the trigger.

'So how does that feel then, Crouch? You're just a common murderer. You thought you were so, so clever … but she was cleverer, wasn't she?'

Another step. 'You bastard,' Crouch growled. His finger was trembling over the trigger, his teeth gritted. 'I don't believe you. You're lying to try to save your miserable life.'

Crouch was breathing hard, panting, the tic in his cheek dancing angrily. He was about to shoot, Whiting knew it. Somehow, he knew. He was about to pull the trigger, unleash that clinical, murderous bullet.

Whiting again edged to his left. Another step from Crouch. But it wasn't enough. Nearly, but not quite. Just a couple more.

The life of Marcus Whiting was running out, he thought. He was about to die. He was surprised to feel the fear subside, as though his mind had resigned itself to his fate. He was calm, almost detached from the reality of that gun barrel, just inches from his forehead. It was the last sight he would see. He wondered how he would be remembered.

The thought angered him and stirred a resistance. Could he buy himself just a little more time, to see if justice could be done? Wasn't it his duty to try? An idea flashed into his mind. He inched further to his left. Just a few more seconds …

'And there's more,' he managed, trying desperately to keep his voice steady. 'Do you want to know something about the first woman, Crouch? That first woman you think you saved.'

'What? What, you bastard?'

Another step forwards. He was almost in the doorway. The gun was shaking in Crouch's hand now, so close to Whiting's brow, that finger so very tight on the trigger.

'That's not quite what you believed either,' Whiting continued, thinking desperately. Another step from Crouch. Was it enough? It had to be. Time had run out.

'But don't take my word for it. I've got something to show you. It's in my pocket ... if I can get it? I wouldn't want you to think I'm going for a weapon.'

A slight nod from Crouch. The gun was still pointing straight into Whiting's brain. Slowly, gently, he reached his right hand down, as though moving carefully to his pocket and scratched his side.

A violent, echoing crack split the stillness. Crouch's eyes opened wide for a brief second, then he pitched sideways, fell. Whiting sprang forward, kicked the pistol away, savoured the beautiful sight of it skidding across the hallway carpet, clanging into a radiator pipe, spinning, then settling, out of reach.

Crouch lay on his back, crumpled, staring up at him, blinking fast, his eyes wild with shock. He was panting, gasping, trying desperately to catch his breath. One hand scrabbled at his stomach, searching for the wound, the pumping blood emptying the life from his body. The other was on the silver cross, holding it, rubbing it hard in his shaking grip. He shuddered and writhed, pulling desperately at his shirt, fingers searching the taut, sweating skin for the bullet hole.

Whiting stood over him, shook his head.

'No easy way out for you, PC Crouch,' he hissed. A black-clothed marksman appeared at his side, looked down at the gasping figure.

'That was a baton round,' Whiting continued. 'You're just winded. You'll be OK in a few minutes. There'll be a nasty bruise, but that's it. You'll be just fine to stand trial.'

Chapter Twenty-five

THERE WAS A KNOCK at the door of his office and Adam looked up from the interminable drugs surveillance report. The sight was a surprise. He hesitated, then beckoned the man in. It was Whiting, wearing a dark grey suit and navy tie. Adam rose from behind his desk and Whiting held out a hand. Adam hesitated again, then shook it tentatively, without warmth or feeling, just professional.

'I won't keep you long, Chief Inspector,' said Whiting, and Adam noticed he was trying to keep the hiss from his voice. He didn't move to sit down, stayed standing by the open door. 'I just wanted to say goodbye.'

Adam gave him a questioning look.

'Well, all right, it was a little more than that,' the IPCA man added.

Adam nodded. 'I hear congratulations are in order,' he said. 'On the promotion.'

Whiting rubbed his hands together thoughtfully. 'Thank you. It means of course I'll be spending most of my time behind a desk in Cardiff. So it's unlikely I'll see you again. I don't suppose either of us will worry too much about that.'

A silence. The two men looked at each other.

'It's fair enough,' said Adam eventually. 'Your promotion I mean. I have to say it was a well-run case. I take it you deliberately let the word get out that the investigation was all but over and Crouch would be reinstated, cleared of any crime?'

Whiting's face formed that cold smile, the oddly small teeth exposed. 'I don't see the point in false modesty Chief Inspector. Yes, I did. And it worked. It flushed him out. I thought if he was driven in what he was doing he'd have a taste for it. After two murders, I doubted he'd give up his killing easily. I had evidence the Chanter woman was seeing someone else and wanted rid of Richie Hanson, but it wasn't enough. It wasn't proof. I told Crouch about it in order to get him talking. I had to have something concrete and fortunately it worked. That talk in his house provided the proof of how he'd gone about his murderous plot.'

Adam nodded. 'Clever. But you took quite a risk. With your life. I have to say, it was … very brave. Stopping him being shot by putting yourself in the marksmen's way. Then getting him talking and goading him out into the open so they could stun him.'

'Indeed. But …'

'But what?'

'But I saw no other way to resolve the case. To do my …'

Adam noticed Whiting stopped himself from finishing the sentence. He didn't comment, instead asked, 'You were wired up?'

'Yes. I was carrying a tiny microphone and recorder. It's given me all I need. I wanted Crouch's laptop, but it's still missing. I'm guessing he suspected someone was trying to trace him and he got rid of it somewhere between the allotment and his home. The two women are still denying it, so there'll have to be a trial. The first one, the Bodmin woman, may well get away with manslaughter. She genuinely was being abused by her partner, so could plead provocation. But Chanter's will definitely be a murder charge. I think we've got enough evidence to convict them both, and Crouch too, now. If I hadn't let Crouch believe he was going to get away with it, he wouldn't have broken cover and gone back into his chatroom.'

Adam tightened his tie. 'I have to hand it to you, it was clever and …' he hesitated, '…brave too. You got your man. I know Claire was involved, but she won't say anything about what happened. She says it's a matter for you if you want to tell us.'

He stared at Whiting, nodded to emphasise his words. 'She's very loyal like that, even when her loyalty can be misplaced. Did she know what you were doing? Or did you use her?'

Whiting flinched. 'I don't care for the word "use", Chief Inspector. From the start she struck me as a very talented and dedicated officer who knew her duty. I believed that even if she weren't on the case officially, she would be unlikely to let it go, especially if she had a strong motivation to prove herself. I gave her that. Let us say simply that … I banked on reading her personality correctly and stood back to see where it would lead. I raised the computer link between Crouch and the two women to put it into her mind, but I think she would have seen it anyway. I didn't intend to remove her from the investigation in the way I did, but knowing about her relationship with that journalist, when the photo of Crouch came out it was too good a chance to miss. I was originally planning to find another pretext.'

'That hurt her very much you know, Whiting.'

'I appreciate that, Chief Inspector. I only hope she can see it was for the greater good. It's sometimes the way in our business of deception.'

'You could just have taken her into your confidence.'

Whiting shook his head sadly. 'I've made that error before. My job makes winning the confidence of police officers rather problematic. Sometimes it's necessary for the people who are working for you to be unaware of that.'

The IPCA investigator reached into his jacket pocket, produced a white envelope. 'Would you be so kind as to pass this on to her please?'

Adam reached over the desk and took it. 'What is it?'

'It's a letter. It explains what I did and why. I've also taken the liberty of making my thoughts on her talents clear. I've sent a copy to the Chief Constable too, requesting Claire be commended.'

'She'll appreciate that. Thank you.'

Another silence.

'Well, if that's all you wanted to say …' began Adam.

'There is just one further matter, Chief Inspector. I heard you were considering resignation.'

Adam sat wearily back in his chair, let out a long breath. 'How did you hear that?'

'Just police station gossip. Even I get to hear it now. Some of your colleagues have actually started speaking to me. They said I wasn't as bad as had been made out. I took that as a compliment.'

Adam managed a tight smile, despite himself. 'Yes, it's quite true. I still haven't decided what to do.' He gestured to the reports, folders and memos filling the red plastic in-tray on his desk. 'I don't seem to have much heart for this any more. I keep asking myself – what's the point? The letter's written. It's in my drawer. I'm just deciding whether to submit it.'

Whiting sat down opposite Adam, reached into his pocket for a few pence in change and placed them on the chair next to him. 'You blame yourself for Nicola's death?'

Adam looked down at the floor. 'I do. If I'd been alert and doing my job properly I would have arrested Gibson when he did his security guard act. Anyway, regardless of that, I should have found her sooner.'

Whiting studied his thin fingers, flexed them back and forth.

'This is none of my business,' he said softly, 'as you will no doubt tell me. But you shouldn't blame yourself. Your senior officers agree. There have been no complaints or criticism whatsoever about how you conducted the investigation. That business of Gibson at the leisure centre could have taken anyone in. It would me. It did your … friend, that journalist. You did everything you possibly could to find Nicola. More than everything in my view. And I think …'

'Thanks,' Adam interrupted. 'I appreciate the sentiment. But I'd rather not go back over it, if you don't mind.'

Whiting stood up, gathered the coins from the chair. 'Of course. I understand. But, for what it's worth, I think you're a fine detective and the police service would be much poorer without you.'

Adam just stared. 'And don't take my word for that,' continued Whiting. 'It's the talk in the canteen too. You're held in high regard, Chief Inspector, by all who know you and work with you.' He paused for a second. 'And I mean … all.'

Whiting held out his hand and Adam got up and shook it, this time with a hint of honest feeling.

'I still think what you did to Chris was wrong,' Adam

added.

'And I still disagree,' said Whiting smoothly, sliding out of the office and shutting the door.

Dan lay on his bed, Claire next to him, Rutherford on the floor, the dog's tail thumping softly against the carpet. It was such a reassuring noise, for him the sound of home. It was all he'd longed for during those cold and despairing hours on Dartmoor. Even his ankle had stopped aching. Just a bad sprain, the doctor had said, with the usual implication that her patient was a hypochondriac. A couple of days rest would see him fine.

Claire had been wonderful, fussing over him, bandaging his ankle, cooking him supper. It wasn't the best curry he'd ever had, spinach and potato madras, not enough meat and not hot enough for him, but that scarcely mattered. He was being looked after by the woman he …

And there he'd stopped the run of thought. By this woman he … was very fond of. He would leave it at that. For now, at least.

Dan was still wondering what she was going to say earlier, when she'd first got to the flat and seen him. He must have looked a dreadful state. He could see the shock in her eyes. He'd opened the door and she'd flung her arms around him, swept him into the bedroom and cuddled into him. He thought she was crying, could only half hear her through the muffling fleece he wore.

'Don't go scaring me like that again,' she'd said. 'When I heard someone had been shot on the moor I thought it was you. I don't ever want to go through that again. I still need you. I … I …'

Her words had tailed off. I what? he kept thinking. I what? He knew what he wanted it to be. But if she said it, what would he do then?

Lizzie phoned and the moment had been broken. She always had such magnificent timing.

He'd answered the call with heavy resignation, expecting a savaging for missing that outside broadcast, when they'd left

Princetown to go down to Evil Coombe to search for Nicola. He had his justifications ready but she'd been surprisingly understanding. We got Loud to haul some other police inspector in front of the camera for a live update she'd said, and used your lunchtime news report again. It was fine.

The ratings had soared because of their insight into the Nicola case. His insight he thought, but didn't say. Lizzie was only sorry it had ended the way it did. Dan had been about to agree, that Nicola's death was a dreadful tragedy, but she'd gone on to lament that the shooting of Gibson had denied them the chance of covering the story all over again at his trial. Dan didn't say anything. It was pointless.

He was expected in the office later, too, she made that clear. He could rest for a few hours, but that was it. She wanted him live in the studio tonight to talk about what had happened in the final hours of the hunt for Nicola and what it had been like in the old tin mine.

Dan shuddered at the thought. It was the last thing he wanted to relive.

The memories wouldn't leave him, kept playing in his head. He was dreading his dreams, didn't want to sleep alone in the coming nights. Adam in despair, bending helplessly over Nicola's lifeless body in that black hole of a cave. Gibson swaying and dropping after the volley of hissing bullets, the blood oozing from his chest. Gibson's gun pointing at him, that feeling of expecting the shock of a fatal shot.

He wondered if he'd ever get over all that had happened. And would he ever stop feeling that if he'd been cleverer, made more of an effort, Nicola Reece would still be alive?

Dan reached down and stroked Rutherford, cuddled Claire closer. He screwed his eyes shut to try to leave it all behind, the gunshots, the cold, the darkness and the death.

He'd have to see Nicola's mum soon too. He had something to ask her.

Epilogue

IT WAS THE WEEK before Christmas and a classical sweep of pure snow had settled on Dartmoor. Children tumbled and screamed, dived and sledged, cut swathes in the white canvas with their rolling, gathering snowballs, the tracks leading to a sentinel army of smiling snowmen, standing a frozen watch. Rutherford joined in the children's cries with a crescendo of yelps and barks, danced around them, his padded feet flying across the shining carpet as he chased the hurtling melee of delight.

Claire held Dan's gloved hand tightly as they plodded up the old mine track towards Higher Hartor Tor. The frozen ground creaked and crumped under their stomping feet. Bill, the young stonemason Dan knew from his days covering the environment, followed, occasionally throwing a stick for Rutherford. It was the first time Dan had been back here since Nicola's death. He'd been waiting for the moment, knew it must come, and had finally found the strength to face it. But he was still tense with the memories.

They neared the top of the hill and he readied himself for it, tentatively turned his head, looked over towards Evil Coombe. His eyes ran down the valley to where Gibson's little tent had stood, but all he could see now was a long furrow of sleeping snow, punctuated by the occasional grey granite boulder. Claire followed his gaze silently, knew what he was thinking and squeezed his hand harder. He had no idea what he should be going through. Pity, regret, sorrow, fear, anger, hate, he'd expected something, but nothing came. All he felt was hollow.

Claire stood with him, allowed the minutes to pass, let him take it in, then tugged gently at his hand. They turned away without a word, back towards the old Eylesbarrow mine. The black mouth of the adit was blocked now, packed with black soil, pitted with granite rocks, covered in a grid of rigid wire mesh. A group of children kicked snow at each other alongside it.

'Have you got any particular stone in mind?' asked Bill, scanning the ground.

'No,' replied Dan. 'Take your pick. Whichever you think will work. There are plenty to choose from. But fairly close to the entrance to the mine please, that's all I'd ask.'

The stonemason's stout frame worked its way through the granite boulders littered around the tumbledown remains of the mine. He bent over, checking them for size, occasionally running a hand across a craggy surface pockmarked with green moss, feeling the texture, brushing off some powdery snow.

'This one,' he said, kneeling by a stone about five feet long by a couple wide. 'It feels like a good size for a young girl. Is it OK?'

It was just an ordinary piece of Dartmoor granite. 'Fine.'

'And you want to keep it simple? Just Nicola Reece, 1999 – 2008?'

'Yes please. It's what I agreed with her mum.' He tried to forget his suggestion of adding the word sorry. 'Just a simple memorial.'

'Fine,' replied Bill, fumbling a set of tools out of his rucksack. 'I won't be too long if you want to go off for a walk. I know what you loving couples are like.'

'We'll stay with you,' said Dan, looking at Claire. 'I'd like to watch you carve it.'

They strolled over to the ridge looking back on the valley. The snow seemed to have settled everywhere, a uniform layer of white across the expanse of the upland. A couple of Dartmoor ponies chewed at some stray grass poking hopefully through the snow. They tossed their chestnut manes in the yellow sunlight as if in disapproval of the meagre pickings.

'Did you ever find out what the dispute between Mr Breen and Whiting was about?' asked Claire. 'I've often wondered. I heard gossip, but nothing concrete.'

Dan wound an arm around her. 'It's a strange story. Just between you and me? Adam told me as a friend.'

'Of course. As ever.'

Dan gently kissed her cheek. 'Adam had an old detective inspector who used to mentor him when he was a sergeant, just like you. His name was Chris Golding. Adam says he was the best he ever worked with and taught him most of what he knows.'

Claire turned, then nuzzled into his side. 'What happened?'

'Apparently this Chris was pretty driven. He couldn't bear letting criminals off the hook. Old school, I think you might call it. But he went a bit too far one day in making sure he had good evidence against a suspect.'

'It happens. Not so much these days, but it happens.'

'Yeah, I know that now,' said Dan with feeling. 'Long gone are the days when I thought the police were clean and straightforward.'

'Sometimes you have to fight dirt with dirt.'

Something in her voice made him want to ask what she'd done that wasn't entirely scrupulous, but another time, he thought. Maybe he wasn't ready to hear that yet, and certainly not today.

'Yep,' Dan replied. 'But I've already learnt the golden rule is – don't get caught. Chris did.'

Claire smiled knowingly. 'Spot on. What did he do?'

'His mum was a victim of one of those distraction burglaries. You know, when a couple of men turn up at someone's house? One of them says they've got a report of gas leaking, or water, something like that. He keeps the person talking while the other goes over the house and steals whatever they can find under the pretext of looking for the leak.'

'Uh huh. Low and nasty. Usually aimed at older people.'

'Yep. Hence Chris's mum. She had some jewellery stolen, which his Dad had given her. He'd died a couple of years before from cancer and she was distraught. Chris went after the guys who did it.'

'And?'

'He got them, but he didn't have any evidence. So he created some.'

'How?'

'He got one of them in to the interview room and gave him a real going over. Adam was there. He remembers it almost word for word. He says it was quite a pasting the guy got, threats, violence even, the whole works. But he was a professional criminal and knew they didn't have anything on him. So he kept denying it and Chris had nothing.'

'What did he do?'

'He suspended the interview and got the guy a cup of tea. He made out he'd given up. After that, they let him go. But then he took the mug and planted it at the home of one old man who'd been a victim of a similar distraction burglary. Chris went round to see him again under the guise of re-interviewing him to see if he could get any more evidence. He suggested to the man the burglars took up his offer of a cup of tea. The guy was quite confused and basically agreed. Chris planted the mug, and there's your evidence. A nice DNA profile from the saliva and some of the guy's fingerprints. Chris had made sure he'd wiped his own prints off.'

Claire didn't say anything. Dan looked down at her, trying to read her expression, but it was inscrutable.

'What went wrong?' she prompted.

'This guy's lawyers demolished it in court. The old fellow wasn't up to being a witness and couldn't confirm the mug was his, had been in the house, anything. There'd been a hint of Chris doing things like that before so an investigation was launched. It was the time when police standards were getting tighter. Or more politically correct, some might say. Anyway, whatever. Whiting came in and got him.'

'How? Surely Mr Breen didn't say anything?'

'No. He just stonewalled. He took the classic politician's way out and told Whiting he couldn't remember what happened. But Chris made one big mistake. The interview with the burglar was recorded on video. The mug was clearly visible. Whiting confronted him with it and, according to Adam, gave him a choice. Resign from the force with your reputation intact and take a good pension or be charged. Chris quit. Adam says he'd about had enough anyway. He didn't like the modern emphasis on criminals' rights and all the legal hurdles and red tape the police were facing. He always used to say a man forfeits his rights when he turns to crime. It was the victims he cared about. He lives in New Zealand now, according to Adam.'

Claire looked at him, her head tilted on one side. 'So Whiting didn't actually follow the rules then, did he? He gave this Chris a choice instead of just charging him?'

Dan stared at the horizon where the white line of the expanse of snow met the perfect blue of the sky.

'I suppose you're right,' he mused. 'Maybe he'd say he did his duty in removing an unreliable police officer from the service. Maybe he'd say he didn't need to go any further and ruin him.'

He thought back on his encounters with Whiting, all he'd heard about the man, that hissing voice, the tiny teeth and those narrow, flicking eyes. 'Maybe duty isn't a black and white concept, not even to Marcus Whiting,' he added.

Dan reached down and rubbed his ankle. It had fully healed, but still he sometimes imagined a pain there. Perhaps it was the surroundings, prompting his memory.

'You know what it was with him, don't you?' he said. 'I mean, why he was so driven. The duty thing of his.'

Claire shook her head, tussling her black bobbed hair. Damn, that was attractive, he thought.

'No,' she said. 'I'd heard it was something to do with his family, but nothing specific.'

'It was kind of that. He gave an interview to the *Western Daily News* just before he went back to Cardiff. It was an exclusive. I sometimes wonder if he did it to spite me, after the run-ins we had. Lizzie was annoyed we didn't get it. It was a good story.'

Dan almost managed a smile at the thought. It was a creative form of revenge, he had to hand it to the man.

'It made interesting reading,' he said. 'His dad was a civil servant and heavily into duty. But that wasn't the reason. The young Whiting rebelled against his parents, as all good growing lads do. I certainly did.'

'So what happened?'

'The article didn't go into great detail. But he was at a boarding school and apparently some teacher made him a prefect to try to straighten him out. One night Whiting turned a blind eye while a group of lads sneaked out to meet some girls at their school. They had to climb a fence to get in and one of the boys fell off and broke his back. He's had to use a wheelchair ever since. Whiting blamed himself and thought that if he'd done his duty – as his dad had drilled into him – the lad wouldn't have got hurt.'

Claire stamped her walking boots against a granite boulder, dislodging plates of snow. She scooped some up and rolled it into a tiny snowball, threw it down the valley. Dan wondered what she was thinking.

'Has Mr Breen said anything more about whether he's going to quit?' she asked finally.

'He'll only say he's still thinking about it.'

'Do you think he will?'

Dan leaned back into her. 'I genuinely don't know. Nicola's death has really hit him. He won't stop blaming himself. I think he's wondering if he's up to the job. But I'm only guessing. Every time the subject comes up he just goes quiet and says he doesn't want to talk about it. I think he finds it hard that we were so close to saving her. She'd only been dead a little while when we found her. It was that blow on the head that did it. The scientists say she'd just about freed herself from the ropes around her ankles, but stumbled and fell over them as she tried to stand up. She hit her head on some piece of metal from the old mine workings and the injury, combined with the shock and cold, killed her. She was already freezing from having been out on the moor and in the mine for hours. If we'd have got there an hour or so sooner, we would have saved her.'

A crow cackled as it wheeled above them, a swooping black dart in the azure sky. Dan gazed at it as the bird hovered effortlessly, then tilted its wings and landed elegantly on a black rock in the white snow barrow of Evil Coombe.

'How much are you paying Bill to carve the stone?' Claire asked, a fog of her breath drifting over him.

'A couple of hundred pounds.'

'So what are you going to do with the rest of the money

Gibson left?'

Dan stared out across the valley. 'That I don't know. I have been wondering. No one who knows who it belonged to would take it. I don't see the sense in wasting it by burning it or something like that. It just seems pointless. It might at least do some good. I think it'll have to be an anonymous donation to charity. I'll probably give it to one that looks after horses.'

A memory of a story he'd once covered drifted into his mind. 'I know there's a charity which specifically looks after Dartmoor ponies,' he said. 'I'll give the rest of the money to them. It's about the best I can do.'

Dan's words softened as the memories of that night in Evil Coombe and the mine gathered again in his mind. They were all impenetrable darkness, lit intermittently by flares of gunfire and the sweeping beams of flashlights, both revealing only death. The images were always laced with flowing strings of numbers and letters; "law bee sorry, 605, band of gold, 679, Denton and Hyde, Manchester".

He blinked hard, then closed his eyes, but knew they'd still be there, waiting for him. He wondered how long it would be before the visions faded.

Claire nuzzled into his side. 'You did your best you know. Both you and Adam. You must believe that. You did all you could. Come back to me.'

Her voice sounded pleading. She held him tight, then stepped back, found his shoulders and shook them, turned his head with a gentle but insistent hand and stared into his eyes. Dan wondered what she saw there.

'Come back to me,' she said. 'Don't hold it against yourself that you couldn't save Nicola. You did the best you ever could. The best anyone could. Come back to me. Please. You did all you could, that and more. You did your very best.'

'I know,' Dan replied softly, hoping one day he would come to believe it.

About the author…

Simon Hall

Simon Hall has been the BBC's Crime Correspondent in the south-west of England for three years. He also regularly broadcasts on BBC Radio Devon and BBC Radio Cornwall.

Simon has also been nominated for the Crime Writers' Association *Dagger In The Library* Award.

For more information please visit Simon Hall's website

www.thetvdetective.com

The Death Pictures

A dying artist creates a series of ten paintings "The Death Pictures" which contain a mysterious riddle, leading the way to a unique and highly valuable prize. Thousands attempt to solve it. But before the answer can be revealed, the painter is murdered.

A serial rapist is plotting six attacks. He taunts the police, leaving a calling card counting off each victim.

A TV reporter covers the stories and is drawn in by the baffling questions. Why kill the artist when he would soon die naturally? Could it be connected with the rapes? He crosses the line from journalist to investigator, forced to break the law to try to solve the crimes.

ISBN 9781906125981
Price £ 6.99

More great crime books from Accent Press

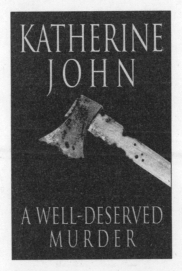

A Well-deserved Murder

by Katherine John

There have always been neighbours from hell. Some
deserve to die, but most people stop short of murder.
Journalist Alan Piper's life is being made a misery by
the people next door. They monitor his every move and
steal from his garden.
His cousin Sergeant Peter Collins suggests CCTV to
solve the problem, but Alan has other ideas.
When Kacy Howells' axe-battered body is found on her
decking, Sergeant Collins and Inspector Trevor Joseph
find themselves wanting to look beyond the obvious
murder suspect.

ISBN 9781906125141
Price £ 6.99

For more information about our
books please visit

www.accentpress.co.uk